Anne Baker

A VIEW ACROSS THE MERSEY

HEADLINE

First published in 2017 by
HEADLINE PUBLISHING GROUP

First published in paperback in 2017 by
HEADLINE PUBLISHING GROUP

1

Cataloguing in Publication Data is available from the British Library

ISBN 978 1 4722 3634 0

Typeset in Baskerville by Avon DataSet Ltd, Bidford-on-Avon, Warwickshire

Printed and bound in Great Britain by CPI Group (UK) Ltd, Croydon CR0 4YY

Headline's policy is to use papers that are natural, renewable and recyclable
products and made from wood grown in well-managed forests and other controlled
sources. The logging and manufacturing processes are expected to conform to the
environmental regulations of the country of origin.

HEADLINE PUBLISHING GROUP
An Hachette UK Company
Carmelite House
50 Victoria Embankment
London EC4Y 0DZ

www.headline.co.uk
www.hachette.co.uk

A VIEW ACROSS
THE MERSEY

Anne Baker trained as a nurse at Birkenhead General Hospital, but after her marriage went to live first in Libya and then in Nigeria. She eventually returned to her native Birkenhead where she worked as a Health Visitor for over ten years before taking up writing. Anne Baker now lives in Cornwall, where she continues to write, and her previous Merseyside sagas are all available from Headline.

Praise for Anne Baker's gripping Merseyside sagas:

'A stirring tale of romance and passion, poverty and ambition' *Liverpool Echo*

'A heartwarming saga' *Woman's Weekly*

'Baker's understanding and compassion for very human dilemmas makes her one of romantic fiction's most popular authors' *Lancashire Evening Post*

'With characters who are strong, warm and sincere, this is a joy to read' *Coventry Evening Telegraph*

'A wartime Merseyside saga so full of Scouse wit and warmth that it is bound to melt the hardest heart' *Northern Echo*

'Truly compelling . . . rich in language and descriptive prose' *Newcastle Upon Tyne Evening Chronicle*

'A well-written enjoyable book that legions of saga fans will love' *Historical Novels Review*

To find out more about Anne Baker's novels visit
www.annebaker.co.uk

CHAPTER ONE

Sunday 29 January 1922

CHARLOTTE MORTIMER RUSHED DOWN to the dining room for lunch and managed to get there just before her brother Glyn. Grandma gave him a forbidding look, because he was a minute late taking his place at the table. 'Have you children washed your hands?' she asked.

'Yes, Grandma,' they chorused.

Jemima Mortimer rang the bell for Ida, their one remaining maid, to bring in the soup tureen. The children's mother, Olwen, had died many years ago, and Jemima had moved in to the family home to help bring them up. Her spinster daughter Harriet had come with her to act as housekeeper.

Charlotte was cold and hungry after walking home from church with the family, but she could see that Glyn was fizzing with excitement and knew why. A steaming bowl of soup was put in front of her. It smelled delicious, but she dared not start to eat until everyone had been served. At eleven years old, she knew that Grandma's ways were old-fashioned and formal – she always called her Charlotte, while to everybody else she was Lottie – but she was also kind and tended to spoil her because she was the youngest of the five children.

'Dad,' Glyn said, 'Philip Royden told us when we came out of church that Uncle Lazlo is home on leave.'

Their father Charles straightened up in his chair, his soup spoon halfway to his mouth. As head of the family, he managed the Mortimer Line, the business that provided a living for them all.

'He's staying at the Adelphi,' Glyn added.

Uncle Lazlo was their father's younger brother. Every birthday and Christmas he sent them cards and gifts, but they rarely saw him because he worked out in West Africa. He seemed a distant, romantic figure. Lottie didn't understand why, but the family seemed to think of him as a black sheep, and she'd picked up occasional references to a cataclysmic row they'd had many years ago that still kept him estranged.

He had further blackened his name by taking a job with Henry Royden and Partners instead of working in the family business. The Roydens lived four doors away along New Ferry Esplanade. Philip Royden was a few months older than Lottie, and a few months younger than Glyn, and was their close friend. He was often round in their playroom telling them stories about life on the West African coast where Uncle Lazlo worked. Lottie and Glyn loved to hear them. Philip also told them that his father was friendly with Lazlo and considered him an asset to their firm. Henry Royden had been at sea school on HMS *Conway* with Dad, and was his competitor in trade and his erstwhile friend.

Lottie looked round at her family. Dilys, her eldest sister at twenty-three, was fashionably dainty and full-figured. She had Celtic colouring – dark curly hair with blue eyes and fair skin – and took after her Welsh mother rather than the Mortimers.

Aunt Harriet had the same round, attractive face, and was placid and smiling and kind, but at forty she was short and dumpy. Lottie's favourite brother Glyn, one year older than her, was square, sturdy and strong like Dad. Twenty-one-year-old Eunice, who was already married, was missing from the table, while Oliver, at sixteen, was away at school.

Grandma was tall and thin, with a long face and a large nose. She had the features of a classical Greek statue, with few wrinkles considering she was almost eighty. She had strong opinions on everything and decided most things on behalf of the family. Even Dad had to bow to her will.

Charlotte was already almost as tall as Dilys, and was still growing; she was thin and angular like Grandma. She would have loved to have silky dark brown curls like the rest of her family, but her hair was straight and pale blond. She loved them all, but somehow she'd always felt she wasn't quite one of them. She didn't fit the mould.

Charles started carving the sirloin of beef. 'With trade the way it is, I'm afraid I might have to mothball another ship,' he worried. 'Probably the *Cheshire*; we just can't get the cargoes.'

The Mortimer Line had once had a fleet of twenty ships. Currently they had three seagoing tramping freighters transporting grain and general cargo round the Mediterranean and the Black Sea, and two smaller coastal vessels transporting slate from the Welsh quarries to the Mersey to cover the roofs of Liverpool.

'Things might pick up soon,' Harriet said, trying to comfort him. The adults were always talking about how poor trading conditions had been since the war, and what a terrible effect it was having on the family's finances.

Glyn cut in to ask, 'Can we phone Uncle Lazlo and invite him to come over and see us?'

Lottie could see from Dad's face that that didn't meet with favour. 'We like to rest on a Sunday afternoon,' he said.

'Then can Lottie and I go over to see him?' Glyn persisted.

There was a shocked silence. 'By yourselves?' Aunt Harriet's eyebrows had gone up. She had grown used to being at the beck and call of her mother and brother, and was no longer paying much attention to her appearance. She'd given in to middle age.

'Could Dilys take us?' Glyn suggested. 'You'd like to come, wouldn't you, Dilly?'

'Absolutely not,' Grandma thundered. She was the power-house of the family, overflowing with vitality. Her eyes were alert and her mind razor sharp, and she considered it her duty to oversee them all. 'We do not want to see Lazlo, and would prefer that you did not either.'

'Why not?' Lottie could see that Glyn was disappointed, but he never knew when to give up.

'We've told you why not,' Grandma said tartly. A foghorn blared out on the river. 'Anyway, the fog is thickening; it won't be safe to go anywhere this afternoon.'

The Mortimer family lived in Mersey View, a large bungalow on the New Ferry Esplanade that Charles had bought when he married Olwen thirty years ago. The tide swept up to the Esplanade twice a day and sometimes splashed over and into the garden. On foggy nights the foghorns could keep them awake.

Once lunch was over, Grandma said, 'You young ones will need to learn to look after yourselves. It's been difficult to get

4

anybody to help in the house since the war, and anyway, we can't afford it any more.' She allotted Lottie and Glyn the task of clearing the table. Dilys was to put away the remains of the food, while Ida washed up. Meanwhile, Grandma, Dad and Aunt Harriet settled beside the fire in the sitting room with the newspapers.

When they had finished their chores, Lottie followed Glyn to the playroom, which had once been their day nursery, and stood beside him looking out at the river. It was a grey, wintry afternoon; the tide was fully in, and without any wind, the water was flat calm. The Mersey was not much more than a mile wide here, but the city of Liverpool was no longer visible in the thickening fog.

'I'm bored,' Glyn said. 'I'd love to go and see Uncle Lazlo. Philip says he's been home several times and takes him out and about. He's jolly and always happy and he gives Philip a good time, but we haven't seen him for years.'

'I wish Grandma would tell us why they won't have anything to do with him,' Lottie said. She'd been asking about him for years, trying to get to the bottom of what had happened. Grandma had said, 'It was all a long time ago; he wouldn't settle down and learn to run the business.' She wouldn't be drawn further.

Aunt Harriet had been more forthcoming. 'Lazlo was wild and rebellious, and made trouble on board a freighter when he was taken on as a midshipman. Charles had to take him into the office, but he was trouble rather than a help there, and after a disagreement, he walked out on us, leaving both his home and his job.'

'But Oliver has left home too,' Lottie said.

'That's different, as you well know,' Harriet replied.

Like his father and uncle, Oliver had gone to sea school on the HMS *Conway* when he was thirteen to be trained as a ship's officer. The boys of the family then furthered their careers by working on Merchant Navy ships. That was thought to be the best grounding for managing the family business; it was learning from the bottom up. Glyn would follow the same path.

'You'll be old enough in September to start on the *Conway*,' Harriet had told him.

'But Oliver is nearly old enough to go to sea now, so he won't be there,' Lottie pointed out.

'That is the family tradition,' Harriet said. 'Then after a few years' experience he'll be taken into the business.'

'Yes, but Dad said there won't be much work for him, so it might be better if he makes his career at sea.'

'Oliver says he'd rather do that,' Glyn said. 'Uncle Lazlo managed to find more exciting work, so why not? Dad never stops complaining about how hard it is for our business to earn money.'

All the family were proud to say they were shipowners, even though the business was much reduced in size and import-ance. Grandma was alone in believing that one day a family member would take over the Mortimer Line and lift it back to profitability and its former glory.

Glyn said, 'Let's see if we can phone Uncle Lazlo.'

Lottie felt a shiver of foreboding. She'd always been close to Glyn, but he was very daring and often got her into trouble.

'Grandma will be cross,' she said.

'I don't care,' he retorted. He fancied a job like Uncle

Lazlo's out in Nigeria and was keen to meet him and hear more about it. 'Come on, let's try,' he said.

They could hear Dilys and Ida talking and clattering dishes in the kitchen. They crept quietly to Dad's study and closed the door. Glyn lifted the phone and asked the operator to put him through to the Adelphi Hotel, while Lottie listened nervously. It seemed an age before he began to speak. 'Hello, Uncle Lazlo. It's Glyn.'

For an agonising moment she thought Lazlo hadn't recognised the name.

'Yes, I'm Charles's son. Yes, twelve now. Lottie and I are bored. Can we come and see you this afternoon?'

Lottie stared out on to the rose hedge in the back garden, her stomach fluttering with nerves. She thought Uncle Lazlo was asking if Grandma had given permission for them to come, and Glyn was sidestepping the question.

'Yes, all the family are fine.'

He put the phone down and grinned at her. Glyn had all the Mortimer good looks, with a dimple in his chin as well. 'Uncle Lazlo said he'd love to see us, and can we find the way? I told him we could.'

Lottie felt uneasy as they crept back to the playroom. Grandma was going to be furious. 'We'll have to tell somebody or we'll get into trouble.'

'That's impossible. They'll stop us going.'

'We'll get into trouble for using the phone, too; we're supposed to ask first.'

'But they'd have said no.'

'We can't just go.' Lottie was aghast.

'Of course we can. Get your coat and don't make any noise.'

'We'll need money.'

'Yes, for fares.' Their money boxes stood one each side of the mantelpiece. Glyn had long since learned how to open them; now he managed to tip six pennies out of his and fifteen out of Lottie's.

'We won't need all that,' she objected.

'Better take it; we have to think of getting home again.'

'Shouldn't we leave a note?' Lottie worried. 'We're supposed to tell somebody where we're going before we go out. They'll miss us at teatime and get anxious.'

'Don't fuss.'

She pulled the middle page out of her homework notebook and wrote: *We've gone to the Adelfie Otel to see Uncle Lazlo,* and left it on the playroom table. 'There'll be an awful row when we get back.'

'Come on,' whispered Glyn. 'I'll say I persuaded you. We'll be in time for the half two ferry if we hurry.'

Once Lottie was running up the garden path to the back gate, it seemed a great adventure. New Ferry pier was two minutes' walk away, past the parade of shops and the post office. It was only when they were passing the entrance to the Esplanade that she could see how much thicker the fog had become. The tide was right in and lapping gently against the bottom of the slipway.

They often travelled this way, and Dad went to work on the ferry every morning. The men working in the ferry house knew them and called, 'It's getting a bit thick out on the river, but the ferry hasn't stopped running yet.'

They each bought a ticket by putting a penny into a machine. 'There's a boat tied up now,' they were told. 'You'd better run.'

Everything seemed different now they were hurrying down the pier, and Lottie thought even Glyn was having misgivings. There wasn't a ripple on the water, and she'd never seen fog as thick as this. All round them other ships were beginning to sound their hooters. The ferrymen knew them too, and waited until they had boarded to rattle up the ramp. They climbed up to the top deck and leaned against the rail as they always did.

Lottie felt a shaft of fear; it was as though they were wrapped in cotton wool. HMS *Conway* and three other training ships were usually visible moored in the Sloyne, a deep-water channel that ran up this side of the Mersey in front of both Rock Ferry and New Ferry. But today they were nowhere to be seen. She knew they'd pass close to them, but though she strained her eyes, she couldn't even make out their outlines. She saw nothing until the buildings at the Pier Head and the terminus for trams and buses appeared through the gloom. Now the fog was yellowish in colour, and she could smell the chemicals in the air. Grandma said the stench came from the chimneys of the heavy industries all round them billowing smoke that couldn't get away because of the blanket of fog.

Glyn gripped her by the hand when they were getting off. He asked the ticket collector, 'What number tram do we need to get to the Adelphi Hotel?' They had to wait for one to come, but they did eventually reach their destination. Lottie had never been here before and felt intimidated; it looked a very grand place.

Glyn asked for Uncle Lazlo at the reception desk, and very soon Lottie spotted a stranger striding towards them. As soon as she saw his smiling face, she felt better. He threw his arms round her and tried to lift her off her feet in a giant's hug.

'My goodness, what a big girl you are now.' He looked a little like Dad and Aunt Harriet, but he was bubbling with good humour and the joy of living, while they always looked worried and dragged down by the cares of the world. He held her at arm's length. 'Can this really be little Charlotte?'

He kissed her, then shook hands with Glyn, man to man.

'I'm delighted you've both come over to see me. I was a little worried because of the fog, but you've got here safely.'

Uncle Lazlo had the body of an athlete, the brightest blue eyes and a deep healthy suntan. He led them into a vast lounge, where they sat facing him on a huge sofa. 'It's teatime,' he said. 'Would you like ice cream or cake? Oh, why not both? This is something of an occasion. I haven't seen you for so many years. Tell me what you've been doing.'

'Philip Royden tells us all about you working in foreign places. I'd like to do that too,' Glyn said. 'But you know what our family is like.'

'You've been given to understand you're destined to run the family business?'

'Yes, though Oliver's not keen to join it.'

'I don't suppose it's going well. How many ships does your dad run now?' They all knew he didn't actually own any outright. The family was reduced to holding shares in the vessels and managing the business on behalf of the other shareholders.

'Three tramping freighters and two coastal vessels, and Dad's worried all the time that he'll have to lay one of those up,' Glyn told him. 'He thinks it'll be the *Cheshire* next.'

Lazlo's smile had gone. 'It's becoming harder and harder for any of us to make a profit.'

'But Roydens are still making a profit, aren't they?'

Charlotte asked, checking up on what Philip had told them. The Roydens had once been shipowners too, but their business had been taken over by Elder Dempster, one of the big Liverpool shipping lines that ran the mail ships out to West Africa.

'Well, the Elder Dempster Line is, and they're using seven of Royden's small ships. They pick up cargo from the mailboat in the large ports and ferry it along the coast and up the rivers to the smaller places.'

'And what exactly do you do out there?' Glyn wanted to know.

'I look after the African end of the business. I see to the provisioning and bunkering of the ships when they arrive, and arrange cargoes of palm oil, tropical fruit and sometimes parrots for them to carry to the great African sea ports of Freetown, Takoradi and Lagos. The Elder Dempster mailboats call in there on a strict timetable to pick up the goods and bring them to Liverpool.'

'I'd like to live in exciting places like that,' Glyn said. 'I don't want to be like Dad, working in that gloomy office trying to get cargoes and worrying because trade is falling off.'

Lazlo pulled a face. 'You'll have an easier time if you knuckle down and do what your father wants. Don't make enemies of your family; you'll find it isn't worth it.'

Lottie wanted to get him off that subject. 'Tell us about Calabar. Grandma says it's the white man's grave.'

'Perhaps it was in the old days, but not any more. We have electric light and running water, and the mailboats bring out bicycles and sewing machines and cars.'

Ice cream in three flavours arrived in glass dishes, and Lazlo told them, 'Help yourselves. Eat as many of these fancy cakes as you can. I'm certainly going to.'

'This is a scrumptious tea,' Glyn said.

All the time they were eating, Uncle Lazlo was talking about life in Calabar, and the way he traded for palm oil to be made into soap; coconut husk that could be made into coconut matting; crocodile skins and grey parrots.

'It's very different from the Mersey. There's very little to be seen on land; it's dense, hot rainforest, palm trees mostly. The inland waterways spread everywhere and they're only as wide as the roads here, but they're deep, so quite big ships can navigate them. You can see ships coming towards you through the palm trees and it looks as though they're sailing on land.'

New arrivals came into the lounge, and they heard them talking about an accident somewhere on the river, and saying that the fog was now so thick that all buses, trams and ferries had stopped running.

Uncle Lazlo jerked to his feet. 'It's time you two went home. Thank goodness for the underground trains; they won't stop.'

'By train?' Glyn asked. 'We live a long way from the station.'

'So you do.'

'We always travel by ferry; we don't know about trains,' Lottie said anxiously. She turned round to look at the windows and was shocked to see how dark it had become. 'Will we be able to find our way home?'

'Course we will,' said Glyn, but she could see he was worried too.

'Oh dear!' Lazlo said. 'This could blacken my name further. I'd better see you safely back. Look, I've been invited to dinner by Henry Royden this evening, but I need to go up to my room to change. Come to the bar and I'll buy you each a glass of lemonade, and you must wait for me down here. I won't be long, so don't go away.'

When he'd gone, Lottie sipped her drink and said, 'I think he's lovely. I don't understand why the family don't like him,'

'He's great fun,' Glyn agreed. 'They don't like him because he's working for the Roydens and helping them make more profit than we are.'

CHAPTER TWO

J EMIMA MORTIMER HAD BEEN determined not to give in to old age, but she'd found that a rest after lunch kept her going until bedtime, so nowadays she allowed herself half an hour. Today, the frequent blare of foghorns on the river made it hard to drop off, and no sooner had she done so than Harriet was poking the fire into a blaze and throwing on more coal.

Jemima yawned and sat up straighter to see that Charles was still asleep and Dilys was reading. 'I thought you were going out,' she said.

Dilys closed her book. 'I changed my mind and decided to stay by the fire. Look at the fog now; it's a real pea souper.' It was already dark outside, and the fog was a greyish-yellow blanket against the windows. 'I'll put the kettle on, shall I? You'll be ready for tea, Grandma.' On Sundays, Ida had the afternoon off and they had to look after themselves.

She had just reached the door when there was an almighty boom outside, somewhere between a crash and an explosion. It was loud enough to hurt the ears and made her cry out with shock. It was followed by a cracking of timbers that sounded almost like shots from a gun.

Charles was jerked back to wakefulness. 'What on earth was that?'

Dilys was already peering out of the window. 'I can't see anything, but it sounded close.'

There were two windows in the room; they all crowded against the glass. 'As close as the garden gate,' Jemima said. 'Just listen to that!' Now they could hear a cacophony of foghorns and bells.

'An accident out on the river,' Harriet said. 'Two ships must have collided in the fog.'

'None of ours are in the Mersey,' Jemima said thankfully. 'It sounds as though there's panic out there.'

'But not a light to be seen!'

'I do hope nothing has run into the training ships in the Sloyne, with all those young lads on board,' Charles said. They were all fully awake now, and anxious. 'I'm going out to see.'

'I'm coming with you, Dad,' Dilys said.

'Put your coats on,' Jemima called after them as she returned to her fireside chair.

Harriet sighed. 'We might as well have our tea; there's nothing we can do to help. I'll put the kettle on.'

It was only when she'd brought the tray into the sitting room and was pouring the tea that she said, 'Where are the children? I gave them a shout.' Usually they came promptly for the biscuits.

'Did they go out with Charles and Dilys?'

'I don't think so.' She opened the door and called again, 'Glyn, Charlotte, it's teatime,' then returned to the fireside to pick up her cup and saucer.

'Quite a disturbance out there,' Jemima worried. 'I've never heard as much noise as this before. I do hope nobody's been hurt.' As she sipped her tea, she felt an anxious niggle about the children. 'They must have gone out with Charles.'

Without a word, Harriet got to her feet and went to find them. Seconds later, Jemima heard her rushing back at twice her former speed, waving a piece of paper. 'They went out ages ago – look at this!'

A page torn from a notebook fluttered on to Jemima's lap. She reached for her spectacles and stared at Lottie's careful writing. *We've gone to the Adelfie Otel to see Uncle Lazlo.* 'Oh my goodness!' She got to her feet. 'They are naughty, after we expressly forbade them to go to him!'

'This will be Glyn's doing,' Harriet said. 'Isn't he exactly like Lazlo?'

They heard the front door slam shut, and moments later Dilys came to warm her hands at the fire. 'There's a problem down on the pier,' she said. 'An ambulance has just drawn up by the ticket office. Dad has gone to see if he can do anything to help, but there's a crowd of people come from the hotel.' The New Ferry Hotel was only a few yards away, overlooking the pier.

Charles was back before very long, his cheeks scarlet with the cold. 'A ship has collided with the pier.'

'A ferry?'

'No, the ferries stopped running an hour ago because of the fog. It was a Dutch steamer, quite a big one. They're saying the crew were drunk, that the captain had gone to his cabin and the crash threw him out of his bunk. He's been taken to hospital.'

'Is the ship all right? Much damage?'

'I don't know. They say the pier is unsafe, but they wouldn't let me near enough to see. Getting to work tomorrow is going to be difficult.'

Harriet said in a matter-of-fact voice, 'The children have gone across to Liverpool to see Lazlo. A more pressing question, Charles, is how they will get back.'

'What?' There was anger in his voice. 'They know we don't want them to have anything to do with Lazlo. Why did you let them go out? Surely you could see the fog was thickening?'

Jemima got up and pushed Lottie's note into his hand. 'You heard me forbid them. I expect they'll be sorry by now that they went.'

'Do they know the way back from the station?'

'Which station? We're an equal distance from Rock Ferry and New Ferry, and none of us ever travel by train. Why would we when we're only a few yards from the pier?'

Harriet shuddered. 'They won't be able to see their hands in front of their faces by now. They'll be terrified.'

'Serves them right,' Charles said.

'I'm worried.' Jemima shivered. 'Will they be able to find their way home?'

'Damn Lazlo,' spat Charles. 'Why did he have to come back and cause more trouble?'

Lottie stood on the steps of the Adelphi and looked at the nearest street lamp sending a cone of yellow into the dark fog. There was almost no traffic and the few cars were travelling very slowly. Uncle Lazlo gripped her with one hand and Glyn with the other as they crossed the road to Liverpool Central underground station.

'This is terrible,' he said. 'I've telephoned Henry Royden

and asked him to bring his car to meet us at New Ferry station.'

Oh goodness, Lottie thought. Dad wouldn't be pleased about Philip's father turning out to collect them in this fog. 'I'm sorry,' she said, 'to put you to the trouble of getting us home.'

'Your grandma would be furious with me if I left you to find your own way back in this.'

'Yes,' Glyn agreed, though Lottie could see he was enjoying the prospect of the train ride. It was a different experience, and the fact that Lazlo was with them meant they didn't have to worry about finding their way.

Mr Royden was waiting for them in his car. He got out and threw his arms round Lazlo in a bear hug. 'Welcome home,' he said. They clapped each other on the back and seemed in high spirits. Lottie knew he was Lazlo's boss, but she could see they were friends too.

He opened the back door. 'In here, you little rascals,' he said jovially. 'Did you enjoy your expedition this afternoon?'

Lottie was not enjoying this part, and she knew Glyn wasn't either; he was sinking lower in his seat. They were about to face Grandma and she was going to be incandescent with rage.

The car stopped at their back gate. 'Come on, you two, I'll come in with you to say hello,' Lazlo said. 'It might help to break the ice. I'll only be five or ten minutes, Henry, but don't wait for me. I can walk along the front to your place.'

Glyn opened the back door and stood back. Lottie's heart was fluttering as she led them through to the sitting room, where the rest of the family were sitting round the blazing fire. They all turned to look at them, their faces full of condemnation. Lottie's spirits sank further.

'Hello, Mother.' Lazlo strode across the room to embrace her, but Jemima remained stiff and unbending. Harriet did too when he bent to kiss her. 'How are you, Charles, old thing? I've brought the children safely home, in case this awful weather got the better of them. Lovely to be back in dear old Blighty all the same.'

Lottie watched her father pull himself to his feet, but Grandma was not to be distracted. 'You two go to your rooms,' she ordered, 'and stay there. You knew you shouldn't go out; you deliberately disobeyed me. As punishment, you'll have no supper tonight.' Lottie clutched at Glyn as she went on, 'And stay in your own rooms, please. There's to be no getting together to play board games.'

'Sorry, Grandma,' they muttered together. 'Sorry, Dad.'

'Dilys,' Grandma commanded, 'would you be good enough to make sure they stay apart; and then perhaps you could set out supper for the rest of us on the dining table?'

Dilys ushered them silently out. 'Oh my goodness, you've done it this time,' she said. Lottie hung her head in shame and went meekly to her room. Once alone, she opened the door to hear better the angry buzz of voices from the sitting room, but it was impossible to pick out any words.

After a while, it seemed Lazlo was leaving, 'I can't stay and argue with you now, Charles, the Roydens are expecting me, but perhaps I could come again tomorrow and . . .'

She thought she heard Dad tell him not to bother.

'I'd like to take you out, Mother, what about lunch tomorrow?' The reply was softer, but she thought that was a refusal too, then Lazlo's footsteps went up the hall and the front door banged shut. It seemed Grandma didn't want to be friends with Lazlo, and Charlotte was little wiser as to what it was all about.

The punishment was what she'd expected, but Dilys had always looked after them. She crept back five minutes later with a pork pie and an apple for each of them. 'Keep quiet, say nothing and stay in your room until breakfast time,' she hissed.

When daylight came the next morning, Lottie opened her bedroom curtains and gasped with astonishment. It was still grey and misty, but the fog had thinned sufficiently for her to see that the end of the pier had been cut right off. It was now in two pieces and the supporting timbers had been knocked askew. Ragged decking hung down on both sides almost to the waves. There was no sign of the vessel that had caused the damage.

She rushed to the kitchen, where Aunt Harriet was preparing breakfast. 'Something terrible has happened to the pier,' she said.

'Yes, a Dutch steamer steered a course straight at it.'

'How will Dad . . . ?'

'He's already set off to walk up to the main Chester road, where he hopes to catch a tram.'

'To take him to a train station?'

'Or to Woodside to catch the ferry there. He's no idea which would be the more convenient,' Aunt Harriet said. 'He's never had to do it before.'

'Poor Charles,' Grandma said. 'He bought this house because it was such a pleasant and easy journey to his office, but if the ferry doesn't run, all that is lost.'

'Please get yourselves dressed and ready for school,' Harriet said.

Glyn had joined them in his pyjamas. 'It makes no difference to us,' he said. He and Lottie went to different schools, but they were on this side of the river and they both walked there.

'Why does Dad need an office in Liverpool?' Charlotte asked.

'Yes, why?' Glyn echoed. 'Our ships mostly use the docks on this side of the river; wouldn't it be better for him to have an office here?'

'The Liverpool address,' Aunt Harriet murmured. 'All the big shipping firms are there; it's where the important business takes place.'

'But ours is no longer a big shipping firm,' Glyn said.

'And Dad is grateful for any cargo these days.'

Grandma sighed. 'I can't get over what's happened to the pier. It will be a major undertaking to repair that.'

'And it'll take ages,' Charlotte said.

Before setting off to school, she went to her bedroom window for another look. The rest of the family kept doing the same. They all found the sight of the wrecked pier unbelievable. It had been built in 1865 and paid for by a wealthy Liverpool sugar refiner by the name of Macfie. A ferry service had been operating since then, turning New Ferry into a destination for day trippers.

Rock Ferry was already a tourist destination, with many hotels and fine shops. It had its own pier and ferry service, and during the summer months the Rock Hotel and the Olympian Gardens on the waterfront offered afternoon and evening entertainment: everything from classical piano concerts to Pierrot shows in a circus-sized marquee.

Both places had taken their names from the ferry service. The two piers were only a mile apart, and the resorts were connected by a fine promenade with a little sandy beach called the Gap. The New Ferry Hotel overlooked the pier and provided spectacular views across the Mersey to the centre of Liverpool. It had a bowling green, flower gardens and picnic grounds.

Ever since Charles had taken over the management of the Mortimer business and moved to his present home, the shipping trade had been growing less profitable. Since the turn of the century there had been competition from other countries, and after the brief boom provided by the Great War, there had been another collapse, driving many companies into bankruptcy. Roads and public transport were being improved, and passengers and goods could travel by rail and road just as cheaply.

Lottie knew her family really missed the ferry service, as did their neighbours, but after months of waiting and hoping and writing to the local newspaper, it seemed no money would be forthcoming to repair the pier.

CHAPTER THREE

OVER THE FOLLOWING MONTHS, Lottie looked out of her bedroom window at the wrecked pier every morning and saw the tides gradually begin to erode it. It served as a daily reminder of their troubles. That September, Glyn left his day school to join his brother Oliver as a pupil on HMS *Conway*, where they were all boarders. He was happy to do this; it was what he'd expected, and he had his friend Philip Royden starting with him. Lottie missed him terribly, missed Philip too. From now on, she was without her two closest companions for most of the year.

HMS *Conway* was a beautiful black-and-white wooden ship that had started life as HMS *Nile* of the Royal Navy in 1876. It had been refitted as a school for boys aged thirteen to eighteen to train them as officers for the Merchant Navy.

Once Charlotte knew that Glyn was there, the *Conway* drew her attention away from the damaged pier. It was one of four training ships moored in the Sloyne. The old iron *Indefatigable* had been refitted as a training ship for orphans and sons of Liverpool seamen to prepare them for life at sea, while the *Akbar*, another handsome wooden vessel, and the *Clarence* were reformatory ships for boys who had fallen foul of the law.

She often heard bugles sounding and bands practising on the ships, and sometimes she saw the boys rowing ashore in skiffs. They played cricket and rugby on a playing field nearby. She gathered that the boys of the *Conway* thought themselves very much superior to the pupils on the other ships.

Because she and Dilys were the only two children left at home, they were thrown together more. Dilys would often suggest a shopping trip for clothes or a visit to the pictures, and Lottie loved going out with her, but she knew her sister was bored. 'Why don't you get a job?' she asked her. 'I wouldn't want to stay home all day with Grandma and Harriet.'

Dilys sighed. 'When I first left school, Gran asked what I wanted to do, but Dad and Aunt Harriet don't believe young ladies should go to work. They think Grandma broke the mould and it wouldn't do for the rest of us. It was easier to have a good time when Eunice was living at home and Dad belonged to the yacht club and we sailed the *Fair Wind*.'

Lottie remembered being taken to the Royal Mersey Yacht Club in Rock Ferry. 'I saw Father Christmas there every year, and they held lovely Christmas parties for children.' She'd heard the family talk at mealtimes about the yacht club, and Aunt Harriet had lots of photos of it in her albums.

'Yes, there was a racing programme, and lots of regattas and suppers and dances and formal dinners. We knew lots of people then, and had a social life. When the war came, there were bandages to roll and comforters to knit, and we all had to help with things like that. Lucky Eunice got married soon after leaving school. I do miss her. That was when I decided I wanted to get a job.' She gave another gusty sigh.

Charlotte said, 'Grandma would be all for it. She trained as a nurse so she could help the sick and the poor. She believes that women, married or single, should have a free choice as to how they spend their time.'

'She thought I should be a nurse too, but I didn't fancy that. Aunt Harriet said what was the point of starting three years' training when I'd want to get married before I finished it.'

'Don't you want to get married?'

'Of course I do.' Dilys smiled. 'You are a little innocent! Nobody has ever asked me, and we girls have to wait for the proposal. Yes, I want to get married, but what chance do I have of meeting anyone when I'm stuck at home like this? Since Dad sold his boat and gave up the club, the family never go out and we never invite anyone here. I'm bored out of my mind.'

'You could go out for a sail in the *Seagull*. I'll come with you if you like.'

The *Seagull* was a fourteen-foot sailing dinghy that was kept anchored in the mud in front of the house. Dad had bought it for them when he sold the *Fair Wind*, as he believed every Mortimer should become a competent sailor. Lottie and Glyn had spent many happy hours in it.

The large keelboats belonging to the yacht club members needed deep water to moor them in, and the club had to run a service to ferry them out to their craft. Little *Seagull*, though, had a centreboard to give her stability, and because she was anchored close to home, she was easier to take out for trips.

'You'll have to watch the tides and the winds,' Grandma had warned them several times. 'It's up to you to act responsibly.'

Dad had brought a book of tide timetables to the playroom

and taught them to read it. 'It's safer to go upstream rather than down,' he told them. 'The ebb tide produces very strong currents and the river is busy. Watch out for other shipping.'

Mostly they didn't venture far. It was safe enough to go out towards the training ships moored in the Sloyne, which provided a large area of water well away from the ocean-going liners, coastal barges, lighters and ferries that filled the main shipping lanes. They always looked out for Oliver on the *Conway*, but rarely saw him, though there were often other boys to be seen. Glyn and Lottie waved to them, and they always waved back. Further upriver was Bromborough Dock, where ships brought palm oil from West Africa to make margarine and soap in the nearby factories. The occasional tanker hooted at them to get out of the way, but they'd never come to any harm.

'Sailing the dinghy won't help me meet anybody.' Dilys was not in a good mood. 'I've grown out of all that.'

'Then you'll just have to get a job. You'd meet lots of new people then.'

'That's what I keep saying. If only they'd sent us to Birkenhead High School, we could have been teachers or solicitors. But Mortimer girls have always gone to Connaught House School in Rock Ferry, because it has a smart uniform that picks us out from the hoi polloi.'

'I like it there,' Lottie said. 'Aunt Harriet said she did too.'

'It's no better than a dame school,' Dilys said. 'I need some training if I'm to get a job, and that'll cost money. You know how they're always moaning that they're hard up.'

'That's silly,' Lottie said. 'If you were earning a living, that would surely help.'

'I pointed that out, but they're old and habit-bound. Dad thinks nothing has changed since Queen Victoria's day.'

Lottie left Dilys fuming. She felt there was nothing she could do to help her. At least she herself went to school every day, and there was plenty going on there.

But the next day, when she was setting the table for dinner, she heard the grown-ups talking. 'It's not good for Dilys to be kept in idleness,' Grandma was saying. 'Surely you can draw out the money for secretarial lessons? That's education, isn't it?'

She didn't catch all of Dad's reply; just, 'I'd rather not.'

Aunt Harriet sounded impatient. 'She'll be getting her inheritance next year anyway. Surely she can wait till then?'

'She probably won't want to work once she has that,' Grandma said tartly. 'She needs more to fill her days now.'

After dinner, while they were washing up, Lottie whispered to Dilys, 'Grandma is on your side. Keep on at them; she knows how to make Dad do what she wants. She'll make him agree. And Harriet says everything is going to be fine for you by next year.'

'Why? What's going to change?'

'I'm not sure; she said something about you inheriting money.'

Dilys laughed. 'Pigs might fly.'

'Have another go at them when we've finished here.'

'I will.' She was drying her hands. 'I'll make their coffee. When it's ready, I'll pass it round and ask them while they're all relaxed.'

'I don't want to miss this,' Charlotte said. 'Make enough for all of us.'

'Grandma thinks you're too young for coffee, and it'll stop you going to sleep.'

'It never does, but I'll put a cup of milk on the tray for me before she suggests that awful camomile tea.'

Dilys returned somewhat downcast moments later to fill the kettle. 'My ideas never go to plan. There's only Grandma and Harriet there; Dad has gone to his study.'

'Never mind, it's them you need to work on.' Lottie helped her carry everything in and then dropped down out of sight behind the sofa. She'd come to understand that her presence tended to inhibit her family.

On her last birthday, she'd been given an outsize jigsaw puzzle of a map of England. The family approved because it was thought to be educational, but it was so big there was no place to lay it out but on the floor. On her birthday night she and Glyn had made a good start on it on the parquet in the corner of the sitting room, where the carpet square didn't reach. But they'd taken so many pieces out of the box that it would be a huge job to move it to the playroom, and she'd been allowed to leave it there.

She often tried to fill in a few more pieces as she waited for meals to be ready, and had completed the part of the puzzle showing Merseyside; that had been easier because the names were familiar. Now, against the clink of coffee cups, she made a start on the London region.

'This is kind of you, Dilys,' Aunt Harriet said. Usually it fell to her to make the coffee.

'I'd like to talk to you both,' Dilys said. 'I have mentioned it before, so forgive me if I seem to be nagging about it, but I'd really like to get a job. I don't mind what I do; I just want to get out and about more, see a bit of the world. If it costs too much to send me to secretarial school, I'd be quite happy to work in a shop.'

'A shop!' Aunt Harriet was shocked.

'A clothes shop. Or one of those big department stores in Liverpool like Bunney's.'

'Getting to Liverpool is difficult without the ferry,' Grandma said. She didn't seem to be helping after all.

Dilys had a defensive note in her voice. 'There are clothes shops and department stores in Birkenhead.'

'There's absolutely no need for you to work,' Aunt Harriet said impatiently. 'It's time Charles spoke to you about your expectations.'

Dilys gasped, and it made Lottie stiffen. 'What expectations do I have? I assume this dull life will go on for ever.'

There was a long silence, then Grandma said, 'How old are you now, Dilys?'

'Twenty-four.'

'Yes, and it's high time you were told about the plans made for you by your mother.'

Lottie sat up straighter; she had not expected anything as exciting as this.

'What plans?' Dilys sounded equally surprised.

'Olwen Thomas had very definite ideas for her children,' Aunt Harriet said stiffly.

Lottie was familiar with that name. Hanging in pride of place on the dining-room wall were two large framed photographs of ships: the *Olwen Thomas* and the *Gwendolen Thomas*. Glyn had asked Dad about them several times, and he was always ready to talk about them. 'They were fine ships,' he

29

said. 'The *Olwen Thomas* was launched in 1880, when your mother was a little girl of five. And when they ordered a new ship to be built, they named it after her sister Gwendolen.'

'Marvellous to have a ship named after you,' Lottie had said.

'It was the fashion.' Dad smiled at her. 'Times were prosperous then because coal heated our houses and was used to power the ships and the trains.'

The *Olwen Thomas* and the *Gwendolen Thomas* had been small colliers carrying coal from their home port of Cardiff. They had been new and clean when the photographs were taken, but Lottie did not rate them all that highly.

From her bedroom window, she'd grown used to seeing the glamorous transatlantic passenger liners run by Cunard and the White Star Line tied up across the water at Prince's Landing Stage in Liverpool. They were known as the greyhounds of the Atlantic. Because there was competition between the shipping lines, they vied internationally over the fastest crossing to New York and the prize of the Blue Riband, and so were occasionally in the news. She'd even seen pictures of them on the cinema newsreel, with flags fluttering, champagne flowing and bands playing. The colliers bore little resemblance to these elegant ships.

Grandma spoke of Olwen's family quite often. 'The Thomases had their problems; the family had been riddled with ill health for years. TB plagued them and they had no sons to carry on the business. Only the two daughters survived – your mother and your Aunt Gwendolen.'

She'd get out photographs of them from time to time, posed studio pictures of two pretty little girls in big fancy hats and uncomfortable frilly dresses. The older one always appeared caring of the younger. Sometimes Lottie was allowed to look through the album of photographs taken on her parents' wedding day, when Olwen was grown up and a great beauty. Her sister had been her bridesmaid and still looked very young.

'Aunt Gwendolen was six years younger,' Grandma told her. 'She married Jeremy Arbuthnot, an important man, a Conservative Member of Parliament no less, and they live in London.' Lottie had never met Aunt Gwendolen, but she'd heard a lot about her.

'The Thomas family made a fortune carrying coal not only round England but to the Mediterranean and Black Sea ports; round the world in fact,' Grandma said now.

'That was all a long time ago,' Dilys pointed out.

'Yes, now we use diesel and electricity. Coal is yesterday's fuel.'

'That's why I don't understand. How can the plans Mum made for us be any good now?'

'I'll talk to your father; it's time he explained it all to you. You have a right to know what you can expect when you turn twenty-five.'

'Expect! Please tell me, I want to know now,' Dilys pleaded.

'Why does she have to wait until she's twenty-five?' Charlotte jerked to her feet to ask.

That drew Aunt Harriet's eyes to her. 'This is none of your business, young lady, it doesn't concern you.'

'Why not?' she asked.

Grandma stood up. 'Because you are still a child. Dilys, I'll ask your father to get the papers out and explain it all to you one evening.'

And with that Dilys had to be content, but it didn't curb her impatience. Later, when she was alone with Charlotte, she sighed. 'I always have to wait and wait and wait.'

'I'll have to wait a lot longer,' Lottie said. 'It'll be years before I'm twenty-five. Never mind, it'll be Christmas soon and Glyn will be home. That'll cheer things up.'

CHAPTER FOUR

CHARLES AND OLWEN MORTIMER had chosen Mersey View for their first home because it was similar to the houses they'd both grown up in: spacious rooms with high ceilings ornamented with intricate plasterwork, and black and white tiles in the hall. The kitchen and bathroom were the originals, and there were two lavatories, both in mahogany cabinets, with a blue pattern inside the porcelain bowl.

The bungalow had been built in 1880 but in the Georgian style, and with eight bedrooms was large enough to accommodate a family in comfort. There was an extensive basement underneath. This was reached by a flight of stone steps going down from the back garden in the London fashion. Looking down, a front door was visible, and a row of similar windows to those in the rest of the bungalow, though these were only three feet away from the brick retaining wall. Very little daylight reached down there, and not even a glimmer of sun. The basement was used by the domestic staff. Charles and Olwen had moved in with a cook and a housemaid, and a gardener who lived out. The house was already old-fashioned, and a little shabby, but it had a faded elegance.

Christmas was almost on them in 1922 when Charles told Dilys and Lottie over dinner that he could not afford a tree this year. Lottie was shocked. 'It won't seem like Christmas.'

'It should,' Harriet said, 'since you've spent the afternoon putting up paper streamers in the playroom.'

Jemima had told them paper chains were tawdry. She felt a few cards along the mantelpiece and a sprig or two of holly tucked behind the pictures was more than enough in the main rooms.

Dilys objected. 'Surely we can stretch to a tree? That's all we need; we've got lots of ornaments and tinsel left over from other years.'

Grandma was tight-lipped. 'Your father is worried about the outlook for the business.'

'Please,' Lottie pleaded.

Jemima's stern exterior hid a kind heart. The following day, she took them to the market and paid for the tree they chose. While they put it up in the playroom, she sank into her armchair in front of the sitting room fire and stared into the flames, deep in thought. Everything was changing, she reflected; this was not the world she'd grown up in. In those days, the Mortimer Line had returned a good profit year after year, going from strength to strength with twenty ships. Everything was set fair: her three older brothers worked in the business and her father was king of all he surveyed.

In her time, girls had not gone out to work, and when Jemima had failed to attract a husband by the time she was twenty, she'd grown impatient and bored with the domestic round. She'd had to fight her family to be allowed to train as a nurse at the Florence Nightingale School in London, and it had opened her eyes to how the rest of the world lived. Added to that, a few years working in the back streets of Liverpool made her realise just how fortunate she was. The appalling conditions and the plight of some of the women and children she'd tried to help had filled her eyes with tears.

She became interested in public health and joined the Ladies' Sanitary Reform Association. Through her work she met Patrick O'Leary, a doctor who was trying to improve the lot of immigrants flooding into Liverpool as they fled famine in Ireland. He had no interest in money or business; his only thought was for the welfare of others. Surprising her family, she fell in love for the first time at the age of twenty-nine. They didn't approve of Patrick, who had no idea how to run an important firm like theirs and was not prepared to try. He intended to continue working as a doctor.

To please her, he changed his name to Mortimer by deed poll before they were married. Jemima counted her marriage very happy, and she was well content with her lot. They had two sons and a daughter, and worked together to help the poor and the sick. In 1894, however, Patrick caught cholera from his patients and died.

Jemima thought that was the end of her world, but it was just the first tragedy of many. Her mother died of a stroke shortly afterwards at a comparatively young age, then during the second Boer War one of her brothers was lost at sea. After the turn of the century, competition in the shipping trade increased and the Mortimer Line was no longer able to make the profits it had done.

Her father was semi-retired when the Great War broke out and was relying on her other brothers to run the business. Both were killed, and in addition they lost eight ships. Her father told her that in future she and her sons would have to run the

Mortimer Line, and this she was determined to do. She promised him she'd do her best to bring the business back to full profitability.

During the war, trade picked up, but there was a shortage of ships as so many had been sunk. Jemima used much of the compensation the firm received for its losses to buy two more ships at very inflated prices. She learned quite soon that that had been a bad mistake. Trade fell away and was showing no sign of recovering.

Of her children, Charles and Harriet were kind, placid people like their father and were hardly suited to trade. Only Lazlo had shown the interest and alert ability needed, but then he'd made that crass mistake and deserted her. Charles was trying to do his duty by the family, but he'd married a fragile wife and their children seemed to be cast in much the same mould. It was too soon to tell with Glyn and Charlotte, but meantime the responsibility was hers. She felt guilty now that she'd failed to keep the promise she'd made to her father on his deathbed to make the business profitable again.

Glyn and his brother came home from the *Conway* bubbling with seasonal joy. Oliver was looking forward to his first voyage as a seafarer, and Glyn was full of stories about his new life.

At dinner the first night he looked round at them all. 'Did you know that the poet John Masefield was once a pupil on the *Conway*?' he asked.

'Yes,' chorused Dad, Grandma and Aunt Harriet. 'I didn't know him though,' Charles added.

Jemima usually dressed for dinner and wore her mother's

pearl necklace. As this was a special meal to welcome her grandsons home, she wore her diamond brooch too. She was always alert and took part in everything; now she recited in a loud voice a line from one of John Masefield's most famous poems, 'Cargoes'.

'That's the Mortimer Line exactly,' Glyn said, and they all laughed. 'But after one voyage to Chile, during which he was seasick, Masefield decided he'd rather be a poet than a sailor and gave up the sea.'

A parcel of books arrived for Glyn and Charlotte, a Christmas gift from Uncle Lazlo ordered through a Liverpool bookshop. They opened it up immediately to find they were about West Africa. One was about the slave trade, a second about the explorers searching for the source of the River Niger, and a third about how trading with the natives for palm oil had started in the Oil Rivers region where Lazlo worked.

They devoured the books, but neither Dad nor Grandma approved. They thought such reading matter could only sharpen Glyn's appetite to follow in Lazlo's footsteps. Aunt Gwendolen, their only remaining Welsh relative, also sent each of them a book, but she misjudged their ages and interests and they were soon laid aside.

To Lottie's delight, Philip came round and invited her and Glyn to a children's Christmas Eve party at the yacht club as guests of his family. Even Dilys found that having their brothers at home enlivened everything. The boys rushed them to the shops to help them buy their presents, and took them out carolling with a group from the church.

Two days before Christmas, however, a crisis arose.

Ida, who had started with them as their housemaid fifteen

years ago, and was now their only household help, was collecting the dishes after their main course at dinner when she suddenly announced: 'I want to give notice and leave immediately. I've been offered a job in a very nice house in Rock Park where they keep a cook as well. She'll be company and I'll be paid more for fewer hours.' She stalked out with their dirty plates, leaving them stunned.

'That means no help over Christmas.' Aunt Harriet was horrified.

Dad groaned. 'I paid her this afternoon *and* gave her a Christmas box. Well, we can't afford to replace her. There are three of you ladies at home all day. You'll have to learn to manage the housework between you.'

Aunt Harriet and Dilys complained, because they all knew Dad was thinking of buying a car to get to work. Grandma spoke of trying to find someone to replace Ida, but nothing would come of that before the big day. She organised them all to produce the usual Christmas fare of turkey, plum pudding, mince pies, trifles and cakes. Charlotte and Dilys were given new lists of household chores and told that in future they were responsible for making their own beds and keeping their rooms clean and tidy.

Neither gave much thought to Ida's departure; their minds were set on the Christmas festivities. Lottie had a marvellous time at the yacht club party; there were games, a magician pulling white rabbits out of his hat, and a magnificent tea. The Roydens were attentive hosts, and Philip hardly left her side He was in sparkling high spirits and helped her pull her Christmas cracker. It tore without a sound and a tie pin fell out.

'A disappointment,' he said. 'I don't suppose you'd ever want to wear that. Let's see if there's anything better in mine.' When they pulled his cracker, it went off with a satisfying bang, and a ring dropped out. 'Just the thing for you, Lottie, a diamond engagement ring.' He slid it on to her finger and patted the back of her hand.

The ring was too big and she had to ask Glyn to put it in his pocket in case she lost it. When she showed it to the family on Boxing Day, Grandma said, 'Trash, you can't wear that. Throw it away,' but Lottie put it in her pencil case to show to some of the girls at school. Philip had called it an engagement ring and slipped it on her finger. Perhaps one day he'd give her a real ring.

Eunice and her husband Martin Sanderson had been invited to lunch on Christmas Day, but she was expecting her first baby and the birth was near. They had accepted provisionally, though the family were speculating anxiously as to whether they would manage it now there was no ferry. At the last moment Martin cancelled because the trains would be running only a limited service, but agreed to come instead on Glyn's birthday, which was Tuesday 2 January.

There were gales after Christmas, but Philip came round to show them a complete set of cigarette cards that his father had collected years ago and had now given to him. He and Glyn tried to collect the current ones from the packets their relatives smoked – they were of famous cricketers at the moment – but his father's set was very special. The cards depicted the flags and funnels of fifty of the world's shipping lines, twenty of them Mersey companies. Charlotte was thrilled to see the

Mortimer Line's green funnel with black and white rings round the top, together with its green triangular flag.

Philip also had a card showing the colours of the Royden fleet, a buff-coloured funnel with black and red rings and a buff and red house flag. 'Sadly,' he said, 'since Dad amalgamated with Elders, our markings are no longer being put on any ship.' But Lottie and Glyn knew that it had been a wise choice that had proved profitable. The Roydens still kept two maids.

'Come and show these to Dad,' Glyn said. 'He'd like to see them.'

They took the cigarette cards to the sitting room, and all the family studied them with interest. They were able to pick out many companies that had gone out of business since the cards had been printed.

The Roydens were taking a group to the pantomime at the Empire Theatre and invited Lottie and Glyn to join them. On New Year's Eve, a party was to be held at their house, and they invited Dilys and Oliver too, as there would be older Royden cousins there.

Lottie was afraid her family believed the Roydens had lured Uncle Lazlo away from them by offering him an exciting job, and that he'd betrayed them by accepting it. Relations between the grown-ups remained cool, though the younger members were getting together more, and she and Glyn counted Philip a special friend.

'I feel very lucky to have my birthday in the Christmas holidays,' Glyn said. 'Much more fun than in term time, and Eunice will be here for lunch.'

Lottie heard Grandma organising that on the telephone.

'Eunice, we've ordered a taxi to meet you at New Ferry station; you must phone us when you are about to leave home so that nobody has to wait too long.'

She was excited and wanted to go with Dad to meet them, but Grandma said, 'No, you stay here with us. There'll be four of them in the taxi already, and Eunice won't want to be squashed.'

Eunice was Martin's second wife, and he already had three children. The two youngest would be staying at home with the nursemaid, but the eldest, seven-year-old Christabel, would be coming with them.

'I told Eunice she was mad to marry him,' Dilys had said, and certainly at the wedding Lottie had thought the groom looked nearly as old as Dad.

'Come on,' Glyn said to Dilys, 'you're envious because she's two years younger than you and she's managed it first. You'd like to get married too.'

'I would,' she said. 'What's wrong with that? I don't want to end up like Aunt Harriet, living in somebody else's house and having to earn my keep by cooking and cleaning all day.'

'No need to feel life is passing you by, not yet.'

'But I'm fussy. I don't want a husband like Martin Sanderson.'

'I think he's nice,' Lottie said.

'He's too old for Eunice and he's used to looking after those three kids; he treats her like another child. He decides everything for her. I reckon she's more tied up and fenced in now she's married than she was at home.'

'You said you liked his moustache.'

41

'Yes, I did. But I want a husband nearer my own age, and he must be the sort of person who will take me out and about so we can have fun.'

'You'll want him to be rich, too, and shower you with jewels,' Glyn said. 'I hope you find the perfect husband.'

Eunice had been introduced to Martin by Aunt Gwendolen's husband Jeremy; he too was a member of the Sanderson family, who owned a factory making toffees. They were particularly known for their excellent chocolate eclairs.

Gwen and Jeremy had married in 1910. They had a fine house in Princes Park in Liverpool but had to spend most of their time in their Westminster flat. They moved in very exalted circles, and since Olwen had died, the Mortimers had seen very little of them.

Martin was a cousin of Jeremy's. He'd been thirty-seven when he met Eunice, and despite his having been married before and already having a family, she had been very keen to marry him.

Aunt Harriet had encouraged her. 'He'll be a good husband to you,' she'd said. 'He can provide you with a full family life and a good standard of living.'

Martin seemed very pleasant and his little daughters were delightful. With his family connection, permission for Eunice to marry had not been delayed. She had joined him in his very nice house in Gatacre, and they'd not seen much of her since.

The family were all in high spirits that morning because it was Glyn's thirteenth birthday and they were very much looking forward to seeing Eunice. Christabel looked very sweet in a red velvet party dress, and they made much of her. She was well behaved but shy, and couldn't be persuaded to say very much. The visitors brought a family-sized tin of chocolate eclairs and a cheque made out to Glyn.

But Lottie could see that everyone was shocked at how much Eunice had changed. Once she'd been the prettiest Mortimer daughter. Now she'd not only put on a grotesque amount of weight, but she was deathly pale and there was a dissatisfied droop to her mouth.

'Unfortunately Eunice has not kept in good health,' Martin told them over the splendid lunch they'd worked hard to produce.

'I wish this baby would hurry up and come,' she said. 'I feel fat and clumsy and I'm tired all the time. I'm fed up with being pregnant.'

'It's almost due,' her husband murmured sympathetically, patting her hand. 'Only three more weeks, darling.'

'How long exactly does pregnancy take?' Lottie asked. Everyone ignored her. She'd noticed before that adults were reluctant to talk about such things in company. They'd wait until they could catch her on her own and then be horribly embarrassing, describing every last detail.

'I feel as though this baby has taken over my life.' Eunice was petulant.

'You must expect a baby to do that,' Grandma said tartly, 'but it won't be for ever. Anyway, once he's born, you'll feel such love you'll just want to hold him in your arms and gaze at him. You won't be able to get enough of him.'

Eunice sniffed in disbelief. 'Martin is at work all day and I'm on my own so much.'

'The other children are with you, dear.'

'What about the nursemaid?' Lottie asked. 'Don't you like her?'

'A baby of your own will settle you down,' Aunt Harriet said.

'Harriet, you know nothing about babies,' Grandma said. She turned back to Eunice. 'Would you like Dilys to come and stay with you for these last few weeks? She'd cheer you up.'

'Yes,' Eunice said. 'Please, Dilly, do come,' and for a moment she seemed near to tears.

'Of course I will,' Dilys said warmly, 'if you think I can help. It'll be deadly dull here once everybody goes back to work. Philip Royden's cousin Brian has asked me to go out with him – I met him at their party – but I'll ring him to put him off.'

'Go and pack your things so you can go back with them,' Grandma said. 'Eunice, it's a fine day, and a breath of fresh air would do you good. Charlotte will take you for a short walk along the Esplanade.'

Eunice was ungainly. Lottie held on to her going down the steep garden steps. The wind felt icy and cut through her coat like a knife. The tide was in, the mud was covered and the waves were pounding against the narrow strip of sand and filling the air with life and energy. It smelled of seaweed and the sea.

'I do miss being at home with you all.' Eunice seemed immediately cheered. 'It's lovely to see the four old ships in the Sloyne again, but how odd to see the pier in two pieces.'

'We're getting used to that, but we miss you too. It's very quiet now you're married and Glyn has gone away to school. Dilys yearns for more fun.' Eunice stared into the grey afternoon but said nothing. 'When she goes too, I shall miss you all desperately, because I'll be the only one left at home.'

Lottie felt troubled by Eunice's visit, and it wasn't just that she'd seemed less content than they'd all supposed.

She and Glyn were alone in the playroom. 'Eunice says it makes nine months or forty weeks to make a baby,' she said. 'I'm ten months younger than you are; that seems to allow very little time for our mother to recover before she became pregnant with me.'

'I was thinking that too.'

'Would that be the reason she died?' Lottie asked. 'Is that what killed her?'

Glyn's horrified eyes met hers. 'No, they've told us it was TB, but let's look at a calendar.'

They went to Dad's study, where there was a big new calendar for 1923 hanging on the wall, and counted the weeks between Glyn's birthday and hers. There were forty-two and a half weeks.

'Surely that can't be right,' Glyn said. 'Mum was ill, an invalid, and it doesn't give her enough time.' They counted again. There was no mistake.

Lottie's stomach seemed to turn over; she felt sick. 'This must mean something terrible.' She'd always felt she wasn't quite one of the family. 'I'm not your sister.'

'Of course you are, don't be daft,' Glyn said. 'Don't go blowing this up into some big drama.'

But the more Lottie thought about it, the more worried she became. If Glyn's mother was not her mother, it altered everything. She was not who she'd believed herself to be.

'Ask Grandma about it,' he said. 'She'll tell you.'

Lottie was scared about doing that. Deep down, she was sure she was right. She'd been led to believe she was Charlotte Mortimer, the youngest child of the family, and she couldn't imagine being anyone else, but she was afraid that she was not who she'd thought she was.

'For heaven's sake.' Glyn was impatient. 'Come on, let's do it now and clear this up.' He took her hand and pulled her to the sitting-room door. Lottie's heart was thumping as he threw it open.

Aunt Harriet was half asleep in her chair beside the fire, but they'd roused her with their noisy entry. Dad was fiddling with the mantelpiece clock, which he'd lifted down to the side table. 'This clock has stopped again,' he said. 'It'll have to go to the mender.'

'Dad,' Glyn said. 'Lottie has some silly idea that she doesn't belong to our family. She thinks she's a sort of cuckoo in the nest. Can you tell her she's wrong?'

'Oh my goodness.' Harriet pulled herself upright in her chair. 'What a silly idea.'

Charles turned round and threw his arms round Lottie in a hug. 'You mustn't worry about things like that. We are your family. You can rely on us to take care of you.'

'There,' Glyn said triumphantly, 'I told you so. It's just some fancy you've got into your head. Of course you're my sister; who else could you be?'

Lottie felt her father's arms tighten round her before he dropped a kiss on her forehead and released her. She felt comforted and reassured by his show of affection.

'Could you two take this clock up to McCarthy's, the clock

repairer on the New Chester Road? I'll give him a ring and tell him it's on the way. He should be able to fix it.'

As Lottie was putting on her coat, Glyn said, 'There you are, what did I tell you?'

'Grandma wasn't there,' she said.

'No, but what difference would that make?'

CHAPTER FIVE

LOTTIE SHARED THE FAMILY pride that they could describe themselves as shipowners. There were vessels of every sort to be seen scudding up and down the river, and she loved to watch them from her bedroom window. She'd asked many times to have the family's ships pointed out to her, but rarely saw them. 'You'll have to go to Morpeth Dock,' Dad would say. 'The *Caernarvon* is unloading slate there today.'

'We'd rather go to the Mediterranean and see the *Cheshire* loading grain,' Glyn would add.

The night she'd heard Grandma recite 'Dirty British coaster with a salt-caked smoke stack', and Glyn had pointed out that that described the Mortimer Line ships exactly, she'd understood that there was nothing glamorous about the family fleet. Later, when she talked about it with Glyn, he said, 'But we're still shipowners, a family of status.'

At dinner on the last night of Glyn's holiday, Lottie asked, 'How did we start in the business, Dad? I know the family have owned ships for hundreds of years, but how did they get the first one?'

He smiled at her; she knew he liked nothing better than to talk about the business. 'A forebear of ours, Lazarus Mortimer, was a master mariner and captain of a schooner carrying cargoes round the world.'

Glyn put in, 'Was Uncle Lazlo named after him?'

'He was indeed; it became a family name. The first Lazarus saw that the Liverpool owners of his ship made a fortune from the cargoes he carried from one port to another on their behalf, and he became ambitious and wanted a ship of his own so that he could earn the profit for himself.'

'At school we learned how the slave trade made fortunes for the Liverpool traders,' Glyn said. 'I hope the first Lazarus Mortimer wasn't involved in that horrible business. Did he carry slaves?'

Grandma barked, 'A lot of nonsense is taught about slaving by people who ought to know better. Liverpool did not invent it; the Greeks and Romans had slaves in prehistory. If Lazarus did carry slaves, then I hope he had the sense to treat them kindly, feed them well and let them walk around the deck during the voyage. Why wouldn't he? Nobody would buy a sick slave; it was to everybody's advantage to have them arrive in good health. And we should be proud that Britain led the world in putting an end to the trade.' She returned to her apple pie and custard to show that the subject was closed.

Lottie pondered. Did that confirm that the family ships had been slavers? She was afraid the Mortimers might have skeletons in their closet, but it was not to be mentioned. Despite Dad's talk of poverty, they were not all that poor. She'd heard there were men without jobs congregating on street corners, and they had no money for food.

She could see that Glyn was opening his mouth again but managed to get a question of her own in first. 'But Dad, a ship costs a lot of money. Was it possible for a captain to buy one?'

'Yes, in the old days ships were small, made of wood, and they had sails. The wind was free; a ship wouldn't have cost much compared to what it does today.'

'But even so . . .'

'Our company started with a single ship, as was often the case. I expect Lazarus would have saved some money and knew one or two people in the trade who wanted to invest, and that way he'd be able to raise the cost of a vessel. He was a master mariner and would arrange his own route, the ports and the cargoes, and advertise for passengers in the newspapers.'

'And when he made more money, he eventually owned all his first ship?' Lottie asked.

'No. Both the ship and the cargo could easily be lost in a storm, so it was safer to own a half-share of two ships.'

'But things are different now,' Glyn said. 'Safer. There are fewer shipwrecks.'

'Very different now. Eventually some of these single-ship companies joined together to be managed here from the port, and that is how L. E. Mortimer and Partners came into existence.'

'But we don't own all of our ships?'

'No, quite the reverse. Ships became more expensive. Iron sailing ships were built, and then steam engines were invented and fitted, and they used coal. Now the latest thing is diesel oil.'

'No private family could buy a ship today,' Grandma said. 'As these advances were made, more people had to be found to invest their money. Years ago, the number of shares per ship was capped at sixty-five.'

'Sixty-five people owned one ship?'

'Yes, and then each share was allowed to be split into five.'

'Good Lord,' Glyn said. 'Then how much do we actually own of the Mortimer Line today?'

'Just a fraction,' Charles said. 'I pay the seamen and the harbour dues, arrange the cargoes and for the ships to be provisioned and bunkered, but for years it's been getting harder to make a profit. Once I managed ten ships; now there are just the three small tramping freighters and two coasters.'

'Is that because you can't get enough cargoes to keep them all working?'

'That's right.'

'And you have to share whatever profit you make with all the people who invested money in the ships?' Lottie said.

'Of course.'

'What sort of cargoes do you want? No passengers, of course, but what do you carry?' Glyn asked.

'We would take a passenger if somebody wanted to travel, and almost any cargo to any destination. We take the goods made on Merseyside all round this country as well as to Ireland and Europe – things like matches, sugar and jam.'

'And potato crisps,' Glyn added.

'Yes, and we hope to pick up a cargo to bring back.'

'Such as?'

'The blue slates from Port Dinorwic cover most of the roofs on Merseyside and can come faster by sea than they can by rail or road. They have been our bread and butter for years, and so have the granite setts that are quarried and finished in North

Wales. We've brought them here in their millions to pave the streets of Liverpool. And the limestone quarry near Colwyn Bay is still sending regular shipments into Liverpool.' Charles sighed. 'Once I could have expected the Mortimer Line to make me rich, but not these days. Everything is changing, and it's not for the better.'

Lottie was in the sitting room saying goodnight to the family when the telephone rang. Aunt Harriet went to answer it and came running back all flushed and excited. 'That was Martin to say Eunice has gone into labour at last.' She'd gone nearly two weeks over her dates. 'The doctor is with her but he says it will be another hour or so yet.'

To Lottie, it felt as though they'd been waiting for the news for ages, and each day that passed had made things seem worse. Eunice's pregnancy had lasted forty-two weeks. That was the exact age gap between herself and Glyn.

She was trying to find the words to ask about it when Grandma said, 'Go to bed, Charlotte, it could be ages before we have more news.'

'The baby might be here when you wake up,' Dad said as he kissed her cheek. 'Off you go, goodnight.'

In bed, she comforted herself with the thought that once the baby was born, Eunice would cheer up and Dilys might come home. She meant to stay awake listening for the phone ringing again with more news, but it was morning when she woke up. Harriet came in to draw back her curtains. 'Eunice had a baby boy, at three o'clock,' she said. 'He weighed eight and a half pounds and they're both fine.'

Everybody was more awake than usual over breakfast.

'We'll all go over to see the new baby next week,' Grandma said.

'What are they going to call him?' Lottie wanted to know.

'Thomas Martin Charles,' Grandma said. 'He'll be known as Tom.'

'Thomas because it was his grandmother's surname,' Harriet explained. 'Martin after his own father. Charles after your father and because it's a Mortimer family name. He will be your first nephew.'

They were all delighted at the news. Lottie thought that with three little girls already, Eunice and Martin must be pleased to have a son. She was looking forward to being taken to see the new baby the following Sunday. It would be a big outing for her, and she wanted to see Eunice and Dilys again. At the last moment she heard that Oliver and Glyn had been given special leave from the *Conway* to come with them. There had been a lot of talk about Dad getting a car, but it still hadn't happened, so they took a taxi to Rock Ferry pier to pick up the boys and catch the ferry across from there.

Charlotte felt immediately that Glyn was not his usual cheerful self. His face had come out in pimples and he seemed distant and troubled. But she forgot her worries about him in the pleasure of meeting baby Tom and seeing her sisters again. Eunice was still in bed recovering, but she seemed very happy and proud to show off her son. Lunch was a very grand meal and Eunice was brought down by her husband to sit at the table. Lottie marvelled anew at her sister's smart home, handsome husband and ready-made family.

There had been talk about Dilys coming home with them, but she said, 'Eunice would like me to stay and help with the new baby for another week or so, and Martin has said I'm welcome to stay as long as I like.'

As they were leaving, Martin whispered to Lottie that Dilys had an admirer, who'd asked her out next week. 'I'll see she comes home after that,' he said, and presented her with another box of the sweets made in his family's factory.

Oliver seemed like a grown man now, and spent his time talking to the other adults. He told them he was waiting for a placement for his first voyage and had asked for a ship going to the far east.

'When my time comes,' Glyn said, 'I will ask for a vacancy with Elder Dempster to work on their mailboat service to West Africa. I want to do what Uncle Lazlo is doing.'

It bothered Lottie that Glyn seemed suddenly changed for no apparent reason. It was almost as though he'd become a stranger, and the close relationship she'd had with him appeared to have gone. On the ferry going back he looked really sad, as though he had the weight of the world on his shoulders. Aunt Harriet tried to jolly him along. 'It must seem strange to find you are Uncle Glyn and Aunt Charlotte to that new baby when you're only twelve and thirteen years old yourselves.' It didn't help.

As they saw the four old ships come closer, Lottie went to stand beside him against the ferry's rail. 'There's something the matter,' she said. 'You're not happy. Don't you like being on the *Conway*?'

'Yes,' he muttered, but he looked even more miserable. Clearly the problem wasn't something he could talk to her about.

The family stood on the jetty watching the skiff being rowed across from the *Conway* to collect the two boys. Once they'd gone, Dad decided that the rest of them would walk home along the promenade.

'I'm tired,' Lottie complained, and Harriet said she was too.

'It's only just over a mile,' Grandma said briskly. 'Come along, you two, it's a nice evening. It'll do us all good.'

CHAPTER SIX

DILYS CAME HOME A WEEK or two later, with a new hairstyle from Eunice's expensive hairdresser. Lottie thought her dark curls made her look prettier than ever and longed to have the same beautiful hair. She thought her own hair looked colourless alongside her sisters', and it didn't help that Grandma insisted on unflattering short pigtails for school.

Dilys was starry-eyed about her new boyfriend, and came to lie on Lottie's bed to tell her all about him. 'His name's Keith Driscoll, he's twenty-six and he works for the Liverpool Savings Bank in County Road. His dad works in their head office in Bold Street. He came to Eunice's house to take me out. He's lovely, really handsome, and he's got a car. I'd never have met anyone like him if I'd stayed at home. I can't wait to go out with him again.'

At dinner that evening, she told the family that she'd been out two or three times with her new boyfriend while she'd been at Eunice's. 'He's asked me out again on Saturday.'

'We don't know this person,' Grandma said severely. 'You should not go out with young men before you've brought them home and introduced them.'

'Eunice and Martin know him, and I like him.'

'Bring him here,' Grandma ordered. 'I want to meet him.'

'For heaven's sake,' Dilys said. 'I'm twenty-four and this is the twentieth century. All that died out with Queen Victoria. He's asked me out again and I'm going whether you like it or not. He's got an Austin Seven and he's taking me to the theatre in Birkenhead.'

Lottie knew that Dilys was enraged, but like the rest of the family she couldn't ignore Grandma's request. She asked Keith to come to the house and collect her. On Saturday she was like a cat on hot bricks as she got ready for the outing, going to great lengths to look her best. Lottie made a point of being in the sitting room with the family when she brought him in.

Grandma shook hands with him. 'I understand you work at the Liverpool Savings Bank. What is your position there?' she wanted to know.

'I'm an assistant at the moment, but I'm hoping to be promoted soon to deputy manager at another branch.'

'And your father?'

'He works for them too, but at their head office in Bold Street. He's their chief accountant.'

It was obvious that Keith Driscoll had their approval, and Dilys was on cloud nine. Lottie herself thought him a nice enough man, though nothing special to look at. Dilys had led her to believe he rivalled Rudolph Valentino.

She stayed up as late as possible to hear how the outing had gone, but was sent to bed before Dilys came back. She tried to stay awake and could hear frustrated words passing between Dad and Aunt Harriet in the hall. It seemed that Dilys was still out and they were getting anxious about her. The next morning her sister didn't appear at breakfast, and the grown-ups were tight-lipped and frosty.

Before leaving for church, Lottie popped to Dilys's bedroom and found her red-eyed and miserable. 'There was a terrible row last night when I got home,' she whispered. 'I'm staying out of the way because they won't stop nagging at me.'

The adults were still talking round the dining table. Lottie tiptoed past the door to the kitchen to see if anything could be salvaged for Dilys's breakfast. A serving of bacon, sausage and tomatoes had been cooked for her and was cooling on a plate. She slid it on to a tray, then found a bread roll and filled a glass with milk. She took it to Dilys's bedroom before joining the family for the walk to church.

When she got home afterwards, Dilys was resentful and out of sorts. 'I'm in big trouble. Not forgiven for being late back,' she said.

'But how was your night out? Was it worth a telling-off?'

'No, it didn't go all that well.'

'What went wrong? Where did he take you?'

'To the Argyle Theatre to see a variety show; Dad and Aunt Harriet don't approve of variety shows, not for young ladies. They say they can be risqué.'

'What's that?'

'Rude jokes, but they were wrong, there weren't any. The show was all good fun, dancing and singing. Gracie Fields was the star turn and she was lovely. Then he took me to the Central Hotel for supper. We had smoked salmon and wine, that was lovely too.'

'I thought you said it hadn't gone well?'

'It didn't. He was getting boring because he talked about himself all the time. He brought me part of the way home in his car, then stopped in Eastcott Road where all those big trees are. All he wanted to do was grope and kiss me.'

'But that's romantic, isn't it? What all boyfriends want to do?'

'I couldn't get him to stop. He was into heavy petting the first few times he took me out, but not as bad as this. He was trying to undress me.'

'Why?'

'Oh God, Lottie! You must have had your talk from Grandma by now.'

She nodded. 'Yes.'

'Well you've heard all about it then. He wanted to anticipate marriage, but we must not risk that. We must stay in control and make sure we have our babies at the right time in our lives. They are a joy when we're married but can cause terrible trouble when we aren't.

'I knew it was getting late and I wanted him to bring me home, but he wouldn't. I got out of the car and started to walk, but he followed me and tried to persuade me to get in again. I was jolly glad to reach the back gate, I can tell you. But don't tell Grandma or Dad. He's a complete rotter and I certainly won't be going out with him again.'

Lottie was envious about the visit to the Argyle Theatre, and incredulous that a friend of Eunice and Martin would be like that, but by Monday Dilys was feeling better. 'Come to the pictures with me,' she said. 'I'm bored out of my mind.'

'I'd love to, but Grandma won't let me go out on a week night.'

'She knows I'm depressed, so she might let you come if we ask her nicely.'

They found Grandma in the kitchen. Harriet was consulting

her about a ham she was boiling. 'Take Charlotte to the cinema? What film is it you want to see?'

'I don't know what's on,' Dilys said. 'I just want to go out.'

'Then no. Charlotte knows she isn't allowed out when she has to get up for school the next morning, and as for you, Dilys, you go out far too often. A night in would do you more good.'

It seemed Dilys had recovered by the time they were sitting down to dinner, because she said, 'Dad, I'd like to get a job. Could I have lessons to learn to type? Once I can do that, I could help you in the office.'

Charles pondered. 'It might save one person's salary.'

'No, I want to be paid.' Dilys was alarmed. 'I want a real job.'

'For goodness' sake, Dilys, make up your mind,' Grandma told her. 'You've dragged your feet about this for years. Nursing would be a good career.'

'Not for me. I couldn't stand bedpans and sick people. I'd hate that. An office job would suit me better.'

'There is no need for you to work at all,' Harriet said. 'Our family are shipowners, and have been since the seventeenth century.'

'Nothing ever happens here,' Dilys burst out. 'I'm bored. Since you've given up the yacht club—'

'Membership wasn't cheap,' Grandma said. 'We were sorry to have to do it, and we all miss it.'

Harriet sighed. 'Everything was so much handier when we lived in Rock Park. There was always something on in the Olympian Gardens, or at the Rock Hotel.'

'Please can I have typing lessons?' Dilys pleaded. 'If I get a job, you won't have to support me.'

Charles sighed. 'I'm your father, Dilys, it's my duty to support you, and secretarial school would mean a further outlay now when trade is poor.'

She was getting angry. 'You keep pleading poverty, Dad, but you're always talking about buying a car and learning to drive.'

Lottie took a deep breath; she wouldn't dare to say such a thing to Dad, but all he did was sigh again.

'Rain is getting into the spare bedroom and I'll have to get someone to look at the roof again, which is why I keep putting off buying a car. As it is, any car would have to be second-hand; I couldn't afford a new one. The lease on the office is coming to an end, and without the ferry, I'll have to find one on this side of the water, but buses can be very tiring and inconvenient. I'm sorry, Dilys, but no lessons at the moment.'

They were all surprised to hear Grandma say, 'I think Dilys is right. If she's bored, she needs a job. Times are changing, Charles, and it did me no harm to work before I got married. Even after you were born, I helped out when your father was busy and needed help.'

Lottie held her breath; she'd been right, Grandma was the one to talk to.

Grandma went on, 'I will pay for you to have lessons, Dilys. You need something to fill your day. I believe you will be more content if you have something to do, and I understand that work of that sort is not too difficult to get once you are a competent typist.'

Dilys leapt out of her chair and threw her arms round her grandmother. 'Thank you, thank you, Grandmama.'

'And Charles, it's high time you talked to her about her expectations. She has a right to know.'

He sighed. 'She has,' he agreed, 'but not now. I'm tired, and it's complicated.'

Dilys didn't have to wait long. The next day there was Madeira cake for tea, but they were allowed only one slice because Grandma believed it would spoil their appetites for dinner. Lottie fancied more, and while she and Dilys were in the kitchen washing up the teacups, she cut another slice.

Aunt Harriet put her head round the door. 'Dilys, go to your father's study. He and Grandma have looked the papers out, and he'll explain about your mother's will now.'

Lottie crammed the last of the cake into her mouth and prepared to follow, but Harriet stopped her. 'This has nothing to do with you, Charlotte.' As an afterthought, she added, 'You're too young to understand.'

Lottie felt frustrated as she put the remains of the cake back in the tin. If her sister could understand, so could she. Why did there have to be so much secrecy in the family? If their mother had made provision for her children, why keep them in ignorance about it?

And if that was the case, it seemed she too would be rich one day, and the thought gave her warmth, comfort and a feeling of security. Why not let them all enjoy these pleasant feelings as they were growing up? It made no sense to her.

Flushed with excitement, Dilys went to the study with a spring in her step. Grandma was there, and Dilys was immediately sent to bring another chair so she could sit down too, but not before she'd glimpsed documents spread out on her father's desk. This meeting seemed very important and very formal.

'This is your mother's will.' Her father pushed it across the desk. 'You and your siblings are joint beneficiaries. I first met your mother's family when I was seeking a cheaper supply of coal. We used it as fuel for our ships at that time.'

'I've always known Mum's family were in coal.'

'Yes, the Thomases had a shipping business similar to ours, and they also had mining interests in the Welsh coalfields, but as you know, they were plagued with ill health. When your mother and I were married, tuberculosis had been taking its toll on them for decades, and there were no sons left to run the business. Your Welsh grandfather sold up while they were still making money, and invested it wisely in other ventures. Your mother and her sister inherited a lot of money from him; it made them rich.'

'He was clever to do that.'

'Wiser than we have been,' her father agreed. 'He couldn't see his daughters running his business, though I believe he was wrong about that: they both had a firm grasp of financial matters.'

Grandma picked up the will. 'Your mother's instructions were that her money should be put into a family trust fund, and the interest paid to her children in equal shares.'

'But why do I have to wait until I'm twenty-five?'

'Because she wisely decided that she wanted you all to reach an age when she could expect you to be sensible with money. So when you turn twenty-five, or on marriage if that is sooner, you will start to receive your share.'

Dilys was put out. 'On marriage? That must mean Eunice is already getting hers.'

'Yes, she's drawn an income from this fund since her wedding day.'

'Why didn't I hear about it? Why didn't she tell me?'

'I told her not to,' Grandma said.

'That's not fair. She's got a husband to buy things for her.'

'That is what your mother decided. Getting married can be an expensive time.'

'But it wasn't for Eunice; she only had to buy her dress. You put on the wedding breakfast here, and her husband already had a smart house and a business to support her. Wouldn't her money just make them richer?'

'Of course, having money does make people richer.'

'Do they have more money than you, Dad?'

He sighed. 'It would seem so.'

Grandma took a deep breath. 'What is laid down in the will must be carried out; that is the law, Dilys.'

'I'm surprised you let Eunice get married,' she burst out. 'Weren't you afraid her husband would run off with her money?'

'No,' Grandma said firmly. 'Martin Sanderson is related to your Aunt Gwendolen's husband, so it isn't as though he was a stranger. Anyway, the inheritance has been arranged in a way that makes it impossible for him to do that. You all get a share of the interest, but none of you can touch the capital.'

Her father said, 'So from your next birthday – that's . . .'

'August the third.'

'Yes, you too will enjoy an income of your own.'

Dilys's eyes were round with surprise and delight. 'Are you telling me I'll be rich?'

'Well, comfortable anyway.'

She was astounded. 'But you're anything but comfortable; you're always complaining of falling trade and shortage of money. Will I be richer than you, Dad?'

'Well, you'll have a more reliable income, and it will be paid every year for the rest of your life.'

Dilys felt dazed by her unbelievable good fortune.

Grandma said, 'You'll never need to support yourself, but that doesn't mean you have to live a life of idleness. You've applied for a place at that secretarial school, and I think you should get yourself a job when you're qualified to do so.'

'I will, Grandma.'

Her father reached for the other documents on his desk. 'These papers give details of the trust fund and the current investments that comprise it.'

'Gosh, there are a lot. This is complicated.'

'It is. The Thomas family arranged for a firm of accountants to oversee it and keep things up to date. You may keep these documents overnight to study them, but I want them back tomorrow to keep here in my safe.'

'Thank you, Dad. You've been very generous to me.'

'It's your mother you must thank. We've all missed her love and care over recent years, but she is the one who has provided for you.'

'Can I keep her will overnight too? I'd like to read it carefully.'

'Yes, but you must return everything tomorrow. I only have one copy, and there's the rest of the family to explain it to.'

'One thing more,' Jemima said. 'Please do not show any of this to Charlotte, or talk to her about it.'

'She'll be bound to ask,' Dilys said.

'Yes,' Charles said, 'but you must not tell her. It doesn't apply to her.'

'Not at this time,' Grandma added.

Dilys rushed to her bedroom with the will, knowing that Lottie was likely to be waiting for her with a hundred questions on the tip of her tongue. Her sister arrived at her bedroom door ten seconds behind her. 'Are you really going to be rich?' she asked. 'How rich do they mean?'

'I've been told not to talk to you about it.'

'But Dilly, you will, won't you?'

'No, they say it has nothing to do with you.'

'That's mean.' Lottie leapt on to the bed. 'You can tell me a bit of what they told you,' she wheedled. 'Where did Mum get all this money?'

'From her family.'

'They were better at business than Dad?'

'Dad always says he should have sold up when the war was over, before the business started going downhill. Like the Roydens did.'

'And now it's too late?'

'Yes.'

'You could tell me more about Mum. Nobody seems to mention her now. Do you remember her?'

'Yes, I was about your age when she died.'

'What of?'

'Tuberculosis; it was rife in her family, she'd been ill for a long time. But you know all that. I didn't see much of her over the last year or two. She spent a lot of time in her room, or out in the front garden on a chaise longue if it was fine. They used to wrap her up in coats and scarves and she'd stay there for hours. It was supposed to cure her.'

'Who looked after me? I must have been tiny then.'

'We had a nanny and a nursery maid, and there was plenty of help in the house. Aunt Gwendolen came to oversee things when Mum was very ill. Grandma had her own house in Rock Ferry then, and Aunt Harriet lived with her.'

Dilys smiled at Lottie and sat down beside her. 'I remember the day you were born. Eunice and I came home from school and Dad took us to see you in a cot by Mum's bed. "Your new baby sister," he told us, and we were allowed to hold you. It happened like that when Glyn was born too.'

She sighed heavily. 'We weren't poor then, Dad was earning plenty of money. Lottie, don't you have any homework to do? I'd like to read the things Dad has given me.'

'Tell me about Mum's family.'

'She was brought up near Cardiff in a house called Dolwen, and she and Auntie Gwen could speak Welsh.'

'Tell me about their business. It was bigger than ours, wasn't it?'

'Get lost.' Dilys suddenly swept her off the bed. 'You know all about the *Olwen Thomas* and the *Gwendolen Thomas*, and the Thomas Line; Dad never stops talking about them. I need peace to read these documents.' She flapped them at Lottie.

'Why did Dad say it was no concern of mine?' Lottie asked. 'If Mum left her money to be shared amongst her children—'

Dilys put her out of the bedroom. 'You've got to grow up first.'

CHAPTER SEVEN

A s THE SUMMER HOLIDAYS DREW near, Glyn wrote home to ask if he might bring a friend to stay for a few days. *His name is Ralph Kingston*, he wrote, *and his father is a senior captain working for the White Star Line. He lives in Heswall.*

Lottie didn't like the idea – she wanted Glyn to herself when he was at home – but Dad said yes. 'Come and help me make up a bed for him,' Aunt Harriet said to her. 'We'll carry the camp bed into Glyn's bedroom. I expect they'd prefer to be together, and it'll save me airing and dusting the spare room.'

As soon as she saw Ralph, Lottie took a dislike to him. He was blond and good-looking, but he seemed to take all Glyn's attention. They were full of plans and arranged all sorts of expeditions that excluded Lottie. She was afraid he'd taken her place in Glyn's affections.

Philip Royden came round to see Glyn, but he was given short shrift too. It seemed Ralph had pushed everybody out of Glyn's affections. Philip sat in the kitchen with Lottie and they finished off a Victoria sandwich she'd found in a tin, though she was afraid Harriet might be cross.

'We might be moving house,' he told her. 'Did Glyn mention it?'

'No!' It seemed Glyn was taking no interest in anything but Ralph. 'Where are you going?'

'Mum and Dad are looking for somewhere in West Kirby.'

'But why?'

'Dad thinks New Ferry is becoming isolated, and it's getting shabby. Some of our neighbours are moving out too.'

'It's true,' Lottie said. No money had been found to repair the pier, and without the ferry service, New Ferry's time as a convenient, high-class residential district for Liverpool's successful businessmen was over. Neither could it continue as a pleasure venue for day trippers. Without the passing trade, the little post office and most of the shops in the parade by the pier would close down. The hotel had changed hands, the only trade was in the bar and it had become a pub. The district had become an idle backwater doomed to grow shabbier with time.

'But won't you miss the river?'

'Not now the ferry has closed.'

'I'll be sorry to see you go.'

'I like it here.' Philip pulled a wry face. 'I don't really want to leave. I'm going to lose my friends.'

'Don't lose me,' she said vehemently. He shook his head and wouldn't meet her gaze. After a silence, she added, 'And don't lose Glyn; we don't want to be left here on our own.'

He looked up and smiled. 'I won't,' he said, and she knew he was looking for companionship too.

They walked upriver along the beach to the shore fields, where there was a clay pit where bricks were made and shipped to Liverpool to build houses.

'Come down to our house tomorrow,' Philip said as they parted company. 'We'll go for another walk or something.'

Philip's mother was always welcoming, and the following day she gave Lottie lunch. In the afternoon a new naval ship was being launched from Cammell Laird's yard, and they went to Rock Ferry promenade to watch it. Lottie saw Glyn and Ralph in the crowd that had gathered.

She realised that Grandma too had taken a dislike to Ralph, and was surprised. Glyn's bedroom was next to hers and she occasionally heard giggles and scuffles from there. One night she was woken up in what seemed the middle of the night by a huge commotion. It was so loud it brought Dad to their door. She gathered that the camp bed had collapsed, and it pleased her to think Ralph had been thrown on to the floor. She turned over to go back to sleep, but the incident seemed more serious than that, because the next moment, Grandma had come to deal with it.

She lifted her head to listen. Grandma's strident voice was laying down the law in no uncertain terms, but the house was solidly built and she couldn't hear enough to find out what they'd done, and couldn't imagine what it could be to cause all this trouble.

The next morning, when she got up to go to the bathroom to wash, Aunt Harriet was in the passage, fully dressed and looking very serious, 'Get dressed, Charlotte,' she said. 'Don't disturb the boys, and go straight to the dining room for your breakfast.'

'What happened last night?' she asked.

'Just do as I say.' Her lips were in a hard straight line. Glyn's bedroom door was firmly shut and there was silence within.

At breakfast, the rest of the family looked equally solemn. 'What's happened?' Lottie asked.

'Never you mind,' Dad told her.

It seemed he didn't intend to go to work straight away; there was something important he had to attend to first. Lottie was curious and waited to find out more. She was really shocked when she realised he was ringing Ralph's parents. It seemed he wanted them to take Ralph home before the agreed stay of a week was over. She knew he and Glyn must have done something seriously wrong. She'd picked up that whatever it was might be against the law, but she couldn't think of anything it could possibly be. Glyn was completely honest.

Ralph's parents arrived an hour later to collect him, and Grandma took them and the boys to Dad's study, where the two families had a long discussion behind the closed door.

Only Lottie and Aunt Harriet were excluded. 'What is going on?' Lottie asked, but Harriet sent her out with a shopping list to buy what she called a few basic essentials. Lottie felt it was to get her out of the way, and her curiosity burgeoned.

When she returned with the bag of shopping, it was all over. Grandma and Aunt Harriet were having a restorative cup of coffee in the kitchen and Dad had gone to work.

'Where is Glyn?' Lottie asked.

'In his room,' Grandma said, and as she hadn't been forbidden to go and see him, she knocked on his door.

Glyn was hangdog and upset. He looked as though he'd been crying, and she couldn't remember him ever crying before. He believed in the stiff upper lip and didn't want to talk about what had happened, but Lottie knew she'd get more from him than any of the grown-ups and persisted. She could see he was embarrassed and struggling to find the words, but eventually he muttered, 'Ralph and I are homosexuals.'

'What's that?' She'd never heard of it and didn't know what he meant. She still couldn't see what it was that had turned the family upside down.

Jemima felt very strongly that Charles should have taken Glyn aside and spoken to him clearly and directly about what had occurred. The boy must be worried; this was something that should not be brushed under the carpet and forgotten. She was annoyed that Charles thought that by telling the other lad's parents and sending him home, he had done all that was required of a father.

She went to Glyn's room and knocked on the door. She heard no invitation to enter but went in anyway. He turned from the window, the look on his face telling her he wanted to be left alone. She knew she was right to be concerned about him. She put an arm round his shoulders and drew him to the bed. 'Let's sit down.'

He shook her arm off but sat down beside her and stared at the floor.

'You haven't been yourself for some time,' she began. 'You've seemed troubled. Have you been thinking that you may be homosexual?'

He jerked his head up to look at her, his mouth open, but said nothing.

'Most schools like yours are a hotbed of feelings about this.'

'I know I am,' he burst out. 'Isn't that what all this fuss is about?'

'It is.'

'I'm sorry, Grandma.' He was the picture of misery.

'I want to talk to you about what's happened because I think you might well be wrong. You're only twelve, too young to know.'

'I'm thirteen,' he corrected, 'since January.'

'Yes, thirteen, you must forgive my lapse of memory, but you're still a young boy and a long way from being grown up. I know Ralph Kingston thinks as you do, that you'll be all in all to each other for the rest of your lives, but the decisions you make at thirteen will be long cast aside by the time you're twenty-one.'

He looked truculent and pursed his lips.

'Feeling like this can be part of growing up—' Suddenly Jemima got up and opened the door. Lottie stood there, looking downright guilty at being caught out. 'Come in, Charlotte, I thought I heard you there. I'm talking to Glyn about growing up. No doubt you guessed, and as you are growing up too, you are right to be interested. It'll do you no harm to understand the stages of development we humans go through as we become adults.'

Lottie stood her ground. 'No, I don't want . . .'

'Come.' Jemima took hold of her hand and led her to the bed, then sat down between them. 'There's no need for either of you to be embarrassed.' They were shrinking into themselves and neither would look at her. She could feel discomfort like a wall between them. 'I came to explain to Glyn what homosexuality is, since it has caused something of an upheaval here recently.

'Everybody knows that we humans have to develop physically into adults,' she said. 'But we also have to develop mentally and emotionally, and that isn't so easy to understand. Think of Eunice's baby. At the moment he is aware only of himself. He can feel hot or cold or hungry or in pain, and he'll demand immediate attention to his needs. But soon he'll come to recognise his mother and his nanny and will be aware of the affection they show him. As he grows older, he'll learn to love his family. At school he'll discover how to play with other children and make friends, to be part of a team and expect only a fair share of attention from others.

'We all develop in the same way. At first we like to play with children of the same sex; we understand them and enjoy the same games. Now that you're teenagers, you've done all that and developed further emotionally, so your thoughts and your feelings—'

'Lottie isn't a teenager,' Glyn broke in furiously.

'She will be in another couple of months, and I don't want to go through all this again then. As I said, you have both been changing. You're seeing other people in a different light and you are making friends and forging attachments to people outside the family, but you still prefer your own sex. That's the stage you've now reached, Glyn. You've forged an attachment to Ralph, you feel love for him.'

Glyn's head sank lower. He was staring at his feet.

'And what of you, Charlotte? I've spoken to you before about the physical changes you're experiencing in your body as you grow into a woman. But what of your emotional changes?'

Lottie's cheeks were burning, a deeper and deeper red.

'It's in their teenage years that girls tend to have crushes on the games mistress at school, or perhaps another older girl. I know I did. Both of you need to understand that these sorts of feelings are a normal part of growing up.'

She was disappointed at their lack of response. 'But you

wait and see. Eventually most of us go on to fall in love with someone of the opposite sex. That's the way we humans develop into adults.'

They were both silent for a long time. Eventually Glyn muttered, 'But what causes this homo thing?'

Jemima felt she'd reached him at last. 'A proportion of us don't take that final step in our teens, and though it may not seem a big thing, it causes those affected more trouble than almost anything else. Older and wiser people than you misunderstand homosexuality; the law certainly does. It's complete nonsense to make it a criminal offence. We all have personal feelings, and homosexuals aren't evil as was feared in medieval times; they are just normal people whose feelings are different.'

'You're not cross with me?' Glyn asked.

'Of course not! It upsets me to see you so troubled about something that may never happen. My advice to both of you is to stop worrying about this. Wait and see how you feel in a year or two; you'll probably be thinking along completely different lines by then.'

'Grandma,' Lottie said, 'are you saying women can be homosexuals too?'

'Yes,' she said, 'it's exactly the same for our gender, but women who love other women are called lesbians.'

She got up and left them, and Glyn breathed a gusty sigh of relief.

Lottie felt Grandma had touched on an important truth when she'd spoken about girls having a crush on the games mistress at school. In her case it was Miss Laidlaw, who taught them art.

She'd discovered her name was Laura, and yes, she did feel love for her. She was young and pretty and more down to earth than the other teachers. She'd awakened in Lottie a love of art that hadn't been there before, and she was now trying to paint ships in a cloud of mist like Turner had. She'd also dragged Glyn to the Port Sunlight Art Gallery as Miss Laidlaw had recommended. But she'd never mentioned it to anyone, least of all to Miss Laidlaw herself, and never approached her except for advice on art, though that didn't stop her admiring her from afar.

Yet Grandma had said it was normal for children to prefer to play with friends of the same sex, but she had always counted Philip as her best friend. So she wasn't normal there.

Glyn got off his bed and went to look out of the window. 'What a rumpus you caused,' Lottie said. 'What an upheaval.' He was keeping his face turned away where she couldn't see it. 'Talks from Grandma can be so embarrassing,' she went on, 'but it's done with now. Let's go down to the shore; the tide's just gone out and there'll be crabs in the mud.'

He still looked very down. 'Grandma says we mustn't catch them and bring them into the house. Last time she could hear their claws scratching on the playroom lino as they crawled round.'

'We won't,' Lottie agreed. 'Grandma's very wise, she understands everything. Are you coming?'

'Leave me alone, can't you?'

Lottie went to see if Philip was at home and could think of something interesting to do. His mother had gone out and his father had told him to pack his toys and books ready to move to their new house. He'd got them all over his bedroom floor and was trying to decide what he'd grown out of or no longer needed.

She started to tell him about the rumpus Ralph Kingston had caused, and that he'd been collected and taken home.

'They'll only have been playing with themselves,' Philip said. 'If boys are caught doing that at school, there's always a dreadful fuss. They tell us that terrible retribution will follow if we persist. That it's evil and we should be ashamed of ourselves.'

'Just for playing with yourselves? Boys together? Grandma says all children prefer to play with children of their own sex, and it's only when we're grown up that we take an interest in the opposite sex. Yet you play with me.'

Philip sniggered, then laughed outright. 'I don't, Lottie, not in that way. That would be worse.' He grinned at her. 'A lot worse.'

Lottie laughed too. 'But I don't understand what all the fuss is about; why Ralph was sent home in disgrace.'

Philip stifled another giggle. 'If your grandma hasn't explained that to you, I don't feel I should,' he said.

CHAPTER EIGHT

DILYS WAS LATE COMING back from a visit to Eunice. They'd kept dinner waiting for fifteen minutes, but Grandma's patience had given out and they started without her. No sooner had Lottie cut into her lamb chop than she heard the back door slam and Dilys come rushing up the hall.

'I'm sorry I'm late, Grandma,' she said.

'Your dinner is in the oven keeping warm.'

Dilys made haste to fetch it. 'Sorry, Grandma,' she repeated as she returned to the table. Grandma believed they should always be punctual.

'I hope you have good reason to be late,' she said. 'It keeps us all waiting and can spoil the meal.'

'Yes, Eunice is pregnant again, she's upset. I've been trying to cheer her up.'

'Upset because she's pregnant?' Grandma's eyebrows went up. 'How old is little Tom?'

'He'll be two in January,' Charlotte said.

'Well I think she's very fortunate. A two-and-a-half-year gap between confinements is considered good timing, both for the wife and the children.'

'It's not the timing,' Dilys said. 'I don't think she wants another baby.'

'Oh dear!' Grandma laid down her knife and fork. 'I'm sorry she's upset, but I did explain fully to her what marriage was about. She assured me she was ready for it. Children are what she must expect.'

'There are four already in that house.'

Lottie had been listening with interest. 'Can't she stop having babies when she's got enough?'

Grandma gave her a stony stare and said, 'Do eat up, Dilys. What do we have for pudding, Harriet?'

That Christmas, nothing seemed the same. Oliver had accepted a position as third officer on board a tramping freighter bound for the Far East. The captain would pick up cargo from one port and carry it to another. He did not expect to be home for a couple of years.

Dad had not renewed the lease on his office in Liverpool. 'It would be more convenient for me to have an office on this side of the water,' he said. So instead he'd rented one in a back street near the entrance to the Morpeth Dock in Birkenhead.

When Lottie and Glyn opened their presents on Christmas morning, they found that Uncle Lazlo had sent each of them a crystal set in kit form. It came with instructions on how to build it, apparently a simple task. The British Broadcasting Corporation had just been set up in Savoy Hill, and had started broadcasting with the call sign 'This is 2LO calling'. Suddenly a crystal set was what everybody wanted, and when Philip told them he'd also received one from Uncle Lazlo, they asked him to bring it to their house so they could build their sets together. He came the day before Glyn's birthday, and the three of them unpacked their kits on the table in the playroom.

'It's the latest technology,' Glyn said. 'The kit is just a box containing a piece of galena crystal and a coil of thin and springy wire. All we have to do is place the wire on the surface of the crystal and delicately adjust it to find the spot where we can hear a radio signal.'

'You'd wonder how it's possible to hear things from London with one of these,' Lottie marvelled.

'The box must be the detector,' Philip said, his brown eyes sparkling with interest. 'And these headphones convert the radio waves into sound waves that can be picked up by the human ear.'

Lottie looked at Philip's neat head of chestnut hair close against Glyn's darker brown curls as they argued earnestly about the aerial the sets would need. She and Glyn had already discussed this with Dad, and twenty yards of wire had been procured for them. Philip and Glyn climbed up into the loft to lay it out, and immediately Lottie could hear crackles and music through her set.

'Mine's working,' she shouted excitedly.

They took the sets to the living room so Grandma and Aunt Harriet could listen in too; they were instantly hooked. Dad had said he didn't believe it would be possible to hear anything. He had to keep adjusting the wire as he kept losing the signal, but he listened through the headphones for a long time and said he thoroughly enjoyed the concert.

Glyn and Philip returned to school and took theirs with them. Charlotte hated to see them go, but she found her set gave her something different to do. Aunt Harriet was so impressed she borrowed it often.

Now that Dilys was old enough to draw an income from the

trust, she often took Charlotte shopping with her. She bought her a new dress as well as several for herself. She wanted a crystal set too, and found they cost only a few shillings.

Back at school, Lottie found her classmates were beginning to talk about the handsome boyfriends they had. Some even had photos they passed round. She told them about Philip. He was good fun and reasonably nice-looking, and sometimes if he caught her eye in church on a Sunday morning, he would wink at her.

The Roydens' old house had been divided into two separate dwellings, which were advertised for rent, and two new families had moved in. Both had several children, but the oldest was barely above toddler age, far too young to be companions for Lottie. Philip didn't forget her, though; in the summer holidays he'd come back to see her and Glyn.

'Do you like your new house?' she'd asked.

'Yes, it's very smart, and bigger than the one we had here. Come over and see it; Mum says I can ask you both to tea.'

She and Glyn had been very impressed with the new house. It was modern and airy, and everything looked sparkling new and fresh. The River Dee could be seen from the upstairs windows, and it was only a short walk to the train station.

The Roydens were not their only neighbours to move. Sometimes she walked home from school with Emily Warren, who lived further along the Esplanade, though she was two years older than Lottie and didn't always deign to speak to her. The Warrens' house was up for sale too, and Emily said they were moving to Heswall.

'Are we going to move, Dad?' Lottie asked him that evening.

'No, we can't afford to,' he said. 'Anyway, we like it here, don't we?'

'Yes,' she and Dilys chorused, but secretly Lottie wished they could move closer to the Roydens.

One Saturday Dilys suggested to Lottie that they go over to see Eunice. Her second pregnancy was now showing, and she didn't look well. She was lying on a chaise longue in the conservatory when they arrived, but sat up immediately when two small children followed them in.

'Hello, Tom,' Dilys said, pulling the little boy on to her knee.

'You remember Frances,' Eunice said. 'Martin's youngest daughter.'

Lottie patted her knee invitingly, but Frances shook her head.

'You'll have some tea?' Eunice asked, and went to see about it.

'She looks awful,' Dilys whispered. 'Matronly, almost middle-aged, and she's only twenty-four.'

Eunice returned with a nursemaid, who took the children away, and shortly afterwards a tea tray was delivered by a housemaid.

'You need to take more care of yourself,' Dilys told her. 'You're letting yourself go to seed.'

'I've got a lot to do,' she murmured, 'a lot of responsibility. You've seen the children; they're into everything, a real handful.'

'You've got a nursemaid,' Dilys said. 'It's not as though you have to do everything yourself. And Frances is at school now, isn't she?'

'Yes, she started last September.'

'Your hair looks a mess. It needs cutting. If you make an appointment with your hairdresser now, we'll take you.'

Eunice looked uncertain. 'I don't know . . .'

'Come on, what's the problem?'

'I have so much to do, and I'm tired all the time.'

'That's because you're pregnant. Can't you tell that husband of yours to lay off? He surely can't need any more children; this will be his fifth.'

Eunice's blue eyes filled with tears. Dilys shot over to her and threw her arms round her. 'I'm sorry,' she said. Eunice put her head down on her shoulder and wept.

Lottie pushed her hankie into her sister's hand. 'Is there a problem? Something we don't know about?'

'It's just me; everything's getting me down at the moment.'

Dilys insisted on ringing her hairdresser, but Tuesday was the earliest appointment she could make.

Eunice had recovered by the time they were going home, and they persuaded her to walk with them to the station. They had to pass her hairdresser's, and Dilys said, 'You used to go to one of the top salons in town, they did a much better job for you. Made you look more stylish.'

Eunice shook her head.

'Why here, for heavens' sake?'

'This is handy.'

'You could do with some smarter clothes. They do maternity wear in the shop where I work. Why don't you come over on Monday and I'll help you choose something?'

'No, it doesn't matter what I wear now; nothing can make me look smart.'

Dilys looked at her thoughtfully. 'What you really need is to go to a Marie Stopes clinic to stop yourself getting pregnant all the time.'

For a moment Eunice stared at them, looking stricken. 'It's a bit late for that now,' she said, then turned and fled back the way she'd come. They watched her hurrying away with head down and shoulders hunched.

'Oh my goodness! You've upset her,' Lottie said.

'It needed saying. Eunice is worse off now than she was at home with us.'

Lottie felt upset for her sister. 'You're right, she should never have married Martin. Is it that he's just too old for her?'

'I thought that was it at first, but I don't know . . . She has enough money to buy whatever she wants and do what she likes, but she's turning herself into a drudge.'

'She isn't happy.'

'She's very unhappy.'

'But why?' Lottie pondered. 'Do you think she's lonely?'

'I don't know. Martin doesn't spend much time with her. I thought he'd be at home today.'

'They have a lovely house and she's waited on hand and foot, yet she's complaining of having too much to do and too much responsibility.'

'They have an extravagant standard of living, far better than we have at home, but she had that dress when she was pregnant with Tom.'

'She isn't spending much on herself,' Lottie agreed. 'I don't think she's in love with Martin any more, and she just can't be bothered to smarten herself up. That must mean the romance has worn off.'

Dilys sighed. 'Well there's not much we can do about that. But once this baby is born, I'm going to drag her to a Marie Stopes clinic.'

Within a month of coming into her inheritance, Dilys had bought herself an Austin Seven, and a youth from a local garage had given her driving lessons. It hadn't taken her long to learn.

Once she'd completed her course at the secretarial college, she found a job in the office of Robb Brothers, a large department store in Birkenhead. She settled down quickly and was soon much more content with her life.

One dinner time she told the family, 'I get the best of both worlds there. On my way up to my office, I walk through the shop and see all the latest styles.'

'And buy most of them,' Grandma said wryly.

'But I get a discount on what I buy.'

That made Aunt Harriet cluck with impatience. 'As if you need it.'

'Auntie, if you tell me what you want, I could buy things for you,' she said.

'There isn't much I need,' Harriet sniffed. 'Not at my time of life.'

Dilys now had plenty of men friends, and according to Grandma, she went out and about with them far too often and came home far too late. She talked of setting herself up in her own home, but Dad was keen for her to stay with the family.

After a year, because her father was still talking about buying a car but had done nothing about it, she gave him the Austin and bought herself a smart red Morgan two-seater.

'A fast sports car is more my sort of thing,' she told Charlotte. 'After all those years of boredom, I'm going to enjoy everything I can from now on.'

For Lottie, being driven round by Dilys in that magical car was pure heaven. One day she hoped to have one like it herself. 'I'd like to learn to drive,' she said. 'Will you teach me when I'm seventeen?'

In the summer of 1925, Eunice gave birth to her second baby with far less fuss from the family than when she'd had her first. The following Sunday, when baby Edgar was three days old, they all went over to see them in the nursing home.

Eunice seemed subdued and said she didn't feel well yet. Grandma insisted on lifting the baby out of his cot to inspect him. 'You should be happy,' she told her. 'The waiting and the pain of the birth is all behind you now. You have a lovely, healthy, bouncing boy. Eight pounds five is a very good weight.'

Eunice muttered something about the hard work of bringing up yet another child.

Grandma's voice rang round the room. 'You need to pull yourself together, Eunice. If you feel like this, you must not go on adding to your family. Five is more than enough for anyone. Have you talked to Martin about it? You must get contraceptive advice now, and this is the place to do it. If he won't take the initiative, then you must. And do it before you go home.'

Eunice's face was scarlet against her pillows. Harriet's cheeks flamed too, and even Dad looked uncomfortable. 'I will,' she muttered.

Grandma went on, 'Can I safely leave it to you? Or do you want me to have a word with one of the midwives while I'm here? Be sure to ask for an appointment at the clinic. It's silly to be embarrassed. If you don't sort it out, you'll only have yourself to blame if you find yourself pregnant again.'

Lottie could feel her toes curling up and could see from Dilys's face that hers were too.

Suddenly Grandma said, 'I'm going to do it for you. I'll only worry about you if I don't,' and headed briskly for the door.

Tears were running down Eunice's face. Lottie took hold of her hand. 'Grandma's right,' she said.

'You need this,' Dilys added.

Lottie was coming to the end of her school days, and one evening after dinner Grandma said, 'I hope you've given some thought to what you want to do when you leave school. You need to start off on the right foot, get settled, not find yourself bored like your sisters.'

'I've thought a lot about it,' she said. 'I'd like to be involved with ships and shipping. That's what interests me. I'd like to work in the family business.'

They all looked a little shocked. 'I'm not sure that's a good idea,' her father said. 'It isn't making much profit these days.'

Harriet was shaking her head. 'It's rough down on the docks, no place for a girl like you.'

'What about nursing?' Grandma asked. 'Caring for others is a good career for a girl.'

'I couldn't,' Lottie said. 'Dilys couldn't do that sort of work and neither could I. I want to be part of what I see going on all round me: the ships and the river, the family business.'

Dad was shaking his head. 'I don't know how much of the business will be left in another year or so. Trade is bad, cargoes are increasingly difficult to get. There are thousands on the dole and ships are being laid up. I don't know if it can survive.'

'It's survived for the last two hundred years, Dad,' Dilys said. 'Trade won't always have been booming.'

'It's what I'd like to do,' Lottie said firmly.

Grandma sighed. 'Perhaps we could stretch to a secretarial course for you too,' she told her. 'You could make yourself useful in any office if you could type and do shorthand.'

Charles said, 'If you're serious about wanting to learn to run the business, you can start by coming to the office with me on Saturday mornings and in your holidays.'

'I'd love to,' Lottie said. 'Thank you.'

In the autumn of 1926, she left school and started at the same commercial college Dilys had attended. She was happy and got on well, but what she really enjoyed was the time she spent in Dad's office. It made her feel like a proper grown-up to be there.

She was surprised at how small the office was. Her father had rented just one room and a slit of a kitchen, where she learned to make the frequent supply of tea he seemed to need. He had one employee working for him: a water clerk called Ivor Smith.

Her father was friendly with Ted Pascoe, who occupied the office next door. He was the shipping agent for an international oil company, and employed a secretary called Miss Porter.

On her first Saturday morning, Lottie was feeling a bit out of her depth, and was pleased when Miss Porter put her head round the door. 'Hello,' she said, 'I'm Dorothy.' She had long red hair, which she wore in one thick plait, and a smiley face.

'Your dad has asked me to show you where the ladies' cloak-room is,' she said. She was very friendly, and Lottie took to her.

When the holidays came round at the college, Aunt Harriet cut sandwiches for Lottie's lunch as well as Dad's. Dorothy came in and said, 'Mr Pascoe goes to your office every lunch-time to eat his sandwiches with your dad, and afterwards they walk to the Queen's Head for a glass of beer. Why don't you come to our office and eat your lunch with me?'

'What about Mr Smith?'

'He's usually out on a job visiting some ship or other on the docks. Sometimes he goes home for lunch.'

Dorothy was vivacious, a mine of information and full of chatter about her social life. Lottie wished she could be out and about as much as her new friend was.

Lottie came home from college one day to find a fraught atmosphere at home. Dad had come back early to show Grandma a report in the financial pages of his newspaper.

Harriet pushed the crumpled pages in front of her to read. It appeared that Richards and Frayne, a well-known Liverpool confectionery firm, had bought the Sanderson business. 'Taken it over lock, stock and barrel,' she said.

'It's strange that Martin hasn't mentioned it.' Dad was troubled. 'He must have been having talks about this for some time.'

'And where does that leave him?' Grandma asked. 'They may not want him to run it now. I've rung Eunice,' she went on, 'and stranger still, she knew nothing about it, but I've asked them to lunch on Sunday, so we can find out what's been going on.'

They came as expected and brought four-year-old Tom, as well as Edgar, who was a very active toddler and wanted everybody to play with him.

Martin said, 'I'm sorry, I couldn't tell you that we'd decided to sell the business. Profits have been falling off over the last few years, so we felt that selling it was the best course, but it all had to be kept very quiet. Richards and Frayne are hoping to turn it round and make a profit. We didn't want to publicise the news of our losses.'

'But doesn't that mean you are out of a job?' Jemima asked. 'We have been worrying about that.'

'No.' Martin smiled. 'I'm happy to say the new owners want me to continue working for them. Nothing is going to change for me.'

Grandma pulled a face. 'Except you are now an employee rather than an owner.'

Lottie would never have said anything quite so pointed, but Martin was still smiling. 'Yes, and it takes a lot of worries off my shoulders.'

She thought it had been a storm in a teacup and that Dad and Grandma had worried themselves unnecessarily.

Mrs Royden sent Lottie a note saying that her Uncle Lazlo was staying with them while on leave, and inviting her to tea one Saturday to see him. She was delighted, though Glyn was on the *Conway* and she'd have to go alone.

Dad wanted to use the car, and Dilys was going to see Eunice, but she'd long since learned to get about by herself. She telephoned Mrs Royden and told her she'd come by train. At the station, she heard someone calling her name, and when she turned round, she was surprised to see Philip.

'Lottie? Hello, it is you! I hardly recognised you, you look so grown up.' He gave her an enthusiastic hug and thumped her on her back.

'I wasn't expecting to see you here,' she said. He'd grown into a young man since she'd last seen him, slim with an athletic build and glowing with strength and health. He was still a little taller than her, though she'd caught Glyn up in height. His brown eyes shone with the friendliness she remembered so well. He took her arm and stepped out briskly in the way he always had.

'What's your news?' she asked as they walked.

'I'm leaving the *Conway*.'

'Glyn is waiting to hear which ship he'll get,' she said. It was usual for the *Conway* to find them placements on a seagoing ship at this stage, as a voyage was considered the best route to further their experience.

'I've persuaded Dad to let me go out to the Oil Rivers with Lazlo and work there. I'm thrilled; it's what I've always wanted. I think Glyn is envious.'

'How long will you be away?'

'Two or three years if they're happy to employ me there, but the Elder Dempster mailboats run twice a month, so I could get a passage home at any time. Lazlo came home because he wasn't well – that's why he's here now – but he's getting better with proper medical treatment.'

She was quite shocked when she came face to face with Uncle Lazlo. He looked thin and pale, but he swept her into his arms in a giant hug as he'd done before. 'Is this little Lottie? Quite a young lady now, my goodness, yes. Almost grown up.'

'Lovely to see you again, but I hear you've been ill.'

'There was an epidemic of yellow fever on the rivers, but I'm over it now.'

She wondered if he really was; he looked older than Dad, with a yellowish tint to his heavy suntan, but he was still full of energy and fun.

Mrs Royden produced a tea of home-made scones and a Victoria sandwich, and Lottie told them about the secretarial course. 'Dad said he'd give me a job when I've passed my final exams.'

'So they've persuaded you to join the family firm?'

'It was my idea. Dad was against it; he said the business might not exist in another year or so.'

'Oh dear, things must be even worse than I thought.'

Philip smiled. 'The river is in Lottie's blood.'

'Must be,' Lazlo said. 'Well, this time I'm taking Philip back with me; he's going to give me a hand out on the Coast.'

Philip smiled at her. 'He's fitting me up with lots of cotton shirts and shorts.'

'We still have to get you a camp bed and a mosquito net,' Lazlo said. 'Then I need to buy more shirts and socks for myself and pack everything up.'

'Are you fit enough to go back already?' Lottie asked.

'Yes, life out there is what I know. There's nothing for me here, unless it's retirement.'

At 5.30, Philip walked her back to the station. She'd had a lovely afternoon; the three of them had hardly stopped talking. 'Will you spend all your working life out there like Uncle Lazlo?' she asked. She didn't want to think he would.

'No, the idea is that I go out for a few years to learn how to run the business.' A few years sounded a long time to her. 'I'm looking forward to it.'

At the station, he pecked her on her cheek in much the same manner his mother had when she'd said goodbye.

Lottie decided that only a romantic fool would think Philip was interested in her. He wasn't thinking of girls at all; his mind was totally on the adventure he was about to have. He'd been a childhood friend, but now that he was grown up, it was pointless expecting anything more from him.

CHAPTER NINE

GLYN CAME HOME AND told them he'd asked for and been given a placement with Elder Dempster to sail on the *Accra* as the fourth officer. It was a vessel specially built for the West Africa trade and carried passengers, mail and cargo. 'She's a beautiful ship,' he told Lottie, 'a liner painted white for the tropics, and the splendid thing is, because she's a mailboat, she keeps to a strict timetable. Liverpool is her home port, so I'll be back every month and I'll have a few days of home leave regularly.'

'Will you see anything of Uncle Lazlo and Philip when you're out there?'

'I don't know. I'll only go as far as Lagos, and they're stationed further along the coast at Calabar. I had a letter from Philip the other day. It's in my luggage; I'll find it for you to read. He loves being out there, it sounds very interesting.'

When he'd gone, Grandma said, 'He didn't mention that it would be good experience to fit him to run the company.'

'I don't think that's his plan,' Lottie said. 'He'll leave that to me.'

Lottie was delighted to welcome Oliver home from sea. He'd begun as third officer on the *Ocean Traveller*, but recently he'd written to say he'd been promoted to second officer, that he was enjoying life at sea and planned to return to the same ship for another voyage. He'd grown taller and looked very manly, but he seemed almost a stranger in his own home.

Eunice would soon be twenty-seven, and Martin had invited all the Mortimer family to a lunch party on the Saturday nearest to her big day to celebrate it. Oliver had arrived home three days beforehand and was pleased he'd be able to go with them.

Dilys was shocked. 'I'd have thought a big party would be the last thing she'd want. Whatever is Martin thinking of? She's so tired looking after all those children, I'm sure she'd have preferred a quiet restaurant lunch.'

The party was in full swing when they arrived. Martin welcomed them with smiles. As soon as she saw the sophisticated gathering and the glasses of champagne that were being handed round, Lottie knew that Grandma would not approve. This was very definitely not how they celebrated birthdays at home.

Eunice looked stony-faced and in no mood to celebrate, but she'd had her hair done, and was wearing a new scarlet party dress. 'How are the children?' Grandma asked her. 'Are we not to see them today?'

To please her, Tom and Edgar were brought down briefly to be shown off. They were accompanied by Martin's three daughters in pretty party frocks, Christabel now tall and leggy at twelve. Martin tried to dispatch them back upstairs, saying it wasn't a suitable occasion for children. 'Daddy,' Christabel said, 'I'm no longer a child, and as both my grandmothers are here today, I would like to be allowed to stay to talk to them.'

'Perhaps for a little while,' Martin said, signalling for the nursemaid to take the other children away. 'I should introduce you to my family,' he said, turning back to Grandma. 'Come this way.' He led her across the room, Christabel and Lottie tagging on behind.

'We've met already,' Jemima reminded him frostily, 'when you and Eunice married. Hello, Laura, how are you?'

Christabel said, 'Granny takes us to her house in the school holidays. I can see Lake Windermere from our bedroom window there, and we have an uncle who takes us out in his boat. It's lovely.'

For the first time Lottie realised that Eunice was Christabel's stepmother, and what that entailed. 'You must have been very young when your mother died,' she said to the girl.

'I was five. My mother was killed in a traffic accident. She drove into a bus,' Christabel said matter-of-factly.

That made Lottie shiver with empathy; she wasn't the only one to be brought up without her mother.

A few friends as well as family had been invited, and Lottie was aware that one young man kept looking at her. He was not handsome in the accepted sense – he lacked the even features and smooth hair she admired in Philip – but his dark eyes seemed to search her out and follow her round. She was talking to Eunice when Martin brought him over. 'This is Roddy Onslow,' he said. 'He's asked to be introduced to you. He's a distant cousin of mine.'

Roddy's dark eyes held her gaze and a wide smile lit up his face. Immediately she found him more attractive. He refilled her glass and took her into a corner. 'You're Eunice's sister?' he asked.

'Yes, and also sister to Dilys and Oliver, not to mention Glyn, who can't be here today. I'm the youngest in the family.'

'You don't look much like the others.' He smiled. 'Perhaps a little like Oliver in the face, but you're a different build to your sisters.'

She smiled and answered as Grandma always did, 'I'm a one-off,' though she was beginning to think she was more like Dilys than she used to be. Roddy was tall and thin, noticeably taller than she was. She liked that.

He told her he was twenty-two and a management trainee in the family confectionery business. 'I'm following in Martin's career footsteps.' She told him about her Saturday job with Dad, and how she hoped she'd soon be working full time.

An elegant buffet lunch of smoked salmon and quail's eggs followed. Charlotte found Roddy both attentive and attractive. There was a heightened intensity about him, and his brown eyes kept looking into hers. She sensed he was interested in her. Her heart wobbled when he turned to smile at her again. He had perfect teeth and longish hair that flopped over his face. She thought he was lovely and decided this was what the girls at college meant when they said they were smitten.

A magnificent cake was brought in, and they all sang 'Happy Birthday'.

'Smile, can't you?' Lottie heard Martin whisper to Eunice as he pushed her forward to blow out the twenty-seven flickering candles. It took her several attempts. 'Well done,' he said, and refilled the glass she was holding. 'Many happy returns, darling.'

The French windows were open on to the terrace, and without a word Eunice turned and darted outside. Lottie heard the tinkle of breaking glass and saw Dilys run after her. The rest of the guests seemed not to notice, though, and the volume of noise returned. It was mid-afternoon, and Lottie could see that Grandma was restive and wanted to go home. She felt torn between anxiety for Eunice and hope that Roddy would ask if he might have her phone number so he could get in touch. She feared he'd just leave and she'd never see him again.

Five minutes later, he put the question to her with another wide smile. It made a thrill run up her spine and her heart turn right over. She scribbled the number into his diary when he offered it with a pencil.

She saw Eunice return with Dilys in time for her to say goodbye to Grandma. She looked as though she'd been crying. Lottie kissed her cheek and thanked Martin. Roddy was ready to help her into her coat and into one of the two taxis Martin had called to take the family to the station. His dark eyes burned into hers as he raised his hand to wave goodbye.

As soon as the taxi turned the corner, Grandma was loud with condemnation. 'What a flashy show that was. Who is Martin trying to impress? I do hope Eunice had more sense than to allow her money to be spent in that way.'

Lottie felt all churned up about Eunice. Clearly her marriage wasn't the romantic, bliss-filled affair she'd supposed. But she felt guilty, too, for being excited to have met Roddy, and for thinking it had been a glamorous party of the sort that took place on board the big transatlantic liners she'd seen in the river. She'd enjoyed it all.

'I wish I could have a party like that for my birthday,' Dilys said quietly.

'I expect Oliver thought it wonderful too,' Grandma went on, still breathing fire; Oliver was in the other taxi with Dad and Harriet. 'He couldn't take his eyes off that little blonde girl. Who was she?'

'I don't know,' Dilys said. 'I think her name was Patsy. Can't blame him really, Grandma. I don't suppose he sees many girls when he's away.' Lottie was glad Oliver had deflected Grandma's attention away from her and Roddy. 'Not girls of the right sort.'

'Such a terrible waste of money when so many people are in real need,' Grandma grumbled on. She thought champagne decadent.

Once back home, she said to Lottie, 'Make a pot of tea for us, my dear. We won't need any cake; I'm sure we've all had enough fancy food for today.'

Dilys joined her in the kitchen to help, and whispered, 'Eunice was terribly upset, wasn't she? She threw that glass of champagne right across the terrace.'

'Why was she upset? Because she didn't want a party?'

'It was just that Martin got it all wrong. I told him so. He said he thought a party would cheer her up.'

'He doesn't understand her.'

'No, Eunice doesn't want any more babies, she says she hasn't been the same since Edgar was born.'

Lottie poured boiling water into the teapot and set it on the tray. 'Poor Eunice. Although Grandma says that's part of being married, she has sorted it out for her.'

'Marriage doesn't have to be like that. Oh Lottie, you're such a little innocent.'

*

Charlotte couldn't get Roddy Onslow out of her mind and lingered near the phone in the front hall willing him to ring. The next day after lunch, Grandma had gone to rest on her bed, and as Lottie had to complete a task ready for class on Monday, she went to the playroom to do it.

She heard the phone ring, but Oliver went to answer it and she wondered if he was expecting a call too. The next minute he was at the playroom door. 'That fellow you were talking to at Eunice's party wants to speak to you,' he said.

The strength seemed to drain from her knees, but she managed to pull herself to her feet and run to the phone.

'Hello, Lottie.' The sound of his voice sent a thrill up her spine. 'If I call for you, will you come out for a run in the car with me this afternoon?'

'I'd love to.'

When he came, she took him in to see Dad and Aunt Harriet. He told them he planned to take her boating on the lake at Raby Mere, and they gave the outing their blessing. She was thrilled to sit beside him in the Austin Seven. 'My dad has a car like this,' she said. 'I've learned to drive it. Dilys paid for me to have lessons for my birthday'

Roddy laughed. 'This is my father's. I'm saving up to buy a car of my own, but I want a decent one.'

It was quite a chilly afternoon, and most of the boats remained moored, but he hired a skiff for an hour and she found she was better at rowing than he was. She'd had more practice. They had afternoon tea in the cake shop, then spent the rest of the evening in the car. Roddy's kisses seemed to set her on fire. She wanted to know all about him and his family, and he held her in his arms as they talked. Never had time passed so quickly, and when he drew up near her back gate, she could hardly tear herself away from him. When he saw Dilys's Morgan two-seater, he said, 'I'm impressed with that. It's gorgeous.'

It was 10.15 when she went in. Charles said, 'Did you have a good time? Grandma's gone to bed now, but she said I was to remind you that in future you are to be home by ten. If you're going out with this fellow again, please do watch the time. We get anxious about you when you're late.'

'Sorry, Dad,' she said, and kissed him goodnight. She spent a long time reliving the thrills and excitement of the afternoon before she went to sleep, but she woke early feeling full of energy for the new day.

Roddy telephoned her that afternoon when she returned from college. 'I missed the last luggage boat last night,' he said. 'I had to leave the car in Hamilton Square, but I was able to get home to Liverpool all right on the train.' There were bridges to cross the Mersey further up river but, without driving for miles, the only way for a vehicle to cross from Birkenhead to Liverpool was on the luggage boat. Although a road tunnel had been started it would not be finished for several more years, but a railway tunnel had been built and a train service had been running since 1903. 'My father was furious with me because it meant he had to go to work on the tram this morning. I'll have to come back now to collect the car, so I was wondering if you'd come to the pictures with me. It'll have to be the first house.'

'I'd love to,' she breathed.

It disrupted the family routine, as she couldn't have dinner with them at the usual time, and Grandma wasn't pleased.

'You must eat properly,' she said. 'We'll dish up your dinner and you can warm it up when you get home.'

Lottie didn't like to go hungry. She made herself an extra sandwich at teatime. As she slid into Roddy's car, she felt his arms pull her closer to kiss her. It was bliss.

'We hardly have time to go to the pictures,' he said. 'I daren't miss the last luggage boat tonight.'

Charlotte didn't mind that; all she wanted was to be with him. He took her to a pub for a drink, though she knew Grandma would be horrified about that. Afterwards he bought them both fish and chips, and took her home in good time.

The months began to pass. Glyn had a few days' home leave every month, and that too became routine. Lottie finished her college course and went to work full time for Charles. Because she'd been going to his office regularly, she felt the change was almost seamless.

Roddy wanted to take her out every night. 'You can please yourself now you're a working woman,' he told her, but she knew Grandma would never allow that. Nevertheless, she went out with him at least twice during the week, as well as Saturdays and Sundays.

Grandma shook her head. 'You need to get your rest if you are going to work as well. You would be wise to cut it down to only once during the week.'

A few days later, Roddy said, 'I'd love to take you to the pictures on Friday and somewhere we can dance on Saturday, but I'll have to come over on the train as my father wants to use the car himself on both those nights.'

She said, 'I'll ask Dad if I can borrow his, but I'll meet you off the train with or without a car.' Roddy's family didn't have a phone at home, and he was not allowed to have personal calls at work. Usually they arranged their next meeting before they parted, but Roddy often rang her for a chat on the days they didn't meet.

She put the phone down and went to the sitting room to ask her father.

'I usually play bowls on Friday evening,' he said. 'I suppose you could drop me off at the park and I could walk home. It isn't that far.'

'And what about Saturday night? Will that be OK?'

She thought Dad would have been more than willing, but Grandma said, 'I don't think it's a good thing for your boy-friends to rely on your relatives to provide transport. If a gentleman asks you out, he should be happy to arrange the whole outing and pay for it. He does pay, doesn't he?' Lottie was curling up; she'd been paying her share of the expenses. 'I'm afraid I have a suspicious nature. I don't always feel that your friends are suitable people for you to know.'

'Grandma, Roddy always offers; he wants to pay, but he doesn't earn very much.'

Jemima clucked with disapproval.

Lottie had never felt so alive. She'd fallen head over heels in love with Roddy Onslow, and he seemed equally enamoured with her. Over the last few months, he'd been in contact either by phone or letter almost every day, and he took her out as often as he could. His touch thrilled her and his kisses made her heart turn over. He had a way of holding her close while his eyes searched hers; she felt she'd found her soulmate.

He'd been invited to Sunday lunch more than once, and had conversed with her father about the current dire state of business. Grandma had talked to him about his relatives, and he'd passed on snippets of news about Martin Sanderson and Jeremy Arbuthnot. Lottie felt that connection had helped her family approve of him as a boyfriend.

He'd told her he loved her, and though he hadn't actually asked her to marry him, he'd dropped hints that had left her tingling with anticipation.

'I don't have much to offer you,' he'd said more than once. 'I'm afraid I don't earn very much, though I'm hoping for promotion soon.'

'I'm not that interested in money,' Lottie said, 'and I can work. I'd be happier doing that than sitting around in idleness.'

'I hope you'd be taking care of our home.'

'These days plenty of people do both.'

'But wasn't Eunice given her inheritance when she married? Won't that happen to you?'

'She was, but I'm not sure what will happen when it's my turn.' Lottie pondered on the problem yet again. 'My family believe in keeping us in ignorance until the last moment. Dilys knew nothing about it until shortly before her twenty-fifth birthday, and I'm sent out of the way when they talk to her and told it doesn't concern me.'

'But I understood Eunice to say all her siblings would get an equal share.'

For Lottie, that brought all the doubts she'd had about Olwen being her mother thundering back. 'Possibly,' she said vaguely.

As Roddy's twenty-third birthday drew near, he told her

he'd delay the celebration until the following Saturday so he could share it with her. 'My father says I can borrow his car, so I'll come over in the early afternoon, and we'll have a celebration dinner in a restaurant, just the two of us.'

Lottie looked forward to it all week; if he brought his car, it gave them a place that was almost private to put their arms round each other. She enjoyed that more than anything else.

She met him at Woodside in the early afternoon, and she could sense an undercurrent of excitement in him. 'I'll take you somewhere quiet,' he said, 'where we can talk.'

He drove out to Hoylake, along the beach road to Dove Point, and parked facing the sea. It was a fine bright day, but with the cold wind, there was nobody about.

His eyes were sparkling when he put his arms round her. 'I'm in a fever of impatience,' he said, 'but I'm anxious too. I can't wait any longer to find out what you think. I want to know that we'll always be together. You know I'm madly in love with you.' He was smiling at her. 'Will you marry me?'

Lottie pulled him closer. 'Yes, yes, you must know I love you too.'

'Oh Lottie.' He kissed her again and again. 'I'm delighted. Thrilled. I want us to be married just as soon as we can.'

The rest of the afternoon passed in a whirl. 'We have so much to arrange, so much to talk about,' he said. 'I'll have to ask your father's permission because you're only eighteen. Will he agree, do you think?'

'It's Grandma who decides everything in our family,' she said, 'but she agreed to Eunice marrying when she was twenty, so yes, when she sees how much I want it, I think she will.' She was fizzing with excitement and knew she had a permanent smile on her face. 'But I work for Dad now and that's a complication. I'm sure he'll want me to carry on.'

'Perhaps we can find somewhere to live close to his office.'

'But then you'll have a long journey to work.'

'Your office is close to the Birkenhead ferry, isn't it?'

'Not that close.'

'And there's the underground train too. It won't be difficult. I won't care how long it takes if I can live with you.'

Roddy had booked a table for dinner at the Royal Rock Hotel in Rock Ferry, and he ordered a bottle of champagne. 'To celebrate our betrothal,' he said.

'I'd like to get everything settled tonight.' Lottie was up on cloud nine. 'But if I take you in to ask Dad and Grandma for permission, we'll need to be home by half nine at the latest so you can go home on the luggage boat.'

'Let's try and make it a little earlier,' he said, his gaze playing with hers across the table. 'I don't want to rush that.'

They didn't linger at the table, and a little later, brimming with excitement, Lottie led Roddy by the hand to the back door and through to the sitting room. Dad was pouring himself a nightcap; Grandma was knitting a blue cardigan for herself. Lottie danced across the room to kiss her.

'Grandma, Roddy and I want to get married,' she announced, pulling him forward. Harriet let out a little gurgle of surprise.

Roddy looked shy now. 'I've come to ask your permission, sir, er . . . Mrs Mortimer. I'm thrilled that Lottie has agreed to marry me. I love her and I'll do my best to make her happy.'

She was still holding his hand as they waited for the answer, but it was dismay she saw on Grandma's face. 'Dad? You're pleased for me?'

He wouldn't look at her. 'You're very young, Lottie.'

Roddy's hand twisted round to tighten silently over hers. 'What does that mean?' she asked.

Grandma slowly put her knitting down and stood up. 'You haven't known each other very long. I think it would be wiser if you got to know each other better before you considered marriage.'

Lottie suddenly felt sick with disappointment; she'd thought it a mere formality. 'But why? You gave Eunice permission when she was twenty, so why not me?'

'You are only eighteen, and I thought you were keen to work in the family business,' Jemima said. 'Charles says you're learning fast and he's finding you very useful.'

'I am,' he confirmed. 'You're doing well, Lottie.'

'I'm not going to leave you, Dad. I'll have to carry on working.'

Harriet cleared her throat in the awkward silence that followed.

Roddy's cheeks were scarlet. 'I'm afraid I'm not earning all that much yet, but I'm hoping for promotion soon. And I'm not a complete stranger to you. You know some of my family; we're already connected by marriage. Eunice and Martin . . .'

'And Aunt Gwendolen and Uncle Jeremy,' Lottie added.

'Both Lottie and I are very serious about this. I'll take good care of her. I'm sure we are both ready for marriage.'

'Yes, Roddy, but we would prefer you to wait until Charlotte is a little older.'

'Dad?' she wailed. 'Please . . .'

'No,' Grandma said. 'We understand you've come to an agreement, and you can consider yourselves engaged if you wish, but marriage, no, not in the immediate future. Put that right out of your minds.'

Lottie was speechless. She watched Grandma turn to Roddy. 'I don't think there is anything to be gained by arguing the pros and cons tonight.'

He gasped out, 'I'm . . . I'm terribly disappointed. May I ask for permission again? Say in a few months, when we've all had time to think it over?'

'No.' Grandma was at her most severe. 'You must accept that I mean it to be final. In less than three years, Charlotte will be of age and will not need our permission. I don't think that is too long for her to wait.'

'With all due respect, Mrs Mortimer, may I ask why?'

'I think my way is wiser. Charlotte is very young. And the same can be said for you too, Roddy. Promotion will come to you in due course, and perhaps then you'll be able to afford to marry.'

Lottie felt searing disappointment, and Roddy looked bereft.

'Now,' Grandma went on, 'I understand how you feel, and I know how tempting it is to show each other how deeply in love you are, but I absolutely forbid you, Roddy, to defile Charlotte by anticipating the physical side of marriage.'

Roddy's gaze was on the carpet. Lottie felt she should have expected this, and was kicking herself.

'Do not for one moment forget the risk of bringing a child into this world before you can adequately support it and care for it. And do not imagine either that you can bring the date of your marriage nearer by getting her pregnant. Am I making myself clear? Roddy, would you be good enough to go home now? We'll say goodnight.'

Lottie gasped in horror, but was proud of the way Roddy reacted. 'I'm sorry you don't think more highly of me, Mrs Mortimer. I truly love Lottie and believe I can make her happy.' Without looking at anybody, he turned on his heel. 'Goodnight to you all.'

Lottie ran after him with scalding tears running down her face and caught up with him as he was opening the back door. 'Don't go yet, we haven't said goodnight.'

'Your grandmother doesn't approve of me,' he said angrily. 'She doesn't want us to marry.'

'She'll come round to it.' Lottie clung to him. 'I'll make her.'

'I truly love you, and want to be with you forever.' He held her close.

'Even if we have to wait until I'm twenty-one?'

'Of course,' he vowed. 'We're engaged, aren't we?'

They walked up the garden together. Dilys drove past them, parked and went straight indoors. Lottie followed a few minutes later with a heavy heart. When she reached the sitting room, Dilys had already heard the news and got up to give her a sympathetic hug.

'I'm sorry,' Grandma said, 'but we do believe it would be wiser if we all got to know him better.'

'But I don't understand why,' Lottie burst out, 'You gave Eunice permission, so why aren't you doing the same for me?' That really rankled. 'We love each other. We don't need to get to know one another better. Roddy even belongs to the same family as Martin, and we already know them.'

Her father was sympathetic. 'Charlotte, it's easier to tie the knot than it is to untie it. We want you to be really sure.'

'I am sure.'

'Eunice doesn't appear to be as happy as we'd hoped; as we had expected,' Grandma said. 'I'm sure you will have noticed.'

Lottie looked at Dilys. 'Yes.'

'And that makes us wary of putting you in the same position. If you truly love each other, to wait for a few years does not seem too much to ask.'

Lottie felt chastened; she'd said the same thing to Roddy.

As she and Dilys went to their bedrooms, she asked, 'Did they make Eunice wait at all?'

'To start with she was told a year, but she walked down the aisle within ten months. I am a bit anxious about her.' Dilys had always been close to Eunice. 'Nothing cheers her up. I took my car over today and drove her out to Croxteth Country Park. She said she'd like to see the gardens, and it was a lovely sunny afternoon, but she'd soon had enough and wanted to go home.'

A few days later, Grandma followed Lottie to her bedroom. 'I need to have a little talk with you,' she said, sitting down on her bed, 'before things go any further.'

Lottie had always dreaded Grandma's little talks. She went to the window to put as much distance between them as she could. 'Come and sit down here beside me,' Grandma commanded. Reluctantly she did so. 'You have a serious boyfriend . . .'

'I have, and I don't think you are being fair to me and Roddy.'

'Nothing in this world is fair, Charlotte. Some girls are born beautiful and some are plain. Some are given a good brain and some are not. Some are born to riches and some are paupers. There's not a lot we can do about some of those things; we have to make the best of what we've got.'

She paused, and Lottie closed her eyes, knowing the worst was yet to come.

'I've already told you why we don't want you to marry until you're older. You must see how discontented Eunice is with her lot.'

'But I'm not Eunice. I think I'd be very happy with Roddy.'

She heard Grandma's gusty sigh. 'You see me as an old lady, out of touch with everything, but I was young once. I know how you feel, full of love for that young man.'

'Yes, and he loves me.'

'You heard what I said to him. It's that warning I want to repeat to you. You must not anticipate marriage.'

'Oh my goodness!' Lottie felt the heat rush up her cheeks.

'Do not get impatient with me,' Jemima told her. 'This needs to be said. Experience tells me that while couples like you and Roddy can go on to lifelong happiness, others just as deserving head for disaster.

'The human race would die out if young people were not given this deep urge to procreate, but in life there is a right time for everything. You are both young and should enjoy the freedoms of youth now. There is plenty of time later for the responsibilities of marriage, a husband, home and children. A child is another human being. Do you feel ready to take on the burden of providing everything another person will need?'

Lottie felt terrible. 'No,' she said, in order to shut her grandmother up.

'You do understand what I'm saying? You must not allow your young man to enjoy the state of marriage before the wedding. Human nature being what it is, he'll probably try. You may be tempted too, but if you've any sense you will resist.'

Grandma got to her feet. 'In other words, do not let any so-called lovemaking get out of hand.'

CHAPTER TEN

LOTTIE STARTED TO COLLECT fancy nightdresses and tablecloths for her bottom drawer. 'I wish we lived nearer,' she said to Roddy, 'so we could see more of each other.' He lived on the outskirts of Liverpool, and that entailed a lot of travelling across the river.

It took her several months to accept that she'd have to wait years before they could marry. Roddy commiserated with her, but said, 'We'll just have to be patient. We can do it. We will.'

The upside was that she was enjoying her job, and her father told her he was pleased with her work. She often drove him to and from the office, and because they were spending so much time together, she felt closer to him. She was coming to understand how the business functioned, and its present position, and could appreciate his anxiety about the future.

Ivor Smith, their water clerk, gave in his notice, and she saw how shaken and upset Dad was about that. 'It looks horribly like rats leaving the sinking ship,' he said. 'He's gone to a firm that pays better.'

'We don't really have enough work to keep him busy,' she pointed out. 'You could manage it yourself. Anyway, I'd like to visit the ships with you and learn what has to be done.'

'You?' He smiled. 'It's a man's job. A man's world. Women

113

can't visit ships and trail round the docks. It just isn't done.'

'Why not? There's no real reason why women shouldn't do that. I need something new to take my mind off having to wait years to marry Roddy.'

'It wouldn't be safe for you to walk round the docks by yourself.'

'I could drive down, get as close to the ship as possible. Nobody has ever attacked you down there, have they?' Getting Dad to make a decision was never easy. 'Come on, Dad, you could teach me. We could easily manage this business between us.'

'Well you can't go there in those high heels and dainty skirts. Have you got any trousers?'

'Dilys has slacks; she'll lend me a pair.'

'What are slacks?'

'Trousers; you've seen her wear them when she goes rambling with that club she joined.'

'All right, tomorrow then, and wear them with a plain pullover.'

But after lunch, when he came back from the pub with Ted Pascoe, he was undecided again. 'Ted's offered another solution,' he told her. 'He says he could manage more work, and could act for Mortimer's too. He's said he'll take us on his books. Then I could close this office, and any bits of paperwork I'd still have to do could be done at home.'

Lottie was alarmed. 'What about me? That would put me out of a job. No, I want you to carry on. I want you to teach me to be a water clerk.'

'Ted thought of that; he's offered to take you into his office.'

'But that'll be for clerical work.'

Charles sighed. 'We need to think this over carefully. We have to move with the times.' Lottie knew her father was disheartened after seeing trade go down year after year.

They went home early in the afternoon, as Grandma had to be consulted about everything that affected the business. Harriet was just taking their afternoon tea tray into the sitting room, and returned to the kitchen to make another pot while they explained the situation.

Jemima straightened up in her chair. 'My family have been shipowners on the Mersey for two hundred years,' she said, not for the first time. 'My father managed L. E. Mortimer and Partners successfully all his working life. He would turn in his grave if we didn't run the business ourselves. Besides,' she went on, 'the lease on the Birkenhead office has five more years to run, and we could end up paying rent on it whether you use it or not.'

Lottie relaxed; it seemed her job would be safe.

'Companies registered in the Far East are undercutting us all the time,' Dad said.

'I know that. We've been through difficult times before and survived.' Grandma was impatient. 'We'll survive this.'

Lottie brought up the problem that had started this: the loss of their water clerk. 'I want Dad to teach me what has to be done,' she said, 'and then I can help him with that job too.'

Harriet said, 'You can't walk around the docks on your own.' But Grandma was still flushed with indignation that Charles felt it was possible to close the office, and agreed that she could do it.

Brimming with triumph, Lottie waited for Dilys to come home to ask if she could borrow her trousers. When she tried them on, she found they were baggy round the waist and hips and decidedly short in the leg.

Dilys giggled and pulled them lower until they settled round her hips. 'You look like Charlie Chaplin,' she said.

'I'll have to wear them tomorrow.' Lottie eyed them ruefully.

'We'll go to the shop on Saturday afternoon and I'll fix you up,' Dilys said. Her discount at Robb Brothers certainly came in handy.

The following week, the *Denbigh* docked with a cargo of slate from Porthmadog. Charles picked up the personal mail for the crew, together with the money to pay them off, and took Lottie with him when he went on board.

Their two small coastal freighters had been built in North Wales and traded mainly between Porthmadog and Liverpool. They brought slate out and carried groceries, clothing and almost everything else produced in the north-west on the return journey.

Lottie had only seen the ships rarely, and then from a distance. On closer inspection, she said, '*Denbigh* looks quite shabby, and she's covered in slate dust.'

Charles said, 'That's unavoidable, but it'll wash off. Underneath, she's smart enough. I provide paint and the crew has to maintain the ship properly, otherwise our customers wouldn't entrust their cargoes to us. They have to believe our ships are seaworthy and their goods are safe with us.'

Lottie knew he'd arranged to have the present cargo unloaded, and another of groceries delivered to the ship in two days' time for the return journey. The hatches had been opened in readiness and the derricks were in place. Captain Davies greeted her father like an old friend. They were taken to his cubbyhole of a cabin and given cups of strong tea laced with condensed milk and plenty of sugar.

The duties of a water clerk were to look after the needs of the ship, but today nothing unusual was reported. The crew were not in need of a doctor or a dentist, and no new hands had to be hired. Those who lived in Liverpool had leave to visit their families, and would return for the next trip.

Over the following weeks, Lottie learned about advertising for future cargoes, and how to arrange for bunkering the ships and restocking them with food and other necessities. She found it more interesting than office duties, though she often helped Dorothy Porter when she was overburdened with paperwork. The next-door office was usually much busier than they were. She also got to know the captains of those of their vessels that came regularly into port. Captain Jones of the *Caernarvon* teased her, 'You're the first ever female water clerk I've known in thirty years at sea, and no water clerk is more welcome aboard than you. You always have a smile for us.'

On Sunday mornings, her one day off in the week, Lottie wanted to go swimming, but Grandma insisted all the family attend the morning church service. Not to be ready to walk up to St Mark's at ten o'clock could cause unwelcome arguments. Once she persuaded Dilys to get up early and go with her, but Dilys decided swimming before breakfast and church was not for her. 'I'd rather spend the time in bed,' she said.

Lottie was bemoaning this in the office the next day when Dorothy said, 'I'd like to come with you.'

'Marvellous. What about next Sunday? None of our ships

will be in dock, so Dad won't need his car. I'll borrow it and pick you up.'

Dorothy was becoming more of a friend. 'Great,' she said. 'Where do you go, is it Byrne Avenue baths?'

'Yes, indoor swimming, so it doesn't matter what the weather's like.'

The following week, a letter arrived for Grandma, which she passed round the breakfast table. 'It seems your Uncle Edward has died,' she said. 'His funeral will be next Friday at midday.'

'Poor old Edward,' Charles said. 'He was a distant cousin of yours, wasn't he?'

'Yes, they say he'd been in a nursing home for the last three years,' Jemima said, 'and he'd reached the age of ninety-three.' She pushed the letter back into its envelope. 'We ought to see it as a happy release. I knew him only slightly and I don't feel up to travelling to Buxton. You could go, Harriet, to represent our side of the family? Would you like to?'

'Not really, I only remember meeting him once.'

'But you should,' she urged. 'Charles can't go, he has to work, but midday is a convenient time; you can get there and back in a day without any trouble. It's a pleasant train ride to Buxton, something different for you to do.'

'I'd like to go to Buxton,' Lottie said, 'but I have to go to work too.'

'Of course you do, don't be silly.' Grandma never minced words.

Harriet came down to breakfast on Friday morning smartly dressed in black from head to foot. She was going to catch the bus to Rock Ferry station, and wouldn't be home till the evening.

Lottie arrived home from work at the same time as Dilys, and they headed straight to the kitchen. They were surprised to find Grandma there in some disarray. 'What's happened?' Dilys asked. 'Has the stove gone out? It's cold in here.'

Grandma was agitated. 'I've had a terrible day,' she said. 'I've not had so much as a cup of tea since breakfast.'

'Harriet raked out the stove and got the fire burning up before she made the porridge this morning,' Dilys said. 'She asked me to bring in a bucket of coal to speed things up.'

'It's the stove.' Jemima sounded full of frustration.

It was a monster of a range that had been in the house since it was built, and the fire was never allowed to go out because of the difficulty of starting it up again. They relied on it to provide hot water and hot meals and everything from morning tea to late-night cocoa. Harriet called it the Pest, and complained it was temperamental and had a voracious appetite for coal, and it needed black-leading every week. Long experience had taught her to control it through its complicated system of flues and dampers.

She'd pleaded for a modern electric cooker, and there was plenty of space for one, since the only other equipment was a brown stone sink and wooden draining board. But both Charles and Grandma had deemed that an unnecessary expense and praised the excellent roasts and sponge cakes the old stove turned out.

On the plus side, it also provided an airing cupboard, and the kitchen was the warmest room in the house, which they all appreciated in winter.

Grandma was cross. 'I know Harriet reminded me to keep an eye on it, and stoke it, but I forgot and it went out.'

'We all need a cup of tea now,' Dilys said. 'Is there a fire in the sitting room?'

'Yes, but . . .'

Dilys was filling the kettle. She took it into the sitting room, levelled the burning coals there and sat it on top. 'Shouldn't be long. Didn't you think of boiling the kettle in here?'

'I didn't think it was safe.'

'Is there cake or anything?' Lottie asked. 'Aunt Harriet usually makes scones on Fridays.'

'Well she's not here, is she?' Grandma said irritably. 'Another problem is that she made a casserole and asked me to put it in the oven at three o'clock. So now there'll be nothing ready for dinner.'

Dilys fetched the teapot. 'What time will she be back? I'm going to the pictures with a girl from work tonight.'

'That's another thing,' Grandma exploded. 'She rang up an hour ago and said that Cousin Olivia was making a big fuss of her because she hardly ever sees any of us. She's persuaded Harriet to stay longer and have a meal with them tonight. She won't be home till ten.'

'Well, we'll have this cup of tea,' Dilys said, 'then I'll go out and buy us all fish and chips. Did you know there's a new chippy opened up in that row of shops just beyond the Great Eastern pub? I've heard they're very good.'

'A chippy? What is the place coming to?' Grandma said faintly.

'It's keeping up with the times,' Dilys said. 'Here's Dad; get him a cup and saucer, Lottie, and fill the kettle while you're there so we can all have a second cup.'

Lottie leapt up to oblige and came back saying, 'I think it's rather fun to make tea in here like this, and I found these Marie biscuits to go with it.'

When Dilys returned home from the cinema later that evening, Harriet was alighting from a taxi at the back gate. 'Grandma's really missed you today,' she told her.

In the sitting room, Harriet noticed the kettle singing on top of the fire. 'You've let the stove go out,' she said.

'It's got a mind of its own,' Jemima wailed. 'I've had a harassing day. Make a cup of tea for your aunt, Dilys. She'll be much in need.'

Harriet was in good spirits. She looked revitalised and had rosy cheeks. 'Everything went as planned,' she said. 'Cousin Olivia thought Edward more than ready to throw off his mortal coils. They made much of me and send their love.'

The next morning, although it was Saturday, Lottie and Dilys got up early to help Harriet relight the stove, so they could have tea and boiled eggs for breakfast.

Charles was reaching for more toast when he said, 'We really must get you an electric stove, Harriet. This one works very well, but without staff, it's a lot of work for you.'

'Absolutely,' Dilys said. 'Harriet has far too much to do. Nothing in this house has been changed since Queen Victoria's day. If you can't cope here, Grandma, you shouldn't expect Harriet to do it. There are lots of modern inventions that would cut down the work. We need a Hoover and an electric kettle too. It would make life easier for you, too, when the rest of us are out.'

'That sounds marvellous,' Harriet said, 'and if we could send our washing to the laundry as well, I'd be in clover.'

'We have a washerwoman every week,' Jemima said. 'I'm told that's cheaper than using the laundry. It's not as if you have to do any washing. Mrs Hobbs does it in the basement, so she's no trouble to any of us.'

'She uses up all the hot water and always wants more. I boil kettles for her and run them down.'

Grandma stared at Harriet over her specs. 'We should enter Edward's death in the family Bible, before we forget.' She stood up. 'You need to come too, Charles, to lift the Bible down.'

Lottie trailed behind them to the music room. It was cold, and smelled of damp. She'd been told that at one time Olwen had played the grand piano, but now it was unused and out of tune. Dilys and Eunice had had lessons when they were young, but they'd lost interest; the Mortimers were not musical. There had been no money to pay for music lessons for Lottie and Glyn.

Dad lifted down the family Bible and put it on a side table. It was coated with dust. 'Charlotte, please fetch a duster,' Grandma said.

She scurried off and returned with a cloth. The Bible was bound in leather and had a brass clasp. She tried to slide it off, but it was stiff. Dad did it for her. She opened the book at the title page and wrinkled her nose at the musty smell it gave off. Why had she never thought of looking in it before? Her heart beat a little faster at the thought. It was a traditional family Bible providing space to enter the name of each family member at birth. It started with Lazarus Octavius Mortimer, who was born in 1746 and died in 1790. Lottie felt her interest quicken. She could see the records had been carefully kept, though the ink had faded in places. They would surely pinpoint her position in the family tree.

But Aunt Harriet was bringing pen and ink and she had to get out of the way. She watched Grandma turn the pages to find the entry for Uncle Edward, and Harriet carefully recorded his death. 'Don't touch it until the ink dries,' she warned.

Lottie waited until Grandma and Harriet had gone to the kitchen, then she riffled through the pages to find Grandma's name: Jemima Martha Clarissa Mortimer, born 1845. She'd been told many times how Grandma was allowed to train as a nurse when she showed no sign of attracting a husband, and how she'd met Patrick O'Leary through her work and married him in 1872. It was noted here that at the time of his marriage he'd changed his name by deed poll to Mortimer.

Lottie was enthralled. How unusual was that? It meant that Grandma did not have to be Mrs O'Leary. She had gone from being Miss Mortimer to Mrs Mortimer. No doubt the Mortimer family was deemed to be more important than the O'Learys.

Grandma's children were listed: Dad first – he was Charles Edward, born in 1873 – next Uncle Lazlo in 1878, and then Harriet Jemima in 1882. This was the important bit. In 1896, Dad had married Olwen Myfanwy Thomas, and all their children were listed. Charlotte ran her finger down the page: Dilys, Eunice, William – who had died when he was seven months old – Oliver and Glyn.

She straightened up with a gasp. Her name had not been added! That must mean she'd been right all along, she wasn't a Mortimer! Or had they just forgotten? Dilys had said she and Eunice had seen her in a crib by Olwen's bed on the day she was born, so she had to be her mother. If only she was still alive and Lottie could ask her.

She turned the pages to find the date of Olwen's death, but the only entry for her was her marriage on Dad's page. This was the Mortimer family Bible, and it seemed other people were only mentioned where they touched the Mortimers. Was that intentional, or just an accidental omission?

Suddenly it seemed important that she knew exactly when Olwen had died. She was buried in the churchyard at St Mark's, and every Sunday Lottie went with the family to the morning service there. Often they took flowers from the garden to put on her grave, and she knew the date she sought was engraved on the headstone.

She didn't want to wait until next Sunday, so she slipped her coat on and ran up the back garden. Once in the churchyard, she went straight to Olwen's large and expensive gravestone. The gold lettering was fading now, but still legible:

Olwen Myfanwy Mortimer, née Thomas, died aged 36
Dearly beloved wife of Charles Edward Mortimer
12 May 1874–9 October 1910

Charlotte was stunned. She'd been born on 5 October that year. Why had she never noticed before that Olwen had died only four days afterwards? Glyn had been born at the beginning of that year, and Olwen had been an invalid for some time. She supposed it was possible that Olwen was her mother, but it hardly seemed likely.

But if she was, and she'd died only four days after giving birth to her, then Lottie must have contributed to her death, and that was a fearsome thought.

She ran home telling herself she had to stop thinking like this. One minute she was sure Olwen was her mother, and the next she was quite certain she could not have been. It was getting her nowhere, but at least she could be sure of her father. He'd always been her anchor, unfailingly kind and affectionate, just as a father should be.

Lottie spent a restless night turning the problem over and over in her mind, and decided she had to know one way or another. She would have to confront Grandma and ask her directly.

In the morning she was still half asleep and late down to breakfast. They were all in a rush and she knew this wasn't the right moment. She'd wait until the evening.

It was a busy day in the office, and she and Dad were later than usual coming home.

'I'm glad you're here,' Harriet said as they walked in. 'Dinner is ready. We agreed it would be earlier tonight.'

Lottie remembered then that Grandma had told her she could have an extra late night this week to go to the cinema with Harriet. She didn't have many friends, and Dilys had agreed to go with her to the Lyceum to see Alfred Hitchcock's new thriller *Blackmail*. It was the first full-length talkie made in Britain, and Harriet had never been to a talkie before. Then Dilys had cried off because she wanted to go out with some boyfriend, and Lottie had been more than happy to take her place.

'You haven't forgotten, have you?' Harriet was anxious.

'No,' she said. It had been pushed from her mind, but she

wasn't going to let it stop her speaking to Grandma. She could tell her in five minutes all she wanted to know, and then she could relax and enjoy a night at the pictures.

Her stomach was churning as they sat down in front of their plates of stew and mashed potatoes, but the moment had come and she'd prepared a few sentences to get things started. 'Grandma,' she began. 'I'd like you to tell me about my parents. I've always believed that Dad and Olwen are my parents and you are my grandmother, but—'

Jemima thundered, 'Charlotte, I am your grandmother. You need have no doubt about that.' Every knife and fork had gone down; they were all looking at her. 'What has suddenly brought this on?'

'The family Bible – my birth isn't entered in that, though everybody else's is. And I checked the date Olwen died, and I don't think she could have been my mother, unless giving birth to me killed her.'

'Put that right out of your mind; that isn't the case at all. Right, we need to have a little talk, but let us have our dinner in peace first.' Jemima picked up her knife and fork again and began to eat.

Harriet burst out, 'Charlotte and I are going out after dinner. You said she could come to the pictures with me.'

'So I did. Then our little talk will have to be put off until tomorrow.' Jemima had a healthy appetite and was tucking in.

'Grandma, no, please can't you just tell me now?'

'No, I can't, this will take some time to explain. Harriet, you can go alone to the cinema for once, or you can put it off to another day.'

Harriet was taken aback. 'We could go tomorrow instead, Lottie. That film is showing all week.'

'Good. All right then, Charlotte, I'll talk to you about your parents after dinner.'

Lottie helped Harriet clear away and wash up. Then they made a pot of coffee and carried the tray in. Harriet poured out and handed the cups round.

Stiffly upright, Grandma sat on the edge of her armchair, the most comfortable in the house. 'Come and sit by me, Charlotte,' she said, indicating the armchair next to her. 'As you've asked about your birth mother, we'll tell you all we know about her circumstances.'

'Thank you, this has hardly been out of my mind since I realised exactly when Olwen died.'

Jemima took a deep breath. 'My conscience has been pricking me; I should have explained all this to you some time ago. As you know, our family is closely connected to the Thomas family. Olwen's sister Gwendolen is married to Jeremy Arbuthnot. He is a Member of Parliament, and they both spend a lot of time in London when the House is sitting. When they come to their Liverpool house, he goes often to Southport to deal with matters in his constituency, and Gwendolen is left on her own. She doesn't have a real marriage and I'm afraid she had an extramarital affair.'

Lottie could feel the intensity of Grandma's emotions; of Harriet's and Dad's, too. She said, 'Gwendolen is my mother, isn't she?'

The three of them stared at her in shock.

'Good gracious!' Grandma said. 'I didn't realise you knew.'

'I didn't know,' she said. 'I guessed.'

'Yes, well, we would have been very much against Gwendolen's marriage if we'd known Jeremy was a homosexual. He kept that very quiet, and has continued to do so even to this day.'

'He was such a charming man,' Harriet said. 'He'd progressed in his career; people looked up to him. I thought Gwendolen was doing very well for herself.'

'He was proud of being a Member of Parliament, and of having such a good reputation,' Grandma said. 'Poor Gwendolen, I doubt she knew before . . .'

'Why would he want to marry her if he's a homosexual?' Lottie asked. 'Didn't you say men like that were attracted to other men and not to women?'

'Why indeed?' Jemima shook her head. 'I hate to think. You must understand that Olwen and Gwendolen were orphaned when they were in their teens. The Thomas family was decimated by tuberculosis. Both girls were quiet and retiring, and I think Gwendolen was always a worry to Olwen. It wasn't just her general health, though she was pale and often ill. She relied very much on her older sister and needed to turn to her for support. I was afraid she'd never learn to stand on her own two feet.'

'Mother, you didn't know her that well,' Charles said. 'She was clever; I thought her quite a strong-minded person.'

'Well you may be right, because when she met Jeremy Arbuthnot, she fell head over heels in love with him and was determined to marry him. We all thought he'd make her an excellent husband and be the anchor she needed. He seemed to dote on her. She was twenty when they married, and he was fifteen years older.'

'As you know, he is distantly related to us,' Charles said. 'His mother was a Sanderson, I believe.'

'He was already the Conservative Member of Parliament for Southport, and had been brought up in Liverpool. We were impressed that he'd qualified as a solicitor and yet had chosen to make his career in politics.'

'Olwen was pleased with the match,' Charles said. 'She was already ill and wanted to see her sister settled.'

Grandma sighed heavily. 'Unfortunately, the marriage turned out to be a big mistake. Jeremy Arbuthnot misled us all. I blame myself. It never entered my head that he could be homosexual. He kept it very well hidden. I can only think that he married Gwendolen as a screen for his homosexual activities.'

Lottie gasped with horror.

'He was always concerned about his reputation,' Charles said. 'I suppose he had to be, because he's so much in the public eye.'

Grandma seemed to relax a little. 'The law is very much at fault. It does not understand why some people become homosexual. It certainly makes life difficult for them.' She sighed. 'I write letters of explanation to the newspapers when they publish reports of arrests in public lavatories, but they don't print them. The law brands homosexuals as criminals. In the eyes of the Church they are evil, and all because they are different. It's a medieval idea that has persisted to the present day. Sorry, Charlotte, I'm afraid I'm on my hobby horse again. I hope one day everybody will come to their senses about this.'

'Are you saying he married Gwen even though he didn't love her?' she asked. 'To hide that he was . . . ?'

'How could he love her? He couldn't see her as a wife in the normal sense. He saw her as a screen. He had to hide his homosexual activities from his constituents and the general public.'

She seemed to suddenly collapse.

'I'm sorry, I find raking over these bad times very wearing. Upsetting.'

'Grandma, you haven't told me about—'

'I think I'll have an early night.' She got to her feet. 'I'm going to bed. Goodnight.'

Harriet said, 'Mother, would you like to have your cocoa in your room? I'll make it now.'

When they had both gone, the room was very quiet. Charles looked at Lottie, his gaze agonised.

'I've never quite fitted into the family, have I?' she said, tears prickling her eyes.

'Of course you have.' He got up and came to put his arms round her. 'You've always felt like a daughter to me.'

'Dad,' she said, 'you feel like my father, but you aren't, are you? You can't be. Gwen was Olwen's sister.' His arms tightened round her in a hug. Lovable old Dad, softly spoken, gentle and dutiful; he'd never let anybody down, least of all his wife, and especially not in that way.

'No, love, I'm not, but I've tried hard to be.' His eyes were misting over too. He gave her another hug. 'Grandma hasn't told you the whole story. It's your Uncle Lazlo you need to hear about now.'

He led her to the sofa and they sat down together.

'Gwen was alone so much in Liverpool that when Lazlo came home on leave, Olwen asked him to try and cheer her up.

I suppose it was inevitable that they'd fall in love; they were both lonely people. In those days, there were very few white women out in West Africa, just a few missionaries' wives.

'Lazlo had returned to Africa before Gwen realised you were on the way. She wrote and told him, but he was thousands of miles away by then. I suppose there wasn't a lot he could do. He couldn't ask her to go out there, because there were no hospitals or maternity services as we know them. And Gwendolen was another man's wife.'

Lottie shuddered. What a predicament she'd been in.

'It was a worrying time for us all. By then, Olwen was very ill. She saw Gwendolen as her responsibility and wanted her here with us. She lived with us for about four months, and you were born here. It was meant to help Gwen through the birth, and give her time to think about her choices and what she wanted to do.

'Jeremy let it be known that Gwen was here to help her sick sister and her family,' Charles said. 'Olwen died while she was here, and that was added stress for us all. Gwen decided that she'd return to Jeremy and take you with her. We all thought he'd welcome you, because the world would see a child as confirmation that their marriage was normal.'

'But he didn't?' Lottie could feel tears rolling down her cheeks.

'You were only there a few weeks. Gwen said he found it hard to accept another man's child as his own, but he was trying and she meant to persevere. She wasn't well, but she had a nanny to help, and she kept you away from Jeremy as much as possible. But then one day he turned up here and asked us to look after you. He said Gwendolen was too ill to take care of you, and was afraid you'd catch her illness. She was very upset at parting from you.'

Lottie wiped her eyes on her sleeve.

'Grandma can't unbend enough to give anybody hugs,' he said softly, 'but she does love you. We all do. Are you all right?'

'Yes, Dad, I'm fine, thank you. I think I'll say goodnight now.' She reached up to kiss his cheek, and found that his face was wet with tears too. 'This is all too emotional for Grandma,' she said. 'Getting that way for us too.'

She went towards the kitchen to make some cocoa, but Dilys had come home and was there with Harriet being brought up to date on the evening's happenings. Lottie couldn't face any more emotion, so she went straight to her room, where she found that Harriet had put a cup of cocoa on her bedside table.

She got into bed quickly. The cocoa had gone cold, but she hardly noticed as she settled back to think things over. Grandma would be very concerned about the family's reputation, and want this secret to be kept as dark as Uncle Jeremy's. The whole story had fallen into place as Dad had been speaking. Lazlo was her father; that was why he'd been banished from the bosom of the family all this time. She remembered the presents and cards he'd sent her over the years, how pleased he always seemed to see her, and the way he'd toss her up into a great bear hug when they met.

She reached for a handkerchief and switched off her bedside light. Although Grandma had answered some of her questions, she'd opened up a Pandora's box of more. Not that it really mattered; she knew all she needed to, and the hardest part was accepting that Dad wasn't really her father.

CHAPTER ELEVEN

G LYN MORTIMER SHIVERED IN the cold grey light of an English dawn, but counted himself lucky to be on watch as the *Accra* nosed past the old fort at New Brighton and into the Mersey estuary. It was good to see the familiar brown water and the strong current taking him home.

They'd picked up the pilot off Anglesey and would now go straight to the Prince's Landing Stage to disembark the passengers. He could see the Liver Building taking shape in the morning mist, and tried to pick out the shape of Mersey View on the opposite bank. He'd always known that seafaring was in his blood, and this first voyage to West Africa had confirmed it. His senior officers had told him he was coping well.

The *Accra* ran to a regular timetable. They'd spent five days in Lagos to disembark passengers and unload cargo, followed by the reloading of both for the homeward journey. Uncle Lazlo had come up to see him and had shared a meal with the crew. The next evening he'd treated Glyn to a night on the town, dinner in his hotel and plenty to drink. 'These are the bright lights of life on the Coast,' he'd said. 'There's nothing in Calabar apart from the club, and Fernando Pó is like stepping back into the last century.'

Glyn had enjoyed seeing the sights and the teeming crowds

on the streets, but thought the food on the ship was better. 'I'll have a great deal to tell the family,' he'd said. He was looking forward to seeing them all again.

Even though he was in the Mersey, Glyn knew he wouldn't be able to go home immediately. The *Accra* would have to vacate her berth on the landing stage and go to a dock to unload the cargo. She would be in port for ten days, and a small number of officers were required to be on board to oversee the work. They took it in turns to do this.

When he did go home, three days later, Grandma and Harriet welcomed him and told him he'd grown into a handsome young man. Lottie and Dad came back from work some ten minutes after he'd arrived. He was delighted to see them all again. 'You're taller than me now,' he said to Lottie, 'a real beanpole.'

'But you've got the shoulders of a young bull,' she said. 'They wouldn't suit me.'

Glyn wanted to take her out for a meal, somewhere exciting, and perhaps to a nightclub, but he understood Aunt Harriet and Grandma were preparing a special dinner to welcome him home and knew he couldn't, not tonight.

'I love being at sea, and the West African coast is a fabulous and interesting place, but I miss civilisation too. Tomorrow night,' he said to Lottie, 'I want to take you out to enjoy the fleshpots of Birkenhead.'

'Charlotte has to work,' Grandma told him. 'You mustn't keep her out late.'

'But it'll be Saturday,' he said. 'We can both sleep off any excess.'

'I go swimming on Sunday mornings,' she laughed. 'I pick a

friend up at eight o'clock, so I'll not be sleeping in.'

'I'll come with you,' he said. He intended to get as much pleasure as he could out of his leave.

He found that Lottie already knew the best places to go, and let her decide where to dine and dance. He enjoyed it all, though she told him he wasn't much of a dancer. It was very late when she drove him home.

Early the next morning, he heard her moving about in the next room. It was not quite daylight and seemed miserably cold. He decided he'd give this swimming trip a miss. She swept into his bedroom. 'Come on, rise and shine.'

'Changed my mind,' he muttered, and snuggled deeper under his blankets. The next moment he felt the bedding being dragged from him. 'Hey! Leave me alone.'

'No. You said you'd come, and you'll feel more alive if you do. I'm going to put the kettle on. Kitchen in five minutes, OK?'

Reluctantly he started to dress; he'd forgotten just how cold this house could be. In the kitchen, Lottie pushed a cup of steaming tea into his hand and poured out more to take to Gran, Harriet and Dilys. 'Dad doesn't like tea in bed,' she told him.

In the car, Glyn drowsed in the front seat, musing that Lottie was doing well to have learned to drive and beguiled Dad into letting her borrow his car. 'We're going to pick up my friend first,' she said. 'Her name's Dorothy.'

'What's she like?'

'Always happy, good company. I like her.'

'Is she pretty?'

'Yes, she has lovely red hair, which she wears in one long, thick plait.'

'You mean ginger?'

'Sort of. Dad likes her too.'

Glyn wasn't sure she'd be his type. He didn't care for ginger plaits. 'She sounds just a kid.'

'She's a year older than me.'

'Older than I am, then?'

Lottie pulled up in front of a semi-detached villa and shot up the path to knock on the door. 'Could you get in the back seat, Glyn?' she said.

It was a tiny car and it was a struggle to slither his bulk into the back. A girl ran down the path and got in beside Lottie. A beret covered her head, and he caught only a glimpse of a hawser-like rope of hair before it disappeared behind the front seat.

When his sister introduced them, she said, 'Hello, Lottie's told me a lot about you,' and chatted on about something that had happened at work that excluded him.

The baths seemed cold and clammy and the electric lights were on. He shivered as he changed into his swimming gear and hurried to get into the water, Lottie had assured him it would be warm. He jumped in making a great splash, and it was freezing. He was not surprised to find there were few swimmers.

He turned to watch for the girls. They came out together. Lottie looked like a skinny beanpole and wore a serviceable swim cap, but Dorothy was magnificent in a scarlet bathing suit, with her arm-thick plait swinging below her waist. Hollywood couldn't do better than her.

They walked round to the deep end and one at a time dived in elegantly from the springboard, coming down the pool to

136

join him with powerful overarm strokes. 'Race you back,' Lottie said.

'Why not two lengths?' he suggested. They agreed and waited for him to line up beside them.

He soon regretted it. He was struggling to keep up. On the *Conway*, where the ability to swim had been thought essential, he'd been one of the best. As they turned, he lost more ground, and both girls finished well ahead of him.

'You're getting lazy,' Lottie said. 'You used to be better than this.'

'I'm out of practice,' he said, and felt he'd been taken down a peg. 'Dorothy, you're like a fish in the water.' He could hardly drag his eyes away from her. 'Like a mermaid,' he told her when he thought Lottie was too far away to hear.

'Time to go home,' Lottie said, long before he felt ready. Both girls ignored the steps to get out. He was full of admiration as he watched Dorothy swing herself up to sit on the side. He managed it at the second attempt.

Back in the car, Dorothy had released her hair from its plait and it hung in damp tendrils down her back. She looked more like a mermaid than ever. Glyn made himself ask, 'Are you on the phone at home?'

'No,' she said.

He'd already decided he mustn't let this chance go. 'Will you come out with me this afternoon? I know it's quick, but I only have six days' leave. Lottie will vouch that you'll be safe enough with me.'

Dorothy turned round and her smile was radiant. 'I'd like that, thank you.'

He was thrilled. 'I'll pick you up at two o'clock.'

After they'd dropped Dorothy, Lottie looked at him and raised her eyebrows. 'You're not a homosexual after all, then. How long since you decided that?'

Glyn gave her shoulder a playful punch, even though she was driving. 'Come on,' she said, 'I want to know. When did you stop thinking you were?'

'Grandma was right. Pretty soon afterwards.'

'And what about that pal of yours; was his name Ralph?'

'The same.'

She glanced at him; his cheeks were scarlet. 'Come on,' she said. 'Grandma thinks we should understand everything about our own bodies and minds and brings the most embarrassing things out into the open, so why can't you?'

'Oh God, Lottie! Give over.'

'No, I want to know how homosexuals feel. What exactly did you feel for Ralph?'

'You told me you felt the same for your teacher, Miss Whatshername.'

'Laidlaw. Not the same. I sort of admired her from afar,' Lottie said, 'but wanted us to be closer.'

'I liked Ralph. We all like some people more than others. He was a friend.'

'It was more than that.'

'I suppose there's a degree of intimacy in any friendship. At school we all talked about it and some paired off. We didn't see any girls for months on end. There were absolutely no women in our world. At sea, men have to look after themselves. It's different when we get home.'

'And that's it?'

'Absolutely. I don't like opening up about that time.

It's a bad memory. I want to forget it.'

'OK. I'm glad you like Dorothy, though. You couldn't have chosen better.'

After lunch, she dropped him outside Dorothy's house and went to Hamilton Square to meet Roddy. It was a cold afternoon and she suggested they go to New Brighton for a walk along the prom. He agreed, but very soon he was shivering and complaining it was too cold. When it started to rain, they ran across the road to the nearest café and had hot chocolate. Afterwards they returned to the car, where they spent an hour with their arms round each other. Later, he took her to a pub. She didn't count the afternoon a great success.

When she got to the office the next morning, Dorothy rushed in to see her, bubbling with excitement. 'I think your brother is lovely. We had a marvellous time yesterday.'

'What did you do?'

'We walked round the upper park and then the lower park, and fed the ducks. There was hardly anybody there.'

'Didn't it pour with rain?'

'Yes, we sheltered in the boathouse. We had it all to ourselves. When it got dark, I took him home for tea.'

Lottie thought it sounded as though Glyn had had a better time than she had.

'He's asked me to go out with him again tonight. Did he tell you?'

'No, he didn't get up for breakfast. I took it to his room. Aunt Harriet likes to get everything cleared away quickly. He's probably still asleep.'

Charlotte took the cover off the typewriter and got on with

a few letters Dad had given her to do. She was glad they'd hit it off. Glyn needed a friend to come back to, and who better than Dorothy?

The following Wednesday evening, Lottie when to meet Roddy's train. She glimpsed him in the crowd surging out of the station and knew he was in high spirits. 'Lottie, love.' He threw his arms round her and kissed her. 'Good news, I've got the promotion I was hoping for.

'Marvellous,' Lottie was thrilled for him. 'It's come sooner than you expected.'

'Yes, and I'm delighted.' He beamed at her. 'We'll be able to afford to get married.'

'So there'll be nothing for Grandma to complain of; nothing to stop us as soon as I'm twenty-one.'

'Nothing at all.' He hugged her again. 'But first I'm being sent to our Head Office in Manchester on a month's management training course.'

'When?'

'Next week.'

'Oh, I'll miss you.'

'I'll miss you too, Lottie, but it will be worth it. We must have a celebration dinner.'

He took her to the Central Hotel where there was a three-piece band and a tiny dance floor. It was, Lottie thought, the sort of place Martin would approve of. They were both in high spirits and really enjoyed it, though Roddy had to catch the last train back to Liverpool at 11.20, and Grandma was very cross because she was so late home. Even the news of Roddy's promotion did nothing to sooth her temper.

Once Roddy had gone to Manchester, he wrote lovely letters to her, and she spent a lot of time thinking about him. She was a little uneasy that he'd made such a point of asking about her family finances and she hadn't put him right. She knew she was letting Grandma's suspicions about him get to her. But she was in love and didn't want to upset any of the plans they were making. He'd have his promotion and they could afford to get married.

CHAPTER TWELVE

THE WRECKAGE OF NEW Ferry pier had finally been demolished, and the view from their house had changed for the better. But more and more of their neighbours were moving away from the Mersey to the newer, smarter suburbs on the banks of the River Dee.

'I can't bear to see the district going downhill like this,' Harriet complained. 'It seems New Ferry is no longer considered a desirable place to live.'

'It'll do for us,' Charles said. 'It'll have to.'

Lottie had been working for the family firm for over a year now and was still enjoying it, but she understood why her father was depressed about its future profitability. Ted Pascoe, the shipping agent in the next-door office, was very much busier. So busy, in fact, that Lottie was being asked to help Dorothy Porter more often. Ted paid her for her time, and she enjoyed that too. Dorothy had become a firm friend.

In October, Charlotte had her nineteenth birthday. Dad said, 'I think you're capable of handling most things the captains ask for now.' Thereafter she mostly visited the ships on her own.

As Christmas drew closer, there was the usual round of parties. Philip's mother rang Lottie to tell her they were making a round trip on the mailboat to Lagos over the holidays and hoped to see something of Philip while they were there. She sent her best wishes. 'She's told you so you won't think she's dropped you from their Christmas party list,' Charles said.

On the Sunday before Christmas, Martin and Eunice invited them over for a meal. It was a traditional family Sunday lunch, and Eunice seemed proud to show off her two young sons and the growing girls. She assured them all that she was well and happy.

'She doesn't look all that well,' Grandma commented.

On Christmas Eve, the *Claremont* was due in after a voyage of eighteen months tramping round the Russian and Baltic ports, collecting and delivering cargoes wherever her captain could get them. She was returning home with her holds full of pig iron, copper and cheap glassware, but nothing would be unloaded until after the holiday.

At home, they'd been getting ready for weeks. Lottie and Dilys had tucked holly behind the pictures in the downstairs rooms, put the Christmas tree up in the hall and decorated it. Aunt Harriet had iced the Christmas cake and made several other fancy cakes, as well as mince pies.

Captain Donkin of the *Claremont* hoped to come in on the early tide and be tied up before eight o'clock. It was a dark, dank and completely unseasonable morning, and Lottie got up early to drive down to Morpeth Dock. She was pleased to see that the *Claremont* had come in on time and the gangway was already down.

She shivered as she parked her car and went up the gangway. She hadn't been on this ship before, and the crew seemed surprised to see a girl. Captain Donkin greeted her at his cabin door. He was a big, burly man in his forties, his uniform pressed and his shoes polished. She knew all the ships' officers abandoned their old pullovers and spruced themselves up when they came into port. She put out her hand. 'Happy Christmas,' she said. He shook it, but with no show of enthusiasm.

'Miss Mortimer. Is Mr Smith no longer with you?' She noticed that he kept his hand in front of his mouth, and couldn't speak clearly.

'No, I have taken over as water clerk now.'

'Your father did tell me, but a young girl like you? Mr Smith was very efficient and very obliging.' His expression said he wasn't expecting the same from her.

'Dad has helped me arrange for an immediate delivery of Christmas fare for the crew who will be staying on board,' she said. 'Turkey and Christmas pudding.'

'Thank you, they'll be looking forward to that, but I'm in difficulties, as you've no doubt noticed.' He pursed his lips. 'I do hope you'll be able to help me. I dropped my false teeth in the john in Murmansk and haven't been able to enjoy a meal since.'

He retreated to his desk and opened a drawer to bring out an upper denture broken in two pieces. Looking embarrassed, he pushed them towards her. 'Could you possibly get it mended for me?'

She looked at the denture, trying to hide her distaste. This was not something she'd been asked to do before. 'I'll try.'

'If you could do it before my Christmas dinner is cooked, I'd be really grateful.' His face said he thought it unlikely that she could. 'I can't chew meat without these. It's been a trying time.'

'I'll do my best.' Lottie put the pieces in her bag. 'There's something else I need to do first.'

Dad had gone with her to the bank yesterday to draw out cash to pay the wages. Five crew members were being paid off, and he had already hired others to replace them after the festive season. Three more were going home for the holiday. After she'd paid over the wages, Lottie went back to the office and organised a launch to take the men across the river to the Liverpool side, and booked two of them into the sailors' home.

That left the problem of the captain's false teeth. She had no idea how to go about getting them mended, but she must if he was going to believe she was capable of being a water clerk. She took the pieces out and tried to fit them together on her desk, hoping that it would never be her lot to wear such monstrosities. Ted Pascoe had false teeth, so she went next door to ask his advice.

Dorothy giggled when she saw them; Ted thought it funny too. 'He'll have to postpone his Christmas dinner,' he said.

Lottie wasn't laughing; she was afraid holiday high spirits had already taken over in their office. 'If you broke your dentures, where would you go to get them mended?' she asked.

'I'd go back to my dentist; he made them.' Lottie had no idea who had made these. Dad had said Captain Donkin came from Tyneside.

It occurred to her then that Grandma had false teeth. She'd know what to do. She went back to her own office to ring her. It took Jemima a moment to think. 'You need a dental technician. A dentist measures you up, but he doesn't make them.'

'Do you have the phone number of a technician I could ring?'

'I'll find one for you by the time you come home.'

'No, Grandma, I need it now. Captain Donkin is desperate to eat again. He'd like them in time for his Christmas dinner.'

'All right, I'll look now and ring you back.'

Feeling hot with impatience, Lottie sat looking at the receiver on her desk. What if Grandma failed to come up with anything? She took down some trade directories from a high shelf; perhaps she could find a firm of dental technicians here. Before she could open them, Grandma rang back with a number.

'I had some new teeth made last year,' she said. 'They weren't as comfortable as I'd hoped and I sent them back twice to be filed down and smoothed off. I dealt with a Mr Standish and found him obliging.'

'Thank you, Grandma, you're a mine of information.'

'He might not be there today, though; it is Christmas Eve.'

Lottie rang the number immediately and felt fortunate when Mr Standish himself answered. 'I'm Charlotte Mortimer,' she said. 'My grandmother Jemima Mortimer has recommended you.'

'I remember Mrs Mortimer,' he said. Most people did.

She explained Captain Donkin's difficulty. 'Would you be able to fix his dentures today?'

'It depends on how damaged they are. If we have to make a new plate, it will be impossible.'

'Could I bring the pieces over to show you?'

He paused, and she thought he was about to say no. 'I intend to close at lunchtime today. You'd have to bring them in straight away.'

'I will,' she said eagerly.

'But I can't promise to have them ready by tomorrow. We have to keep dentures overnight to make sure the glue has set properly, and any new work will need filing and polishing.'

'I understand.' When he told her he was speaking from the dental hospital in Liverpool, her spirits sank, but she said, 'Thank you, I'll set out right away.'

She drove to the station and took a train across. She knew roughly where the dental hospital was, and jogged along the pavement when she got off. She was breathless when she arrived, but Mr Standish was waiting for her.

'It's a simple break through the plate,' he said, fitting the pieces together.

'Is there any chance they could be ready for tomorrow?'

'Tomorrow is Christmas Day. It would mean I'd have to come in to work.'

'Please,' she pleaded. 'The captain is miserable about his teeth, and he thinks I'm useless at my job because I'm a girl. I'm the first female water clerk he's come across.'

'All right, ring me in the morning about ten o'clock to see if I have it ready. What is your address and phone number? You've come from Birkenhead? Will you be able to get over here tomorrow?'

'Yes, I saw a notice in the station saying that normal Sunday service is running.'

Christmas morning was like no other. Lottie was woken early by Dilys playing carols on her gramophone. Breakfast was more relaxed than usual, and when she got through to Mr Standish at the dental hospital, he told her that he'd managed to repair the denture.

'Excellent,' she said. 'I'll set out straight away.'

Grandma said, 'I'm impressed that you're showing such willingness to work on Christmas Day. Captain Donkin should be pleased with the service he's getting.'

There was nothing festive about the weather. It was cold and grey, a miserable morning with little traffic and hardly anybody about, but the church bells were ringing.

Mr Standish said, 'You've been quick. Good, I'll be able to go home again now.'

Lottie went straight to the *Claremont*. She'd never seen the dock with every crane idle before. As the captain watched her come up the gangway, a huge smile spread across his face. 'Have you had my denture fixed?'

'Yes,' she said, handing it over. 'Happy Christmas.'

'You're a marvel,' he said, and kissed her cheek, 'a ruddy marvel. It'll certainly be a happy Christmas for me now. You deserve a present for this, you really do.' He rushed her to his cabin and pressed a bottle into her hands. 'Russian vodka,' he said, 'the genuine stuff. I hope you like it. Happy Christmas to you.'

When she got home, everybody tried to read the label, which was in Russian, and Dilys wanted to try the contents. 'Quite unsuitable for young ladies,' Grandma said, and took the bottle from her. 'Your father will know somebody who would like this.'

The family seemed to think that Lottie had made a huge sacrifice by collecting the false teeth on Christmas Day. It made her feel good that she'd managed to please everybody; quite triumphant, in fact.

CHAPTER THIRTEEN

TOGETHER WITH MANY OF the other passengers, Lazlo Mortimer and Philip Royden were hanging over the ship's rail looking down into the turquoise bow wave made by the MV *Accra* on her homeward journey. Lazlo thought he'd glimpsed the flash of flying fish in the foam, and yes, there they were again.

'The ship must have disturbed a large shoal,' Philip said, as suddenly fifty or so small silvery fish were soaring up above the water only to dive again, their place taken by another wave of fish in flight, and then another. They both leaned further over, watching for the glistening flashes, totally fascinated.

'Marvellous,' Philip said.

But then they were gone, and Lazlo was left mourning that he was leaving this bright and sunny world on his final voyage home. He had lived on the Coast for twenty years and hated to think he'd never see the place again, nor his friends at the club, nor Emmanuel who had been his cook and general factotum for all that time. Most Europeans retired from the Coast when they reached the age of forty-five, and he was already fifty. He'd caught yellow fever in the outbreak they'd had five years ago and been sick on and off ever since. He couldn't stay any longer. He had to make a new life for himself in Liverpool, though he had nothing to bring to it but the mistakes he'd made in the past.

Things were very different for Philip. After a successful two and a half years in Calabar, which he'd enjoyed, he was looking forward to getting back to civilisation and taking up where he'd left off.

Lazlo had been assured that a job awaited him in Elder Dempster's head office, but he viewed that with some trepidation. He'd had leave every couple of years, of course, but never enjoyed it much. He no longer felt at ease in England. He couldn't cope with the bustle of traffic, the big shops, the cold weather, and everybody else being engrossed in their own homes and families while he had nothing.

To tell the truth, he'd found the weeks of leave difficult to fill. He was always invited to spend a few days with Philip's parents, his friends Henry and Fiona Royden, and this time would be no exception. He had another friend who'd retired from Calabar and now lived near Cheltenham, so in the past he'd visited there for a few days too, but after that he'd moved to a hotel, or sometimes booked a voyage, often as the only passenger, on a small freighter going to some warm and distant place in the Far East. It was a man's life on board a ship like that, and the crew were always ready to talk. But this time it would be different: he was home for good.

Twenty years ago he'd messed up everything. At the time, he thought he'd had the most enjoyable leave ever and found his soulmate. He'd been planning to make that his last tour. He wrote to Gwen daily, keeping his letters like a diary, because the post only went at two-week intervals when the mailboat sailed. It was over two months before he knew he'd fathered a child.

He worried and worried about whether he should throw up his job and go home. Things were complicated because Gwen was already married, but it was not the sort of marriage she'd envisaged. They'd continued to write to each other, trying to decide things, but he'd let it drag on too long.

She eventually told him that her husband had asked her not to write to him, and she thought the best thing they could do was to have a clean break. So he hadn't gone home until his next leave was due.

He'd tried then to see Gwen and his daughter, but he'd had an almighty row with her husband and received a punch on the nose. On top of that, his own mother had disowned him. She'd told him he'd let his family down, and not only had he ruined his own future, but he'd ruined Gwen's life too.

He had a daughter he hardly knew and had seen only on rare occasions, and now he had to think about making amends. Down in his cabin, he'd started a letter to his mother, apologising yet again and asking if she would meet him for lunch at the Adelphi. He'd tried to do this before and she'd refused, but surely after all this time his sins could be forgiven and forgotten?

That left Charlotte, of course. He still thought of her as a child, but she'd be a young woman of twenty by now, and Mother would have told her the story of her parentage and of his bad behaviour. He was curious to know how she felt about him. Perhaps she would help him settle? But most of all he wanted to see Gwen again and make his peace with her.

*

Lazlo received a warm welcome from Henry and Fiona Royden, and after a day's rest he went into the city to visit the head office of the Elder Dempster shipping line. He wanted to meet Arthur Bellingham, who would be his new boss, and see where he'd soon be working.

India Buildings was a nine-storey neoclassical building in the heart of the commercial area. Everybody was very pleasant to him, shaking his hand and envying him the four months' leave he had before he'd start. It all seemed very alien. There weren't many buildings above two storeys in Calabar.

He shivered as he came out into the damp cold of a grey morning. He'd decided he must find himself somewhere to live, and as he'd have to come here every day, he needed it to be close. The buildings here housed shipping offices, banks and insurance firms. He needed to find an estate agent, but they'd not have their offices in a prestigious area like this. He started to walk into town, but the buildings were still like skyscrapers and all he could see were more offices, elegant restaurants and fine jewellery shops.

He changed direction and headed south towards the docks, and suddenly, in another block of offices, his attention was caught by a name that he recognised printed in gold letters across a window. It made him feel guilty just to see it. *Arbuthnot and Dodd, Solicitors. The Merseyside Family Legal Service.*

Gwen's husband! He was reminded of Jeremy's profession before he became a Member of Parliament. He hadn't realised he was still practising. Well, if he was to buy a house, he would need a solicitor. On the spur of the moment, he went inside. Several clerks were working in silence at their desks. A young woman smiled at him. 'What can we do for you, sir?'

'Would Jeremy Arbuthnot be in at the moment? He'll know who I am. The name is Lazlo Mortimer.'

'He's not arrived yet, but he is expected shortly. Mr Sanderson, his partner, is already here.'

Lazlo knew that wasn't the name he'd seen written on the window, but he said, 'Ask him if I can have a word, would you?' A few moments later, he was being shown into an inner office.

A fair-haired man in early middle age got up from behind his desk and came forward with his hand outstretched. 'I'm Martin Sanderson.'

The name rang a bell, but for a moment Lazlo couldn't place him. He shook his hand; the man had a welcoming grip.

'I don't think we've met before, but my wife was a Mortimer; her name is Eunice.'

'Oh goodness me, yes.' Lazlo had heard of her marriage. 'She's my brother's child, my niece.' He was explaining how he'd lived abroad for years but had now retired and needed to buy a house when the door swung open and Jeremy Arbuthnot breezed in.

Lazlo got to his feet; he'd have known Arbuthnot anywhere. He was a big man in every way, tall and broad, very smartly dressed in a pale grey suit. Gwen had said he was a homosexual, but there was no hint of that in his appearance.

Arbuthnot's facade of self-confidence slipped. 'Mortimer?' He was staring at him, screwing up his face.

'Yes,' said Lazlo, putting out a hand. 'It's me. How are you, Jeremy? You look very prosperous.' His hand was ignored. Jeremy continued to stare at him. 'I'm glad I've met you like this,' Lazlo went on. 'How is Gwendolen? After all this time, would you mind if I came to see her? As an old friend, just to say hello.'

There was hostility on Arbuthnot's face. 'Yes, I would mind. Don't you come anywhere near my wife. I'm not having you sniffing round her and making trouble for us again.'

Lazlo felt shocked. 'I don't want to make trouble. I've apologised for what I did. The last thing I want is to upset you or Gwen. I've retired from the Coast. I have to settle here now and I want to make friends. Can't you forgive what happened?'

'No, I want you to stay well away from me and mine. I can't have you interfering with our lives again.'

Lazlo had hoped for a better reception than this. 'Jeremy, I'm no longer the young, hot-blooded Lothario I was. I've calmed down in middle age. But if you can't be a real husband to Gwen, can't I at least be her friend?'

'How dare you? Gwendolen does not want to see you. She's put you right out of her mind.'

Lazlo took a deep breath and tried to keep calm. 'Surely we can act in a civilised manner and put the past behind us. I'd very much like to know how she's fared. It's been twenty years, for God's sake.'

'Absolutely not! I see no reason for us to have any contact.'

Lazlo felt a shiver of indignation. Arbuthnot had treated him in a similar manner at the time, but he hadn't expected his anger to fester all this time. 'What about Charlotte, her daughter?'

'Gwendolen does not have a daughter. Now please leave.'

Sanderson said uneasily, 'Jeremy, do be careful.'

Lazlo made one last effort. 'Could I not speak to Gwen on the telephone, and perhaps ask her to meet me in town?'

'Did you not hear what I said?' bellowed Arbuthnot. 'Get out now before I throw you out.'

Lazlo could feel his own temper rising. 'People in glass houses shouldn't throw stones.'

'What are you saying? Don't you dare threaten me.'

Lazlo could see him coming closer with clenched fists. 'I wouldn't risk it if I were you,' he said, making for the door.

'Do your damnedest,' Arbuthnot retorted. 'You can't hurt me.'

Lazlo felt thoroughly riled by the meeting and was glad to gulp the cold air outside. A magnificent cream sports car was drawn up against the kerb; it had not been there when he'd gone in. Did it belong to Jeremy Arbuthnot?

He took a closer look. It looked very expensive and the badges told him it was a Mercedes Benz. It still smelled new. There was a copy of *The Times* newspaper on the passenger seat, though nothing to pin the car definitely to Arbuthnot, but he thought it was his.

By the look of things Jeremy Arbuthnot was an important man who had made his mark in the world and was enjoying a high standard of living. Unfortunately, he hadn't mellowed with time, and it made Lazlo dislike the man more than ever. He felt he'd made a mess of that meeting and should have been more careful. It made him even more determined to talk to Gwen. He might need to come here again, so he looked up for a street sign. He was in Duke Street.

He needed a cup of coffee after that, and he found a smart refreshment room on the opposite side of the road and ordered one. It was still far from lunchtime and there were few customers; he sat at a table in the window to get his breath back.

Ten minutes later, he saw Arbuthnot drive past in the cream sports car. He had a passenger with him who could have been Martin Sanderson, Eunice's husband. Lazlo was afraid he'd lost touch with everything. He hadn't known they were in business together.

As an MP, Arbuthnot would earn a salary of £400 a year, but his lifestyle suggested he was spending more than that, so he'd need another source of income. Gwen was probably underwriting their expenses; she'd inherited money from her family.

Lazlo couldn't stop thinking about Gwen. He was hoping to see a lot of his daughter, and he wanted to see her mother too. Jeremy Arbuthnot was not going to stop him trying to do that. He felt he had to make his peace with Gwen, if only to set his own mind at rest.

CHAPTER FOURTEEN

A WEEK OR SO LATER, on a cold, dark Monday evening, Lottie was helping Aunt Harriet dish up the roast beef left from Sunday lunch, with warmed-up Yorkshire pudding, when Dilys came home. She'd never looked prettier, with sparkling eyes, a wide smile and dancing brown curls. 'I'm engaged to be married,' she announced, and laughed.

Jemima nearly choked on her glass of sherry. 'To whom?' she demanded. 'We had no idea you had a serious boyfriend. You never bring your friends home these days.'

'I will now, though I don't think you're likely to approve of him. His name is Alec Middleton, he's a schoolteacher and never likely to earn a fortune. And he's three years younger than I am.'

'Good gracious! Are you sure?'

'Quite sure. His father was a riveter at Cammell Laird but lost his job when they lost that big contract and had to lay off some of their workers.'

Charles said, 'I don't know if it's wise to rush . . .'

'A sudden affair . . .' Grandma began at the same time.

'It isn't sudden.' Dilys laughed again; she was effervescent with excitement. 'I've known Alec for two years and I've been thinking it over for most of that time. Like Queen

Victoria, I've had to propose to him.'

Lottie threw her arms round her. 'Congratulations, I wish you happiness and the best of everything. At least you can go ahead in your own time.' Grandma had put a firm brake on Lottie's marriage, and it had been postponed indefinitely.

'Yes, fortunately I don't need anybody's permission, and with my inheritance, Alec and I won't starve.'

'Bring him to lunch next Sunday.' Grandma was at her most severe. 'We need to meet him.'

Lottie knew Dilys was on edge; she wanted her family to like Alec and give their blessing. She'd persuaded Harriet to make a special effort with lunch and produce leg of lamb with apple pie and custard to follow. Lottie swept and tidied round to make the place spotless, while Dilys got out the best tablecloth and cutlery. With everything organised, Dilys went to fetch Alec in her car. He did not have one of his own.

Grandma liked her sherry bone dry and it was never offered to anyone else in the family, but she'd bought a bottle of sweet sherry as well; today she was aiming to please her guest. Lottie put out the two bottles with the Waterford crystal glasses on the silver tray, before going to the kitchen to help Harriet with the final preparations for the meal.

The whole family waited in an atmosphere of trepidation; they all wanted this to go well for Dilys. When Lottie heard them come through the back door, she straightened up ready to greet them. Her first impression of Alec was that nobody could disapprove of him. He was tall and good-looking, with a pencil moustache, and he was wearing a smart suit and tie.

Dad offered Lottie a glass of sherry, and she sat down with it, feeling awkward. Alec looked a little stiff, but then they all did except Grandma, who could cope with any social situation. Dad got him talking about the worsening economic situation and seemed pleased to find him knowledgeable. Alec started to tell them about his work as a primary school teacher, and gradually they all relaxed.

Afterwards, Dilys suggested taking him for a walk. He thanked them for lunch, and complimented Aunt Harriet on her cooking. Once they'd gone, Grandma said, 'Better than I expected. He's quite an intelligent fellow, his manners are all right and he's got some conversation. Dilys is going to need her inheritance, but he seems a reasonable fellow. She'll be all right with him.'

Charles said, 'I think he's a newspaper-and-slippers man.'

'Then he's like you, Dad,' Lottie said. 'I like him.' She was glad he'd passed the family's inspection.

On Tuesday night, Dilys came home wearing an engagement ring and held out her hand to show it off to the family, who were sitting round the fire.

'I hope he hasn't been spending all his money on fripperies when he needs to set up a home,' Grandma said.

'No, it was his mother's; she died a few years ago,' Dilys said. 'He had it cleaned and altered to fit me.'

'That was sensible.' Grandma held on to her hand, assessing the ring. It was three small diamonds on a gold hoop. Lottie could see from her face that she didn't like it. Eunice did have a much nicer one.

Lottie was envious when she saw Dilys going ahead with her arrangements to marry Alec. They started to look at small houses to rent near his school, and Dilys came home to tell the family all about them. She was even more envious when a week or two later Dilys brought a sheaf of documents back and announced, 'We've decided on a small semi-detached house in Bebington, and instead of renting, we're going to buy it on a mortgage.'

'A mortgage?' Grandma's eyebrows shot up. 'With your income, you should save up and buy outright. It wouldn't take you long.'

'I'm thirty-one now and I don't want to wait any longer. They're just starting to build it. The foundations are in and the brickwork is going up. We'll be married just as it's finished and move straight in.'

'Is it on an estate?'

'Yes.'

'Let me see those brochures.' Grandma took them with her to read in the sitting room. 'Your father and I need to discuss this.'

'They don't,' Dilys whispered when she'd gone. 'Thank goodness I'm past the stage of having to persuade Grandma that I'm making the right choice.'

'I wish I was,' Lottie said. 'You are lucky.'

'Your turn will come. It's taken me a long time, and Grandma isn't going to like our house.'

She was right about that. Over dinner Jemima told them, 'It's like a doll's house. You'll need one each. Have you worked out how tiny the rooms will be?'

'Alec likes it. He was brought up in a house that size.'

'Still, they will have a house of their own,' Harriet said.

'Can I have a look?' Lottie picked up the brochure. 'Roddy

and I would be thrilled to have any house. It looks jolly nice in the pictures.'

She hadn't the slightest idea what sort of house she and Roddy would be able to afford. Now she'd learned that Olwen wasn't her mother, she thought it unlikely she'd have a share in the income she'd willed to her children. She pondered on it for a while, and then told herself she was a fool to not to find out definitely one way or the other. She remembered how cagey Grandma and Dad had been about telling Dilys about her share. They were doing the same to her.

The following evening, Dad was carving the chicken they were having for dinner to celebrate the fact that Oliver had come home on leave again. The family always welcomed him back and were glad to hear his news. The bread sauce and vegetables were being passed round the table.

Lottie decided it was a good moment to bring it up. 'Grandma, and Dad,' she said. 'Am I right in thinking there will be no inherited income for me when I'm twenty-five?'

The chatter ceased. Harriet looked shocked and every eye fastened on Lottie. 'If Olwen is not my mother, then I won't be entitled to a share, will I?' She'd taken them unawares, and they both hesitated.

Then Grandma said, 'No, you won't. There'll be no money from that source for you.' It was what she'd expected, though she'd hoped otherwise.

'What's all this about inherited income?' Oliver wanted to know.

'Oh, it's a dead secret. We're told not to talk about it,' Dilys said. 'You have to be twenty-five before it's whispered to you.'

'Lottie knows, and she's not twenty yet.'

'She's nosy,' Dilys said, winking at her, 'and she's here all the time and finds out about everything.' She explained about their mother's will, with some help from Grandma.

Jemima said, 'Your father and I were only saying last week that it's time we mentioned it to you, Oliver. When is your birthday?'

'He'll be twenty-five in March,' Lottie reminded them.

'But why keep it a secret?' he demanded. 'It's marvellous news. I can't believe—'

'Indeed it is excellent news,' Jemima said, 'and nobody could be more pleased for you than I am. But I've lived long enough to see for myself that if a child is handed an adequate income to keep them in comfort, they may not make much effort to earn an income for themselves. I believe boys try harder if they have to stand on their own two feet, and in the long run they get more satisfaction from doing that.'

'How much will I get?' Oliver's face glistened with expectation.

Dilys told him to the penny. 'We all get an equal share.'

'And Eunice got hers from the date she was married?' He looked amazed. 'I did wonder, Dilly, how you'd managed to afford such a great car.'

'I'll get the documents out after dinner,' Charles said. 'You'll want to study them.'

'If you'd got married, you could have had it early too,' Lottie told Oliver.

'Hard luck that there's no inheritance for you,' he said gently. Dilys had taken him aside earlier and filled him in on what had happened while he'd been away.

'I don't mind about the money,' she said. 'It's the fact that I believed you were my real family.'

'We are your family,' Jemima thundered. 'We have looked after you all your life, and will continue to do so.'

Lottie was blinking hard and she could see that Dad was doing the same, but this was no time for tears. Oliver and Dilys were in the mood to celebrate.

Lottie was still meeting Roddy regularly, and sometimes on a Sunday both he and Alec were invited to lunch. But while Dilys was going full steam ahead with her marriage plans, Lottie fretted about having to wait.

Dilys had taken her to see the house, and while it was small, she thought it would suit the newly-weds perfectly. She hoped that one day she might have something similar. Dilys often brought full carrier bags back from the shop and took them straight to her room. 'Are you getting your trousseau together?' Lottie asked. 'Can I see what you've got?'

'Yes, I suppose you can. Come along then.'

She pulled open two of her drawers, and Lottie was impressed by the luxurious nightdresses and underwear. She had new shoes and blouses too, and today she'd brought her wedding dress home in a huge cardboard box. She opened the box and shook out the folds of cream duchesse satin in order to hang it in her wardrobe. 'Oh, it's absolutely gorgeous,' Lottie breathed in admiration.

'It's very traditional, plain and slim-fitting.'

'But such rich and lustrous material. I bet you have lots of people to advise you on what fits and what looks best.'

'The whole of the fashion department,' she laughed.

'Will you be my bridesmaid, Lottie?'

'I'd love to,' she breathed.

'We've decided on a quiet wedding and you'll be the only bridesmaid, so we can choose pretty much any colour and style. When can you come to the shop so I can show you what we have?'

'If we're not busy, Dad'll let me come any time.'

She went the following afternoon and had a lovely time in the shop with Dilys. They chose a chiffon dress in palest eau de nil.

'What colour is that?' Dad wanted to know when they went home.

'Pale green,' Dilys said. 'Come on, Grandma, you and Aunt Harriet must have new outfits too.'

'Yes, I'll ring my dressmaker.'

'You should come to the shop. There's absolutely no need to fuss with dressmakers these days, and no more black for either of you.'

They went together on Monday morning, as Dilys said the shop would be quiet then. She managed to persuade Grandma to buy an afternoon gown in lavender-coloured silk brocade. Aunt Harriet looked elegant for once in a two-piece in soft blue delaine.

The next day, Dilys was delighted to hear that their house was expected to be completed before Easter, which was sooner than she'd dared hope. Her wedding plans went into overdrive. 'It means we can be married during the school holidays,' she said. 'I'm seeing Alec this evening; we need to get organised now.'

'I'm looking forward to having the wedding breakfast here,' Jemima said. 'It seems a long time since we entertained. How many guests will you invite? We had sixty or so for Eunice, but it was July and it meant we could spill out into the garden. Easter can be cold.' She got out a pad and pencil.

'Thirty at the most,' Dilys said firmly. 'Just our two families and a few friends.'

'You can cater for thirty, can't you, Harriet? Could we do a sit-down meal?'

Harriet was taken aback. 'Well I don't know. Eunice had caterers in.'

'So will I,' Dilys said. 'Don't worry, I don't want any fuss. It'll be a simple buffet.'

Within a few days, she was writing out the invitations. 'Alec's school breaks up at midday on the Wednesday, and we can take over the house the same day. The next day is Maundy Thursday, and I hope the carpets and some of our furniture will be delivered then. The vicar has agreed to marry us at eleven o'clock on Easter Monday. We'll have the wedding breakfast and leave on our honeymoon around four o'clock. That will give us lots of time to get to Southport.'

'How long a honeymoon will you have?' Lottie was thrilled that everything was about to happen for her sister.

Dilys laughed. 'Anybody would think it was you getting married! Alec has booked for three nights. We want to get back to sort the house out.'

'It'll be very different to Eunice's wedding,' Aunt Harriet said.

'But far less expensive,' Jemima retorted. 'Martin wanted champagne and lobster. I told him that was ridiculous and we'd buy a ham. He ordered a case of champagne and had it sent here.'

'I can promise you Alec won't do that.' Dilys looked radiantly happy. 'I'll see to everything, Grandma.'

'You shouldn't do everything too cheaply, not for your wedding.'

Dilys laughed. 'You complain that Eunice and Martin spent too much on fripperies, and now you're saying I'm too economical.'

'Your money is a gift from your mother; she'd want you to enjoy what it can buy.'

'Money doesn't buy what I want Grandma. I just want to settle down with Alec in a place of our own.'

'Very romantic,' Grandma said.

'I understand perfectly,' Lottie breathed. 'That's all I'd ever want with Roddy.'

A week or so later, Jemima opened a letter from Glyn at the breakfast table and read out extracts to the family. *By happy good fortune, the* Accra *will be in port over Easter, and I'll ask to have Dilys's wedding day as part of my leave. Also, Uncle Lazlo has retired, and both he and Philip Royden are home for good now. Ask Dilys to send Philip an invitation, and what about Lazlo? Should he be invited too?*

'What do you think, Dilly?' Lottie said. 'Are you going to invite Uncle Lazlo?'

CHAPTER FIFTEEN

LAZLO WAS TRYING TO settle into his new life in England, but was finding it hard. He was staying with the Roydens while he looked for somewhere to live, and Philip and his mother had taken him shopping to buy clothes more suited to the English climate. They also thought he should get a car, but the traffic looked heavy after all the years in Calabar, where most of the traffic was waterborne. They'd had a few hundred yards of tarmac road between the jetty and their settlement, but beyond that it had soon petered out into dirt track. They'd had a small lorry and a pickup, and he'd driven those to move goods about. The truth was he was a bit nervous about driving through the streets of Liverpool.

Philip, though, was keen to own a car, and could afford one after his spell abroad. 'It's rumoured that soon we may need a licence to drive and we'll have to sit a test to get that. It would be better for us to start driving now.'

Lazlo added a car to the list of things he must get, but for the time being he obtained train and bus timetables. His first bus trip alone was out to Gwen's house. He was determined to see her but was wary of falling foul of her husband and meant to avoid trouble if he could.

From the road he took a good look at the house, hoping the

neighbours wouldn't take him to be a common thief. It hadn't changed much in the last twenty years. He knocked on the door and peered in at the front windows, but it was clear that no one was at home. Neither was there any sign of Jeremy's car. The house had been built before cars had become commonplace, but there was a large detached garage in a style meant to blend in. He was afraid it could be in there.

When he saw that there was a back gate, he went through it into the garden. He was very impressed with that; it was large and immaculately cared for, with colourful borders and flowering shrubs.

His heart was pounding as he approached the garage from behind and stood on a convenient upturned plant pot to look through the high window. The garage was bigger than he'd surmised, with room for three cars. There were two vehicles inside, but neither was the car he'd seen Jeremy driving. One was a large saloon, and the other a more mundane and older car, both black. Most cars were black. Neither of these would be easy to follow in traffic. This was bad news; it hadn't occurred to him that Jeremy would have more than one car.

He was scribbling down their registration numbers on the back of a bill he found in his pocket, when the cream-coloured sports car pulled up outside the fancy iron gates at the front, and Arbuthnot's large figure got out to open them. Lazlo swore under his breath as he slid back out of sight behind the garage. The car pulled up on the gravel as near to the front door as it could get, and Jeremy used his key to let himself into the house.

Lazlo's nerves were jangling. That had been a near thing, and now he'd have to try again.

When he returned to the Roydens' house, he found a reply to the letter he'd written to his mother waiting for him: *Thank you for your invitation, I shall be pleased to have lunch with you at the Adelphi Hotel. I agree, the time has come to forgive you and forget the past.*

Immediately he asked Fiona if he might use her telephone; he wanted to get things moving. 'Hello, Mother. Thank you for your letter . . . I'm very pleased. Are you free to have lunch with me tomorrow? . . . Good, I'll book a table.'

He made a point of arriving at the Adelphi before her, and watched for her from the main entrance. He knew he must handle this better than he had his interview with Jeremy Arbuthnot, but when he saw her crossing the road from Central Station, he thought she looked stern and stiff and was not all that hopeful. He went out on to the front steps as she climbed slowly up; she was showing her age.

'Mother, I'm glad you've come.' He put his arms round her and tried to give her a hug, but she felt ramrod stiff and wouldn't yield. 'Now that I'm home for good, I want to heal this breach and see something of the family.'

'I've told you that we'll all be glad to do that.'

Lazlo found it hard going until she'd had a glass of sherry and he'd got her to the table. With a glass of wine poured out in front of her, he dared to ask about Charlotte.

'She's well and working in the business. She knows that Gwen is her mother, and Charles told her that you are her father. She and Charles have always been close, so that's been hard for her. He's kept a special eye on her. I think he started by feeling sorry for her. When she was little, he used to give her rides on his back round the playroom; he didn't do that with his own children. And now she's working as his water clerk and they're getting on famously, so don't think you can just come home and claim her as your daughter. Charles might resent that.'

Lazlo sighed. 'And what about Gwen, how is she?'

'There's nothing I can tell you about her; we haven't seen her for years.'

That shocked him. 'Why not? I thought you'd keep in touch. Look after her.'

Jemima was frowning. 'Her husband didn't want contact with our family, not after what you'd done, and of course, Charlotte was here. The last thing he needed in his position was any hint of scandal about his family.'

'So Gwen was abandoned by us all?'

'There was less reason to keep in touch once Olwen died. Eunice sees her from time to time, though. Her husband is some vague relation of Arbuthnot's.'

'I understand he's his business partner.'

'No, Martin isn't a solicitor. He worked for the family confectionery firm, and though they were taken over by somebody else a few years ago, they've kept him on.'

Lazlo shook his head. 'I've seen them together. Spoken to them. They seem to be business partners.'

'That's as maybe. Come to lunch on Sunday and make your peace with the rest of the family.'

Lazlo was pleased he was to be allowed back into the family fold, but he was worried about Gwen now.

The next morning, he meant to take another look at Arbuthnot's business premises. His mother had said Martin wasn't a solicitor, and his name certainly hadn't been in evidence on the office window. He wished he'd asked the staff about Mr Dodd while he was there, because now they might recognise him if he returned to ask questions.

He was up and out early, and the cold air reminded him that he should wear a pullover. As soon as he turned the corner into Duke Street, he thought he recognised Arbuthnot walking ahead of him, head held high and swinging an elegant cane. His suspicions were confirmed when the man went straight into his office.

Lazlo retraced his steps because he hadn't seen Arbuthnot's car. It was a huge thing, like those that raced on the Brooklands track near London, and it would stand out anywhere. He didn't think Jeremy would have come on the bus.

He eventually found it in a connecting street where there was practically no traffic. He deliberated whether to go out to Arbuthnot's house again to try and see Gwen, or keep a watch on his office. It started to rain, and as there was a convenient coffee shop where he could keep the office in view, he decided to do that. He made his cup of coffee last as long as possible while the rain grew steadily heavier.

Lazlo felt bored and frustrated, and was sorry he hadn't tried to catch a bus out to Gwen's house, but at least this gave him time to think. He couldn't see where Martin Sanderson fitted into Arbuthnot's solicitor's practices, and he had the feeling that something was wrong there.

He knew that all businesses had to file a copy of their annual audited accounts at Companies House for taxation purposes, and that these records were open to the public. Henry Royden would know how to access them. He decided to take a taxi to Henry's office and ask him about it.

When he arrived, he found that Philip was there and his father was about to take him out to lunch. 'Why don't you join us?' Henry said.

'I'd like to,' Lazlo replied, and told him why he'd come. Before they set out, Henry telephoned a friend who worked in the Liverpool Chamber of Commerce and asked him to organise the enquiry.

During the meal, Lazlo regaled the Roydens with an account of his morning, which he felt he'd wasted. 'I really must start looking for a place of my own.'

'There's no hurry,' Henry said hospitably. 'You've been away a long time and we are enjoying your company. Also, you are giving me a clear view of the present conditions out in Calabar, and that's useful for the business.'

'Philip could do that for you,' Lazlo said.

'Dad has more faith in what you tell him,' Philip pointed out.

Philip had spent much of lunch talking about the new car he'd ordered, which was now ready to pick up. 'Dad was going to come with me,' he told Lazlo, 'but now he says something has come up and he has to go back to the office. Would you come with me to collect it?'

'Of course,' Lazlo said. He needed to find out more about cars.

He was very impressed. The Morris Cowley was a two-seater with a canvas hood and a dicky seat behind. 'How much did this cost?' he asked.

'Two hundred and fifty pounds.'

'Not bad.'

'Dad has given me a few lessons,' Philip said, 'but I'm a bit nervous of driving it.'

'That's a problem we share.' Lazlo grimaced. 'Everything looks so alien after living out on the Coast, and I don't want to bump a new car.'

Philip sat in the passenger seat and the salesman explained the knobs and pedals to him while Lazlo tried to take it all in from the back seat. Then Philip took the salesman's place at the wheel and off they went.

To Lazlo, Philip seemed cool and confident. 'It's exhilarating,' he said. 'Good fun. You should get yourself one, Lazlo.'

He almost decided he would; he wasn't enjoying travelling by bus, and Philip seemed to find it easy to manage, even in the centre of the city.

'I'm a bit worried about getting it on and off the luggage boat,' he told Lazlo. 'I meant to wait for Dad to finish work so he could come with me, but since you're here, I think I'll try it. There'll be less traffic now.'

'I'm not sure I'll be much help,' Lazlo said. 'The only thing I could do is push.'

Philip laughed, but in the event he found he didn't need any help.

A car certainly seemed to be a tempting prospect. But first Lazlo needed to look for a home of his own, and to make contact with Gwen.

CHAPTER SIXTEEN

D URING MEALS WITH THE Roydens, Lazlo was able to talk to Philip about following Jeremy in his car to find out where he was going. He hoped that that way they might be led to Gwen. 'We should be able to pick him up either at home or at his office.'

'I'll be happy to help with that,' Philip assured him.

In the meantime, Lazlo decided he must do something about his own affairs; he needed to find a home for himself as soon as he could.

The next morning he went into Liverpool again with Henry and visited an estate agent that he recommended. Soon he had an array of brochures to look at, but he really didn't know what to choose. He'd thought of buying a house, but now decided it might be wiser to rent a flat or a few rooms to give himself time to look round and see what was available.

He saw two flats but he didn't like the area of high buildings and canyon-like streets. The flats he looked at were dark and seemed to get no real daylight. Only those on the top floors stood any chance of getting sun.

He was assured that public transport to India Buildings would be easy, as it was close to the bus and tram terminal at

Pier Head. That persuaded him to look at a small furnished house in the suburbs.

He bought a newspaper and ate lunch in a small café, which wasn't very good. Then he called another taxi to take him to the house. He was sitting back watching the passing buildings, which seemed ugly and unwelcoming, when his taxi was held up in traffic. 'There's been an accident,' the driver said.

They crawled on a few yards and Lazlo was very surprised to see the cream-coloured Mercedes Benz sports car pull over and park just ahead of him. Jeremy Arbuthnot got out and started to walk on along the pavement. The taxi crept forward for another fifty yards or so, and all the ire Lazlo had felt during their meeting returned. The man had been unreasonable, a thorough pain in the neck; Lazlo had been chasing round for the last few days looking for Gwen when Arbuthnot could so easily have told him where she was. She couldn't be far, because Eunice had seen her several times. She said they were quite friendly. He'd find her eventually.

Suddenly Jeremy disappeared inside what appeared to be a public lavatory, and Lazlo stifled a smile. Poor sod, was he seeking a partner? He'd heard that in England, the unfortunate homosexual had to look in such places to find like-minded friends. Round the next corner he could see that a lorry had lost part of its load. The police had arrived; one officer was directing a single line of traffic past an ambulance. Another was just getting out of a car.

Lazlo's mind lit up with the need to get even with Arbuthnot. Hadn't he said disparagingly, 'Do your damnedest', as though he thought his high status put him beyond any harm Lazlo might inflict? Big-headed, pompous ass that he was.

'Stop,' Lazlo commanded the driver, and wound down the window. 'I want a word with that policeman.' He signalled to the officer, and he stepped closer. 'Would you please check the public lavatory round the corner? I've just seen something that is against the law. Please don't delay, it could be happening now. Drive on,' he said to the driver before he could be asked to give a name and address.

He laughed silently as the taxi sped on, now free of the hold-up, though he felt he'd descended to schoolboy games by informing on Arbuthnot like that. Soon came the feeling that although the man had been obnoxious, nobody deserved such a punch below the belt. He regretted what he'd done, it was unkind. It turned the afternoon sour and he did not like the house he'd come to see.

Back in the city, he was dropped off near another café and went in for a cup of tea. He studied the adverts in his newspaper and discovered it was possible to get lodgings with breakfast and evening meal provided. He had no idea how to cook or clean; up to now he'd had Emmanuel to take care of all that. Lodgings sounded an easier option, and less permanent. He found a telephone and rang the number in the paper. The landlady sounded reasonable, so he went to see the place. It didn't look too bad from the outside: a Victorian house of four storeys, a little shabby perhaps.

The landlady was plump, with rosy cheeks and a contented face. 'The room is let at the moment, but he's given notice and will be leaving at the end of the week,' she said. 'He's Irish, and the job he's been doing is coming to an end, so he's going home.'

She shot up flight after flight of stairs so quickly Lazlo had trouble keeping up with her, and threw open the door of a large attic room. Two small windows allowed him a distant glimpse of the Mersey across half a mile of rooftops; he liked that.

'A lot of things here belong to Mr Murphy,' she said, 'but all the furniture remains.' He saw a double bed, a wardrobe, a sofa and a desk as well as several upright chairs, small cupboards and side tables.

'There are two other lodgers here,' she went on. 'Quiet and pleasant men who've been here for a long time.' She showed him the bathroom, which was two floors down and felt cold and clammy, with the original large fittings. 'We all share this,' she said. 'The family too.'

Lazlo knew it wasn't ideal, but he was tired of looking round. 'I'll take it for a month,' he said, and they agreed he would move in next Monday.

'Breakfast is at seven o'clock.' She smiled. 'Cooked if you want it. Evening meal is at half six.'

It would do until he could find something to suit him better. He couldn't batten on the Roydens' kindness indefinitely, so he paid her in advance for two weeks. He thought he could do without a car while he was here. He didn't know if he'd be allowed to park outside overnight, and anyway, it might not be safe to do that.

When Charlotte drove Charles to the office the next morning, he was in his usual relaxed mood. They chatted about how well Harriet's plans for the garden were coming on. They'd both been roped in to help plant more bulbs earlier in the spring so as to have flowers in bloom on Dilys's wedding day.

When they arrived, he sat down to glance over *The Times*, which he had delivered here. Lottie unlocked her desk, took the cover off her typewriter and settled down to type two letters Dad had dictated to her the day before. Suddenly she heard his sharp exclamation of surprise. 'What is it, Dad?'

'Nothing that need concern you,' he said, rapidly folding the newspaper and putting it in his out tray to take home. Charlotte thought he looked embarrassed, even agitated, and was afraid something really bad had happened.

'I'm going to have a word with Ted,' he said as he went out. 'I won't be long.'

She wondered if something had gone wrong with one of their ships, or had another shipping line gone bankrupt? Whatever it was, he was in no mood to tell her. A few moments later, it occurred to her to open up the newspaper to look for herself. She scanned the business pages slowly; they were full of bad economic news, but she found nothing to account for Dad's sudden change in behaviour.

She took a couple of letters she'd typed for Ted Pascoe next door and had a chat to Dorothy. When she returned to her desk, her father was talking to Grandma on the phone. He put the receiver down quickly and seemed silent and a bit withdrawn for the rest of the morning. Though she asked again what was troubling him, he said, 'Nothing.' She concluded it did not concern shipping or business, or he'd have explained at length.

At lunchtime she ate her sandwiches with Dorothy as usual, and Dad and Ted went to the pub. Later, Charles suggested leaving early, and they were home in time for afternoon tea. He always took his newspaper home for Grandma and Harriet to read; apart from the local *Echo*, it was the only one they had. Today, it seemed they'd bought a copy of every newspaper published, and they were spread all over the sitting room. The rest of the family seemed equally agitated.

Charlotte tackled Grandma. 'What is all this about? You're trying to keep something from me, but I'm grown up now, and I want to know.'

'Of course you do, dear,' Jemima told her. 'There's no mystery, and nobody is trying to keep anything from you.' She handed one of the newspapers to her. 'Read this.'

Harriet said, 'It's about Jeremy Arbuthnot, Aunt Gwendolen's husband. Such a disgrace.'

Lottie started to read, still mystified:

Jeremy Arbuthnot, Conservative Member of Parliament for Southport since 1904, and a prominent member of the government when his party was in power, was arrested in a men's convenience in the Everton district of Liverpool yesterday, together with another man. They will both appear in court charged with indecent homo-sexual behaviour.

The next morning Lazlo went into Liverpool with Henry on the train, and then walked to Jeremy Arbuthnot's office. If he was at work, the coast would be clear for Lazlo to go to the house again and see if Gwen was there. He felt a burst of excitement when he spotted Jeremy's car parked at the kerb.

On the slow bus journey out to the house, he practised in his head what he would say if Gwen was in. He got off the bus and was thirty yards from the front gate when a dowdy middle-aged woman came out and walked away from him. Could she be a daily cleaner, working only in the mornings? But he needed to be careful; perhaps there were other staff.

He went straight to the impressive front door and rang the bell. No one came, so he rang again. As before, the place seemed deserted, so he did what he'd done on his last visit, going out of the front gate and round to the back, keeping out of sight amongst the trees. There was a pleasant terrace and several glass doors into the main rooms, while the kitchen door and domestic offices seemed to be on the side.

The back of the house was not overlooked and there was nobody about. He tried the glass doors, but both were securely locked. Then he noticed that a kitchen window had been left ajar. He climbed on to the windowsill, put his hand inside and opened a lower larger window, then climbed across a wide sink into what appeared to be a room used for laundry. Slowly and silently he crept round a whole suite of kitchens, larders, storerooms and a housekeeper's room before reaching the main hall.

He stopped to listen, but there was no sound. He was sure now that there was no other domestic help here, but he was breaking and entering, and that thought set his nerves on edge.

'Gwen?' he called from the bottom of the stairs. 'Gwen, are you here?' The only sound was the thumping of his own heart.

He toured the downstairs rooms, calling her name. There were several sitting rooms, a library that seemed to be a study too, and a large and elegant dining room. They were all empty. He went up the main stairs two at a time and threw open every door. Only two rooms looked as though they were in use. In one, he found a dressing table set with cut-glass pots and a silver-backed brush-and-comb set. The wardrobe was full of what must be Gwen's clothes. That brought him to a standstill. He could sense her presence, but she was definitely not here.

In Jeremy's room too there were lots of fine clothes. In the adjoining dressing room a suitcase had been left on the floor. It was empty, but was it a clue that the two of them had gone somewhere else?

He felt a desperate urge to get out of the place while the going was good, but since he wouldn't want to come again, he must look at everything while he had the chance. He went downstairs to the library and sat at the large partner's desk to think. Did Jeremy have a safe? Yes, there was one set into the wall behind one of the bookcases. It had a keyhole, but without the key he couldn't open it.

Back at the desk, he started opening drawers. Only the top one was locked; in the lower ones Jeremy kept some of his business files. Lazlo flicked through the documents. Here were all the details he could ask for about Arbuthnot's business, but he was too nervous to concentrate on figures. He replaced everything just as he'd found it.

The place was giving him the creeps. He returned through the kitchen window, but found it impossible to fasten the catch so left it ajar as it had been. He didn't breathe normally again until he was on the bus going back into the city. It had been a hard day, and once again he'd failed to see Gwen.

Frustrated, he went into town to buy the largest and most expensive box of chocolates he could find for his mother. He wanted to show his appreciation at being invited back into the family fold. It was raining again, and he ducked into a gents' outfitter's to buy a raincoat, which he put on straight away. He saw umbrellas there too, and chose a large one. He thought he could hide behind it when he was hanging around Arbuthnot's premises.

He saw a fine display of Easter eggs in the window of Bunney's department store and went in and chose two, one for Charlotte and the other for Dilys, the bride-to-be. While they and the box of chocolates were being packed up, he decided he'd buy another for Harriet, as he didn't want her to feel overlooked.

It was almost more than he could carry, and he'd had rather a disappointing day, but very soon now he'd come face to face with Charlotte for the first time since she'd learned that he was her father.

CHAPTER SEVENTEEN

DILYS HAD ALWAYS WORRIED more about her sister Eunice than any other member of her family. 'I'm concerned about her happiness,' she said. 'She seemed down last time I saw her. It's Saturday tomorrow and we have a half-day off. I'd like to go and see her. Try to cheer her up a bit.'

'I'll go with you,' Charlotte said.

'Good idea,' Dad said. 'We're all anxious about Eunice.'

Lottie and Dilys took sandwiches to work just as they did on weekdays, and Dilys brought hers to Lottie's office so they could eat together. 'I'm glad we're going over,' Dilys said. 'I rang Eunice in my morning break to tell her we were coming, and she sounded worse than ever.'

Lottie made them a pot of tea. 'What's she bothered about now?'

'It seems that Martin is furious with Uncle Jeremy. He came over a week or so ago on business and they had an almighty row, and then Uncle Jeremy was arrested for homosexual behaviour in a gents' lavatory in Everton. It was in all the newspapers.'

'Oh yes!' Lottie couldn't forget reading that story. 'That came as a shock to Dad and Grandma too; no wonder they're all upset.'

They tidied up and locked up the office, then set off. Dilys parked her car in Hamilton Square and they caught the train. 'I do wish they'd hurry up with this new road tunnel under the river; it would make life a lot easier.'

'They say they started tunnelling a couple of years ago,' Lottie said, 'but I've heard nothing about it since.'

'Let's hope they're getting on with it. It can't come soon enough for me. We've had a train tunnel for over three decades, so we know it's perfectly possible.'

Eunice lived in a pleasant leafy suburb, and when they rang the bell, the front door was opened by a housemaid in a black dress and lacy apron. Lottie found it hard to understand how her sister could be unhappy living in luxury like this. Eunice came running downstairs to greet them, followed by Tom. 'I'm so glad you've come over. Providence must have brought you.' She'd taken no care at all with her appearance and looked pale, stressed and nervous. She ushered them towards a small room that Martin called her boudoir, then turned to the child and said, 'Tom, go back to Nanny.' Once he had run off, she shut the door carefully.

'Has something happened?' Dilys asked.

'Yes, it's one thing after another. There's no peace, Martin and Jeremy were tearing each other apart before he was arrested. Now he's back and forth to the police station, and he's absolutely furious with Jeremy.' Eunice blew her nose and mopped at her eyes.

'It's quiet enough here at the moment,' Dilys pointed out.

'Martin's gone to work. He reckons Jeremy has ruined his career and reputation, as well as his own and that of his family. He's at his wits' end.'

'Come and sit down,' Dilys patted the seat beside her, 'and tell us why Martin thinks his career is ruined. I don't understand.'

'He's scared.'

'Well he's bound to worry about what'll happen to Jeremy.'

'I'm scared too, and so is Auntie Gwen. She's here; Martin went to fetch her this morning.'

'Here?' Lottie felt her heart jerk. 'Why did he bring her here?'

'She isn't well and he says Jeremy is worried about her being alone.'

Lottie couldn't believe her luck. She was about to see her mother at last. The hours of wondering about her, imagining what she was like, would soon be over.

'What's the matter with her?' she asked anxiously.

'Flu, we think, and she's not sleeping. But with her past history, there's always the fear that it could be TB.'

'So where is she?'

'She's in bed, resting. Martin says it's best to keep her away from the children in case it is something infectious.' Eunice shook her head in despair. 'Gwen says she doesn't want to be here.'

'But you can look after her now,' Lottie told her.

'I don't know what to do. It was Martin's idea to bring her here. I suppose she comes here quite often, so he thought it would be the best place.'

'Does she?' Dilys was surprised. 'I didn't know that. I haven't seen her for donkeys' years, not since Mum died. She came to look after us when Mum was ill.'

'I've never seen her, and she's my mother,' Lottie said wistfully.

'You have, she looked after you when you were a small baby,' Eunice said. 'I remember that, but I don't believe that story about her being your mother. Both Martin and Uncle Jeremy say she isn't. She wanted babies but they didn't come, she was too ill.'

Lottie was getting more anxious. 'Why don't you take us up to say hello?' she asked. 'Where is she?'

Eunice was near to tears. 'We don't really have a guest room any more. I allowed Christabel to use it, but now she's having to share with Emily, and she's not too happy about it.'

'You have a big family.'

'And the nanny has to have a room too.'

Lottie followed them up the fine staircase. The curtains had been drawn in the bedroom and it was in semi-darkness. A tall, gaunt figure in a frilly housecoat had lifted the curtain and was looking out of the window. 'Aunt Gwendolen,' Eunice said, 'we have visitors come to see us. You remember Dilys, my eldest sister?' Dilys went forward to kiss her. 'And this is Charlotte, the baby of the family, now grown up. She doesn't remember ever seeing you.'

Lottie could see Gwendolen peering at her. She went closer, full of curiosity, meaning to kiss her too, but let out a little squeal of alarm when she saw that her mother was silently swaying, and would have collapsed on the floor if she hadn't caught her in her arms to hold her upright.

'Oh my goodness!' Dilys and Eunice rushed to help. They manoeuvred Gwendolen on to the bed and laid her down. 'What's happened?'

'She must be really ill.' Eunice was wringing her hands. 'What can we do?' But Gwendolen was already stirring.

'She fainted,' Dilys said.

'Thank goodness she's coming round.' Lottie felt shaken. 'Shouldn't you call a doctor?'

'We've had him out to see her.' Eunice was rubbing her aunt's hands. 'He gave her a tonic and pills to help her sleep. He said the only other thing that would help was peace and quiet, and plenty of rest. I thought she was getting better.'

'Then why did she faint?' Lottie wondered.

'How are you, Auntie?' Eunice asked. 'How do you feel?'

Faintly they heard, 'I'm all right.'

Lottie watched her sisters put a pillow under Gwendolen's head and cover her with the eiderdown to make her more comfortable, but all the time the woman's anguished eyes stared up at her.

'Would you like a drink of water?' Lottie asked her.

'Please.'

Eunice, clearly upset and very much on edge, went to get it. 'Martin said she should have another of the sedative pills if she needs it.'

'No.' Gwen could hardly get the words out. 'I took one half an hour ago. Just a drink.'

Lottie raised her up and held the glass for her. She took tiny sips, and when she'd had enough, she said, 'Sorry, I don't know what came over me.'

Dilys said soothingly, 'You're not at all well. We should leave you to have more rest.'

Eunice was pulling the curtains back into place. 'You must try and sleep now.'

'No,' Gwen murmured. 'Charlotte . . .'

Lottie felt transfixed. Gwen was clasping both her hands,

but Dilys took her elbow and drew her away, then led them downstairs to the little sitting room.

Dilys and Eunice were upset and carried on worrying about Gwen, but Lottie hardly took in what they were saying. She felt transfixed by the frail figure she'd come face to face with upstairs. Whatever Eunice thought, she knew Gwen was her mother, and now she'd met her at last! She couldn't get that thought out of her mind.

Eunice asked for a tray of tea and cake to be brought, and gradually they all calmed down, but Lottie felt she couldn't go away without seeing Gwen again. She needed to talk to her.

She drained her cup. 'I want to go to the loo, Eunice. I'll go upstairs and just peep in to see if Gwendolen has settled.'

'Don't disturb her if she's asleep,' Eunice said. 'She's so worried. A little sleep would do her good.'

Lottie sped silently up the stairs. The bedroom door had been left an inch ajar, and she pushed it wider. Gwen's eyes were closed and her breathing was slow and regular, but was she really asleep? Feeling full of pity and love, Lottie crept closer, taking in every detail of her grey hair, her arched eyebrows and the beads of sweat standing out on her pale lined skin. 'Mother?' she whispered, but Gwen didn't stir.

She'd taken her housecoat off to reveal a Victorian-style white cambric nightgown with high neck and long sleeves, all pretty pleats and gathers. One of her hands was outside the covers, small, white and wearing only a wedding ring. Lottie was tempted to touch it. There were so many questions she wanted to ask, so much she wanted to tell her. 'Mother?' she whispered again, but Gwen's eyelids remained closed.

Charlotte tiptoed out; she couldn't wake her up. She'd come back again tomorrow and have a really good chat.

Downstairs, she found that Eunice had become agitated again. 'Martin wants her here but this isn't where she wants to be. I can't cope with this, and neither can Auntie Gwen. You've got to help us.'

'We have plenty of empty bedrooms at home,' Charlotte said. 'We should take her there so that Grandma can look after her.'

'But we've come on the train,' Dilys said. 'I don't think she's well enough for that. We should go home and talk to Grandma. Then I could bring Dad's car over later on to collect her.'

'Tonight,' Eunice said. 'Please come for her tonight.'

Lottie and Dilys went home to find the house full of the delicious scents of baking. 'How is Eunice?' Grandma asked. 'Better, I hope.'

'No, she's in a terrible state,' Lottie said. Harriet was clearing away the remains of afternoon tea; the family had enjoyed freshly made scones with strawberry jam.

Dilys told them what had happened. 'Eunice wants us to bring Gwen here,' she said. 'We've got to help them, Grandma. They're all so frightened there.' Lottie could see the family were shocked.

Grandma recovered first. 'Is Gwendolen really ill, or is she just nervous because of what's happening to Jeremy?'

'We don't know,' Dilys said. 'According to what the doctor told Eunice, it's nothing that rest won't cure, but she collapsed in a dead faint when she saw us.'

'Oh dear!' The colour was draining from Grandma's face.

'Charles,' she said, 'she is your sister-in-law; we have to help. Eunice can't stand stress of this sort. She hasn't the strength to help anybody. Gwendolen will have to come here.'

'Eunice wants her to come tonight,' Lottie was saying when the phone rang. She was nearest the door and went to answer it to find it was Eunice, who was so distressed she could barely speak.

'Martin's come home. He wants to speak to Grandma. He reckons we girls are panicking for no reason.'

Jemima went out to the hall, bristling with irritation; they all crowded round to listen. 'Charles and I will come over to fetch Gwendolen tomorrow,' she told Martin. 'We will be more than happy to take care of her.'

Martin interrupted, and all they could do was watch Jemima's face and surmise what he was saying.

Eventually she put the phone down and almost felt her way back to her armchair. She looked bemused. 'I've not heard Martin speak with authority like that before. He says there is no call for us to do anything. Jeremy has been given bail and has taken Gwen home. He will be able to look after her himself, and if necessary he'll hire a nurse to help. He sends his thanks to you and Dilys for trying to help, but now he's home there's absolutely no need for you to worry about Gwen.'

'He is her husband,' Charles said, 'and home is the right place when you don't feel well.'

CHAPTER EIGHTEEN

ALL THE FOLLOWING DAY Lottie was uneasy about Gwen, and she knew Dilys was too. Her sister had taken her aside and said, 'Eunice thinks Gwen is afraid of Jeremy. Perhaps they all are.'

That evening, Dilys brought home the plans of her house and spread them over the kitchen table. She'd taken Lottie more than once to the building site where the new house was going up, but so far she'd seen only foundations and brick walls. Everyone drooled over the plans, so she said, 'I'll take you all to see it now it's progressing. When can you come?'

'Any evening,' Harriet said, and Dad and Lottie nodded in agreement.

Later that evening, Dilys went to Alec's and mentioned that she would be taking her family to see the house. 'I'll meet you there,' he said. 'We can show them round together.'

His mother said, 'Why don't you bring them all round here afterwards for a bit of supper? It won't be anything fancy.'

His parents had been to one of Grandma's Sunday lunches, so they had all met, but this was the first time Dilys's family had been to his home. She decided they'd need two cars, and arranged with Dad that Lottie should drive his.

It was a cold, damp evening and the air felt heavy with

moisture, but even Grandma got out to look round the site. Lottie could visualise how the house would look now. The roof was on and the windows were in, but the bathroom fitments were waiting to be installed and the front garden was a sticky mud bath. Around it were several other houses in the same state.

She could see Grandma was not impressed, but the happy pair were brimming with excitement and anticipation. She wished she and Roddy had reached this point, and had to tell herself it was no good feeling envious. Her time would come.

Alec's parents lived in a similar modern semi-detached house, but their estate looked mature; the houses were smart and the gardens all neatly trimmed. She thought their house was lovely, so light and fresh, and much easier to keep warm and clean than their own.

They had laid on a buffet meal, and it wasn't really the squash with eight people that Grandma had predicted. There was a jolly party atmosphere and they stayed quite late. Lottie thought they'd all enjoyed it, and Alec was gaining family approval. All the talk was about wedding plans.

On Sunday morning, Lazlo travelled to Mersey View by bus. He found it quite a long walk from the main road. It made him realise how much his family must miss the ferry service that had run almost to their front door. He was walking down the back garden when he saw Charlotte picking mint.

She straightened up and waved the bunch of mint at him. 'It's for the lamb. Hello, Father – I understand that's who you really are.'

'Yes.' He felt ill at ease with her big blue eyes searching his face. She was taller and prettier than he remembered, quite beautiful, but not like her mother. He wanted to kiss her, greet her as a father would after all these years away. As an uncle he wouldn't have hesitated. 'So they've broken the news to you at last. Did it come as a shock?'

'Not really. I've had niggling feelings for years that my place in the family was not quite the same as Dilys's.'

'Are you saying you were worried about who your parents were?'

'Yes, as it happens, but I've got used to the idea now.'

'I didn't face up to my responsibility to you and Gwen. I stayed a thousand miles away and that's been on my conscience for years. Your grandma has forgiven me. I hope you will too.'

'Of course.' She smiled. 'The family gave me a happy upbringing. I've nothing to complain about there.'

'I'm glad about that, and what did you think of me?'

She beamed at him. 'You were the exciting uncle who sent us all lovely presents. You had broken out of the family mould and made us realise we could do the same if we wanted to.' But now he could see she was blinking hard, so it had troubled her.

'I still fiddle with that crystal set from time to time, and so does Glyn, though the family have a valve set now. We had hours of fun from them.'

'It's a comfort to have it all out in the open,' Lazlo said. 'I know where I stand now.'

She nodded and looked embarrassed. 'I'm sorry, but I can't call you Dad. Charles has always been my father. He's been great, and I work for him now too.'

He laughed and kissed her cheek. 'Just call me Lazlo, that's probably the best. Now I'm retired and home for good, I hope we can see more of each other.'

'I'd like that.' She looked up at him shyly. 'D'you know, I'd hardly have recognised you. You've grown a beard.' It was thin and grey across his cheeks, but there was plenty of it round his chin. 'It makes you look distinguished, and very much a seafaring man. You'd better come in and say hello to the rest of the family.'

He presented the gifts he'd brought and was introduced to Dilys's fiancé. He seemed a sensible lad, but his presence meant Lazlo couldn't ask about Gwen. Mother would not want to discuss family problems in front of him. Or was Alec more part of the family than he was himself?

He couldn't help but notice that the view through the windows was different. 'The pier's gone,' he said. 'Without it you can see much further down the river.' Nothing in the house had changed over the last thirty years, but his family had. Mother was still the matriarch in charge, but she looked really old now, and poor Harriet was even more drab and middle-aged.

Charles brought out the sherry bottles for the ladies. 'Would you rather have a beer, Lazlo?'

'Yes please. I want to thank you, Charlie,' he said, 'for taking care of Charlotte. She tells me you've been a caring father.'

His mother boomed out, 'In your absence we've all had to help bring her up.' They were not at ease with him, nor he with them.

'Did you know Jeremy Arbuthnot has been arrested?' Jemima changed the subject. 'Caught in a public lavatory with another man, and charged with committing an act of gross indecency.'

'What?' Lazlo was shaken to the core as he realised that he was responsible for this outcome.

'You knew he was a homosexual, didn't you?'

'Yes, yes, of course, but . . .'

'We kept some cuttings from the newspapers if you want to see them. They're on the desk in the study. Charlotte, would you get them?'

Lazlo was almost overcome with guilt. He could feel the sweat standing out on his brow and could hardly see the print when Charlotte pushed the cuttings into his hand. He hadn't meant to cause trouble like this for Jeremy, and of course it would have an effect on Gwen and all the family. What a childish, stupid thing to have done. He'd been totally thoughtless.

It was only when they sat down to lunch that he realised they no longer had any help in the house. He found it hard to believe they could manage without it. The lamb was delicious, and Sunday lunch was the substantial meal it always had been. Afterwards there was a flurry over clearing away and washing up. Lazlo felt awkward; this wasn't something he was used to.

'Take your father to the sitting room, Charlotte. He's in our way here,' Jemima said. 'Tell him about seeing Gwendolen. He'll want to know all about her.'

'You've seen her?' Lazlo was more than glad to follow Lottie and poke the sitting room fire into a blaze. 'I understood none of you had had so much as a glimpse of her over the years.'

Anne Baker

'We haven't. I saw her for the first time the day before yesterday. Dilly and I went to see Eunice, and found Gwen was unexpectedly there. She recognised me as her daughter, I could see it in her face, but we couldn't talk. Dilly and Eunice thought she needed rest, and they had me out of her room before I could say anything.'

'How was she?'

'Not well. Really she looked quite ill, but Eunice isn't well either, and we felt she wasn't looking after Gwen properly. Dilly wanted to bring her here, but Martin rang us later that evening to say Jeremy had taken her home and there was no need for us to do anything.

Charles joined them. 'It's very worrying,' he said. 'According to Eunice, Martin's been acting a bit strangely since this business with Jeremy, and she and Gwendolen are very upset by it all.'

Lazlo felt another wave of guilt wash over him, but the last thing he wanted to do was to let the family know he'd caused Jeremy to be arrested. He couldn't believe he'd been such a fool. Instead he told them about going to Jeremy's office. 'Martin was there too,' he said. 'He appeared to be one of the staff. No, more like another boss. I got the feeling that something odd is going on there. I'm going to take another look at the place once I've moved into my lodgings.'

He started to tell them about his new accommodation; it was a safe subject. 'It will take me at least two journeys to move my belongings over there. I came home with three suitcases,' he said, 'but Philip and Fiona have taken me shopping, so now I have much more.'

'Lottie could give you a hand,' Charles said. 'She can drop

me at the office in the morning and then use my car to take you over. There'd be enough room on the back seat for all your stuff, wouldn't there?'

'Yes,' Lottie said, 'I'll be glad to, though it won't be a quick journey, because we'll have to go over on the luggage boat.'

Their kindness made Lazlo feel even worse.

The next morning, Lottie went to the Roydens' house to pick Lazlo up as arranged. It was Philip who answered when she rang the doorbell. She beamed at him. 'Lovely to see you,' she said, expecting to be thumped on the back and given a hug. 'It seems ages. You look very well.'

He was the picture of health. His shoulders had broadened and he had a good tan, but he was not smiling. 'How are you, Lottie?'

She felt saddened. His years abroad had made him almost a stranger. Lazlo was bringing his luggage downstairs and they both went to help him, and by the time Lottie had loaded it on to the back seat, Philip had disappeared and Fiona had taken his place.

She presented Lazlo with a cake in a fancy tin. 'In case you don't get enough to eat,' she said. 'You can use the tin for biscuits when the cake has gone.'

'You've been very kind.' Lazlo kissed her goodbye feeling touched. He was very impressed with the way Charlotte had packed his things into the car, and she was adept at handling it and driving it on and off the luggage boat. It made him feel inadequate; he wasn't up to doing that and it was not good for his ego.

He managed to direct her to his lodgings, and she carried

half his possessions up all the flights of stairs. He saw her looking round, taking in the details of his new home. She didn't seem to like it. 'You don't approve?'

'Yes, I do, I can see its attraction for you, a place of your own. It's clean, a crow's nest, high up with a good view, and you don't have to worry about cleaning or cooking.'

'Yes, but it's an odd feeling to know that all I possess in the world is here in these bags and cases,' he said.

'Can I help you hang your things up in these cupboards?'

He steered her towards his new purchases, and emptied his less savoury belongings into the many drawers. 'That's better, it looks more settled now.'

'It's not very warm here,' she said. 'Have you checked your bed?'

He did so. 'All cleanly made up, but . . .' There were three thin blankets and a cotton bedspread.

'If I were you, I'd go out and buy an eiderdown before tonight,' she said. 'And a couple of cushions for this sofa wouldn't go amiss.'

'Will you come with me if we do it now?'

'Why not?'

She led him briskly down to the car, and they were outside George Henry Lee's and looking for a parking spot within minutes. She knew the way round the shop and took him to the right departments. She also seemed to know by instinct what colours would look best in his room.

They'd started to serve lunch in the café, and he suggested they eat there before going back. She had a good appetite and ate as much as he did, and he was beginning to feel that he should be very proud of his daughter; she was practical and capable, a real chip off the Mortimer block.

Back at his lodgings, she helped him unwrap his purchases and set them out. 'These cushions brighten the place up,' she said. 'Make it look more homely.'

'They do.'

Lazlo was pleased with the effect, but later, when it got dark, he realised there was only one central light in his room, which made it difficult to read in bed. Neither would there be any point in buying one of the attractive reading lamps he'd seen in the shop, as there was nowhere he could plug it in.

That night, he was more than glad of the thick eiderdown Lottie had taken him to buy, but he didn't sleep well. His conscience was heavy; he couldn't stop thinking about the trouble he'd landed Jeremy Arbuthnot in, and it was undoubtedly making things more difficult for Gwen.

He was not dissatisfied with his new home. Tea and biscuits had been served downstairs at nine p.m. for those who wanted them, and for a few extra shillings a week, his landlady was willing to bring his breakfast of fried egg and sausage up to his room. It meant a leisurely start, with the added advantage that his fellow lodgers had gone to work and he could spend as much time as he wanted in the bathroom. He was going to be quite comfortable here.

The next day he went back to Henry Royden's office to see if he had checked the credentials of Jeremy's business. 'Yes, the Merseyside Family Legal Service is a legitimate company, and it trades at the address you gave us. It was established in 1909; that would be before Arbuthnot got into Parliament. Perhaps he keeps the business in case he's voted out.'

'Yes, I suppose he has to think of that.'

'Francis Dodd retired two years ago, and now it's owned solely by Arbuthnot.'

'No mention of Martin Sanderson?'

'None at all. It makes an average profit for that type of business, and last year Arbuthnot took it all out.'

'And you're thinking it would be more usual to leave a proportion of cash there to meet the firm's expenses?'

'Yes, it would. He might have a need for ready cash.'

'Haven't we all?' Lazlo smiled. 'But Francis Dodd's name is still shown as a partner on the window. Is that usual after two years?'

Henry shook his head. 'I don't know of any legal requirement to remove it, but if it means a new plate-glass window, it could be an expense he's putting off. Perhaps he's seeking a new partner.'

'It looks as though he's found one in Martin Sanderson, but why isn't he listed as such in the annual accounts? I find that odd.' Lazlo couldn't decide whether it was important or not, but he had more pressing things to think about.

CHAPTER NINETEEN

Easter was almost on them. On Maundy Thursday, Lottie was typing in the office when Charles opened his newspaper. She heard him gasp in surprise. 'There's another piece about Jeremy Arbuthnot in here today,' he told her.

She got up and he passed it to her folded to a middle page. It gave his name and address, repeated that he was the Conservative Member of Parliament for Southport, and related that together with Albert James, he was charged with gross indecency in a public toilet in Everton. *Both men have been bailed and their case will be heard at Liverpool Crown Court on a date in July.*

'More will come out at the hearing,' Charles said. 'How the mighty have fallen. He'll have problems living this down. I think he might have to resign from his seat.'

'Grandma says they'll send him to prison.' Lottie went back to her desk.

'That remains to be seen.'

'What about my mother?' Lottie said. 'She must be finding this difficult, but she's not contacting us for help.'

'No,' he sighed, 'she isn't.'

Lottie thought that strange.

At home, she felt the burgeoning excitement and anticipation as they all saw to the hundred and one last-minute preparations for the wedding. That same day, Dilys was given the keys to her new house, and everything seemed to go into overdrive.

Jemima had said, 'You can take some pieces of furniture from here; we have rather too much anyway.'

Dilys had chosen a mahogany bedstead in the Georgian style that needed only a new mattress, and six dining chairs and a folding Sutherland table that when fully opened was the right size for her dining room. She'd hired a man with a van to transport it all to her new house. Lottie helped her wrap old blankets round the furniture, then she and Dilys followed the van in her car.

Alec's school had broken up for the holiday, and he was there as carpets and curtains were being delivered. Lottie helped hang curtains for an hour or so, but then left them to it.

She was expecting Roddy to return home in time for Easter. She hoped to see him though it looked like being a busy weekend for her. He telephoned to say that his family had big plans to welcome him back, but confirmed he'd be at Dilys's wedding and that he couldn't wait to see her again. Both Glyn and Oliver had time off over the Easter holiday and were expected home in time for dinner that evening. Harriet was roasting a joint of beef to welcome them. Lottie always looked forward to their visits, as they seemed to wake the family up, and they always took her out on at least one night during their stay.

Glyn arrived first and caused a flurry of noise and excitement as he swept them into hugs. He'd brought coconuts and a couple of pineapples for Grandma, which pleased her. On his last trip home he'd brought mangoes and avocado pears and she'd viewed them with suspicion, though Lottie and Dilys had eaten them.

'Philip has invited both of us to a ball at the yacht club tomorrow,' he told Lottie, all smiles. 'It's the beginning of the sailing season, and there'll be racing during the day – do you want to go to that too?'

'Charlotte needs to help her father on Saturday; he's expecting a ship to dock,' Grandma said. 'And we still have plenty to do to prepare for this wedding.'

Oliver's arrival caused even more of a stir. He'd always seemed an adult to Lottie, and he made a huge fuss of Dilys as the bride-to-be.

Lottie had to help Harriet with the meal and felt a little like Cinderella. She was also concerned about what she could wear to a ball. She hadn't been to a dance for a long time, and now that she considered herself grown up, her old party frock defin- itely wouldn't do. Anyway, the only occasions she'd worn it had been at the yacht club, and Philip had seen it more than once already.

'Dilys will lend you one,' Grandma said. 'She buys a great many.'

That didn't please Lottie either, though Dilys threw open her wardrobe and said, 'Take your pick.' Lottie was four inches taller than her sister, and didn't have any of Dilys's curves. She toyed with the idea of wearing her bridesmaid's dress, but before the wedding? And it wasn't exactly designed as a ball gown.

Dilys said, 'This one is probably your best bet.' She pulled a blue crêpe de Chine dress out on its hanger. 'It was too long for me and I had the hem taken up, so we can easily let it down again. Try it on.'

Lottie remembered admiring it last year when Dilys had worn it, but would it fit her? She liked the colour, and the material was lovely, but she clutched a handful of empty cloth at her waist. 'Miles too wide,' she said, disappointed.

'Come and find Aunt Harriet,' Dilys said. 'She may be willing to take it in for you. It's princess style, so it shouldn't be difficult.'

Harriet looked hot and busy in the kitchen, but she was always obliging. 'Yes, I could do that. It's just a matter of making the darts a little deeper. Take it off, turn it inside out and put it on again, then Dilys can pin the darts so it fits you. But after dinner, please; everything is ready now.'

Lottie unpicked the hem and Dilys pinned the darts. 'I'm very grateful,' she said. 'I'm giving you a lot of work and it will all have to be put back to fit you.'

'No, you keep it,' Dilys said. 'I've worn it a few times already, and I don't think I'll be going to many balls after I'm married. Alec isn't the dancing sort, and anyway I've got several other party frocks.'

'At least you don't have this problem,' Lottie said to Glyn. 'Your evening dress doesn't change. Nobody could look at you and say that's last year's suit.'

He laughed. 'Harriet has let the trousers down as far as they'll go, but they won't fasten round the waist. I've had them since I was fifteen and grown a bit since then, but it doesn't matter. I have a dress uniform to wear on the ship so I can join the passengers on formal evenings.'

Lottie was excited all day, remembering the Christmas parties at the yacht club that the Roydens used to invite her to. It seemed ages since she'd been anywhere as grand as that.

Glyn asked Dad if they could borrow the car. 'Yes,' he said. 'Provided Lottie drives it.' She saw Glyn pull a face. 'She's had more experience than you,' he added.

'That's not surprising, since I spend so much time at sea.'

'Every situation has its disadvantages,' Grandma said tartly. She found a velvet cloak for Lottie to wear, black on the outside and scarlet inside. 'You'd better keep that too,' she told her. 'I have no occasion to wear that sort of thing any more.'

'Parties and dances have never been your sort of thing, Mother,' Harriet said.

The Royal Liverpool Yacht Club had their headquarters at Rock Ferry to take advantage of the deep water and large area of safe sailing in the Sloyne, well away from the commercial traffic in the shipping lanes.

'Everything looks familiar and yet it isn't,' Glyn said as they went inside. 'It's a long time since we came to the children's parties here.'

Philip was waiting for them near the door of the clubhouse. 'Wow, you look fantastic,' he said, kissing Lottie on the cheek, and she could see the admiration in his eyes. She thought he'd got over his earlier stiffness, and he certainly looked very handsome. He was wearing his Merchant Navy dress uniform.

The yacht club did their members proud on formal occasions like this. The club house was beautifully decorated with flowers, and an excellent band was playing music that set her feet tapping. The glittering scene before her lifted her mood of anticipation to one of pure pleasure. Philip was a good host and saw that she had a glass of sparkling wine.

She had a few words with his parents and found Lazlo was

with them. 'Lovely dress,' he whispered to her. 'You're the belle of the ball.'

Philip was doing his best to introduce Glyn to some girls, and he did what was expected of him and asked one of them to dance. Philip took Lottie on to the floor. 'Glyn tells me you have a boyfriend,' he said.

'Yes, you must meet him. In fact you will, as he'll be at Dilys's wedding.'

'It sounds as though he's already well in with your family,' he said. 'A major disadvantage of working abroad is that the best girls have all got fixed up while I've been away. I should have known you'd be snapped up.'

She laughed. 'That doesn't mean I'm going to forget my old friends. You'll be home for some time now?'

'I'm staying put from now on. I'll be working in the Liverpool office when my leave is up.'

The music was lively, the beat invigorating, and Philip was all smiles and anecdotes, thoroughly enjoying himself. Lottie was having a wonderful time, and was never off the dance floor. She had a dance with Glyn, one with Lazlo and another with Henry Royden, but for the rest of the evening she felt she was floating round in Philip's arms. The atmosphere was electric.

They all ate supper together, a magnificent buffet of expensive treats that Grandma rarely allowed at home. All round them the keen sailors were chatting about the racing that had taken place earlier in the day. Lottie heard praise lavished on the skills of the winners. One of them, the owner of the *Lady Rowena*, was an acquaintance of Henry's and stopped at their table. He told them that his firm was transferring him to

Toronto to manage the office there and that he needed to sell his yacht. 'I shall be sorry to part with her,' he said. 'She handles beautifully.'

'There you are, Lazlo,' Henry said. 'If you want to buy a yacht, the *Lady Rowena* is on offer.'

He shook his head. 'I've more important things to buy first,' he said. But he found a brochure in the entrance hall giving all her details and brought it back to the table to study.

It seemed to whet Glyn's appetite for sailing. 'Why don't we take the *Seagull* out on the river tomorrow, for old times' sake?'

'An excellent thing to do on Easter Sunday,' Philip said. 'What about you, Lazlo, do you fancy a sail on the Mersey?'

'I don't think so, too cold. Count me out.'

'Just us three, then. What time is the tide tomorrow?' There was no problem finding out about that in the yacht club, and it was arranged that Philip would come to their house.

The band returned and Lottie was immediately led out on to the floor again by Philip, but after another enchanting hour they were tired and hot. He ushered her outside. 'For a breath of cool air,' he said. They were alone and his arms came round her, and almost spontaneously his lips found hers.

A second later, she was pushing out of his embrace. What had seemed so right a moment ago now seemed hopelessly disloyal to Roddy.

'Sorry.' Philip had stiffened up again. 'I keep forgetting you're engaged to another man. I've always thought of you as . . . Well, you know.'

'We are still friends,' she insisted. 'You must meet Roddy and we'll have a night out together.' She could see immediately that that was not what he wanted to hear. 'Come on,' she said, 'this sounds like the last waltz; let's dance it for old times' sake.' He took her in his arms again, but the joy and exhilaration had gone.

It was two o'clock in the morning when Lottie drove Glyn home. 'It was a wonderful evening, wasn't it?' she asked. 'Did you enjoy it?'

'Yes, I did, but none of the girls are a patch on Dorothy. I'd have enjoyed it more if she'd been there.'

Lottie had found Philip wonderfully good company. Being close to him had intoxicated her. What was the matter with her? Either she was in love with Roddy or she wasn't. She'd promised to marry him, and believed she'd love him till eternity. She was wearing his ring. Philip had bewitched her. She mustn't think like this, mustn't compare them. She'd committed herself to Roddy.

The *Seagull* had been stored on its trailer at one end of Dad's garage all winter. Lottie and Glyn had discussed the cleaning and checking over it would need before pulling it down to the launching ramp near the old pier house. Philip arrived mid-morning in his father's car, which had a towing bracket, but cleaning the dinghy up took more time and effort than they had expected, and even with Philip's help it was a rush to catch the tide.

It was a fine, bright day, with a strong breeze, just right for a sail. The waves were white-tipped and gave the boat a bit of a buffeting, but Lottie loved to feel the wind blowing through her hair. They sailed down towards the yacht club and met several large keelboats out on the river, then went round the historic training ships to wave to the boys. There was a church service being conducted on the deck of the TS *Indefatigable*, and the sound of the band playing hymns drifted across the water.

As they tacked back upriver towards Bromborough Dock, they found they were being followed by a large Palm Line freighter bringing palm oil to the soap factory. 'The *Takoradi Palm*,' Glyn laughed. 'I saw her recently in Lagos harbour.'

'I've seen her many times out on the Coast,' Philip said. 'We'd better get out of her way.'

It was teatime when they moored *Seagull* opposite Mersey View and paddled back across the squelching mud. Lottie was damp and untidy, and her skin felt tight from the wind. They took Philip home with them to wash his feet in the bathroom and replace his shoes and socks. They'd missed Sunday lunch and were all hungry now. In the kitchen, they made roast beef sandwiches from the remains of the joint and took them with a pot of tea to their old playroom.

'Just like old times,' Philip said as he was leaving. Lottie walked up the garden with him to his car. 'It's good to be back, but I feel I've lost touch by going away for so long; lost all my friends.'

'Everybody remembered you last night,' she said. 'Lots of people came up to say hello.'

'Yes, but I'm no longer out and about with friends. Glyn is working and only has limited time to spend with me. I feel as though I've been thrown back on the family for companionship. Like Lazlo.'

'I'm still your friend.'

'Yes, and don't think I don't value that.' He got into the driving seat and started the engine. 'But actually, you're the biggest loss of all. You're engaged to this other fellow.'

He was away before she could say anything in answer to that. It made her feel she'd let him down.

By the following day, Easter Monday, the strong breeze had dropped. The weather was exactly what they'd hoped to have for Dilys's wedding: a sunny spring day.

Family spirits were buoyant until Martin telephoned the bride to say, 'I'm very sorry, Dilys, Eunice isn't well enough to come. She had a fever during the night and I've called the doctor in to see her. She feels terrible about missing your wedding and I feel I ought to stay at home with her.'

'What about Christabel? Couldn't she bring the other girls across?'

'I think it would be safer if they stayed here. Eunice is very disappointed and so are the children. We were all looking forward to it very much. We wish you the very best, Dilys. You know that.'

It caused a big worry at breakfast. Dilys was upset. 'Poor Eunice, she must be feeling dreadful.'

'What a good job she decided she didn't want to be matron of honour,' Grandma said. 'At least she hasn't bought a special gown.'

'I did invite her to be,' Dilys said, 'and I suggested having Christabel and Tom as attendants, but she was afraid the others might be jealous, and as they are quite a tribe, she'd have had to bring the nanny to look after them. I'm very glad now I decided to just have you, Lottie.'

'Christabel will be upset about this,' Lottie said. 'She was looking forward to today. When I last spoke to her, she was going on about the dress she was going to wear.'

For Lottie, the day of her sister's marriage seemed to pass in a romantic haze. The church was decorated with spring flowers and Dilys was everything a bride should be. As Lottie walked down the aisle behind her, she exchanged little smiles with Roddy when she passed the pew where he was sitting. She was sure that, like her, he was longing for this occasion to come for them.

Alec looked the perfect groom. Nobody could doubt his love for Dilys; it was in his voice as he made his vows. The wedding march swelled as they walked back down the aisle, and even Grandma had tears in her eyes.

The bride and groom clung together on the church steps to have their photographs taken, and as they all walked back to the cars, Roddy came up to Lottie, his lips touching her cheek in a butterfly kiss. 'I do love you,' he whispered.

Back at home, the caterers greeted them with trays loaded with glasses of sherry. 'This is not an occasion to give all your attention to your fiancé,' Grandma told Lottie. 'You must mingle with the guests and help to make them feel welcome.'

Lazlo and Philip came to say hello and each kissed her cheek. 'I'm so glad you're both at home and could come today,' she said.

'Wouldn't have missed it for the world,' Lazlo told her.

Philip was ill at ease. 'You look wonderful, happy and on top of the world,' he said.

'I am. It's not every day my sister gets married.'

'It was a lovely wedding.' He was trying to smile, but he seemed strangely stiff and formal. 'Dilys was a radiant bride, and the ceremony couldn't have gone better.'

'If Grandma organises anything, it goes like clockwork, as

you know. Roddy is here today; I'd like you to meet him. Let's see if we can find him.'

They found him alone, staring out at the river through the sitting-room window. She introduced them. 'Congratulations,' Philip said. 'Glyn tells me that you and Lottie are going to be married.' Neither looked comfortable.

'We are,' she said, 'but Grandma says not until I'm twenty-one.'

'I can see it doesn't please you to wait,' Philip said sadly.

The caterers provided delicious finger food, Dad gave his little speech and they had champagne for the toasts. Charlotte found that everybody relaxed and laughed with the groom, whose speech was humorous and more practised. It was a lovely party with all their friends and family round them, even if Harriet reminded them that Eunice and Martin had had lobster and smoked salmon for their wedding breakfast.

But Lottie was trying to divide her attention between Roddy and Philip, and neither seemed pleased. It made her feel uncomfortable, her eyes going from one to the other. She was glad when at last Dilys came to ask for her help to change into her going-away outfit.

'You're leaving so soon?' Harriet asked.

'Who would want to spend more time eating and drinking and making small talk when they could be alone?' Dilys whispered as they went to her bedroom.

She had chosen a very smart suit in mid-blue, with a pretty blue hat. 'I think this really suits you,' Lottie told her. 'It's lovely.'

'I hope to get plenty of wear out of it,' the bride said, and they both giggled.

'Grandma would be proud to hear you say that.'

Dilys had decided they would not need a car in Southport; there would be lots for them to do within walking distance of their hotel, and to drive would be a distraction. She'd asked Lottie to take them to the station. Oliver had tied three balloons and Dad's old boots to the bumper, and they were waved off with good wishes ringing in their ears.

All the way there, people turned to look and wave, and the bridal pair waved back, still fizzing with high spirits. Lottie drew to the pavement right outside Hamilton Square station and got out to kiss her sister goodbye. No point in going further; they wouldn't want any more of her company. On the way home, she decided she wanted her wedding to be exactly like Dilys's.

She put Dad's car in the garage and removed his boots and the balloons from the bumper. Tomorrow morning they'd be going to work.

It was a bright and sunny afternoon, and some of the guests had spilled out into the garden. Harriet had ensured they had plenty of flowers in bloom, and the garden was awash with colour. The first person she saw was Dad, walking across the grass to meet her with a look of horror on his face. 'Are those my boots?' He wore them regularly when he went to the docks, but now they were scuffed and covered with deep scratch marks. 'What have you done? They're hardly wearable now.'

'Not my fault, Dad.'

'Let me have them. Philip is looking for you. He's over there talking to Harriet. Go on.' She felt his hand on her back.

'Quite like old times to be here,' Philip said. 'Everything looks exactly as it used to.' But Lottie sensed that he thought she and everything else had changed. The other guests were melting away now, leaving only the Mortimers and those close to them.

'I'd better look for Lazlo and go too,' he said. 'I'll just find your grandma to thank her.' Then, more awkwardly, he added, 'I wish you the best of everything, Lottie. You know that.'

Glyn came up. 'I'm glad I've caught you, Phil,' he said. 'Would you take Dorothy home? Drop her off on your way?' He had hold of her hand.

'Of course, I'll be glad to.' Philip smiled at her. 'We had a good chat earlier, didn't we? See what I mean, Lottie? All the best girls get snapped up.' He dropped a light kiss on her cheek. 'Don't forget me.' He turned, and headed for the door with Dorothy. Lottie watched them stop for a word with Harriet and then Grandma.

Beside her Roddy said, 'You're lucky to have a family that can afford to live like this.'

Grandma came and flopped into her usual armchair. 'All this standing about is very tiring. I'm no longer up to it.'

'It was a beautiful wedding,' Roddy told her. 'Dilys must be delighted with all the arrangements her family made for her.'

'It's exactly the sort of wedding I want for us.' Lottie smiled at him.

'That would be wonderful,' Roddy said. 'I can think of nothing that would improve it, and with a new home all set up and ready to move into, what better start to married life could Dilys wish for?'

'She's paying for that herself,' Jemima said drily. 'Charlotte is not going to be in Dilys's financial position.'

Roddy looked taken aback, but recovered quickly. 'No

matter, we'll manage. I have my promotion now. Did Lottie tell you?'

'Yes, congratulations. Harriet is putting the kettle on. I'm sure you're both as much in need of tea as I am. Do stay, Roddy, and have a cup with us.'

Lottie already felt drained by the emotional impact of the wedding. Now she felt guilty that she hadn't told him herself. She'd not forgotten that once Roddy had asked for assurance that Eunice and Dilys were her sisters and she was afraid he was relying on her having a similar income. She couldn't forget Grandma's suspicions. After they'd had tea, she led Roddy out to the car to run him to the station.

'I've got the impression that Dilys and Eunice aren't your sisters after all,' he said. 'Is that right?'

She sighed. 'Yes, goodness only knows why the family kept it from me, but I've recently found out that Lazlo is my father. It's all been a bit wearing.'

She stole a glance at him; he was biting his lip. 'But they are your half-sisters? You share the same mother?'

'No, my mother was Gwendolen. Their mother was her sister.'

He twisted in his seat to look at her. 'Oh! Does that mean you won't share the same inheritance?'

'I'm afraid it does. Getting a home together is going to be harder for us. But at least having to wait gives us plenty of time to save and you have your promotion.'

'Yes,' he said. 'It does.'

CHAPTER TWENTY

FOR LOTTIE, THE NEXT morning felt a little flat. At breakfast, the family talked about Eunice. Grandma was worried about her. 'She must be really ill not to come to the wedding,' she said. 'I tried to ring her last night to see how she was, but the operator told me her phone appeared to have been left off the hook.'

Lottie and Charles were a little late setting off to the office, but it didn't matter because they weren't busy. She'd brought a piece of wedding cake for Ted, and she did some typing to help Dorothy out. She couldn't stop talking about the wedding.

Dad was expecting the *Caernarvon* to dock about lunchtime with a cargo of slate from Pwllheli. Late in the morning, the phone rang. Charles picked it up and said, 'Captain Jones, shouldn't you be on your way here?' Lottie knew that meant trouble, and watched her father's face as she listened to one half of the conversation.

He sighed as he put the phone down. 'They've been delayed because of trouble with the engine,' he told her. 'They're just about to set off now, and he expects to dock about seven this evening. A damn nuisance.' It meant they'd have nothing much to do this afternoon and would have to work this evening.

'Dad, can I use the time to go over to see Eunice? Martin will be at work, so I'll be able to talk to her on her own.'

'Yes, that's a good idea. It'll set our minds at rest, and you can count it as time off in lieu.'

'I'll be back in plenty of time to go with you to the *Caernarvon*.'

'I'll ring Harriet and tell her we want dinner at six. Be back in time for that,' Charles said.

Ted was going into town and offered her a lift to the station. Before leaving she tried again to ring Eunice to tell her she was coming, but the operator told her the phone was still out of order.

It was another lovely spring morning, and with the leaves freshly out on the trees, Gatacre was looking its best. Lottie was looking forward to relaying the news of the wedding. Her older sisters were close, and she thought Eunice would be very upset at having missed Dilys's special day.

It was the housekeeper who opened the door to her, but Eunice was behind her in the hall. Lottie knew as soon as she saw her that there was more trouble. 'Thank goodness you've come,' Eunice whispered. 'Martin's at home, working in his study; don't let him hear you.'

The house seemed unusually quiet. 'Are the girls not here?'

'No, they've gone to spend a few days with their grandmother in Windermere.' Eunice drew her towards her little sitting room. She'd been crying, and her eyes were red and puffy. 'I was about to ring you,' she said, 'but Martin says our phone is out of order.'

'It is; we've tried to ring you. What's the matter?'

'Aunt Gwendolen is here; she came back this morning. She's been in an accident – well, no, she hasn't, but that's what

217

Martin decided we should tell the staff. She's bleeding and covered with grazes and bruises.' Eunice was near to tears.

'What's happened to her?'

'It looks as though she's been beaten up, had a good hiding. I think it must be Uncle Jeremy; she's frightened of him.' She shuddered and mopped at her eyes. 'Come and talk to her. Martin's put her to lie down in the spare room.' She led the way upstairs.

Gwen was lying on the bed, covered with the eiderdown. Lottie's jaw fell open when she saw the fresh large graze oozing blood on her forehead and another below her left eye, which looked swollen and sore. Her nose had been bleeding. She peered up at Lottie. 'Is it you, Eunice?'

'No, it's Charlotte.' Brimming with tenderness, she sank to her knees and threw her arms round her in a hug. 'Your daughter.'

Tears were rolling down Gwendolen's face. 'My daughter? Charlotte? Thank God you've come.'

'Did Uncle Jeremy do this to you?' Lottie was choking with pity.

'She's been beaten up,' Eunice wept. 'Auntie Gwen, show her, push up your sleeves.'

Lottie was horrified to see vicious red weals and more grazes.

'What are we going to do?' pleaded Eunice. 'I'm afraid Uncle Jeremy will come to get her. We're both afraid. I want you to take her now. Where is the car?'

'Dad's using it. I came by train.' Lottie was shocked. She'd walked in on what seemed to be a crisis for her mother and Eunice. She had to stay calm and think.

'Martin says reporters have been round to their house pressing for more details about Jeremy. He's afraid they'll come here.' Eunice looked terrified.

Gwen had closed her eyes again. Lottie took hold of her hand. 'Gwen, Dad and Grandma want you to come and stay with us,' she said. 'We have plenty of space and we'll all make you very welcome.' She glanced at Eunice. 'Do we need to pack her things?'

Eunice gestured towards her handbag. 'She's not staying with us.' For the first time Lottie noticed her coat over a chair. 'She only came this morning.'

'Early, you mean?'

'I wasn't dressed, yes.'

Lottie could feel her heart pounding like a drum. 'Is this the first time he's hurt you?' Gwen's face was blank. 'Or has it been going on for some time?'

'It's only since Uncle Jeremy was caught,' Eunice said. 'That's what started this awful trouble.'

'Never mind, Gwen, you'll be safe with us. Lazlo is home for good and he's hoping to see you soon.'

Gwen's eyes flickered open. They were full of pain.

Lottie said, 'We'll need a taxi. Eunice, please call one.'

'The phone isn't working.'

'Try it again. If not, I'll go out and find a phone box.' She turned back to Gwen. 'Come on, let's sit you up and get your shoes on.'

She was aware of a car drawing up in a flurry of gravel at the front door below, and then voices in the hall. Had she left it too late? An angry Martin appeared at the door holding Eunice by the arm. 'Charlotte, please don't interfere.'

'I want to take her home with me. It's what Dad and Grandma want. We'll look after her.'

'Gwendolen,' Martin said, 'you've been in an accident. You need medical attention. Jeremy is making all the necessary arrangements for you to have it.'

He turned to Lottie. 'Jeremy's problems have come as a shock to her, poor dear. She wandered out into the road and was knocked down by a car. Unfortunately, it might have affected her mind too. She's tormented with fears and has some strange ideas.'

At that moment Jeremy Arbuthnot joined them. 'Who are you?' he demanded belligerently of Lottie.

Martin explained, and he looked at her with glazed eyes, then took hold of his wife's hand. 'Gwen, darling, there's nothing to worry about. The doctors will get you better.' He looked Lottie in the eye. 'I've booked her into a nursing home so she can have complete rest and those cuts can be treated.'

Lottie was suspicious. 'Which nursing home?' she demanded.

'It's called the Highground, in Carlton Road. It has a good reputation, much the best place for her.'

'She wants to come home with me,' Lottie insisted. 'We'll see she has the best medical attention.'

'Everything has been set up for her at the Highground,' Martin said. 'It's no longer a case of what she wants but what she needs. It wouldn't be safe to delay treatment.'

'I'm afraid Gwendolen has played on Eunice's nerves for no real reason,' Jeremy said, 'and the last thing we want is for you or your family to worry about either of them.' He was helping his wife into her coat.

'Yes,' Martin agreed. 'As you can see, we are doing our best for her.'

Jeremy guided Gwen out to his car. 'I'm taking her straight to the nursing home.'

Martin looked at Lottie. 'I think the best thing for Eunice is a little rest on her bed. Do be sure to tell your family that they have absolutely no reason to be concerned about either Gwendolen or Eunice. Our side of the family are taking good care of both of them.'

Lottie found herself politely put out on the front step and no longer able to think straight. To see Gwendolen and speak to her and then find she was powerless to stop her being whisked away by her husband was unbelievable, and she certainly couldn't agree with Martin. She had more to worry about than she'd ever had.

She started to walk towards the train station, but then thought about Lazlo. He was desperate to get in touch with Gwen; she had to let him know what was happening, but there was no way of doing that without going to his lodgings. She knew she ought to go home to speak to Grandma, and there was the *Caernarvon* visit to think of, but perhaps she'd have time to see Lazlo before going home.

She was just coming to a bus stop when a double-decker drew up and a couple of passengers got off. She was able to ask the conductor if it would take her in the direction of Upper Parliament Street. 'We go right down there, love,' he told her, and she felt she was in luck. It wasn't going to take her that long to get there.

Lazlo's landlady answered her knock. 'Mr Mortimer is not in,' she said. 'I haven't seen him since early this morning.'

It wasn't her lucky day after all. 'I need to give him an urgent message,' she said. 'Could I borrow a sheet of paper and a pencil from you?'

Obligingly, the landlady gave her a writing pad and invited her to sit at her kitchen table. *Telephone me at home*, she wrote. *I've seen Gwendolen this afternoon and she needs help.* Then she ran up to the top of the house and pushed it under his door.

It was five o'clock when she reached home. As she hurried down the back garden, she saw Dad's car. She could smell cooking and went to the kitchen. Dad was having a cup of tea at the kitchen table and Harriet was peeling potatoes.

'How is Eunice?' he asked. 'Is she feeling better?'

'No.' Lottie sank on to a chair. 'She was in tears the whole time and in a terrible state. Aunt Gwendolen was there; she'd been beaten up and was all bleeding cuts. She seemed confused. I think she'd been hit on the head. Dad, she looked terrible. You've got to help.'

Grandma joined them in time to hear her tell them all that had happened.

'They're both scared of Uncle Jeremy. I knew it was a crisis and wanted to call a taxi to bring her here, but Martin was at home and Uncle Jeremy came and said he'd arranged for her to go to a nursing home. He took her away from under my nose and I couldn't stop him.'

She could see they were all shocked. Grandma recovered first. 'This is very high-handed of them.'

'They probably think they're doing their best for Gwendolen,' Harriet said.

'You'd better air the guest room, Harriet, and make up the bed, just in case. I'll ring Eunice now to see how she is. I'll tell her I'll come and see her tomorrow morning, and that we're very happy to have Gwendolen here if this is where she wants to be and the doctors agree.'

She went out to the hall, but was back in a few moments looking more worried than ever. 'Their phone is still out of order.'

'Do you think you should try to see Gwendolen tonight?' Charles asked. 'I could come with you.'

'No, you have to pay a visit to the *Caernarvon*.'

'Yes, but Lottie is worried, she thinks it could be urgent.'

Jemima paused to think. 'Where was he taking her?'

'He said to the Highground nursing home, in Carlton Road,' Lottie said.

'You two have to go to work tomorrow; I'll go over to Eunice's on the train in the morning and we'll go to this nursing home to see how Gwen is settling in.'

'It might be the best place for her,' Harriet said. 'It could be what she needs.'

'It won't do her any harm to spend one night in a nursing home.' Jemima straightened her shoulders. 'I'll bring her home with me, if that's possible. Harriet, time is going on. How soon can you have dinner on the table?'

'Charles asked for it to be ready at six o'clock, and it will be.'

Lottie felt fraught and knew the rest of her family did too. 'I could go down to the *Caernarvon* on my own,' she said, 'and then Dad, you could go to see Gwen.'

'No you could not,' Grandma barked. 'You can't go walking about the docks by yourself in the dark. Charles will go with you. We don't want any more problems at the moment.'

'Dinner is ready.' Aunt Harriet started to serve up the beef casserole, and they all helped to take the dishes into the dining room.

As soon as dinner was finished, Charles and Lottie put on their coats and went to the docks. Usually Lottie enjoyed visiting ships with Dad, but tonight she was troubled and couldn't stop thinking about her mother. When they arrived, the berth was empty; the *Caernarvon* had not arrived. She could see her father was surprised. 'We're late, where is she? I hope Captain Jones hasn't had more trouble with the engine.'

'Had we better go to the office, Dad, to see if we can contact him?' They had wireless telegraphy equipment there, so they could keep in touch with their ships.

It took only a few minutes to get to the office, but by then Lottie could see her father was very worried indeed, and family concerns were wiped from her mind.

'Something must have gone wrong,' he said. 'It's only a short journey from Pwllheli, and Jones is reliable; he usually arrives on the dot.'

Lottie had developed more expertise than her father with wireless telegraphy, as he mostly left it to her to make contact. It always took a little time and she could see he was fretting. These days it was possible to speak directly to ships, but their equipment was old-fashioned and didn't always work well. Although Charles had talked of replacing it, he had never got round to it, and they still had to use Morse code.

At last she could hear the crackles and knew she was through. She was learning Morse code, but Dad was quicker than she was at sending and reading messages, and she let him take over. She wrote down the letters as he said them aloud. She was afraid this was going to be more bad news.

As the sentences took shape, she could see that the *Caernarvon* had had a fire in the engine room as she was rounding Anglesey. That the crew had managed to put it out, but half-speed was the best they could get out of the engine. They were now in sight of New Brighton and expected to dock in half an hour.

'Has anybody been hurt?' she asked, and watched Dad tap out the question. Yes, came the answer, there were two with serious burns and several more were suffering from smoke inhalation and minor burns.

'Ring for an ambulance,' Dad told her. 'They'll all have to go to hospital. First thing in the morning we'll need a marine engineer from Vickers to assess the damage. I only hope it's confined to the engine room. Can you look out our insurance policy? I hope that'll cover most of it.'

'We can't do much about that until tomorrow,' she said. 'Is there anything else before we go back to the dock?'

'Ring Grandma, she'll want to know. Tell her we'll be late home.'

Lottie did as he'd asked.

'Come on,' he said. 'I want to stop at the Queen's Head and get a couple of bottles of brandy. They'll all be shaken up.'

The ambulance had arrived and the *Caernarvon* was tying up when they arrived at the dock. Once on board, Lottie could hardly breathe for the acrid smell of burning. It was strong enough to taste.

'Thank God slate won't burn and the cargo will be all right,' Dad said.

Lottie watched horrified as the chief engineer and one of the able seamen were stretchered to the ambulance, followed by three smoke-blackened walking wounded. The ambulance driver told her he was taking them to Birkenhead General Hospital, which was nearby.

'Write down their names and contact details,' Charles said to her, then handed some money to one of the walking wounded and told him to make sure the three of them came back to the ship in a taxi.

'Always do that,' he said to Lottie. 'Most of the crew are from Pwllheli and won't know where they are.'

They inspected the damage in the engine room, which seemed to be extensive. In the captain's cabin, Charles opened both bottles of brandy, then sent one to the crew's quarters. Captain Jones produced three glasses, but while her father merely wetted the bottom of the glass for her, he himself joined the captain in a restorative drink. She didn't doubt he needed it as much as anybody.

'We'll have to go back to the office,' he said afterwards. 'I need to speak to the engineer's family if I can, and you must send a telegram to the seaman's wife. You know the sort of thing, very much regret to inform you. Add our phone number and invite her to ring for more details. Give the number of the hospital too.'

Lottie was tired as she drove home. 'You did very well tonight,' he told her. 'I couldn't have managed without you.'

Harriet had gone to bed, but Grandma had waited up for them with cake and cocoa. They were both hungry and tucked in, their tiredness forgotten. Jemima wanted to hear every detail, and questioned them both minutely before telephoning the hospital to enquire after the injured.

'Two of the men have been admitted, their burns have been

dressed and they're as comfortable as can be expected,' she reported.

'We'll ring again in the morning.' Lottie yawned and reached for another piece of cake. She could see her grandmother was too edgy to sit still.

'I'm worried stiff about Eunice and Gwen,' Jemima said, and that brought all Lottie's earlier fears thundering back. 'I feel guilty that Eunice had to cope with her. You and I should have done more for her, Charles.'

'It's not your fault, Grandma. She hasn't seen you for years, and probably didn't realise how stressed Eunice has become.'

'She knew you were here,' Jemima said slowly. 'But without contact, she didn't know how things had progressed. I do blame myself for not keeping in touch.'

'I've had enough, Mother. I'm going to bed,' Charles said, 'and you should too, Lottie. We'll have to be in the office early tomorrow. We've done nothing about the cargoes booked to go out on the *Caernarvon*. Will you remember to ring the suppliers and tell them to hold things up, as she'll be late sailing.'

'Yes, Dad.' Lottie got to her feet. 'Goodnight.'

'I'll give you a few minutes to get through the bathroom,' Grandma said. 'Goodnight, dear.' It was after midnight.

CHAPTER TWENTY-ONE

JEMIMA MADE SURE THE family were up early the next morning and told Harriet to provide a breakfast of eggs and bacon to set them up for the day. Charles and Lottie needed to leave early, and Jemima made an effort to be ready so they could give her a lift to the station.

Lottie was very busy all day. Dad gave her the job of paying the crew's wages and seeing to the needs of the *Caernarvon*'s crew while he put in hand the work needed to repair the engine and the fire damage. He had to forgo his trip to the pub with Ted Pascoe at lunchtime. Instead, they ate at their desks.

It usually took two days to turn the ship round for another trip, but on this occasion, the professional estimate was four days. 'Not too bad,' Charles said. 'When I first saw it, I thought it would take longer.'

'Dad, is it still OK for me to have the car this evening?'

'Yes, you can drop me at the hospital,' he said. 'It was a good idea of yours to phone and ask if I could come and see the men out of visiting hours. I'll get a bus home afterwards, but don't you be late back.'

'I won't, I'm shattered. It's not just today; we were very late going to bed last night.'

'Yes. I wonder how your grandmother got on in Liverpool.'

They'd not had time all day to think about the problems Eunice
and Gwendolen were facing, but to Lottie it felt it like a heavy
black cloud waiting in the background.

Jemima found travelling to Liverpool in the rush hour an
exhausting business. When she arrived in Gatacre, a dour-
looking housekeeper let her in and showed her into Eunice's
boudoir while she summoned her from the bedroom. She was
still in her dressing gown and seemed bemused and very much
on edge.

'I'd like a cup of coffee, Eunice, please.'

'Of course, Grandma. I'll get Hilda to make some.'

'Who is this Hilda?'

'Our new housekeeper. Martin sacked Beryl. He thinks
Hilda is better.'

'What do you think? I would have said it was your job to
hire the staff. How are the children?' she continued.

'Edgar is here, but all the others are in Windermere with
Laura. Tom's gone with them this time.'

'Don't you miss them? What do you do all day?'

She seemed at a loss. 'I don't know. I play with Eddie
sometimes.'

'Will you take the girls shopping for clothes when they get
back? Christabel must enjoy that.'

'Laura sees to all that in the holidays, and Martin takes
them to buy their school uniforms.'

Jemima's spirits sank. Eunice didn't seem much involved
with her family. She was young, and should be full of energy,
going out and about, doing things. An immaculately laid tray
of freshly brewed coffee was produced promptly. They were

employing at least two people in the kitchen, because Jemima could hear them talking. That was unusual in this day and age.

'So what is all this I hear from Charlotte about Aunt Gwendolen?'

Eunice shook her head, and said apathetically, 'She came round here yesterday morning after being injured in a car accident.'

'Charlotte said that was a falsehood Martin had told you to tell the staff.'

'Yes, I think it was a story to hide that Uncle Jeremy had beaten her up.'

'Good gracious, girl, then what happened?'

'Uncle Jeremy came round and took her away. He said he was taking her to a nursing home. He thought she'd be better off there where she'd have nurses to look after her.'

'Eunice, I am a trained nurse, I can look after her.'

Her granddaughter said nothing. Her big green eyes looked nervously up at her and quickly away. Jemima couldn't help but feel sorry for her. She wasn't enjoying life, and she seemed cowed, very different to the boisterous young girl she'd once been.

'Why don't you go and get dressed while I pour myself another cup of this coffee? I would like to go and see Gwendolen. You should come too. It would settle both our minds. Is this nursing home far?'

'Not very, but we'll need a taxi.'

Half an hour later, they set off to the Highground nursing home. When she saw it, Jemima approved; it was a pleasant-looking building surrounded by lawns and high trees. The large board at the gate assured them that patients would be treated by qualified staff in luxurious surroundings, and have their every need attended to. Visitors were welcome at any hour.

Jemima decided to dismiss the taxi. 'We'll want to spend some time with Gwendolen; it's a very long time since I've seen her.' They rang the bell, and when a maid answered it, she said, 'We've come to see Mrs Gwendolen Arbuthnot.'

The girl seemed at a loss. 'I'm sorry, I don't recognise the name. Has she recently come in?'

'Yes, last night.'

'Erm, I'll get a nurse to come and speak to you,' she said and rushed away.

The nurse came. 'Mrs Gwendolen Arbuthnot, you said? I'm sorry. We don't have a patient by that name. She's not known to us.' Jemima was shocked. 'There's another nursing home, the Connaught, at the end of the road. Could she have gone to that one?'

'Possibly,' Jemima said. Eunice seemed only half awake and it wouldn't surprise her to find she'd made a mistake. Then she remembered that Charlotte had named the same place. 'Sorry to have troubled you.'

As they crunched down the gravel drive, Eunice said, 'I'm sure Martin said the Highground.'

'Don't worry.' Jemima took her arm. 'We'd better go and see if she's in the Connaught, since we're close.' Perhaps there hadn't been a room free at the Highground; she should have asked about that. But it turned out the staff at the Connaught had not heard of Gwen either.

Eunice looked close to tears. 'Don't upset yourself,' Jemima said. 'We'll find her. We'll have to ring Martin.'

'He doesn't like me ringing him at work. He asked me not to.'

'Well, there's no other way to find out. Is there a phone box near here?'

'I don't know, Grandma. I don't normally come in this direction. The school and the shops are the other way.'

'We'll walk back towards your house, and if we come across a phone box, we'll use it.' Now Jemima was worried about Eunice too. This was not the behaviour of a happily married young woman. 'The walk will do us good,' she said, and quickened her step. 'We haven't come far. I don't suppose your phone has been mended yet?'

'It was working fine this morning. I don't know what happened to it yesterday.'

Had Martin just taken it off the hook so it couldn't be used? Something was very wrong here.

Back at Eunice's house, Jemima sat down in the hall. 'Would you get Martin on the line for me, dear?'

'He won't be pleased.' Eunice was reluctant. 'I really don't think we should.'

'But I don't want to go home without seeing Gwendolen, so he'll understand the need for it.'

Eunice asked the operator to put her through, and though that didn't take long, it took an age to get Martin to the phone.

'Hello, I'm very sorry to disturb you,' Jemima said, 'but Eunice is confused about which nursing home you took Gwendolen to last night.'

'The Highground,' he said. 'It's one of the better ones round here.'

Jemima was so shocked she couldn't speak. She could hear Martin's voice giving more details about it, praising the treatment there. It took an effort to pull herself together.

'Martin,' she said firmly, 'Gwendolen is not at the Highground. Eunice and I have been there and tried to see her. And she's not at the Connaught either. Where is she?' There was silence. 'Are you still there? Don't be silly, Martin. What is all this about?'

'You don't need to worry about Gwendolen. At the last minute she said she didn't want to go to a nursing home.'

'Martin, I understand she'd received a beating from somebody and had cuts and bruises on her face and body. Eunice says Jeremy attacked her.'

'Oh dear me no. Poor Gwen! She was in a motor accident in town and has been very confused in her thinking since.'

'I am going to take her home with me, where she can have the peace and quiet she needs.'

'She asked Jeremy to take her home. He will see she has the medical treatment she requires. He can't do enough for her.'

'That is not what you said a minute ago, not what Charlotte and Eunice understood would happen. You said he was taking her to a nursing home. I would like to see her and make my own judgement. Where is she?'

'Jeremy is looking after her. He is her husband and he's taking good care of her. Leave it to him, Jemima.'

She was choking with indignation. She knew old age was robbing her of the ability to think on her feet, but she mustn't let him get away with this. 'I would like to see her while I'm here in Liverpool. Please don't beat about the bush. I want to know where she is.'

'At home, as I've said.' Something in his voice made her doubt that.

'If she is not, I'll come down to that factory where you work, and I won't leave until you tell me the truth.' Her knees felt weak, but she was ready to breathe fire as she put the receiver down. She knew he was telling her out-and-out lies.

Eunice had been hovering beside her and had picked up the gist of what Martin had said. Tears were rolling down her face. 'I was afraid Uncle Jeremy was up to something. Aunt Gwendolen is terrified of him. I don't think she trusts him.'

Jemima was appalled. Dilys had been saying for weeks that she was worried about her sister, and yesterday Charlotte had been quite right to raise the alarm about Gwen. Jemima could feel her strength deserting her. She should have done something about this long before now. Charles would have come with her if she'd asked him to – he felt a responsibility for Gwen – but of course he had his own worries today.

'What are we going to do?' Eunice implored.

'I shall go alone to Gwen's house, and if she isn't there, I shall go and see Martin at work and pin him down.'

'Please leave Martin alone,' Eunice wept. 'Don't upset him any further; it'll all rebound on me when he comes home.'

'Eunice, dear, we have to do something.'

'I wish this hadn't happened to Uncle Jeremy. One thing has led to another. It's upsetting everybody, causing turmoil.'

'I need something to eat quickly – a sandwich, and more coffee. No, a glass of milk would take less time.'

'Grandma, lunch will be ready in half an hour and I've

told them you'll be here for it.'

'Tell them to delay it until I get back. Hurry them about the sandwich and milk.'

Jemima wanted to wash her face and freshen up; she had to make herself more alert. 'Write down the address of Gwen's home and Martin's factory for me, and then call a taxi.'

She tried to think while she ate her cheese and tomato sandwich. She was afraid things were worse than she'd ever imagined. When she heard the taxi come to the door, she drank down the rest of the milk and picked up what remained of the sandwich to take with her. 'The best thing for you to do is to go and lie down until I come back,' she told Eunice.

What she needed was a plan, but there was no time for that now. It seemed only minutes before they were drawing up outside the Arbuthnots' house. Twenty years ago, she'd paid one or two visits to Gwendolen here. The house had been repainted recently, though she believed they'd spent most of their time in London over recent years.

The hinges on the front gate seemed well oiled, and there was a gardener clipping the front hedges. The garden looked almost manicured, with a colourful display of flowers. She went to the front door and rang the bell, but nobody answered. She turned to find the gardener approaching her. 'They've gone away for a holiday,' he said.

'Do you know for how long?'

'They said about two weeks.'

'Right, thank you. When did you last see Mrs Arbuthnot? Was she here over the last few days?'

'Yes, she was. They went away this morning. I helped them load the suitcases into the car.'

'Thank you.'

It was as she'd supposed: Martin had lied to her. It looked as though he did exactly what Jeremy Arbuthnot wanted him to do. She returned to her waiting taxi and set off for Martin's workplace. She was afraid she'd been badly taken in by him, that he'd lied about many things and had been doing so for years. Where did that leave Eunice? And where were they hiding Gwen?

They'd all thought Martin a charming man when he'd been courting Eunice. His relationship to Jeremy, though distant, had seemed to give him added respectability. It had reassured the family that he would be a suitable husband for Eunice. Now it seemed they had been very wrong. Jemima blamed herself; she should have been more vigilant.

She quailed at the thought of looking Martin in the eye and trying to extract Gwen's whereabouts from him. She was unlikely to succeed, but felt she had to try. At least in his office he wouldn't want to make a fuss. His secretary could be close and he wouldn't want her to overhear them.

She took stock. Eunice was not only unhappy but agitated. Was that because she'd tried to shoulder Gwen's troubles? Did they have a shared problem? It seemed likely. As the taxi drove across the city, she tried to work out what she should say to Martin. He must surely be expecting her to come.

The Richards and Frayne factory buildings were impressively large and had been freshly refurbished. Jemima went up the steps of the main entrance. Once inside, she approached the reception desk. The two girls sitting behind it lowered their sandwiches out of sight, and one of them smiled at her and said, 'Good afternoon. How can I help you?'

'I'd like to see Mr Sanderson. Could you please direct me to his office?'

'I'm afraid none of the Sandersons come here any more. The arrangement was that they'd do that for the first year to guide the new owners through the handover period, but it's been several years now.'

Jemima was at a loss; she couldn't take that in. She ran her tongue round her lips. 'I'm asking for Martin Sanderson; he still works here. He's my grandson-in-law. I spoke to him on the phone this morning. He was taken on permanently when the new management took over.'

The other girl spoke. 'I know who you mean. I saw him in the office this morning.' She nudged her colleague. 'It's just the name that's the same; this man has nothing to do with our old bosses.'

Jemima could feel herself swaying. This was worse than she'd supposed. It was terrible.

Both girls leapt to their feet. 'Are you all right? Come and sit down for a moment.' Once she was seated, with her arms supported on the desk, the room stopped spinning. 'Would you like a glass of water?'

'No, I'll be all right, thank you.' Jemima made an effort to pull herself together. 'It's just age catching up with me. Yes, quite all right now.'

'I'm afraid it's our lunch hour and many of the staff go out. Let me see if I can find Martin Sanderson for you.' She took some typed lists from her desk drawer. 'Here he is, he's one of our salesmen. Most of the time they're out on the road, but I'll buzz through to the sales department to see if he's in at the moment.'

Jemima felt a second shock wave as the girl picked up her phone. She buzzed several times but her call wasn't answered. 'I'm sorry,' she said, 'but it is lunchtime. Everyone's out.'

Jemima pulled herself to her feet, feeling too old to be meddling in the affairs of others. She managed to say, 'Thank you for your help. You've been kind.'

'Are you sure you're all right?'

'Yes, I have a taxi outside.' One of the girls supported her to the door. All she wanted to do now was to get away from this place. The driver saw her coming and opened the car door; she got in and collapsed on the seat, feeling a failure. She'd not found out where Gwen was, and she'd opened a whole new can of worms.

Back with Eunice, her appetite had gone; she couldn't swallow the fish pie.

'Don't you like it, Grandma?'

'It's beautifully cooked, it's just me.' She couldn't bring herself to tell Eunice what she'd found out about her husband. Afterwards she said, 'I feel exhausted, I need to rest.' She also needed time to think.

Eunice took her up to her bedroom and drew the curtains. 'Have a sleep, Grandma; shall I wake you in an hour? We all rely on you too much. We forget you're not as young as you were.'

Jemima sighed; she hated to be reminded of her age. Right now, she had to keep going for the sake of her family. Here she was, in the bedroom Eunice shared with Martin Sanderson, having just discovered he'd been lying to them about what he did for a living, and had been for years. Probably ever since he'd taken up with Eunice. The only connection he had with the Sanderson family who'd owned that big factory was that he had the same name. He was employed not in management as he'd told them, but as a salesman! Did Eunice know this?

She thought not; hadn't she said that Martin had asked her not to phone him at the office? He'd had to discourage that because she might find out the truth from his colleagues. Even so, it was amazing he'd managed to keep it from her for the whole of their marriage.

There was no way Martin's salary as a salesman would allow him to live in the extravagant style he did. He must have concocted all these lies to make himself more acceptable as a husband. Jemima shivered. What a fool she'd been to give Eunice permission to marry him. He'd hoodwinked them all. She should have been more careful, especially as Eunice had come into money as soon as she married.

Gwendolen had money too, and Dilys had told her she was cowed and ill and in much the same state as Eunice. They'd all assumed that after she'd handed her baby daughter over to Charles and Jemima, her marriage to Jeremy had continued in the same vein as before, but it was beginning to look very much as though things had changed dramatically. They should have kept in touch with her, made sure she was all right. Jemima blamed herself; she couldn't believe she'd been so remiss.

What she really wanted to do now was call a taxi to take her to the train. She wanted to leave Eunice in ignorance. She believed strongly in the ties of marriage, and though Martin was undoubtedly taking advantage of Eunice's money, the capital that generated her income was legally tied up and he wouldn't be able to touch that. How could she tell her the truth about her husband? Poor girl, how would that make her feel?

CHAPTER TWENTY-TWO

B Y THE TIME EUNICE RETURNED to draw back the curtains and wake her up, Jemima had decided it would be cowardly not to tell her.

She had to think of Gwendolen too. When Jeremy's case was heard in court, there was no knowing what might become public knowledge. Jemima believed now that Jeremy had married Gwen not only as a shield for his homosexuality, but also for her fortune. If Eunice understood that, she must surely be suspicious about Martin's motives too. If she did not, it would be better for her to hear it from her grandmother, rather than pick it up from a newspaper report or common gossip.

She pushed her feet into her shoes and went to find her granddaughter in her boudoir. Four-year-old Edgar was playing with a train set on the floor. Eunice said, 'Gladys is making us some tea.'

'Thank you. We need to talk,' Jemima nodded towards the child, 'and it would be better if he were not here.'

'I thought you'd want to see him.' Eunice was biting her lip.

'I do. It's just that it's better that children don't hear too much.'

'Oh! Eddie's too young to understand,' she said. But when Gladys brought in the tea tray, she said, 'Will you ask Betty to come and take Edgar back to the nursery?'

Once the nanny had taken Eddie away, Jemima reached for her tea. It was hot and strong and she'd never needed it more.

'Eunice, I'm worried about both you and Gwendolen. I told you over lunch what I did this morning, but I was tired and upset when I got back. I didn't tell you what I'd found out about Martin.'

Eunice's cup crashed back on to its saucer; her hands were shaking. 'What?'

'Did you know he was a salesman, out on the road trying to get orders from sweet shops for boiled sweets and chocolate eclairs? He doesn't help to manage that company as he led us to believe.'

Eunice wouldn't look at her now. She sniffed miserably and took her handkerchief from her sleeve. 'The company was taken over. Jobs are very hard to find with so many out of work. Martin had to take what they offered. He says it's better than nothing and he quite enjoys it.'

'Is that what he told you? I learned that he's no relation to the erstwhile owners of that factory; he just shares the same name.' Tears were rolling down Eunice's face now; she couldn't stop them. 'He's always been a salesman, hasn't he? He deliberately lied to us.'

She moved over to sit beside her granddaughter and put her arms round her shaking body. 'How long have you known?'

Eunice whispered into her shoulder, 'Since the business was sold.'

'That's how many years ago now? Three?'

'Four.'

'Why didn't you tell us?' Jemima held her away so she could

see her face. Eunice shook her head, deep in misery. 'Was it because you were ashamed of his lies? You knew we'd be upset?' She shook her head again. 'Or did he ask you not to tell us?'

'He didn't want you to know.'

Jemima drew in her breath sharply; so Eunice had colluded with him! 'Jeremy Arbuthnot is a Sanderson on his mother's side, but now we can only assume that Martin lied about his relationship to him too. They were just partners in fraud. And now it seems they have taken Gwendolen from here, possibly without her consent, and aren't prepared to tell us where she is. You should have told me long ago what was going on.'

'I hardly know myself. Martin doesn't tell me everything.'

'Gwendolen has been coming here over the years, but you never mentioned it to us.'

'I haven't seen so much of you since I married.'

'You've seen a good deal of Dilys and Charlotte. Gwen has stayed here with you recently. She must have said something about her own circumstances. Did Jeremy take her away so she couldn't tell you more? Charlotte said she was covered in cuts and bruises; what did she tell you about those?'

Eunice's face was ravaged; she mopped silently at her eyes with a sodden scrap of lace. Jemima felt in her pocket and offered her the man-size handkerchief she preferred to use herself.

'This has blown up beyond your control. You need help, Gwendolen needs help, but unless you tell us everything, what can we do? Come on, sit up and dry your eyes. Drink your tea.'

Jemima returned to her own cup and drained it. She refilled it, then turned to fill Eunice's.

At last Eunice began to speak. 'Aunt Gwen was at her wits' end. She's frightened of Jeremy, scared stiff. He's asking her for money all the time, and he thumps her if she won't give it to him. Beats her up.'

'Oh my God!' Jemima sat up straighter, though this was what she'd suspected. 'How did she get on with Martin?'

'She's frightened of everybody, including him.'

'That doesn't surprise me. Are *you* frightened of him, Eunice?'

'No, he doesn't hit me or anything like that.'

'I should hope not, but is he kind to you?'

'He's not unkind, if I do as he wants.'

'But he makes you anxious, nervous?'

'Yes.'

'What are you anxious about?'

'His temper. It flares up in a moment, and I never know what he'll do next.' Jemima was trying to get her head round that when Eunice went on, 'He was angry when he found Dilys and Charlotte had been here and had spoken to Gwen. I don't think he wants you to interfere in any way.'

'You're right about that. He's made sure I can't by taking Gwen away.' Jemima was fraught. Jeremy and Martin had made it almost impossible for her to help Gwendolen in any way. But she couldn't allow this to continue.

'Grandma,' Eunice's big eyes were full of desperation, 'I think I might be expecting another baby.' Tears had been running down her face for some time; now a bout of crying overtook her.

'Eunice! I thought I'd sorted that out for you. You said you'd been to the Marie Stopes clinic. Didn't they fit you with a cap?'

243

'Yes,' she sobbed, 'but Martin didn't like the idea. He thinks it's interfering with God's will.'

'I didn't know Martin was religious.'

'He isn't really, but he argued against it every time I wanted to use it. Then he took it away and destroyed it. What am I going to do?' Eunice implored.

Jemima felt stiff with yet another shock. She pulled Eunice close in a hug of sympathy. This was beyond her too. But she had to do something.

'Eunice, I have always respected the sanctity of marriage and believed it should be for life. I've brought you girls up to do likewise. But circumstances can arise that make it difficult. Today has changed my mind. Martin is a manipulative liar. He appears to be thinking of your welfare, but he isn't. To take the cap you got from Marie Stopes was cruel. I think it would be safer for you to come home with me. We could pack a few things now. We'll call a taxi and take Eddie with us.'

She jerked away. 'Leave Martin, you mean?' Her eyes were wide with shock at the enormity of that move. 'And what about Tom? I didn't think you'd suggest . . .'

'You could leave Martin a note and say I've taken you for a little holiday. A rest. Tom is perfectly safe with the girls. It would give us all time to decide on the best thing to do.'

'Martin wants me to stay with him. He says he loves me and the boys.'

'But what do *you* want? Do you love him?'

Eunice stared silently back at her, her eyes red and swollen.

'I couldn't leave, not right away. Not on the spur of the moment like this.' That triggered another bout of tears. 'He'd never forgive me.'

'Are you sure?' It wrung Jemima's heart to see her grand-daughter like this.

Eunice nodded. 'Not today.'

'Martin won't welcome me here, so I'll have to go,' Jemima said reluctantly. 'But you must think of our home as offering a place of safety if things become unbearable for you. With Glyn and Oliver away, we have plenty of room for you and your family.'

She went home alone, troubled and preoccupied.

CHAPTER TWENTY-THREE

THAT SAME EVENING, LOTTIE had arranged to meet Roddy at six o'clock outside Hamilton Square station. He'd suggested they go to the pictures – Laurel and Hardy were on at the Savoy with Jean Harlow – but that would mean it would be quite late when she got home, and she was tired. Instead she was going to suggest they go for a light meal in a new café Dorothy had recommended, and that they go to see the film at the weekend.

During the afternoon, she really wished she had a phone number where she could contact him. If she had, she'd have asked to put their date off until tomorrow. Still, Roddy was always good company, brimming with good spirits. He'd make her feel more awake once they met up.

She hadn't stopped all day, and she had to rush to get away in time to meet him. She stifled a yawn as she drove round to Hamilton Square. The town hall clock was striking six as she parked as near to the station as she could. The central garden was full of flowers and a pleasant place to wait for a few minutes if she had to. She didn't get out of the car.

Roddy was often waiting when she went to meet him, but tonight, for once, he was late. The trains ran frequently from

Liverpool, though, so he'd be here soon. She closed her eyes for a moment; it would revive her, make her feel better, if she rested for a few moments.

She was surprised to hear the clock striking again. Good Lord! It was seven o'clock; she must have dozed off. But what could have happened to Roddy? He'd never let her down like this before, and she didn't believe he ever would if he could help it. He loved her and was quick to show it. Something dreadful must have happened to him! He could have rung her at home last night, or at the office today. They had an arrangement that if they were out, Ted or Dorothy would rush in to take a message.

She was really worried about him, but there was no point in waiting any longer. Whatever had happened must have been very sudden and he'd not had time to let her know. Perhaps he'd left a message for her at home.

She felt thoroughly shaken up as she drove, and when she parked the car in the garage, she was surprised to see another car she didn't recognise pulled up alongside. She was tired and her mind was a whirl of worry about Roddy. The last thing she needed was visitors. Only rarely did somebody drop in to see Grandma without prior invitation.

She went straight to the sitting room and saw all the family there, along with Lazlo and Philip. Everyone had anxious faces.

'I'm glad you've come back early,' Dad said. 'Very wise. How was Roddy?'

'He didn't turn up.' She couldn't stop her concerns pouring out. 'Something must have happened to him. Has he phoned and left a message for me?'

'No.' Harriet looked at a loss. 'I was expecting you home for dinner.'

'I'm sorry, I forgot to tell you I was meeting Roddy. No matter. I'm hungry, I'll be glad of it now. I'll warm it up.'

Harriet followed her into the kitchen. 'I'm afraid you're too late. Lazlo and Philip turned up as we were ready to eat, and Charles had just told us you weren't coming home.' Dirty dishes were piled up waiting to be washed. 'I'll scramble a couple of eggs for you, or I could do boiled ham and salad.'

'I'll have ham and scrambled eggs if I may.'

'Why not? You go and talk to Lazlo and the others. If you promise to help me wash up afterwards, I'll bring it in on a tray.'

Lottie gave her a quick hug. 'You're an angel, Auntie, the tops. Of course I'll help you later.'

'Come and sit down,' Grandma said when Lottie returned to the sitting room. 'What's all this about Roddy? Why didn't he turn up?'

'I don't know. It's not like him. I'm really worried. It must be something dreadful to stop him coming. He wouldn't just leave me to wait and wait. He could have been run over and taken to hospital.'

Lottie realised they were all looking at her. There was pity on Grandma's face. 'It's unlikely that any disaster has happened to him,' she said in a firm, calm voice. 'You can put that right out of your mind. I've learned a great deal about the Sanderson family today.'

For the first time Lottie felt the tension in the room and realised that her grandmother was distressed, very distressed. Worse, the family were nodding agreement. She guessed they'd talked about this in her absence.

'Roddy Onslow claimed to belong to the Sanderson family. He told us he worked at the same sweet factory. You met him at Martin's house, and it looks as though they're all mixed up in this together. I don't think we can trust anything we've been told by them. It's been a stream of lies over the years.'

'We believe Roddy was trying to con you,' Charles said.

'And I'm very glad we refused to give you permission to marry him,' Grandma added.

'No,' Lottie said; she couldn't accept that. 'You've got it wrong. Roddy isn't like that. He wouldn't do that to me.'

She stole a glance at Philip; his face was full of sympathy, but to have him here hearing all this made her more embarrassed and uncomfortable. It was too personal. Too hurtful. Too raw. 'Roddy wouldn't stand me up.'

'Charlotte,' Grandma said, 'I'm afraid he has, so you'll have to accept it. I now believe Gwendolen and Eunice were both married for their money, and Roddy was hoping to catch you.'

'But I don't have any money, nor any expectations of it.'

'It's a question of what Jeremy and Martin believed you would have, and what they told Roddy. He asked me about your position in the family,' Grandma went on. 'Did he ever question you about that?'

He had. That had troubled Lottie too.

Harriet brought her meal in on a tray. She'd set another tray with tea and cake for the others. Lottie had been hungry when she'd set out to meet Roddy, but now she found the food hard to swallow.

Jemima recounted what she'd done that day. 'I've been finding out a good deal about Jeremy Arbuthnot and Martin Sanderson. They've been telling lies for years, and now we've caught them out. Charlotte, didn't Martin tell you that Jeremy was taking Gwendolen to a nursing home?'

With difficulty, she swallowed a mouthful of ham. 'Yes.'

'But when Eunice and I went to see her, we found she wasn't there. Martin changed his story more than once. Finally he said Jeremy had taken her home and would take care of her there. It's very dangerous to inherit a fortune as Gwendolen did. I believe Jeremy has been living off her money for years.'

'Some would say she was exceedingly fortunate,' Harriet said wryly. 'I wish it had happened to me.'

'I agree with you,' Charles said. 'If I had inherited money, it would make it easier to cut my losses now.'

Lottie felt her heart turn over. Gwen was her mother, and she couldn't help but think of her as she'd last seen her, covered in cuts and grazes. She remembered how she'd felt when they'd first met, the intensity of Gwen's gaze and the way she'd choked out her name as Eunice had led her away. Lottie had been haunted by that look in her eyes ever since.

'Mother,' Charles said, 'I think you're getting things out of perspective.' He turned to Lottie; she'd never seen him look so serious. 'Because Gwen has a great deal of money and can do what she likes with it, your grandma is afraid Jeremy is trying to force her to make a will and leave everything to him, and that once she does that he'll kill her so he can get his hands on it.'

Harriet gasped. 'That's a bit far-fetched, isn't it?'

Lottie felt sick and pushed her plate away. Every muscle in her body had gone rigid.

'There's logic behind it,' Jemima said. 'I think Gwendolen has always given money to Jeremy, but now she's reluctant to hand over all he is asking for, so he's treating her roughly – hence her cuts and bruises.'

'You don't know that, Mother,' Charles said, 'and it's ridiculous to think he might murder her. That's going too far.'

'No it isn't. Charlotte, didn't Gwendolen tell you it was Jeremy who gave her that hiding, caused all her cuts and bruises?'

'Yes. No.' She tried to think. 'I'm not sure.'

Grandma said. 'That's what Eunice told me. I believe Gwen has been generous to him over the years, but now she's met up with her daughter and he's afraid her money may go there. Did she get that hiding because she refused to hand over more? Was it because he tried to force her to make a will leaving everything to him? If Gwen doesn't want to do that there'd be no point in forcing her unless he intends to kill her. He'd only get her money when she dies, and if she's alive she can change her will at any time, so he could still end up with nothing.'

Lottie shivered; she could see the point of that, but even so . . .

'Now Jeremy and Martin are hiding her from us so we can't help her. They've removed her from Eunice's care and lied about her whereabouts. I really am worried about her.'

Lottie was horrified. 'What about Eunice? Is it safe to leave her there? Martin could hurt her.'

'He's already hurt her, but he won't kill her,' Grandma said. 'He'd gain nothing by that. He needs her there to receive her monthly payments. That's the only way he can get hold of her money. He'll keep her tied to him. It's Gwendolen's plight that really worries me. We must find her as soon as we can.'

'Can't Eunice find out where he's taken her?' Lazlo asked. 'She's in the best position to do that.'

'No, you haven't seen her recently,' Jemima said. 'Eunice can't help herself. She's incapable of doing anything. Martin was angry when she told him Lottie and Dilys had been there talking to Gwendolen. He doesn't want us to interfere in any way. Eunice wants everything kept low key to stop him being angry with her. He's reduced her to a shaking, weeping shadow of herself who won't take my advice. Oh, and she's frightened she might be pregnant again.'

'What?' Lottie couldn't believe it. 'For heaven's sake! But you fixed it so she could avoid that.'

'I did. She was given a contraption that would have prevented it, but Martin thinks that's against nature and took it from her.'

'But he knows she doesn't want more children, and that she doesn't like being pregnant. It makes her ill. He's putting his principles above his wife's wishes.'

'I don't think it's a question of principles,' Grandma said. 'As I see it, it's his way of controlling her. Making her do exactly what he wants. Pregnancy drains her energy, takes the fight out of her. She can't bring herself to leave him while she's with child. He's ruining her health and he's spending her money, and I don't know what to do about it.'

'You should have persuaded her to come here, removed her from his influence, even if it's just for a week or two.'

'For goodness' sake, Charlotte, I thought of that myself. I wanted to call a taxi straight away, and put her and little Eddie in it, but she refused. She said Martin loves her and wants her to stay with him. She believes that. He's got inside her head.

Now we've talked about this all evening and we're going round in circles. I'm tired out and can do no more. I'm going to bed.'

Harriet was on her feet. 'I'll make some cocoa and bring it to your room. Do we all want a cup ?'

Nobody refused, and when she'd gone to make it, they all sat in silent contemplation for a few minutes. 'We must do something,' Lazlo shivered, 'and we need to be quick about it.'

'We won't be as busy tomorrow,' Lottie said slowly. 'I could go to the office and clear up any outstanding work, and then go over to see her. See what I can find out. Martin will have gone to work by then.'

'Too dangerous,' Dad said shortly. 'If Jeremy can attack Gwen, he can do the same to you.'

'I could go with her,' Lazlo said.

'So could I,' Philip added.

'No,' Lottie said. 'I'll get far more out of Eunice if I go on my own. If either of you was with me, we couldn't talk about personal things. You could spare me tomorrow, couldn't you, Dad?'

'I'm still not happy about it. Martin may not know what Jemima found out from that receptionist, but he's aware that she knows enough to make trouble,' Charles said.

'He and Jeremy see Grandma as the person most likely to cause the trouble, and Dilys as the next danger. They treat me as though I'm barely out of infancy, too young to bother them much.'

Lazlo drained his cup. 'Tomorrow I'm going out to Arbuthnot's house,' he said. 'That's the way forward. I know you said the gardener told you they'd gone away, Mother, but I believe that may have been a red herring. We'll need to watch the house. We know Jeremy goes out and about in his car, so he leaves her on her own. When he does, I'll go in.'

'I'll go with you,' Philip said. 'I'll bring my car over. It'll be easier to keep an eye on the house if we have that.'

'That's kind of you,' Charles said.

Lottie knew Philip was looking at her, but she couldn't meet his gaze. 'I want to help,' he said simply.

'And we need all the help we can get,' Lazlo said. 'Without a car, it's very difficult to keep a watch on premises. I've tried it. Right, we'll do that and come back tomorrow evening to let you know how we got on. Come on, Phil, these people are exhausted; they need to go to bed.'

Charles stood up too. 'Yes, I'm off to bed too. We're all too tired to think now.'

Lottie saw the visitors to the back door, and as it was a clear moonlit night, she walked up the garden with them. 'Perhaps we could meet you somewhere and bring you home,' Lazlo said.

'That would make it easier.' Lottie remembered what she'd done yesterday afternoon. 'Did you get my note? I pushed it under your door. I went to look for you, but you were out.'

'No, I didn't see anything. I'll look again when I get back.'

'I told you I'd seen Gwen, though I don't suppose it would have helped if you'd known sooner. It's very hard to get in touch with you, Lazlo.'

'I'll have to ring you regularly from now on, and perhaps I'll buy myself a car too,' Lazlo said as he got into the passenger seat. 'Goodnight, Lottie.'

She opened the gate for them before going back indoors. She was more than glad to go to bed, but her mind was on fire with the problems facing them and she couldn't get to sleep. It had really scared her to hear Grandma pour out her worries about Gwen and to know she was frightened. She'd never known Grandma to be frightened of anything.

But worst of all was the possibility that Roddy Onslow was hand in glove with Jeremy and Martin. She just couldn't believe that, not Roddy. She still clung to the faint chance that an accident had overtaken him.

She groped under her pillow for her handkerchief and had a little weep, but whether it was for Roddy, her mother or Eunice, she couldn't have said. The hurts and difficulties were overwhelming.

CHAPTER TWENTY-FOUR

AFTER A RESTLESS NIGHT, Lottie got up the next morning feeling desperate to know the truth about Roddy. She realised now that she didn't know much about his background. He had been invited to lunch at Mersey View several times, but he'd never asked her back to his home. She'd met his parents, but only once. He had invited her and her family to Sunday lunch at the Adelphi Hotel in the centre of the city. He'd said they'd find it a long and tedious journey out to the suburb where he lived, and public transport was limited on Sundays. Everything had seemed all right to her then, and his parents had appeared pleasant enough, but it had been a busy restaurant and they'd been a large and affable party. It had been impossible to ask personal questions.

Breakfast over, Lottie drove her father to the office and tried to focus her mind on what she still needed to do for the *Caernarvon*, but almost everything was now in hand. When Charles went next door to have a word with Ted Pascoe, she decided to do some private telephoning.

Roddy had told her that his parents had no telephone at home, and there was no way she could contact him. She'd had no reason not to believe him – most people did not have a telephone in their home – but if Grandma was right, that could be his way of controlling how their relationship developed. It had prevented her from finding out any more about him and his work. She only knew what he'd told her.

She did know his home address, because on days when they didn't plan to meet he usually wrote to her, and she to him. Grandma believed he was in cahoots with Jeremy and Martin and had told her a pack of lies. She meant to find out.

She braced herself, took a deep breath and lifted the phone. She heard the operator say, 'Number, please.' She remembered that Roddy's father had introduced himself as Harold Onslow. She gave his name and address and waited, pencil poised, trying to breathe normally. Would the operator be able to give her a number?

Yes. She felt weak at the knees but managed to scribble it down. So Roddy had lied to her!

'Trying to connect you,' she heard, and then a click and a female voice repeated the number. She felt an icy block in her stomach. She'd been connected to his mother!

She was so nervous the receiver almost slid through her fingers. 'Could I speak to Roddy, please?' she asked.

'He's at work at the moment. He'll be home this evening around half five, if you want to ring again.' She found it almost impossible to believe he'd lied to her! 'Who shall I say called?'

'Sorry to bother you,' she said lamely and quickly put the phone down. Her head sank into her hands. Roddy had said he loved her, asked her to marry him, and now she knew it had all been a scam. She was angry with herself for being taken in. She'd trusted him. She'd really wanted to marry him. It had been her big romance.

She shed a few hot tears and told herself she was a fool.

What must the family think? And Philip? Her handkerchief was damp, but she managed to pull herself together by the time she heard Dad coming back.

'I've finished everything you gave me to do,' she said. 'Can you think of anything else?' Charles shook his head. 'Then I'd like to go over and see Eunice now.'

'All right. Better ring her first and let her know you're coming. I need to go down to the ship to see how the work is getting on, so I'll run you to the station.'

'Thanks, Dad.'

'Be careful about what you say to her. Grandma thinks she's likely to tell Martin everything. Keep your wits about you, and don't forget you can ring us if you need help.'

On the train, she did her best not to think about Roddy's defection. She couldn't believe she'd stopped Philip kissing her because she'd felt disloyal to Roddy. She was not the sort to be taken in by a scam like that. She'd prided herself on being clear-sighted about other people, when obviously she wasn't. She felt ashamed that she hadn't seen through Roddy when Grandma had.

And what was she to say to Philip? He was making his feelings for her quite clear, but how could she go back now and say she'd been wrong? It was embarrassing to admit to herself that she didn't know her own mind, but to say that to Philip? He'd think she had the feelings of a butterfly.

She couldn't go on like this; she had to pull herself together and think of Eunice's problems. She was determined she wouldn't let tears roll down her face in public, nor appear a dithering idiot in front of Eunice.

She was about to ring the doorbell when Eunice came to the

door to let her in. 'I've been watching for you,' she said.

Lottie thought she seemed more fraught than ever and gave her a hug. She could feel no flesh on her bones. 'You're losing weight,' she told her.

Eunice sniffed, and left a damp patch on Lottie's shoulder.

Grandma had told her to invite Eunice and Martin to lunch on Sunday, because she thought it might help if she talked to him about Gwen. When Lottie passed on the invitation, Eunice said, 'Well, he's very busy at the moment, and I'm not sure he'll be able to spare the time. I'll get him to ring Grandma.'

'Eunice, you've got to help us find Gwen. What has Martin said to you about her?'

'Just that Grandma was making a fuss about her yesterday but there's nothing for us to worry about. Uncle Jeremy has taken her to their London flat, where she'll be very comfortable. But I'm not sure—'

'To their London flat? Grandma believed they were staying up here.'

'They were, but the Easter recess will be over soon, so he wanted to get back.'

Lottie took a deep breath. 'That is something we can check,' she said. 'Do you have her London phone number? We'll try and speak to her.'

'It'll be in the book here.' They were still in the hall; Eunice went to the telephone table and her fingers riffled helplessly through the pages.

As Lottie took the book from her, she noticed a movement at the other end of the hall, where it was darker. Eunice had introduced her to Hilda, her new housekeeper. She had an uneasy feeling she was watching them.

She said, 'Eunice, could you rustle up some coffee for us?'

Once the woman had been dispatched to the kitchen, Lottie lifted the phone and asked the operator to connect them. 'Sorry,' she heard, 'that number has been disconnected.' She hadn't expected that, and the operator was gone before she could ask anything else.

She took her sister's arm and hurried her to her little sitting room. 'Would they disconnect their phone if they were living there?' she said. Perhaps Jeremy was trying to shut off calls from the press or the House of Commons. 'Have you ever spoken to Aunt Gwen on this number?'

'Yes, but a long time ago.'

'Has Martin used it recently?'

'Yes, he speaks to Jeremy regularly, every few days.'

Lottie remembered her father's caution. 'Well, we don't know whether Gwen is there or not. I'd say probably not.'

Hilda brought in a tray of coffee and biscuits. She went out, leaving the door slightly ajar. Lottie got up and clicked the latch shut. 'What happened to the other girl, Beryl?'

'Martin said she had taken money from his wallet and sacked her. I liked her better than Hilda.'

That took Lottie's breath away. 'Have you ever missed anything? Did you ever wonder if Beryl was taking things?'

'No, I thought her honest. She was kind and friendly.'

Charlotte drank the coffee and wondered if that was another thing to worry about. Had Martin brought in somebody to keep an eye on Eunice? But she had to come up with something they could do that might help find Gwen. She went out to the hall and brought back Martin's book of phone numbers to leaf through.

Roddy's home number was here, and also another where he could be contacted. That made her feel sick. She'd been really worried when he hadn't turned up last night, but after all the time they'd spent together, after saying he loved her, he'd cared so little for her feelings that he'd let her sit and wait. She'd believed in him utterly, believed all he'd told her, but he'd set out to trap her into marriage for money that she didn't have.

'Could I have a pencil and paper?' she asked. When Eunice brought it, Lottie made a note of any relevant numbers, though she couldn't see what use they might be.

'What are we going to do now?' Eunice asked.

'I'm going to take you out for lunch. It'll do you good to go out. Had you better tell your staff?'

She followed Eunice to the kitchen. Hilda wasn't there, but the cook was. They were living like lords! Until now, she'd given scant attention to Eunice's household, but now she could see why Grandma was worried about what it was costing.

'What are the boys doing this morning? Grandma is bound to ask after them.'

'Grandma knows that Tom has gone to Windermere with the girls. I think Betty will have taken Eddie out for a walk.'

They went upstairs so that Eunice could change her dress. Lottie remembered coming up to see Gwen, and wanted to see the room she'd used. Perhaps she'd left something behind: a notebook, or some clue as to where she'd gone. But the room was pristine. The bed had been remade, everything had been dusted and the lines the Hoover had made on the carpet were clearly visible.

'Christabel didn't want to use it again?' she asked.

'Martin said she must stay in with Emily. That we need a guest room from time to time.'

Lottie followed Eunice to her bedroom. The impression was of a rather masculine room, and again, everything was neat and tidy. Lottie eyed the double bed, and the bedside table on what appeared to be Martin's side. When Eunice went to the bathroom, she tried the top drawer and was surprised to find it locked. So there were things he kept hidden from his wife!

She edged open one of the drawers in his tallboy, but found nothing but handkerchiefs and socks. This was hopeless. She didn't know what she was looking for; she'd drawn a blank.

She refused to let Eunice ring for a taxi, and together they walked down the main road towards the train station and the suburban shopping arcade, where there were several small cafés.

'Which one do you like best?' she asked.

Eunice shook her head. 'I've only ever come here with Dilys. I think it was that one over there.'

'Don't you come for tea and cakes?' Lottie chose a place advertising hot lunches at relatively low prices. There would be plenty of customers at lunchtime from the nearby jam factory, but it was still early and she led her sister to a window table.

Eunice stared at the menu for a long time. Lottie said, 'You've got to eat.'

She chose an omelette. 'I shall have a big dinner with Martin at home tonight.'

Lottie decided on beef and carrots with dumplings. 'Do you know what will be served, or does it appear on the table in front of you like magic?'

'I think roast pork tonight. Martin usually tells Cook what he wants.'

'*You* should tell her what you want,' Lottie said. She changed the subject. 'Before all this trouble started, did you see much of Aunt Gwendolen and Uncle Jeremy? Nobody in our house has been in touch with Gwendolen for donkey's years.'

'Yes, Martin and Jeremy are friends and they're in business together. They came to dinner occasionally, and we went to their house.'

'So you knew Gwen quite well. Tell me what you know about her.'

'I felt sorry for her. She's had such a lot of trouble in her life.'

Their meal was served. Lottie's beef and dumplings came with potatoes and cabbage.

'Go on.'

'A long time ago, Gwen had a love affair that resulted in a baby out of wedlock, and she felt very depressed afterwards, but Jeremy forgave her.'

Lottie was shocked. 'Eunice, I am that baby. Gwen is my mother. I told you the other day.'

'No, I asked Martin about that again, and he says you're wrong.' Eunice's brow was furrowed. 'He said you're just being fanciful. You're my sister, Lottie, I know you are. I watched you grow up.'

'So what does Martin say happened to the baby?'

'Jeremy insisted she have it adopted.' Eunice seemed convinced by what she was saying. Martin must really have been playing with her mind.

'And who was the father?'

'Martin said she took a lover because Jeremy was homosexual. I tried to ask, but Auntie Gwen didn't want to talk about that.'

Lottie took a deep breath. It sounded as though Eunice didn't know about Lazlo, or couldn't accept that he'd played any part. She wasn't accepting any of it. 'Did Gwen talk about his homosexuality?'

'Yes, I think it tried her patience but she said he couldn't change so she forgave him.' Eunice's apathy had gone; she was more like her old self. 'But he didn't tell her about it before they were married. She'd expected to have a normal marriage, and children, but Jeremy didn't like children, he couldn't stand being near them.' Eunice smiled. 'He used to rail against politicians who kissed babies to get votes.'

Lottie cut into her dumpling. She couldn't get Dad's warning out of her mind. She wanted to prod Eunice to go on, but she had to be careful about what she said. Eunice went on anyway.

'Gwen said that when she married Jeremy, he was thought to be quite a catch. He was an MP and going up in the world. She thought he was rich, because he always lived well. He spent far more on clothes and social occasions than our family ever did, but she soon discovered he couldn't live on his income, and that it was her money that paid for running the house. He wanted and expected the very best of everything.

'They got by for the first few years, but they always had a young man living with them. Jeremy gave out that he was a nephew or some relative of hers. They often went out without her when they were in London. She knew that sometimes they went to a gambling den, because she heard them talking about losing large sums. Gwen had started out by being fairly generous to him. She could afford to be. But then she began to resent being left at home. He rarely took her anywhere, but he expected her to be the perfect MP's wife. During the run-up to general elections, she had to work hard to win votes for him.

'She said almost the worst thing about it was Jeremy's anxiety that his homosexuality might become generally known. As an MP, he could not allow any hint of that to be attached to his name, and it was the same with his business clients. There were always tensions, times when a leak almost occurred. It was a constant worry to him.'

'So it's Jeremy's homosexuality that has dogged their happiness?'

'Yes, it affected everything, though nobody talked about it.'

'Grandma does.' It occurred to Lottie that Eunice would not have heard about that episode with Glyn all those years ago, and he wouldn't want her to know now. 'So they spent most of their time in London?'

'When the House was sitting, yes, but they are involved in a business they run together, and what with Jeremy's legal business being based in Liverpool, and his constituency in Southport, they actually spend a lot of time up here. Jeremy used to come round to our house quite often, and I'd go to see Gwen, or she'd come to me. In a way, we've been thrown together. Jeremy didn't like her making other friends because of what he wanted kept hidden. Martin is much the same with me.'

'But at least he's not homosexual.'

'No, though sometimes I wish he was. He's far too keen on that side of married life.'

They walked home together, and as they passed Eunice's hairdresser, Lottie persuaded her sister to make an appointment. She was well pleased with her visit. Eunice had opened up, and let her own resentments and dissatisfactions show. Lottie had learned a lot about her marriage, but she wasn't sure whether any of it would help her find Gwen.

CHAPTER TWENTY-FIVE

LOTTIE WAS WALKING ALONG briskly, thinking of how Eunice had been caught up in problems with her husband and his family, and how close she'd come to that herself with Roddy. Suddenly she realised a car was pulling into the kerb alongside her. It was Philip, driving his new Morris Cowley, and Lazlo was waving from the window.

'Come on.' Lazlo opened the door. 'Get in with us. You'll have to sit on my knee.'

Lottie felt the blood rush to her cheeks, delighted to see that Philip was smiling at her, his usual friendly self. 'Hello, how did you manage to find me like this?'

'We've been watching you and Eunice for some time.'

'I wanted to get her away from home and encourage her to talk.'

'We trailed Martin round a few sweet shops this morning. It looks as though Mother was right. He seemed to be collecting orders from the shops for more stock. Then we went back to his house and saw you leave with Eunice to go out for lunch.'

'You really have been watching us.'

'Nothing better to do.' Lazlo grinned at her. 'We ate in a snack bar across the road from you. It wasn't much good. We could see you tucking in through the window.'

'But you didn't find out anything useful?'

'Only that we knew where to pick you up. We let you get out of sight of the house first.'

'Thank you, this is a great help to me.' Lottie tried to get more comfortable on Lazlo's knee. 'I had my suspicions about Eunice's new housekeeper. She seemed to be watching me and listening to what we were saying. That's why I took Eunice out.'

'Was that worthwhile?'

'Oh yes, she really let her hair down. She wouldn't have opened up like that if we hadn't been alone. Martin had told her that Gwen and Jeremy had gone to their London home, so I tried to call there but found the phone had been disconnected.'

'Where is she then?' said Lazlo. 'She can't just disappear.'

'Oh! And Martin has convinced her that Gwen isn't my mother at all.'

'You've done very well, Lottie,' Philip said.

'Yes, but I learned nothing that would help us find Gwen.'

'We'll find her,' Lazlo said. 'With all of us on the lookout like this, we're bound to.'

'Where are we going now?'

'Into town. We didn't have much lunch and we could do with a cup of tea. I'm sorry I'm not able to provide that in my new home.'

'Count me out,' Lottie said. 'I need to go home now. Grandma and Dad will be waiting to hear how Eunice is and what I've done.'

'I'll drop you at James Street station, shall I?' Philip said. 'By the way, there is one piece of news Lazlo hasn't told you yet: we went to order a new car for him and found he would have to wait ten days for delivery. So he decided on a second-hand Riley. Only two years old and he can pick it up tomorrow.'

'My goodness, you don't hang about.'

'Philip has let me have a go on this one. I think I'll manage to drive all right.'

'Of course you will. All it takes is a bit of practice.'

'Once I've got it, I'm going to keep a watch on Arbuthnot. He still comes to his office, so he and Gwen must be somewhere close. Perhaps he'll lead us to her. I don't understand why he's trying to hide her.'

'You heard Grandma's theory. It might be too awful to believe, but she's always right.'

Later that evening, Lottie was washing up after their meal and Grandma was setting the table for breakfast when the telephone rang. Harriet went to answer it, swinging her tea towel.

'Mother,' she said, 'it's for you. I think it's Martin, but he didn't say he recognised my voice or anything; just asked to speak to you.' She came back to the kitchen and picked up another plate to dry, then returned to the door, eager to find out what was being said. Lottie joined her to listen.

'Martin, we all of us lead busy lives. If you really are too busy to come on Sunday, what about Tuesday evening? . . . All right, Wednesday then?' Grandma's face was showing outrage as she listened. 'We're all worried about Gwen, we need to know what's going on.'

She listened again, for longer this time. Lottie could see she was making an effort to hold her anger in check. 'Martin, I'm not sure I'm getting the true picture here. Let me speak to Eunice.' Her mouth opened in shock, and then in a very controlled voice she said, 'Goodbye, Martin,' and put the phone down before letting out a wail of frustration.

Charles came to the sitting-room door. 'What did he say?'

Jemima was waving her arms about. 'That Eunice wasn't able to speak to me because she's upstairs saying goodnight to the children. But I know for a fact that he's lying, as she only has Edgar there at the moment. Also, that he and the family have a lot on their plate, a really busy weekend. He hopes we won't be offended but he wants to put it off to another time.'

'So what are you going to do?'

'What *can* I do if he won't come near or even discuss this on the phone?'

'I thought Eunice had told me all her problems,' said Lottie, 'but I'm beginning to wonder if there's more. Gwen stayed with her. They seem to have been supporting each other. I must see her again.'

'That makes me worry about you,' Charles said. 'Jeremy must be feeling desperate now. I don't want him to attack you.'

'Dilys has always been close to Eunice,' Grandma said. 'She would be the most likely person for Eunice to unburden herself to.'

'Perhaps she already knows things that we don't,' Lottie said. 'She was worried about Eunice before we were. She and Alec are due back from their honeymoon today. I'll ring her and see how they got on.'

'You'd better tell her about the latest developments,' Jemima said.

Lottie rang Dilys at her new home. 'We've had a marvellous time, of course.' Her sister sounded full of life and went on enthusiastically about the hotel and all that they'd done. Lottie hadn't the heart to worry her about Eunice when she was so obviously happy.

'You'll have to tell her tomorrow,' she said to Grandma.

That night Lazlo didn't sleep well, anxiety keeping him tossing and turning for hours, but he was up early, ready for Philip to collect him to take him to the garage.

The handsome little green and black Riley was waiting on the forecourt as they walked up. Now that it had been polished up, it looked brand new, and far more robust than Charles's Austin Seven. He liked the look of it.

It took the salesman more than an hour to explain the controls and complete the paperwork, but at last Lazlo was free to drive away. He'd felt some trepidation at the thought of navigating through the centre of Liverpool, but once he was in the driving seat, as Lottie had predicted, he felt more confident.

He'd already noticed that there were not that many cars on the roads. There were far more motorbikes, many with sidecars. There were also buses and trams, but the really heavy trucks and lorries kept to the main roads leading to the docks. Parking he found was easy almost anywhere, and there was no problem about leaving the car overnight outside his lodgings.

But that afternoon was a complete washout as far as following Arbuthnot was concerned. They didn't catch so much as a glimpse of him.

The following day was also a waste of time. That afternoon, over a cup of tea and a scone with Philip in a tea room not far from his lodgings, Lazlo pondered their problem. 'What I don't understand,' he said, 'is why Jeremy has started hitting Gwen now. They've been married for well over twenty years, he's known from the start that she had money, and I'm sure she'll always have used it to enhance their lifestyle, so what has changed? This is a terrible turn for the worse.'

Philip offered no answer and Lazlo could not confide his agony to one so young. He'd told Gwen he loved her, she'd borne him a child, yet by sending the police after Jeremy in that public toilet, he was afraid that he'd upset him to such a degree that he'd lost control and started to knock her about. He could think of no other reason. The last thing he'd ever want to do was to increase Gwen's difficulties; she was the only woman he'd ever loved.

Philip stood up. 'I'm going home. Mum and Dad are expecting guests for dinner. We'll do the same tomorrow, shall we?'

'Yes, and hope for better luck. Come on the train,' Lazlo said. 'We really must find out what Arbuthnot does with his time. We won't need two cars for that.'

He watched Philip walk out, then drained the teapot into his cup and pondered on the past. He'd originally gone to West Africa on the same terms that Philip had done: one tour of two years to learn the business there, on the understanding that he'd return to head office to pursue his career in Liverpool afterwards.

Meeting Gwen had changed his life. He'd fallen in love with her and offered to support her while she divorced Jeremy. He'd wanted to marry her, and had fully expected her to accept. He'd been so sure she loved him, but there were ties that had kept her close to Arbuthnot. Ties that he didn't understand.

He knew she'd felt guilt at loving him and letting Jeremy

down. She had decided to persevere with her marriage, and that had made him seek a permanent career in West Africa. Neither of them had realised at the time that there was a baby on the way. That had altered everything.

When he'd received her letter telling him she was pregnant, he'd offered to return to England straight away. He'd been ready to throw up his career if that was what was needed. He would never have abandoned her. It was his turn to feel guilt well up from his stomach, knowing he'd brought her nothing but trouble.

When he heard she'd given up her baby daughter, he'd been afraid that she cared after all more for Jeremy Arbuthnot than she did for him and his child. He'd told himself he must put her right out of his mind; that she didn't want him. And now that Jeremy was in real difficulty, when he was ill treating her, she was staying close to him. He couldn't understand that, but could a third person ever really know what went on within a marriage?

His mother's theory that Jeremy must mean to kill Gwen had made his blood had run cold. He'd felt as though he had a block of ice lodged in his stomach for hours afterwards.

Suddenly he realised that the tea room was closing and the staff were waiting for him to go. That meant it was 5.30 and time he went home for his dinner, though he no longer had any appetite. He had to do something about Gwen's plight. He ought to alert the police. Get professional help to find her.

He was walking back to his lodgings, trying to throw off his feelings of guilt and fear, when he saw a policeman. 'Where is the nearest police station?' he asked, and was given directions. He told the officer on the desk something of his problem and waited impatiently for an officer to come and talk to him, though in fairness it couldn't have been all that long.

It took him much longer to explain all the details of Gwen's disappearance and for a second detective to come and note them down. It seemed to Lazlo that the more he talked about his suspicions, the more far-fetched they seemed. When he gave them Jeremy Arbuthnot's name and address, even the officers looked as though they didn't believe him. They asked question after question, and by the time he'd signed his statement and was free to leave, he felt as though he'd been put through a wringer.

But he felt better; he had at least done something that might help Gwen. He went home to find that his fellow lodgers had eaten and gone to their rooms, but his landlady had kept his dinner for him and was ready to warm it up. It was a bit dry, but his appetite had returned and he ate with gusto. He felt he'd done the right thing.

Lottie was at work the next day when Dilys rang her. 'Grandma's just been talking to me about how worried you all are about Eunice. You should have told me last night.'

'I hadn't the heart, you sounded so happy. You're still on your honeymoon and you need to get things settled in your house.'

'It doesn't matter when we get the house organised; Eunice is more important. Alec and I will go over and take her out to lunch. I want them to get to know each other better, and I'll find out what she knows about Gwen's whereabouts. Eunice always tells me everything.'

She certainly used to, Lottie thought, but things were

different now. Jeremy Arbuthnot seemed to be menacing them all, and Alec's presence might prevent Eunice from disclosing her secrets.

'Come round tonight and let us know how you get on. Dad and Grandma are very concerned too.'

After lunch, Lazlo telephoned her to say, 'Everything went wrong this morning and I'm cross about it. Philip came over early and we were out at Arbuthnot's house in time to see him set out. We followed him and he drove into town and parked near Central Station. I left Philip to park the car and trailed behind Jeremy into Lewis's, but I lost him in the kitchenware department. It was quite busy.'

'There are stairs straight down to the underground from that department store,' Lottie said. 'He could have gone anywhere.'

'Yes, I know, but we didn't know whether he'd done that or was just shopping. We hung around watching his car and saw him come back, but it was over two hours later, so we are still no wiser.'

'Lazlo, you need patience for detective work.'

'I don't know how the police stand it. I've reported Gwen as a missing person. They're on the case but they don't seem to be making any more progress than we are.'

'They will, but these things take time.'

'It's damn boring. We followed Jeremy when he came back to his car, but he got through some traffic lights and we didn't. I went round to his business, but his car wasn't there; I think he must have gone somewhere else. We'll have another go tomorrow, but for the moment I'm at a loss. I don't know what else I can do.'

'Come round to see us at home tonight,' Lottie said. 'Dilys will be there; she and Alec are visiting Eunice today. Perhaps they'll have more news.'

During the afternoon, Philip phoned her. 'I'm at a loose end, and even Lazlo is depressed. I'd be much cheered if you'd come out with me tonight. I'd be delighted to take you anywhere you'd like to go.'

She felt hot with embarrassment again. She really would have to admit to him that she'd made a fool of herself over Roddy. The thought made her cringe, but she needed to know where she stood with him.

'You're very kind, Phil, but I'm sorry, I can't.' She told him what was arranged for the evening. 'Why don't you come round too, so that you're up to date with what's happening? They've agreed to come at seven thirty.'

'Thanks, I'll do that,' he said.

That evening, their guests started arriving while they were still eating. Dilys and Alec came first, followed soon after by Lazlo and Philip. Lottie smiled at Philip; she was trying to treat him as she would have done if Roddy had never existed. That wasn't difficult with the family all round them.

Harriet had just brought a freshly baked rhubarb tart to the table for their pudding, and each of the guests accepted a slice. Dilys looked well, with rosy cheeks and a light suntan, but her joy of the previous evening was gone. 'I was shocked to see Eunice,' she said. 'She's a nervous wreck.'

'You've said that before,' Lottie reminded her.

'She's getting worse.'

Jemima took a deep breath. 'Dilys, you're closer to her than the rest of us,' she said. 'Had you seen Gwendolen there before she came with those injuries?'

'Yes, she and Uncle Jeremy were invited to dinner when I was living there. Martin and Jeremy were on good terms; they talked business together. I don't understand what's changed.'

'What sort of business? Do you mean the legal practice?'

Dilys shook her head. 'I'm not sure. It was something they were doing that earned money. Eunice and Gwen were friendly. I'd even say they were close.'

'So what did they talk about when the men weren't with you?'

'Women's stuff generally. There was one afternoon when Eunice asked Aunt Gwen about, you know, Jeremy's homosexuality and how it had affected them. It seemed Jeremy had had a young man called Colin living with them for the past six years. And before that there had been someone else.'

'That is interesting,' Lazlo said. 'How did Gwen feel about having these young men in her house?'

'I think deep down she resented it, but she tolerated them for Jeremy's sake.'

'Was she upset because Jeremy showed them more affection than he did her?'

Dilys sighed. 'I think he did show her affection too. They seemed like a normal married couple.'

'They can't have done,' Grandma said. 'They weren't.'

'They were at ease with each other,' Dilys insisted. 'You know, companionable. Jeremy helped her into her coat and opened doors for her. He was always very polite. Aunt Gwen wasn't afraid of him. Not at that point, I'm certain of it. But this isn't getting us any nearer finding her now. What are we going to do?'

'Tomorrow Philip and I will make another effort to find out where Jeremy goes,' Lazlo said. 'I can think of no other way but to follow him and hope he'll lead us to her.'

'And I can only suggest I try again to get more from Eunice,' Dilys said.

'We still haven't made much progress.' Lottie was despondent. She got up to clear the table. 'I'll wash up.'

She carried a pile of used plates to the kitchen. Philip did the same and took the tea towel from Harriet. 'You can leave this job to us,' he told her. 'Your pie was delicious, you deserve a rest. Why don't you go and talk to the others?'

'Mother will want a cup of coffee,' she said, and filled the kettle.

'We'll make it,' Lottie said. She had to talk to Philip about Roddy, get that out into the open. Clear this embarrassment she could feel between them. She'd been screwing up her nerve since she'd asked him to come tonight.

'OK, you want to be alone.' Harriet left and closed the kitchen door behind her.

'What I have to go through to have a private word with you.' Philip smiled, reaching for some cutlery to dry.

'I'm sorry,' Lottie said. 'I know I've made a perfect fool of myself over Roddy Onslow.'

'You mustn't blame yourself. I'm jolly glad you've found out what he was doing. You could have ended up like Eunice married to him.'

'I have Grandma to thank for that. She put the brakes on.'

'Look, I want to help you. I know you're a bit down because

of all that, and you also have this crisis with Gwendolen to deal with, but Lottie, you know how I feel about you.'

'Yes,' she said, and that was another thing she should say to him, but she was too late: he'd tossed the tea towel aside and was coming closer. His smile was tender and loving and she knew he was about to kiss her, a real lover's kiss with his arms holding her tight against him.

Without thinking, she turned her head so his kiss landed on her neck. Instantly he released her and jerked away from her. Lottie felt like crying. He looked bereft, and she knew she'd really hurt him now. 'I'm sorry, Phil,' she said. 'I'm sorry. I'm just not ready for romance. I can't forget how Roddy deliberately lied to me, misled me.' She fumbled for her hankie. 'I suppose you're going to say that's better than feeling I'm still in love with him.'

'You're better off without him, Lottie.'

'I know that, but he's made me feel an utter fool, and I'm just not ready for more yet. I think it has left me half dead inside. Be patient with me. You've always been my friend and I need you more than ever.'

His smile was hesitant. 'That sounds more like the old Lottie.' He gave her a little hug. 'I'm sorry, I shouldn't have rushed you.'

'I wish I'd never set eyes on Roddy.'

'He was out to catch you, doing his best to make you like and admire him.'

'He succeeded.'

'Let me try and do the same. I very much want to succeed too.'

'I've always liked you, Phil, we're good friends, but what

you're looking for now is love.'

'That's true, but there is no better basis for love and marriage than friendship.'

She nodded, unable to speak, afraid that tears were about to pour down her face.

'Why don't you let me take you out one evening?' he said. 'We could have a meal or go to the pictures or something.'

'My mind is overflowing with worry about Gwen. I feel I should concentrate on how we might find her.'

'It might relax you to have an evening away from that, and help you think more clearly. Both you and Lazlo are in a flat spin about this. Your heads must be going round in circles.'

She tried to smile. 'I'll not be very good company, but I'll come out with you tomorrow night. We can't do anything in the evenings anyway that would help with this search.'

'Good. What about a drink at the yacht club? There's nothing special on, but if the weather's good, it's nice to watch the sun go down over the river. Then we could eat there or go into town for a light supper. Dad reckons the food is good at the Central Hotel.'

Lottie nodded, feeling thankful. At least she now knew where she stood with Philip.

CHAPTER TWENTY-SIX

THE NEXT MORNING, LOTTIE went with Charles to the office as usual. They dealt with the morning post and she typed a couple of letters, then about eleven she set off to see Eunice again.

The housekeeper let her in. 'Your sister isn't too well this morning,' she said. 'She's having a lie-in. If you'd wait a few moments in her sitting room, I'll let her know you're here.'

'No, I'll go up,' Lottie said, making for the stairs. 'Martin has gone out, hasn't he? Then there's no need to bring her down here if she isn't feeling well.'

It was already after midday. The curtains in Eunice's room had not been opened; her untouched breakfast tray had been pushed across the double bed to Martin's side. Eunice was struggling to sit up, and Lottie could see she was in a terrible state, her face pale and tear-stained and her eyes red and swollen.

She sat on the bed and threw her arms round her sister. 'What's happened?' She knew immediately that some new problem was worrying her, but it took Eunice some time to get the words out. 'Martin discovered last night that the police are investigating Jeremy's business affairs. He went berserk. He was absolutely beside himself with fury.'

'Why?' Lottie wasn't sure how that would affect Eunice.

'He's in partnership with him, isn't he? The police are asking all sorts of questions and he's afraid they'll come here and start questioning me.'

'But you don't know anything about his business affairs, do you?'

'That's what he's told me to say.'

'You do, then?'

'No!'

Lottie drew back the curtains. 'I came over to take you out to lunch again. If we go out, you won't have to worry about questions from the police.'

'No, I look terrible, I feel—'

'Go to the bathroom and have a wash. You'll feel better when you're dressed.'

The room was a mess, with clothes strewn everywhere. Lottie opened Eunice's wardrobe. It was crammed with smart clothes, and she chose an outfit for her and laid it out on the crumpled bed.

This time they went into town on the bus. As Lottie had hoped, Eunice began to relax and talk as soon as they were away from the house. They went to the restaurant in the Adelphi Hotel. She ordered a glass of white wine for each of them. 'You're pushing the boat out today,' Eunice said.

'Not really. I'm going to order the set business lunch, because you might eat more if the food is put in front of you, and we know it'll all be very nice.'

Lottie tried to show her sister that she was sympathetic, that she realised she was in a difficult position. Within ten minutes Eunice was starting to get things off her mind. 'Auntie Gwen has always had problems,' she said, 'but they took a turn for the worse when Jeremy's live-in boyfriend had an argument with her. He'd been living with them for six years and they were always having tiffs, but this one was the mother and father of a row.

'He had another noisy argument with Jeremy when he came home from work, and the next morning he packed and left without saying a word to either of them. He took some of Gwen's jewellery and also some money with him. Jeremy was furious and blamed her. It led to him trying to find a replacement and getting caught in that public lavatory. Martin was horrified, and of course it has landed Jeremy in big trouble. He'll never recover from this.'

Now that Lazlo had a car, he was getting out and about by himself. Twice he'd been out to take another look at Gwen's house, though he only stayed long enough to assure himself that she wasn't there.

He'd seen a woman on his earlier visit and he'd mentioned her to Dilys, who asked Eunice about the staff Jeremy kept. Apparently they employed a woman who came three times a week for a few hours when they weren't there, to keep the place aired and make sure everything was all right. When they were living there, she did the heavy cleaning. There was also an Irish maid who travelled with them between London and Liverpool.

Lazlo had told the family that he'd reported Gwen as missing to the police. Charles had said, 'It was the right thing to do. We need all the help we can get. Perhaps we'll get somewhere now.'

'But we'll carry on looking just the same,' Lazlo said.

Philip was coming to his lodgings this morning to join him, so he'd had a fairly leisurely start. He was ready to go out when the landlady shouted up telling him that a man was here asking for him. It couldn't be Philip, because she knew him. He went down, and the rather stout gentleman showed him police identification. 'I've been looking into the whereabouts of the person you reported as missing,' he said.

'Please come up to my room.' Lazlo felt the need to distance himself from his landlady, and leapt up the stairs full of eager anticipation. He had to wait on the top landing until the detective came up puffing and blowing. As soon as he opened his door, he was reminded that he'd had kippers for breakfast and the tray containing the bones and dirty dishes was still here. Opening his window a little, he invited the man to sit on the sofa, which faced the other way, so he would not see his unmade bed either.

'About Mrs Gwendolen Arbuthnot,' the detective began once he'd got his breath back. 'I went out to the address you gave us and interviewed the caretaker, a Mrs Gladys Roberts. She assures me that the Arbuthnots went on holiday . . . let me see . . .' He took out a notebook and read off a date shortly after Jeremy had come out on bail. 'She doesn't know when they will return.'

Lazlo tried to explain why he didn't believe that.

'The caretaker tells me that they also employ a gardener and a maid, a Mr Cormack Kelly and a Miss Bridget O'Malley. The caretaker says that all are in receipt of their wages and Miss O'Malley was also given her fare to Ireland, where she has gone for her annual holiday. Mrs Roberts showed me a picture postcard she'd received from her that morning. All seems to be normal there, Mr Mortimer.'

Lazlo attempted again to convey why he was anxious about Gwen.

'I do understand all that,' the detective said. 'Mrs Roberts gave me the name and address of a relative of the Arbuthnots . . .'

Lazlo could already guess. 'Martin Sanderson,' he said.

'Yes, he confirms that they have gone on holiday; that Mr Arbuthnot is in a difficult position, being a well-known person who has been receiving unwelcome attention from the press. You do understand, Mr Mortimer?'

He understood all right.

'We don't believe Mrs Arbuthnot to be in any danger, and we feel you have no reason to worry about her.'

Lazlo felt he'd been let down with a bump. 'That's it, then?'

'For the moment. We'll keep the case on file, of course.'

Lazlo showed the detective to the top of the stairs and went back to collapse on his sofa. He didn't doubt for one moment that Gwen was in danger. Hadn't Charlotte seen her covered with cuts and bruises? Charlotte had a clear head and both feet firmly on the ground. She had told the truth. Martin had pulled the wool over that detective's eyes.

When Philip arrived, he had to relate the bad news to him. It robbed them of any optimism. 'We've got to do something, haven't we?' Philip said,

Lazlo sighed heavily. 'Let's go and have another look at that solicitor's business they appear to be running together. Come on, it isn't far.'

They rounded a corner and Lazlo couldn't believe his eyes.

Jeremy Arbuthnot's car was parked right outside his office. Both men were heartened to have had immediate success.

'Optimism returns.' Philip smiled.

'I'll park where we can keep an unobtrusive eye on the place, and then when he moves we can follow him.'

'With luck he'll lead us to Gwen this time.'

Quite soon, they were surprised to see a police car come slowly down the road and stop outside the office. Two men in plain clothes got out and went inside. 'Gosh, something is happening,' Philip said.

'Yes, they looked like detectives.' Lazlo's faith in the police had dwindled, but he said, 'In anticipation of having some action, let's change places. You're the better driver and we don't want to lose him today.'

They had to wait forty minutes to see the detectives come out, and twenty minutes after that, Martin arrived looking anxious and went inside. They waited and waited. Philip had brought a flask and some sandwiches. They were having an early lunch when the front door opened again and both Jeremy and Martin appeared. They each got into their respective cars and drove one behind the other into the centre of town, parking outside the Adelphi Hotel. 'They're going to have a better lunch than we've had,' Philip said.

'Bad news, this is going to mean more waiting.' Lazlo was afraid the pair would turn round and recognise him, so Philip followed them up the steps and confirmed that they'd gone into the restaurant.

They spent almost an hour and a half watching the crowds of shoppers and taking turns to read the two newspapers they'd brought. 'A leisurely lunch,' Lazlo said.

'Or they've a lot to discuss.'

When the two men came out, they stood by Jeremy's car still discussing something. Eventually they said their goodbyes, and Jeremy drove towards the river. Philip started the car and followed.

'He's heading back to his business premises,' Lazlo said, dreading a further wait, but instead Jeremy led them down to the Pier Head. 'Oh goodness, he's going to join the queue for the luggage boat. We'll have to wait until he buys his ticket and goes back to his car, then I'll get ours.'

'Thank goodness there isn't a boat tied up at the moment. At least we have plenty of time.'

'Better wait a few minutes; you don't want to be the car immediately behind him in the queue.'

'It looks as though this is a slack time to go over to Birkenhead. Only six vehicles will be crossing on this ferry.'

'Look, Philip, I think you'd better do this on your own. He won't recognise you. I don't want him to see me because he'll know he's being followed. Not now, when it looks as though he's going to lead us to Gwen.'

'OK, you go to your lodgings,' Philip said. 'I'll see you there later.'

Lazlo slipped out of the car and strode quickly to the ticket office, from where he watched Philip drive on to the ferry. He felt thoroughly frustrated by this detective work; it was all hanging about. After an interminable morning, he would still see no action today.

He walked towards his lodgings and had a cup of tea and a cake in the nearby tea room. Then he went home, but he had no book to read, and he'd left the newspapers they'd bought in the car. Not that it mattered; he'd read most of them. He fell asleep on his bed.

He was woken by Philp's tread on the stairs, and shot to the door to let him in, full of anticipation that the news would be good. As soon as he saw his face, he knew it was a false hope.

'I'm sorry, I lost him in Birkenhead. There was a mammoth funeral procession taking place there, some recent mayor of the borough. Jeremy got past but the policeman on point duty held me up. I drove round looking for him but he'd got clear away.'

'Can't be helped,' Lazlo said, but he was overwhelmed with disappointment.

That evening, Lottie came home to find that Lazlo had phoned his bad news through to Grandma. She and the rest of the family felt disheartened. She didn't feel much like going out, but Philip came round to pick her up and join in the perennial family discussion about where Gwen might have been taken.

She cheered up when they reached the yacht club. She considered it a treat to be taken there. Philip ordered two glasses of wine and they sat at a table near the window. There were only two or three members in the bar at this early hour, but they all knew Philip and called greetings. It had been a pleasant sunny day and she was sorry the evening had grown too chilly to sit outside, but the view through the window of yachts moored in the river was very pleasant. Beyond them, on the Liverpool bank, the lights were just coming on and winking in the dusk.

Two more men came in, one with a traditional naval beard, and Lottie heard someone say: 'I was hoping you'd be in tonight, Alfred. One of my neighbours is interested in the boat you have for sale. When would be a good time for you to show him over it?'

The newcomer sighed. 'Too late,' he said. 'I wish you'd told me that last week.'

'Why? Have you sold it?'

'I thought I had. Haven't you heard? I let it go to Jeremy Arbuthnot, but his cheque bounced. He's promised to pay, and asked for a week to get the money together, but I've got a bad feeling he isn't going to manage it, so I've been to the bank and this afternoon I went to the police. Unfortunately, neither wants to take any action until his deadline has passed. The thing is, I've got a new job in Toronto and I'm leaving next Wednesday.'

'It's a lot of money to lose,' his friend sympathised.

'More than I can afford.'

'This is the *Lady Rowena*?' Philip asked. Over the years Alfred Hatton had won many races in the club's regattas and was a keen and experienced sailor. 'Where has Arbuthnot taken her?'

'I wish I knew. I saw him head downriver, but once out in the Irish Sea, he could have gone anywhere. The boat hasn't been seen since.'

'This is the first lead we've had so far,' Lottie breathed. 'Though I'd never thought of Jeremy being a sailor.'

Philip tossed the wine that remained in his glass down in one gulp. 'What about Gwen?'

'She comes from a seafaring family and was probably taught to sail when she was young, but I'd say the last thing she'd want as a present is a yacht. I don't think she's strong enough to manage the *Rowena*. Not well enough either.'

'But if they want to hide her where we would never think of looking, what better place than a boat?'

'I was thinking the same,' Lottie said. 'If we can find the *Lady Rowena*, the chances are we'll find my mother.'

'Shall we go and get something to eat straight away, so we can go back to your place to tell your family about this? It gives us a whole new area to search.'

Lottie felt a quiver of excitement. 'Let's head straight home. I know a good place to buy fish and chips in Rock Ferry; we could stop there on the way.'

The shop was near the pier and the ferry house, and as they were hungry, they sat in the car and ate the food straight away.

'Sorry about this,' Lottie said when they'd finished. 'Your car now smells like a fish and chip shop. We've covered the lovely scent of new leather.'

'I'm not worried about that.' Philip smiled. 'I feel we're making progress and I'm so pleased.' He sniffed. 'It has left a bit of a stink, but we'll drive with the windows open and soon get rid of that.'

Lottie could hardly sit still in the passenger seat. 'What a shame we can't phone Lazlo. It would cheer him up to know about this.'

The family were surprised to see them. Harriet and Grandma were clearing away after the evening meal, and Dad joined them in the kitchen to find out what had brought Lottie back early.

'This is the first time we've heard anything of Gwen,' he said. 'Perhaps we'll get somewhere now.'

'It must mean she's on this side of the river,' Philip said.

'That's why Arbuthnot came over on the luggage boat this afternoon.'

'What a good job you got *Seagull* out,' Charles said. 'If we're looking for a yacht, best thing is to take to the water.'

'Where should we start looking?' Lottie wanted to know.

'Well, the West Float is probably your best bet. We have the *Cheshire* mothballed at a berth there, and there are other similar vessels tied up. But you should look carefully round the East Float as you go through. Neither is as busy as we would like at the moment.'

Charles was getting out his tide timetables and his charts of the river to look for a place where the *Lady Rowena* might have been moored so as not to attract attention when the phone rang. It was Lazlo, so Lottie was able to bring him up to date with their news. 'I'll come over early,' he said. 'Do I need to bring my car?'

'No,' she decided. 'Dad has one and so has Philip. We're thinking of using our sailing dinghy.'

Philip took the receiver from her. 'I'll collect you from Hamilton Square station at quarter to seven tomorrow,' he told him.

For once washing-up was abandoned and the kitchen table was cleared so that the charts could be spread out. 'You'll need to search the Birkenhead bank carefully,' Charles said, 'and plan a route so you miss nothing.'

Chapter Twenty-Seven

T HEY WERE LATE GOING to bed, having stayed up
discussing every aspect of the search they planned to
make. In order to catch the tide before it left *Seagull* high and
dry on the mud, Charles and Lottie had to be ready to set out
at 6.30 a.m. It was chilly, dark and drizzling, not a morning
they'd have chosen to be out on the river.

Lottie went prepared for wet weather with a heavy pullover,
sou'wester and oilskins. Harriet had provided her with
sandwiches, a flask of hot soup and another of tea. Philip had
to wait for Lazlo who caught the first early train bringing the
workmen over to Cammell Laird's.

Charles kept *Seagull* well inshore, and when he saw them
coming across the mud, he steered to meet them in the
shallowest water where she would still float. He got out before
they got in. Lazlo took over the rudder from Lottie, and they
headed downriver. She and Philip adjusted the sails for
maximum speed. 'Not much wind today,' Lazlo said. 'It'll be a
slow trip.'

He and Philip were more at home on water than they were
on land, but the high spirits of last night's planning had
evaporated in the cold reality of morning. 'Visibility isn't good,'
Philip said. 'It won't be easy to spot *Rowena*.'

'May be a good thing,' Lazlo said. 'It'll make it more difficult for anybody to see us nosing round. Going about, watch the boom.'

For Lottie, seeing familiar landmarks from the water was a treat, because these days she didn't often come out on the river. She had to strain her eyes to make out the yacht club through the mizzle, though they were passing the huddle of yachts moored in front of it and were close inshore. The big buildings at Pier Head on the Liverpool bank a mile away were lost in the mist.

They were passing Rock Ferry pier. 'The ferries are still running,' she said; she could see one tied up ready to take workers across to the city. They tacked past the boatyard where *Seagull* had been built eighteen years earlier. Because the deep water of the Sloyne stretched all down this bank, there was safe sailing well away from the busy commercial shipping lanes.

The docks used by the big ocean-going liners were all on the Liverpool side of the river. Over the years, ships had increased steadily in size, and that meant the docks had had to be improved and extended frequently. Liverpool was a prosperous port and had had more investment to keep pace with developments. The docks there were all man-made, built from stone and iron. On the Birkenhead side there were natural inlets providing sheltered areas, so the docks extended over several hundreds of acres. But they were old-fashioned, and in the present downturn in trade, many were unused and falling into disrepair.

The rain began to fall more heavily, pitting the muddy swirling water. 'We'll have to start bailing out if this carries on,'

Lazlo joked. The Birkenhead ferry came out of the mist, heading for its berth at Woodside, and Lottie heard the bells ring as it gave way for them. 'This murk is getting thicker,' he said. 'I hope it isn't going to be a real pea souper.' Already they could hear ships ringing their bells to warn of their approach.

They were passing Morpeth Dock, where the Mortimer Line coastal vessels *Denbigh* and *Caernarvon* docked to discharge their slate. 'It's too early for *Denbigh* to be in yet,' Lottie said, but *Seagull* was so small and low on the water, she couldn't see which vessels were tied up.

In order to get into the Alfred Dock, they had to go through a lock, but they were in luck: they could see a freighter man-oeuvring to enter, and they went in at the same time. From there they could sail into the East Float, with its countless wharves and jetties and endless warehouses stretching along the bank. They looked eerie in the mist.

Inside the dock, there were several large seagoing vessels. With their steep sides, they looked immense from *Seagull*'s vantage point. 'Gives me the feeling of being in a cockleshell,' Philip said.

'It's years since I've been here, but nothing much has changed,' Lazlo said. 'This one's Vittoria Wharf.' They all knew that this was the biggest dock on this side of the river, where vessels from all over the world were stationed. They sailed on under the bridge into the West Float. 'That's Canada Creek on the left bank,' Lazlo pointed out. 'Then Ranks Creek. Wheat comes in from Canada and is milled there.

It was an industrialised area, with graving docks, oil tanks, cranes, warehouses, mills and sheds of every sort, many rusting.

Small factories had been thrown up for various businesses that had long since ceased to function. 'It looks a depressing place,' Philip said.

'Especially today through this murk,' Lottie agreed. The further they went in, the less busy it became. 'Look, there's the *Cheshire*.'

'She's not the only mothballed vessel here,' Philip said, looking round.

'It's a positive graveyard,' Lazlo agreed. 'Isn't *Cheshire* one of the freighters you had tramping round the Med and the Black Sea seeking any cargo they could pick up?'

'Yes, but she was costing more in port dues, wages and diesel than she was earning. Dad couldn't find a buyer to take her off our hands. Why don't we go aboard and check that everything is all right? We might as well do something useful while we're here. He's still hoping to sell her on.'

Lazlo altered course. 'At least visibility is improving now.'

'Look,' Philip said excitedly, 'there's a small yacht over there, and two people disembarking. Could that be the *Rowena*?'

Lottie was dropping the mainsail as *Seagull* headed for the dock wall to tie up, and had time only for one glance before the *Cheshire* cut off her view.

'I think it is,' he went on, 'but we'll see more from on top of the dock wall.'

The dock wall was towering above them now, and they were hemmed into the narrow space separating the *Cheshire* and a small tanker. Philip tied up the *Seagull* at the bottom of a narrow flight of steps cut into the sandstone. There were similar flights of steps every hundred yards or so.

'Be quick,' Lazlo called. 'I spotted two people going up the steps over there.'

Philip had reached the top of the dock. 'One is a woman,' he said, 'but I don't know what Gwen looks like, and anyway, it's hard to be certain at this distance.'

Lottie had scrambled up behind him, feeling hampered by her wet oilskins. 'Yes, I think it's Uncle Jeremy and Auntie Gwen.' Her voice was triumphant. 'They're getting into a black car.'

Once the car had pulled away, there was no sign of anybody else about. Philip and Lottie ran along the dock to look down on the yacht moored below. The freighters and tankers dwarfed it. 'We can't see the name from here,' Philip said, 'but this must be the one.'

The steps going down were slippery with seaweed and there was nothing to hold on to, but they all went down to make sure. It was definitely the *Lady Rowena*.

'We've missed them.' Lottie was disappointed. 'Will they come back, d'you think?'

'Your guess is as good as mine,' Lazlo said, 'but at least we've found the boat.'

He tried the cabin door and it opened to his touch. He put his head inside. 'Anybody aboard?' he called. The only answer came from two seagulls squawking over a piece of flotsam. 'Well, it's deserted now, but since we're here, we might as well have a look round.'

Rowena was nicely fitted out inside. There was more than one cabin. 'Two bunks in this one,' Lazlo said, 'and both have been slept in recently. They've been living here.'

'What is this key?' Lottie lifted it from a hook between the portholes.

'There's a lock on the outer door, but they didn't bother to use it,' Lazlo said. 'Try it now.'

Lottie did so. 'It works,' she said.

'We'd better lock up when we go.'

There were other signs that people had recently spent some time on the vessel. The cabins were untidy, rugs and blankets left about, scraps of paper and unwashed mugs.

'They've been cooking here in the galley,' Lottie said. 'There's salt and pepper, flour and sugar in this cupboard, and a few tins of soup.'

Lazlo fingered them doubtfully. 'Perhaps they're always left on the boat.'

'They've taken most of their stuff away with them,' Philip said. 'Except this old paperback, *The Green Hat*, by Michael Arlen.'

'I read it some time ago,' Lazlo said. 'It's good.'

'But does it look as though they plan to return?'

'Don't know.' Lazlo was disheartened again. 'When I think of all the hours we've wasted sitting in a car waiting for action, and when the action happens, we're in a boat and can't follow.'

'Let's go home,' Lottie said. Water had been trickling down under the collar of her oilskins, and she felt thoroughly wet and miserable.

'We'd better stop at the yacht club and leave a message for that fellow telling him where to find his boat,' Lazlo said.

'Yes, Alfred Hatton. Good news for him anyway. Will he have left for Toronto yet?'

'I think he said he was leaving on Wednesday.'

They tied up at the yacht club and got out. Sitting still in damp clothes had made them all shivery, and they welcomed the chance to move about. Feeling like drowned rats, they went to the bar.

'Alfred's not here at the moment,' the barman told them, 'but he might drop in for a drink later. We've had a few in today, but no one went out sailing.'

'Got more sense than us,' Philip said. 'We've found the *Lady Rowena*. Can you let me have a phone number for Alfred Hatton? He'll want to know as soon as possible.'

The barman disappeared for a few minutes, then returned accompanied by the woman who managed the club. She was all smiles.

'I hear you've found the *Lady Rowena*,' she said.

'Yes, she's moored safely beyond the Poulton Bridge at the far end of the West Float. Right up at the top, near Bidston Moss.' That was where originally the open water had degenerated into marsh.

The manager looked at Philip. 'You're Fiona Royden's son, aren't you?'

'Yes,' he said, 'and my friends belong to the Mortimer clan.'

'Right, I'll go and let Mr Hatton have the good news.'

Back in the *Seagull*, sailing the last stretch home to New Ferry, they were all feeling very cold, but the rain had stopped and it was clearing up. There was now a bit more breeze, so they were making better progress.

'You must both come home with me and change into dry clothes,' Lottie said. 'Grandma will be waiting to hear all our news.'

As soon as they arrived back, Jemima ordered Harriet to run a hot bath for Lottie. 'Look at you all, soaked to the skin. I do hope you aren't going to catch cold.'

Charles had come home early, and he sorted out some dry clothes for Lazlo. 'I'll only be five minutes or so,' Lottie said, 'and then you can have a bath too.'

'Sorry, Philip,' Jemima said, 'the hot water won't stretch to you.'

'Don't worry about me,' he said. 'I'll be all right until I get home.'

'No, come to Glyn's room,' Harriet said. 'We can at least find you a towel and some dry clothes. And I've made a stew, so you can all have a hot meal before you go home.'

Over lunch, they discussed the situation. 'We're still no nearer finding Gwen,' Lazlo said despondently. 'We thought we had a real lead but it's just another dead end. Today has been a complete waste of time.'

Philip insisted on helping Lottie to wash up afterwards. 'It gives me a chance to speak to you on your own,' he said as soon as he'd closed the kitchen door. 'I want to take you out again. The last time wasn't all that exciting. Nobody could call one drink and a parcel of fish and chips eaten in the car a big night out.'

Lottie wasn't really in the mood, but felt it would be unreasonable of her to refuse.

'I'll fix something up.' He smiled. 'Saturday all right? We could do with a bit of a treat.'

Philip kept in touch, and at work on Saturday morning Lottie told Dorothy that he had tickets to take her to see *Chu Chin Chow*.

'I'd love to see that,' Dorothy said enviously. 'It was a great hit on the London stage.'

Midway through the morning, Dad folded his copy of *The Times* in half and put it down on Lottie's desk. 'There's a piece here about Jeremy Arbuthnot trying to buy the *Lady Rowena* with a cheque that bounced.'

'Oh dear.' Lottie read the rest of the article. Readers were reminded that Arbuthnot was a Member of Parliament, and that he had been charged with homosexual offences and was waiting for his case to come before Liverpool Crown court in July.

'This will make him notorious,' Charles said. 'There's no way he can live this down.'

On Saturday evening, Lottie got ready and waited with the family for Philip to pick her up. Dilys and Alec came over to discuss the family problem but were also relating snippets of their own news. Lottie wanted to stay to hear more, but Philip said, 'We have to go, we don't want to be late.'

'What are you going to see?'

'*Chu Chin Chow* at the Argyle Theatre,' Lottie said. 'There's a touring company coming from London.'

'Lucky you,' Dilys said. 'We don't seem to have time for any of that now.'

The gathering crowd and the theatre atmosphere distracted Lottie temporarily from her woes. She'd always been thrilled by her visits to the Argyle, knowing that so many famous stars had started their careers here, but as the curtain went up, her mind was so full of worry that for her the play fell a little flat.

'Marvellous,' Philip enthused as they came out. 'I enjoyed it, didn't you? Are you hungry? Let's go and have a bit of supper in the Havana Room.'

Lottie knew it was an expensive restaurant that stayed open

for after-theatre customers – just about the only one in town that did. She was tired and out of sorts, but as Philip wanted to go, she went along with his plans.

Once they were seated at a table she said, 'I don't understand why Uncle Jeremy is trying to stop us talking to Gwen. He must have some reason.'

Her hand was resting on the table and he covered it with his. 'Lottie,' he said gently, 'I don't want to talk about that tonight. I've brought you out to forget it for a while.'

'How can I forget it?' she asked tearfully. 'Gwen is my mother.'

'I know, and we're all doing our best to find her. Lazlo was a bit down today but he's still racking his brains. It'll do us all good to have a rest from that.' Philip touched the menu she was holding. 'What are you going to have? I'm thinking of a sirloin steak.'

Lottie felt overwhelmed. 'I don't want anything. I'm sorry, Philip, but I'm just not hungry. I want to go home.' She got to her feet. 'You haven't ordered anything for me, so I'll go and get the bus.'

'No,' he said. 'It's late, the buses could have stopped running by now. I'll take you home if you want to go.'

'You don't have to.'

'I think I do.'

With extra politeness he helped her back into her coat and ushered her outside. He opened the car door for her in silence, then stared out at the road with a concentration that was hardly needed, because there was little traffic. The atmosphere felt heavy and she knew he was disappointed.

When they came to a halt outside her back gate, he said,

'Lottie, I do understand this is a terrible time for you, but you need to relax.' She knew his arms were coming round her and felt for the door handle to escape. 'It's no good, Phil. I'm just not in the mood.'

'But you are over Roddy? There isn't anyone else?'

'I'm over Roddy but too distracted by everything that is happening with Gwen to think of anything else. I'm just not in the mood.'

'At least the show was good. You enjoyed that?'

Long training from Grandma made her say, 'Yes. Thank you for taking me. I'm sorry, Phil, you must think me an ungrateful pig. Goodnight.' She got out and was running down the garden to the back door before he could reply.

Harriet was making cocoa in the kitchen.

'Do you want one?'

'No thanks, I'm tired. I think I'll go straight to bed.'

On Sunday morning she went swimming with Dorothy as usual, but her friend kept asking questions about the show and about Philip, and seemed to sense that all had not gone well. Lottie knew her brusque replies were giving offence, but Dorothy just smiled and said, 'You must have got out of bed the wrong side this morning, or you've got a nasty hangover.'

The rest of the day passed slowly. Lottie had time to think and knew she'd shown bad manners and ingratitude to Philip, and now she very much regretted it.

On Monday, Dilys had arranged to take her place with Lazlo and Philip so that Dad could rely on Lottie's help in the office. Now that she was married, Dilys was working part-time so she'd have time for household chores, but with Alec at work she wanted to help the family on her free days.

Dilys popped in to see Grandma on her way home. Lottie and her father were already there having a cup of tea. 'The only bit of news I have to tell you,' she said, 'is that Philip has heard from his parents that the story of how you found the *Lady Rowena* is going round the yacht club bar, and everybody is full of praise and sends congratulations. Alfred Hatton set out immediately with a friend to help him sail her back to her berth at the club, and other people were rallying round too. Better still, the member who had a neighbour interested in buying confirmed that the man was still keen to have her.'

'So,' Harriet said, 'something good came of your very wet expedition after all.'

'Not for us,' Lottie retorted. 'We seem to have reached a dead end.'

CHAPTER TWENTY-EIGHT

LOTTIE KNEW THAT THE search for Gwen was on the point of stalling. Dilys had spent the next two days with Lazlo and Philip. They had seen Eunice again but had learned nothing new. When Dilys had to go to work on Thursday, Lazlo spent the day on his own but came over and had a meal with the family that evening. He had no progress to report either.

On Friday, he rang them in the evening and told them that he and Philip had watched Arbuthnot's office and later his house, but that they'd failed to see either of them. They'd had a late lunch and given up.

After that the family showed their frayed nerves during the weekend by losing patience and having bouts of ill temper with each other. Lazlo came to lunch on Sunday and seemed quite depressed. He'd been invited to have supper with the Roydens that evening, and went straight there.

Later that evening, when Lottie was making cocoa, he rang again. 'According to the Roydens,' he said, 'another member of the yacht club, an estate agent, told them last night that he'd been approached by Arbuthnot wanting to rent a flat.'

Lottie's spirits lifted. 'A ray of hope at last. If we could get an address for him that way, it would be marvellous.'

'It certainly would. This fellow apparently showed him round two or three flats and he decided he liked one of them.'

'Do you know where it was?'

'No, but Philip and I will go to see the agent in the morning to try and find out.'

'Will he tell you?' she asked. 'So many people want to keep their clients' business confidential.'

'He was gossiping in the club bar, wasn't he? We can but try.'

At lunchtime the next day, Lazlo rang the office while Charles was next door with Ted Pascoe. 'Philip persuaded the estate agent to give us that address,' he said to Lottie. 'We're going round there now to see what's what.'

'I wish I could go with you.'

'Dilys has come again this morning, though she said she was afraid her time could be better spent scrubbing her kitchen floor.'

'What if Jeremy is there and picks a fight?'

'He can't fight three of us. We're not going to put up with any more of this nonsense,' Lazlo said. 'I'm hoping we'll get to see Gwen this afternoon, and if we can manage it, we'll take her to your house.'

Lottie was on tenterhooks for the rest of the day, and when she told Dad, so was he. 'We should have a family conference to decide what to do next,' he said. 'But you know what Lazlo's like, he'll go in like a bull in a china shop and cause another wave of trouble. Dilys is with him, you said? I hope she doesn't get hurt.'

As they'd heard nothing more by three in the afternoon, he decided that they'd go home early. Both Philip's car and Dilys's were parked at their back gate, and Lottie almost ran down to the house to talk to them. They were having tea with Grandma and Harriet and looked thoroughly out of sorts.

'Another wasted day.' Lazlo was really down. 'We went round to the flat but could get no answer, though the agent had said Jeremy wanted to move in as soon as he could.'

'Were you too quick off the mark?' asked Charles.

'No,' Philip said. 'We trailed back to the agent and he told us Arbuthnot had just phoned him to say he'd changed his mind, he didn't want to rent that flat or any other after all.'

'He was cross,' Dilys said. 'He was complaining about Arbuthnot, said he'd had a wasted day showing him round.'

'I told him we'd wasted weeks looking for him,' Lazlo added.

'The problem now,' Philip said, 'is that he could go to another agent and choose a flat from his list. He's probably done that already and seen a flat he likes better. We'll hear no more of this.'

Lazlo grunted. 'Exactly, and I'm sick to death of hanging about trying to keep a watch on him on the off chance he'll lead us to Gwen.'

'I've always thought that it's through Eunice that we're most likely to get a lead,' Lottie said. 'Martin and Jeremy are involved in this together.'

'But I think Eunice has been told to keep her mouth shut,' Dilys said. 'I've tried to get her to talk, but I can't, and she used to tell me everything. We were great friends all the time we were growing up.'

Lottie knew she was right. 'I've tried to get her to talk about what was happening too, but I can't get her to add anything we don't already know. Yet I get the feeling she could, that she knows exactly what's going on and it's worrying her. I reckon Martin has made her promise to keep quiet.'

'Or possibly Jeremy,' Dilys added.

'I think the time has come to give up,' Grandma said. 'There is a limit to what we can do. I suggest we leave it to the police now.'

'But they're so slow,' Lazlo said. 'I've reported Gwen as a missing person, and Alfred Hatton reported that Jeremy's cheque for the *Lady Rowena* bounced and that he'd disappeared and taken the yacht. But we've heard nothing.'

'We're all worrying ourselves silly about this.' Jemima was indignant. 'Martin is playing games with us. I think you should ask the police what they're up to. Stir them up a little.'

'They're probably doing their best,' Lazlo said.

'I'd do it myself,' Jemima said, 'but I'd have to go over to Liverpool, and you live there.'

'Mother, I'll do it tomorrow.' Lazlo was frosty. 'I want to find Gwen as much as any of you, if not more.'

'I do too,' Lottie said. 'I'd like to try again with Eunice. I think if I keep on at her I'll wear her down. Things are happening in that house that involve her, and I think she'll eventually crack.'

'You could be putting yourself in danger,' Jemima said. 'Look at what happened to Gwendolen. I think you should stay out of it.'

'We can't stay out of it, Grandma,' Dilys said. 'I'm very worried about Eunice. Something has changed her. She's living on her nerves, almost a zombie. I don't think we should leave it to the police. She needs help. Lottie and I could go over together. We'd be safe enough then, wouldn't we?'

'Yes,' Lottie agreed. 'I'd like to do that. Is that all right with you, Dad?'

'It has to be; we need to get this settled now,' Lazlo said.

'All right, we'll go tomorrow,' Dilys said. 'We need to pin her down and make her talk. I'll come here and pick you up, Lottie. Dad, you'll have to cope without her. We'll go over on the luggage boat and get there early.'

'Not too early,' Lottie said. 'I know that Martin drops the children off at school on his way to work. We want them all out of the way before we try and get Eunice to talk.'

The next day, Dilys arrived as Charles was setting out for the office. 'Morning,' he called as he got into his Austin Seven. 'Lottie's ready and waiting for you.'

Everybody was up and bustling round. 'Do you want sandwiches?' Harriet wanted to know.

'No thanks, we'll take Eunice out to lunch,' Dilys said.

Lottie sat in the passenger seat of her sister's car and watched her drive. 'I wish I could persuade Dad to get a car like this,' she said.

'Don't waste your time dreaming of that; he never will.' Dilys giggled. 'Grandma would insist on a saloon car; she'd tell him it would be far more suitable for a family like ours.'

It was a lovely June morning, the sky cloudless, and for once the Mersey was picking up the colour and looked blue instead of muddy. There were several yachts sailing on the Sloyne, and the usual traffic of coasters, freighters, tankers and liners coming in and going out on the high tide.

As they approached Eunice's house, Lottie got out to run ahead and make sure that Martin had gone. It came as a surprise to see that the garage door and the garden gate had been opened in readiness, but Martin's large American saloon was still inside.

She ran back to tell Dilys, who said, 'If those children are going to be at school by nine, he should have gone. We'll wait, he won't be long.'

They waited fifteen minutes. Time had never passed more slowly. 'Has he taken the children to school already and come back?' Lottie mused.

'We'll give him another five minutes and then we'll go in. We can't spend all day waiting in the road.'

Nothing seemed to be happening, so eventually Dilys drove in and parked near the front door. Lottie rang the bell. The door was opened by Hilda with a face like thunder.

Martin's raised voice could be heard from his study. 'Don't be silly, Eunice. The children are old enough to look after themselves. They have no need of Betty.' The atmosphere felt electric. Lottie knew they'd arrived in the middle of a row.

'Please wait in here.' Hilda was trying hustle them out of earshot into the small sitting room.

'Hilda!' they heard Martin roar. 'Get the children into the car. Hurry, we're going to be late.'

The housekeeper ran upstairs, and within moments the children came hurtling down and out of the front door. 'Good morning,' Dilys said as they thundered past. The study door slammed and they were followed by Martin. 'Good morning, Martin.'

He scowled angrily. 'Have to rush,' he said, 'or the children will be late.'

Lottie went to the study to look for Eunice. She was

309

supporting herself against the desk with her head back and eyes closed. Lottie put an arm round her shoulders. 'It's OK, he's gone. What was all that about?'

'Let's go to your boudoir.' Dilys took her other arm.

Eunice straightened up. 'No, Frances is in there. She hasn't gone to school because she's got toothache.'

'OK, we'll stay here,' Dilys said, 'but we want to know what that row was about.'

Eunice snivelled into her handkerchief. 'He sacked Betty. I could trust her; she's been here since Tom was born. He says the children are all old enough to manage without a nanny, but Betty sees to their clothes and does their laundry and keeps their rooms clean and tidy. Who does he think will do all that work if she goes?'

'Eddie's still little,' Dilys said. 'Who's looking after him?'

'Martin found a trained nursemaid for him, Muriel.'

'Then surely she can see to the other children's needs too?'

'You're upset because you're fond of Betty,' Lottie said, perching on the desk.

'The children are too.' Eunice was mopping her eyes, trying to pull herself together. 'You caught us at a bad moment.'

'I'm glad to find you trying to intervene on Betty's behalf.' Dilys gave her a little hug. 'You should tell Martin that you run the house. That it's up to you to decide who works here.'

Eunice sniffed again. 'He wouldn't agree to that. He hired Hilda and the cook and I don't like either of them. I feel they're watching me all the time.'

'Do you like Muriel?

'Not much, but she's only been here a few days; I hardly know her.'

'Insist on keeping Betty,' Dilys said. 'She wants to stay, doesn't she?'

'Yes, but it's too late. She's already gone. He sacked her last night and said nothing to me until I missed her this morning.'

'That's a bit high-handed,' Dilys said. 'No wonder you're upset.'

Eunice blew her nose. 'And there's Frances to think of this morning. Muriel made an appointment at the dentist for her at quarter to ten, but normally Betty would have taken her. Martin says she's quite old enough to get there on her own and go in to school afterwards, but she's miserable and in pain and wants me to go with her.'

'Lottie will take her for you,' Dilys said.

Lottie didn't want to leave just now. Eunice looked thoroughly shaken up, and she was sure she'd be more likely to open up in the aftermath of that row with Martin. But it seemed Dilys understood that too and felt she could handle it alone.

'You can take my car,' Dilys said. 'You wanted to try it, didn't you?'

Lottie did her best to smile. 'Course I'll take her, Eunice,' she said; somebody would have to. She didn't know Frances very well, hadn't seen much of her, but she lived here too, and perhaps knew something of what was going on.

She went to look for her and found her curled up asleep on the sofa in Eunice's boudoir. She was a leggy eleven-year-old with Christabel's pretty face and yellow hair. Lottie put a hand on her shoulder. 'Time to wake up, Frances.' Large blue eyes looked vacantly up at her for a moment, then she sat up with a jerk. 'How's the toothache?'

311

'Better.' Her tongue explored the back of her mouth. 'It's gone. Muriel gave me some aspirin. I could go to school.'

'No, I'm going to take you to the dentist first. She made an appointment for you.'

'I'm all right now, I don't need—'

'Yes you do. Dilys says we can go in her car. Are you ready?' Frances was wearing her school uniform; her gymslip was now crumpled. 'Where are your shoes?'

'I don't know.'

'Come on, we must find them.'

'I want to go to the bathroom first.' Very slowly she stood up. 'I really don't think I need the dentist.'

Eunice brought Dilys in. 'You know you do, Frances,' she said. They settled on the sofa in Frances's place and Hilda brought in the coffee tray.

'Does she know her way to this dentist, Eunice?' Lottie asked.

'Yes, she's been before.'

Frances returned wearing her panama and blazer, and Lottie led her out to Dilys's car. 'I'd like a car like this when I'm grown up,' the girl said as they got in.

Lottie breathed a sigh of relief. Frances wasn't going to be difficult after all. 'So would I,' she said. 'I expect your father will get you one when the time comes.'

'Why d'you say that?'

'Well, he likes to buy you anything you ask for, doesn't he?'

'Not recently. He's suddenly very mean. He's lost all his money. He had to sack Betty because he couldn't afford to pay her wages.'

Lottie held her breath; she hadn't unexpected such an easy

opening. She was afraid of changing the subject, but had to ask, 'Which way at the junction?'

'Turn right. You've learned to drive, so why don't you have a car?'

'I can't afford it. I drive my father's Austin Seven when he'll lend it to me.' Then she added quickly, 'He can't have lost all his money; he hired Muriel not so long ago, didn't he? It can't be that.'

'It is. He says it's Uncle Jeremy's fault. He's done something really bad. He and Daddy were in business together and everything is going wrong. Poor Daddy has been very upset and worried for ages. It cost him a lot of money to get Uncle Jeremy out of prison on bail, and then over Easter he couldn't find the money to pay our school fees.'

Lottie smiled, delighted to find that Frances was a little chatterbox. 'Well, you're all back at school now, so he found the money from somewhere.'

'Yes, he must have done.' She lapsed into silence.

Lottie racked her brain; she had to keep this conversation going. 'Do you like school?'

'Yes, we play lots of games and there's a swimming pool. We've all learned to swim.'

'Lucky your father found the money then.' Lottie took a deep breath. 'So, do you know where Uncle Jeremy is living now?'

'In Princes Park, where he's always lived. He has a lovely garden. This is it, the dentist's.'

Lottie's hands were shaking as she parked at the kerb. Could the girl be right? Lazlo had searched Arbuthnot's house and said that Jeremy and Gwen weren't there. But they had spent time on the *Lady Rowena*. Had Jeremy looked at furnished flats and decided they'd have far more comfort at home? Had they gone back?

She went into the dentist's with Frances and led her to the far corner of the waiting room to sit down. There was only one other person, and he was well away from them. She had to know. 'Have you seen Uncle Jeremy and Auntie Gwen recently?'

'Yes, we all went to see them last Sunday. We had tea there. Auntie Gwen always gives us lovely cakes with cream in.'

Lottie was amazed. 'How is Auntie Gwen? We were told she wasn't well.'

'She seems all right.'

Frances was called in. 'I'll wait for you here,' Lottie said, glad to have time to think. Goodness! Lazlo and Philip had been chasing round for days, and they'd all had a very wet sailing trip, and it could have been so easy. Why hadn't they thought of asking the children before?

Then it occurred to her that Eunice must know all this. Aware that Grandma and the rest of them were searching desperately for Gwen, she'd deliberately kept her whereabouts from them!

The dentist brought Frances out and spoke to Lottie. 'All done. I've taken out one of her back baby teeth. It should have come out on its own, as there's a new one pushing against it. She'll have no more trouble now it's out.'

'Good. Is she's well enough to go straight to school?'

'I don't see why not. You feel fine, don't you, Frances? You've been very good.'

'Right,' said Lottie, 'come on then, you'll have to direct me. I don't know the way.'

The school was housed in a beautiful stone building set in acres of grounds. Lottie drove up a sweeping drive to the front door and Frances jumped out.

'Thank you for taking me to the dentist, Lottie.'

'Goodbye, Frances. Dilys and I will be gone before you come home.'

She sat still for a moment, watching Frances run up the steps and disappear inside. She'd been very lucky. Doing this favour for Eunice had provided valuable information she could use to prod her sister to reveal more. They could get to the bottom of this today.

CHAPTER TWENTY-NINE

BACK AT EUNICE'S HOUSE, a daily woman was washing the front steps. Lottie said good morning to her and walked into the house. Dilys and Eunice were still in her boudoir. Dilys said, 'Could you take this tray back to the kitchen, Lottie, and ask Hilda to make another pot of coffee?'

Lottie couldn't help but notice that Eunice's eyes were even more red and puffy. She was willing to bet she'd found out more than Dilys had. She went back to the small sitting room and threw herself into an armchair.

'You should have told us that Martin was in financial difficulties,' she said. That brought Eunice's head up with a jerk. 'Frances has been telling me he had trouble finding the money for their school fees.'

Eunice started to cry openly. 'Yes,' she said through her sobs.

Dilys looked amazed. 'But what has caused Martin's sudden shortage of money?'

'I don't know.'

Lottie was reluctant to put pressure on her, but felt she had to. 'Yes you do, Eunice.'

Dilys put an arm round Eunice's shoulders and hugged her. 'We want to help you, but we need to know.'

'Martin's had a lot of expense recently. He had to pay for Jeremy's bail.'

'I find that hard to believe,' Lottie said firmly. 'I think Jeremy could pay that himself, and if not, I'm sure Auntie Gwen would.'

'No, she wasn't willing to.'

Lottie froze. Dilys's face showed horror. 'Why not?'

Eunice's eyes filled with tears again; they were rolling down her face. Lottie heard a knock on the door and leapt to her feet to open it. Hilda was there with the coffee tray. 'Thank you,' she said and went to take it from her.

'Will you want lunch today?' Hilda asked. It reminded Lottie that time was going on, and Eunice would not want to be seen in public in her present fraught state. Anyway, they'd cracked it; they could do the rest here. 'Yes please, lunch for three.'

She closed the door and came back. Eunice sniffed. 'Martin was hoping Jeremy would repay the money, but Jeremy's in a desperate state, totally nerve-racked and they quarrelled. We aren't going to see him again.'

'Why is he in such a state?' Lottie wanted to know.

'Well, we're all a bit on edge, aren't we? He's been given a date for his case. It's on the twentieth of July, so not very long now. He says it's like a ticking clock, and as the days go by, it's getting on his nerves.'

'But how does that involve you and Martin?' Dilys asked.

'We're desperately short of money. He's always looking for more.'

'But you get money every month from Mother's will,' Dilys said. 'I know you do; we both get exactly the same. Why don't you use that for school fees?'

'It goes nowhere. We have to pay for the upkeep of this house and the wages for the staff.'

'You've got too many,' Dilys said.

'Isn't that what Grandma thought when we came to Eunice's birthday party?' Lottie said to her. 'That was the day I met Roddy.'

'We thought you were getting on well together,' Eunice said. 'Why did you quarrel with him?'

'They didn't quarrel,' Dilys said. 'He dropped her like a hot brick when he realised she wasn't going to inherit any of Mother's money.'

'It's my fault,' Eunice wept. 'I told him you'd have the same as me and Dilys as soon as you married.'

Hilda came to announce that lunch was ready, but it took a little time to calm Eunice down, and for her to wash her face.

After an excellent lunch of lamb chops, Lottie suggested they all go and visit Gwen and Jeremy. 'Oh no,' Eunice said. 'Martin has forbidden me to go anywhere near them, and I'm to shut the door in their faces if they come here.'

'That sounds a bit strong,' Dilys said.

'Well we'd like to see Gwen before we go home,' Lottie said.

'Lottie,' Eunice said, suddenly frantic, 'don't go anywhere near Jeremy. He could hurt you. It wouldn't be safe.'

Eunice refused to leave the house and, reluctantly, they left without her. Dilys strode out to her car, Lottie two paces behind. 'You and I are going to talk to Gwen, aren't we?' Lottie asked.

Dilys pulled a face. 'I don't know. After what Eunice said,

I'm a bit worried about going there. Grandma will say I'm leading you into danger.'

'Nonsense. We've learned so much today. I'd really like to talk to Gwen before we go home. We'd know the full story then, wouldn't we?'

'We should try and contact Lazlo to go with us.'

'Dad would say he'll go in like a bull in a china shop and start a fight. I think you and I could manage.'

'No. Let's go home. Lazlo will ring you tonight won't he?'

'I couldn't stand another night without seeing her.' Lottie sighed. 'All right, let's go to Lazlo's lodgings and see if we can talk to him.'

'Will he be there? It's nearly three now, and Alec will get home between four and four thirty. I can't be late again.'

'Oh yes, you have a husband to consider.'

'I do, and there's always a queue for the luggage boat at going-home time.'

'Run me to Lazlo's lodgings then, and just wait five minutes while I find out if he's there. If he isn't, I'll come home with you. If he is, you can leave me and I'll come back on the train.'

As they pulled up outside Lazlo's lodgings, Lottie was delighted to spot both his car and Philip's outside. 'Won't you come in and see his room?' she asked Dilys.

'I already have. You're forgetting I've seen a lot of Lazlo recently. I'm going to go home now. Ring me tonight. I want to know what happens.'

Sparkling with triumph, Lottie ran up the four flights of stairs and knocked on Lazlo's door. 'I've got such good news for you, Lazlo,' she sang out when he let her in. 'I've found Gwen.'

He pulled her into a hug. 'Thank goodness. Come and sit down and tell us all. Philip and I are feeling low.'

Lottie perched on the arm of the sofa. 'Hello, Philip, I saw your car outside.' She began recounting all she and Dilys had learned during the day.

'Back in their own house?' Lazlo was surprised. 'I searched through every room once, and I've been back since and I was quite sure they weren't there.'

'Grandma said you broke in like a common criminal.'

'Yes,' he agreed, 'I did, I wanted to make sure that Gwen really wasn't there.'

'We watched the place for a couple of hours once,' Philip added. 'And we never saw any movement.'

'But they're obviously back there now,' Lazlo said. 'We must go straight up and see them.'

Lottie laughed. 'That's what Dad would expect you to do. Eunice warned me and Dilys against going as she said Jeremy could be dangerous. We heeded the warning.'

'Well I'm not going to.' Lazlo stood up. 'Come on.'

'I'll go home,' Philip said. 'Unless you want me to come with you? In case Jeremy turns nasty.'

'We'll be all right,' Lazlo said. 'I'm not afraid of him.'

'Are you sure?' Philip pressed him. 'Lottie?'

She hesitated.

'I'll follow you as a reserve in case of trouble,' he decided, 'but I'll not stay if all is well. It's your family after all, really none of my business.'

'That's very generous of you,' Lazlo said. 'You've been a real ally to me while this has been going on.'

Lottie enjoyed the drive in Lazlo's car. 'I like your Riley. It's far more comfortable than Dad's Austin.'

'Get him to trade it in for something better.'

'He's far too fraught to think about cars.'

'This is the place,' Lazlo said. 'I know the outside of Jeremy's house like the back of my hand. We'll park at the kerb outside, easy for a quick getaway.'

Philip drew up behind him. 'It all looks quiet,' he said. 'Nobody about.'

'I don't see his car,' Lazlo said, 'but it might be in the garage. I think we'll just march up to the front door and ring the bell.'

Lottie could see he felt both excited and nervous, and she did too, her heart hammering. Philip stood behind them like a bodyguard. A middle-aged maid in a black dress with white cap and apron opened the door.

'Good afternoon,' Lazlo said. 'Is Mrs Arbuthnot in? We'd like to see her.'

'Yes,' she replied. 'Please step inside. Who shall I say is here?'

'Lazlo and Charlotte.'

Lottie's spirits shot sky high. They'd found her!

'Is Mr Arbuthnot at home?' Philip asked.

'Yes, he's about somewhere.' The maid was disappearing into a room.

'Shall I leave you?' Philip asked anxiously.

'Hang on for five minutes; let's see what happens.'

The maid was returning, but Gwendolen burst out into the hall ahead of her. 'Charlotte!' She gathered her into her arms. 'And Lazlo. Marvellous to see you both like this, just when I need you most. I've missed so much, but thank God you've come.' Her face was a picture of love and anguish.

321

Lottie had let out a little squeal of delight when she saw her, but now she didn't know whether to laugh or cry, and realised she was doing both at once. She stared at her mother in wonder, and saw that her eyes were wet too. Gwendolen was smartly dressed and her hair had more style than Eunice's, and even Aunt Harriet's come to that.

'You look so much stronger than the first time I saw you,' Lottie said. 'Quite different.'

'I hope I do. I was ill and confused that day. I hardly knew what was going on but I knew it was you. I fainted, didn't I? But Jeremy came out on bail and took me home. And once I stopped taking the pills Martin was forcing on me, I felt more myself. Martin tried again to get money from me, and gave me a hiding when I refused. He tried to tell everybody that Jeremy had done it.'

Lazlo was almost overcome. 'I'm so relieved we've found you,' he said. 'We've spent weeks searching. We've been really worried.'

'Oh Lazlo.' Gwen's broad smile wavered a little. 'I didn't know I was lost.'

'Oh but you were,' Lottie insisted. 'We've all been chasing round. It was as though you'd gone for good.'

'Gwen,' Lazlo said. 'This is Philip Royden, a family friend. He's been helping us look for you. He's here in case Jeremy starts a fight.'

'Poor Jeremy has had all the fight knocked out of him. He's in a terrible state. You've got it all wrong.'

Lottie could see that Philip was ill at ease and unwilling to meet her gaze. 'I'll go now I know you're all right,' he said. 'I'll only be in the way.' He headed for the front door.

'Thank you,' Lazlo called after him. Then, turning back to Gwen, he said, 'We've so much to catch up with.'

'Yes, come and sit down, and I'll tell you what's been happening. Let me get Bridget to make us some tea first.' She shot out of the room. Lazlo and Lottie sat down side by side on the sofa. Lottie knew they were both feeling confused. Gwen returned to sit on another sofa opposite them.

Lottie said, 'If you weren't hiding, I don't understand why you didn't stay in your own home. Why did Jeremy make matters worse by taking the *Rowena* without paying for her? You were living on her, weren't you?'

'Yes, Jeremy was trying to avoid Martin and the newspaper reporters. That's a very long story.'

Lottie's mouth had gone dry. 'Martin?'

'Yes, for years Martin's been blackmailing Jeremy, saying he'll let the world know about the young men he has living with us. Well what with that and waiting for his case to come to court, Jeremy is at his wits' end.'

'Martin's been blackmailing him for money? And he's been paying him?' Lazlo was shocked.

'Yes, at first Martin called it helping a poorer member of the family. Jeremy didn't tell me he was giving him money for a long time.'

'But we thought Martin and Jeremy were friends,' Lottie said. 'Eunice told me they were.'

'So did I at one time, but Jeremy felt no friendship for him,' Gwen said. 'Martin pretended to be friendly, and with hindsight I think that's all it ever was, pretence. It was a ruse to make it easier to extract money from him.'

Lazlo was shaking his head. 'But Jeremy's such a strong

person, physically strong, and a man of the world. A Member of Parliament, a man of some importance.'

'I thought he was strong once, and perhaps he was, but he was pretending to be something he wasn't. He had to hide his homosexuality at all costs, and over the years he began to lose confidence in himself. He's a shadow of the man he once was. Martin got inside his head. But that all ended when Jeremy was arrested, because of course it brought everything out in the open.'

'Yes, yes, of course. It meant Martin lost the power he had over him.'

'Yes, but he continues to harass Jeremy for money. And now I've refused to hand over another penny.'

There was a knock at the door and the maid reappeared pushing a tea trolley. 'Thank you,' Gwendolen said.

When she'd gone, Lottie said, 'I'd like to use your phone if I may. I need to tell Grandma that I'll be late home.'

She returned to find Lazlo pouring out the tea. 'Frances told me you always have lovely cream cakes,' she said as she lifted the plate and handed them round.

Gwen refused a cake. 'I'm afraid Eunice has been bearing the brunt of all this. I used to ask her about you, Lottie, and she'd keep me up to date with what was happening in your life. She was my comfort. Martin harasses her too, I'm afraid; he's very controlling. I was the one friend he allowed her to have.'

'But Eunice told me Jeremy had attacked you.' Nothing was as Lottie had supposed.

'All lies. Martin lies about everything, and he makes Eunice confirm them. That took me in for a while; I didn't realise he'd got into her head too. He controls her as he controlled Jeremy. He plays on their minds, makes them do what he wants.

'I've been anxious about Eunice for some time, so when I was up here in Liverpool, I often went to see her. She confided in me, but I didn't tell her too much about my own difficulties; I was afraid it would worry her more. We were quite good friends, and sometimes she brought Tom and Edgar to see me.'

'I'm afraid I was blind to what was going on,' Lottie said.

'We've all been that,' Lazlo said sympathetically. 'We got it all wrong.'

'A lot of what happened has been my fault,' Gwendolen said. 'I introduced Eunice to Martin and brought all this trouble on her. I now see that as a major error of judgement and feel very guilty. Martin knew from Jeremy that I had inherited money, and I think he was envious. He understood that Eunice was my niece and thought she would inherit the same amount on marriage. He seemed so pleasant and polite to me, and so caring and in love with Eunice. She was very enamoured, as you know, and I was pleased when he wanted to marry her.

'I think he deliberately set out to woo her, believing it would solve his financial problems, but on marriage he found her inheritance was much less than mine and was disappointed. I'm horrified at what he's done to her. Poor Eunice, he's twisted her mind; the relationship between them isn't normal.'

Gwen sighed. 'That morning you and Dilys saw me at Eunice's house, she'd rung me and sounded very upset on the phone. She asked me to come over, and I went alone by taxi. It was Jeremy's first day out on bail and he was doing a bit of gardening. I thought a quiet time in the garden would relax him after being on remand. When I got there, Martin was at home and took me straight to his study.'

'You mean he demanded money from you?' Lottie asked.

'Yes, but the situation had gone on far too long, and knowing he'd lost his power, I was not going to break down and pay his debts. I told him those days were over.'

'Good for you,' Lazlo said.

Lottie felt sick. 'And because you refused, he attacked you?'

'Yes, he was desperate for cash. Still is, come to that. I think he got Eunice to lure me to the house, and when I refused point blank to give him money, he picked up a wooden clothes brush he had in his study and whacked me with it.'

Lottie still couldn't quite believe it. 'It was Martin that did that? We've been blaming the wrong man?'

At that moment she saw the door opening and a bent figure shuffled in.

'I didn't know you had company, Gwendolen,' he said, looking from Lazlo to Lottie. 'I've been doing a bit in the garden but I came in to have a cup of tea.'

'Jeremy, this is Charlotte.' Gwen waved a hand in her direction. 'And you know Lazlo.'

Lottie held her breath. Lazlo had expected Jeremy to make trouble, but he was just staring at her. She turned her face away to hide her blush.

Gwen lifted the teapot and handed it to him. 'Get Bridget to make another pot; we've drunk this one dry. You'll need more milk too.'

They sat looking at one another in his absence, but he was soon back. The silence continued as the housemaid followed him with the new pot and busily refilled the cups.

Lottie took the opportunity to study Jeremy. He'd lost weight since she'd seen him at Eunice's; his clothes hung loosely on him and he was painfully thin. He had wide shoulders but they were stooped, and his shoulder blades stuck out sharply through his pullover. His eyes were sharp, but he dropped his gaze quickly when it met hers. He looked frail and vulnerable, not a man to scare anybody. Yet Eunice had said she was frightened of him, and that Martin was too. Poor Eunice, she was in a state.

Lottie still had a hundred questions she wanted to ask Gwen, and she knew Lazlo had too, but most involved her life with Jeremy, and they were impossible to broach in his presence. Gwen was talking to him about the garden. 'Your peonies and foxgloves look absolutely beautiful this year.'

Lazlo gulped down his tea. 'It's time we went home, Gwendolen,' he said. 'I'd like to come and see you again sometime. Shall I give you a ring so we can fix a convenient time? You don't mind, Jeremy?'

Jeremy grunted wordlessly.

'Grandma would love you to come and have lunch with us one Sunday,' Lottie said. 'I'll get her to ring you about that. Dad would like to see you too, Gwen. He was your brother-in-law and still thinks about you.'

'Am I glad to get out of there,' Lazlo said as they got into his car.

'Me too,' Lottie agreed. 'It got horribly uncomfortable once Jeremy came in.'

'He was embarrassed too. I've never seen a man change so much. He used to have such a commanding presence; he was well over six foot, with broad shoulders, and he walked with his head held high. He appeared to ooze self-confidence, and usually got what he wanted the first time he asked.' Lazlo felt responsible for this change. Telling the police he'd seen Jeremy going into the gents' lavatory in Everton appeared to have lit a fuse setting off consequences he hadn't foreseen. He'd regretted doing that quite soon afterwards, but now he realised how many secrets Jeremy had been hiding.

'I'll come home with you, Lottie,' he said. 'We've got so much to tell Mother and Charlie. We've cracked it now, haven't we?'

'Better if we go over on the train at this time of day,' Lottie said. 'We'd have to queue for the luggage boat, and they stop running quite early, so you mightn't get back.'

'I'll leave my car at James Street station then.'

'And I can ring home from there to let them know you're coming. Harriet likes a bit of warning if she has an extra mouth to feed.'

When she got through, Grandma said, 'Dilys is here; shall I ask her to pick you up at New Ferry station.'

'That would be lovely, but she only has a two-seater.'

'Charles is home; she can use his car.'

Dilys was waiting when they got off the train. 'I thought you were in a hurry to get home?' Lottie said.

'Alec had a teachers' meeting; he got the day wrong. I should have stayed with you. Just my luck not to be there when you finally found Auntie Gwen.'

When they got home, the family found the story hard to believe. 'After all the worry and the time you wasted searching for her,' Harriet said.

Lazlo said, 'Gwen is perfectly happy at home. It's Jeremy who's in trouble. He's worrying about his case, which is coming up on the twentieth of July. He feels it's like a time bomb ticking away the hours before it goes off.'

'But Eunice told me—' Dilys began.

'Grandma,' Lottie broke in, 'I took the liberty of inviting them to lunch one Sunday, and told Auntie Gwen you'd ring her to fix which weekend you want them to come.'

'Good idea. We'll have them next Sunday,' Jemima said. 'The sooner we get to the bottom of all this, the better.'

'Do we have to ask both of them?' Lazlo said. 'It'll be difficult to talk if Jeremy comes too.'

'I'll ring Gwendolen now; she'll understand that.' Jemima bustled out to the hall and they waited in silence until she came back.

'Well?' Lazlo asked.

'She'll come alone next Sunday, and of course, you are invited too, Lazlo.'

'I'd like to be here as well,' Dilys said.

'Dilys, you know you're welcome here any time, but if you could leave Alec at home on Sunday, it would be a help. Eunice is the one in real trouble. We're all very worried about her.'

'Martin is desperate about paying his staff and the school fees and things like that,' Lottie said.

'I'm not at all surprised,' Jemima replied tartly. 'He has absolutely no sense where money is concerned. He's also a liar and a fraudster, and we should never have given Eunice permission to marry him. I think that's one of the biggest mistakes we've made, Charles.'

'He's a con man,' Harriet said. 'He convinced us all he was in love with her.'

'A woman who inherits money attracts men like Martin,' Dilys said. 'I've met a few myself. It's safer to keep quiet about an inheritance like ours.'

'That is exactly what we tried to do,' Jemima said. 'There are too many greedy men wanting to marry girls for their money. Dangerous men like Martin.'

Dilys said, 'How did he find out Eunice would inherit money?'

'He knew Jeremy, didn't he?' Lazlo said. 'Apparently he thought Eunice would inherit as much as Gwendolen did.'

'And now he's disappointed,' Jemima sighed. 'He's a *very* dangerous man.'

'We must help Eunice,' Dilys said. 'Thankfully, she's told me that her fears of being pregnant again are unfounded, but she needs our help now she's going through all this.'

'I tried,' Jemima said. 'I suggested she come here with the boys, either for a short break or permanently. But she wouldn't. She believes he loves her and wants her with him.'

'And what about those three girls?' Lottie said. 'Are they to be left with a father like that?'

Dilys stood up to kiss her grandmother. 'I'm going home.'

Harriet got to her feet too. 'I must see to the dinner.'

She shared out the liver and onions in smallish portions to the family. Lazlo looked as though he could have eaten more. Lottie would have liked more too, but she knew there were more important things to worry about. They might have found Gwendolen, but Eunice was still in danger.

CHAPTER THIRTY

O N SUNDAY MORNING, LOTTIE WENT neither swimming nor to church. She felt she had to stay at home to tidy up and help get the sirloin joint into the oven. She missed Dilys's company peeling the potatoes and shelling the peas. Harriet said, 'At least she'll be here to help dish up and serve.'

Lottie very much wanted to talk to her mother on her own, and she'd changed and was ready by late morning when Gwen and Lazlo arrived. She took her to her bedroom to take off her hat and coat. Gwen sat at her dressing table and took a comb from her bag to run through her hair. 'I'm sorry I've caused you and the family so much worry,' she said. 'I could so easily have telephoned Jemima if I'd known you were chasing round looking for me.'

'I expect I caused you worry and stress when you found out you were having me.'

'You did, but the trouble was of my own making. Mine and Lazlo's.'

'It must have been a very difficult time for you.'

'It was. Charles and Jemima were shocked that Lazlo and I would do such a thing. It came at the worst possible time for everybody. Olwen was so ill, and we knew she'd not live much

331

longer. It also caused a huge upset with Jeremy, but he understood that our marriage wasn't what I'd been expecting. Once I got used to the idea and the furore died down, I wasn't unhappy about it. I thought Lazlo's baby would give me something special for my very own. I thought Jeremy would welcome you because you would make us look like a normal family.'

'But Grandma told me you had to bring me back here.'

'Yes, he resented Lazlo and therefore he resented you. He very much wanted a normal life, and ours is a strange marriage. Jeremy can think only of himself; it's as though he needs two wives. I am the social wife, the one in the public eye, the one he introduces to his colleagues. Colin was kept out of sight, but in his way, he was fond of us both.'

'But you didn't want to keep me.' Lottie had found it hard to deal with that thought. Her mother had handed her over to Grandma to bring up.

'I wanted you very much. I was heartbroken when I had to part with you, Charlotte. You see, I'm not physically strong; none of my family ever were. My pregnancy and all the worry it involved dragged me down, and it was harrowing nursing Olwen through her last months. After you were born, I too became ill. I was diagnosed with TB, the illness that had decimated the rest of my family. I don't know whether I caught it from Olwen, or whether it was always to be my fate. The smoky air of London and Liverpool were no good for me, and the doctors arranged for me to go to a sanatorium in Market Drayton where I spent twenty-two months.'

'So you couldn't keep me with you?' That lifted some of the weight that had been on Lottie's mind.

'No, having spent my childhood feeling ill and without energy, and seeing my mother, brothers and sister die of the disease, I dreamed of you growing big and strong like Lazlo, of running free in perfect health. I knew your best chance of doing that was to bring you here. I wanted Charles to bring you up in the way he brought up his own children. I was right about that; you look supremely healthy.'

'I am. You did the best thing you could for me.' Lottie could feel tears threatening to fall.

'When I left the sanatorium, I wanted to bring you home, but Jeremy persuaded me to leave you here. He said I needed to convalesce and I wasn't strong enough. As time went on, I regretted that. I should have insisted. Not only has it been on my conscience, but it felt all wrong to know you were growing up without me.'

There was a rap on the bedroom door and Grandma swept in. 'Charlotte, you mustn't keep Gwendolen to yourself; we all want to say hello and make her welcome. Lunch is almost ready, and if you come now there will just be time to have a glass of sherry first.'

Jemima led Gwen to the sitting room and Lottie followed. Aunt Harriet and Dilys were in the kitchen making gravy. Lottie had filled the empty grate with flowers from the garden that morning, and Dad and Lazlo were sitting one each side drinking beer.

Dad got up to greet Gwendolen, and Jemima said, 'I've been very worried about you. I went over one day to look for you. Martin said you were ill and Jeremy had taken you to a nursing home, and that's when I discovered Martin had lied and tricked us all.'

'So much must have happened to you,' Lottie said as she handed Gwen the glass of sherry Dad had poured for her. 'Do tell us.'

Gwen sighed. 'I'm afraid you don't know the half of what Martin did to Jeremy. His solicitor's practice hasn't been as profitable over the last year or so; he wasn't giving it the attention it needed, and when he couldn't meet Martin's demands, he took money from his clients' accounts.'

'Gwendolen! That is a criminal offence,' Grandma thundered.

'I didn't know about it for some time. Jeremy was too ashamed to tell me.'

'Oh my goodness, what a fool he is.'

'He's frightened and worried. Then, without telling me, he decided to buy that yacht. Martin has never had anything to do with boats or the sea, so Jeremy thought it was the perfect place for us to hide from him. I didn't approve, but as soon as Jeremy told me, I put the money he needed into his account. I look after most things for him; I have to. But then the police went round to his business and were asking questions. It seemed one of his clients was suspicious about missing funds, and Jeremy was so rattled that he immediately repaid the money.'

Charles sighed. 'And of course that left insufficient funds in his account to meet the cheque he wrote for the *Rowena*.'

'You should have walked out on him years ago.' Lazlo was angry.

'Perhaps I should,' Gwen said. 'Jeremy doesn't look after his bank accounts as he should; he never has. Once he realised his cheque had bounced, he was afraid the police would start looking for the boat. That's when he decided a furnished flat would be the answer. We looked at flats to rent where we'd never be found, but Jeremy would never have settled in any of them. I persuaded him that the best thing was to go home.'

'What a shambles,' Grandma was saying, when Harriet came in, her cheeks red and glistening from the heat of the kitchen.

'Lunch is ready. I've put the soup out for you to serve, Mother. Could you all please come to the table?'

'Oh my goodness,' Gwen said, catching sight of the two sepia photographs hanging on the dining-room wall. 'The *Olwen Thomas* and the *Gwendolen Thomas*. I was six years old when that ship was launched. I didn't care that it was just a small coastal collier, I was very proud of having a ship sailing with my name emblazoned on her hull. How old-fashioned she looks now.'

Gwendolen said little more about her difficulties until they were returning to the sitting room for coffee. She stopped in front of the two pictures to look more closely at them. 'I've been very lucky. My family managed their business exceedingly well.'

'We all did in those days,' Grandma said, standing on her dignity.

'As you know, my father sold his business when it seemed only Olwen and I would be left to run it. It gave us two girls a huge inheritance, enough to provide all we could want throughout our lives. He knew how to control money and took great pains to make sure we understood how the financial world functioned.'

'You may have inherited your family's wealth,' Grandma said sharply, 'but you inherited their poor health too.'

'Yes, unfortunately we did. I know you think it's bad manners to talk about money, Jemima, but I'm sure that is what is at the root of our present problems, and unless I explain, you won't understand.'

'I do understand money matters, Gwendolen.'

'I'm sure you do, Jemima, but this is for Charlotte and Dilys.' She gave her daughter a little smile. 'My father invested our inheritance through a first-class firm of stockbrokers that he'd used and trusted for years. We were told to discuss our wishes with them and nobody else. Our money is as safe as it possibly can be. Jeremy, though, was never taught about finance. He has no discipline when it comes to money. Martin is the same, if not worse.'

'I'd agree with that.' Jemima nodded.

'Jeremy's appetite for spending is voracious.' Gwen smiled. 'I had to take control of our household expenditure. He says I have austere habits.'

'You mean he expected you to provide him with unlimited money?' Charles asked.

'Not unlimited. I don't like to see money squandered, and I've had long practice at refusing to hand it over.'

Charles said, 'Gwen, why did we never realise that you're a very determined woman?'

'Or that Jeremy is at the end of his tether, having to wait for his case to come to court, and knowing he'll probably be sent to prison?' Lazlo added.

'He's very frightened,' Gwen agreed. 'Afraid of reporters asking questions and knowing his answers will be in the papers the next day. He's totally incapable now of looking after himself.'

'He's the very last person who should be deciding government policy.' Grandma was indignant. 'To think of him running the country, passing laws that honest citizens have to keep.'

'Parliament is sitting, but he doesn't want to go near the place,' Gwen said. 'In the past, he worked hard, but I think he gloried in being an MP. He was like an actor playing a part.'

They sat in silence, as though stunned, until Lottie asked, 'Who paid for Jeremy to come out on bail?'

'I did,' Gwen said. 'I knew he hated being in there; he pleaded with me to get him out.'

'Martin told Eunice that he'd paid for Jeremy's bail; that you refused to.'

'I might have guessed. That would be his way of explaining his need for more cash.'

'Eunice is in real trouble too,' Dilys said. 'We should have been taking care of her all along.'

'What are we going to do to help her?' Charles said. 'We need to put our heads together and decide on a plan.'

'She needs to get away from Martin.' Dilys was frowning. 'She's not well. Perhaps I can persuade her to come and stay with me.'

'Nonsense,' Jemima said. 'How can you possibly look after guests? There would be no room for Eunice and those two little boys in that doll's house of yours. You have to work three days a week and you're still a bride. No, our guest room has been ready and waiting for weeks, and we have plenty of space for the boys. Eunice would be far more comfortable with us here, and I can keep an eye on her.'

Dilys raised her eyebrows in resignation. 'We'll see, Grandma. I'll go round there again tomorrow. She needs somebody to talk to. I know I would if I were in her position.'

Chapter Thirty-One

L OTTIE COULD FEEL THE muscles she'd had tensed for weeks beginning to relax. Her mother was safe and well. She could feel the atmosphere at home lightening. Fear and dread were melting away. Jeremy still had his problems, of course, but the family were concentrating on Eunice now. Jemima was ringing Dilys almost daily, hoping to have better news of her.

Lottie was going over to see her mother quite often, and she no longer seemed a complete stranger. Lazlo was doing his best to encourage the family to see more of each other and get on more normal terms. He repaid them for their hospitality by inviting them all to Sunday lunch at the Royal Rock Hotel.

Glyn was expected home for his regular monthly leave again, and Lottie was discussing with Harriet the meal they would cook to welcome him back when it occurred to her that she'd not seen or heard anything of Philip for over two weeks. She raised the subject that evening with Lazlo, who was taking her and Gwen out for a meal.

'I've not seen him for a while either,' Lazlo said. 'Selfish of me really. I've got what I wanted and forgotten about him.'

That was on Lottie's conscience too, but she had to keep her mind on her work, and on Eunice.

Glyn came home with a deep suntan and bounding energy, arriving in time for dinner. He was like a breath of fresh air blowing through the family, all smiles and bursting with joy to see them again. They had a lot of news to tell him and spent ages round the table afterwards listening to his tales of life at sea. He and Lottie cleared away, and long after the others had gone to bed, they stayed up late chatting over the dying coals in the sitting room.

'Sorry to hear you've lost interest in Philip,' he said as they were saying goodnight.

Lottie's conscience smote her again. 'What makes you say that?'

'He's asked me and Dorothy to make up a foursome on Saturday night. He's got a new girlfriend. Her name's Sylvia. I assumed you knew.'

Lottie was shocked. It was the last thing she'd thought likely. But as she agonised about it later in bed, she realised she had only herself to blame. Philip had made his feelings for her clear, yet she'd been rude and thoughtless to him, insisting he treat her as a friend, turning away from his kisses and saying she wanted absolutely no romance. What a fool she was; even as a friend she should have been more aware of his feelings.

Lottie spent a miserable few days; even Glyn's presence couldn't cheer her up. On Sunday morning she couldn't wait to ask him what he'd thought of Philip's new girlfriend. 'An absolute stunner,' he said. 'She's so beautiful that people turn to look at her.'

'Oh! Does she have a job?'

'She's training to be a journalist with the *Echo*, but she also does modelling.'

So she was beautiful *and* she had a glamorous job. That really depressed her. This mistake was worse than believing Roddy Onslow loved her, and this time it was all her own fault. 'You know how I feel about you,' Philip had told her, and tried to kiss her. He'd given her several chances to change her mind. Now it looked as though it was too late.

Late on Monday afternoon, Dilys called round with news of Eunice. Lottie and Charles were not yet home, but Jemima and Harriet were having tea.

'She was totally fraught this morning,' Dilys said. 'She told me that all their staff have left. She doesn't know how she's going to manage to run the house on her own.'

'We have no staff and we manage,' Jemima reminded her tartly. 'You have no staff. It's not the end of the world.'

'It is to Eunice; she isn't used to cooking and cleaning, she's never done much in the house. She was all weepy because Martin expects the same standard of food and service from her. Also, school is breaking up for the summer holidays this week, and she'll have the children to look after as well.'

'We'll do our best to help,' Grandma said. 'Anyway, the girls usually spend their holidays with their maternal grandmother.'

Dilys pushed her hair off her face. 'I haven't explained it properly, Grandma. This is a real crisis. By the afternoon, Eunice got round to telling me that the staff had walked out because Martin hadn't paid their wages last month. He doesn't have the money for rail fares to send the girls to the Lake District. To the confectionery firm that employed him, Martin was never more than a member of the sales team. He'd been successful but, recently, he'd been acting strangely, and his sales had fallen so sharply that the sales manager felt the need to investigate. When he called on the sweet shops that had once been good customers he found their products were still being stocked, and they were well pleased with Martin Sanderson. He was now delivering their orders personally, and giving them better discounts than before. Further investigation revealed they were losing stock from their warehouse.

Martin's only excuse was that he was overworked and behind with his paperwork. He was dismissed without notice. He has no income whatsoever.'

Lottie and Charles arrived home in time to hear Dilys say, 'There's no money for the school fees next term. Martin literally has no money for anything. Not even food.'

'I see. I could have predicted this,' Grandma said. 'But Eunice does have the income her mother left her. I hope you reminded her that I've said she can always come here with the boys.'

'I did,' Dilys said, 'but she can't look after those three girls as well. When I asked about them, she just wrung her hands and wept. We can't leave them there with their father. I wanted her to try and get in touch with their grandmother, but she wouldn't; she leaves all that to Martin.'

'You will have to do that,' Grandma said.

'I know. I copied Laura's address and phone number from their address book, and I'll try and ring her when I get home. She needs to know what's going on here.'

Lottie felt stunned. It hardly seemed any time since she was envying Eunice's house and standard of living. Now she felt sorry for her.

'Poor Eunice is a wreck,' Dilys said. 'She doesn't care about her appearance any more and had yesterday's dinner down the front of her smock. Right, I'm going home to ring the girls' grandmother, then I'll fix up our spare rooms so Eunice can bring her boys to stay with me. I'll feel happier having her where I can keep an eye on her for the time being.'

Harriet and Dilys went to the airing cupboard for spare bedding, and Lottie helped carry the sheets and blankets to her sister's car. Whatever had made her think the family troubles were over?

The next morning, Gwen rang Lottie at the office. 'I'm frightened,' she said, panic in her voice. 'Can you get hold of Lazlo and bring him here?'

'What's happened?'

'It's Jeremy, he's at his wits' end. For months he's been talking about revenge, getting his own back on Martin. He hates him, and blames him for all this trouble he's in. Now he's telling me he's going to kill him. He's planning to poison him.'

Lottie was aghast. 'Are you sure?' There was no mistaking her mother's fear, but it all sounded very far-fetched.

'Jeremy is in an awful mess. The days are flying past and I know he's feeling desperate about the court case. He means to poison Martin before then.'

Lottie tried to steady her nerves. 'But how can he? What sort of poison?'

'He's just showed me a package marked "Cyanide". He had to sign a register to buy it, and give a reason for wanting it. He told me he'd written down that it was to kill moles in his garden.

He's swearing to get his own back on Martin, give him what he deserves.'

'We've got to stop that,' Lottie said, 'and not just for Martin's sake. If Jeremy attempts to poison him, the fact that he bought cyanide and openly signed the register for it will be enough evidence to hang him.'

'I know. I've pointed that out but he doesn't seem to care. Can you get hold of Lazlo? He said he'd come round tonight, but it could be too late by then.'

Lottie at last felt the urgency of this. 'I'll do my best,' she said, 'but the only way I can do it is to go to his lodgings, and that takes time.'

'As fast as you can. Please. I'll try and keep Jeremy here.'

When Lottie told her father what was happening, there was a look of total disbelief on his face. 'No, love,' he said, giving her a comforting hug. 'When people say they're going to kill someone, it's just a figure of speech. I can't believe Jeremy is serious.'

'Gwen believes he is,' she said. 'I'll have to find Lazlo.'

She was already lifting the phone to ring Philip. She thought perhaps he'd know where he was, might even be going to meet him. If he wasn't at his lodgings, she wouldn't have any idea where he was, and she'd have to go to Gwen's on her own.

It was Fiona who answered. 'I don't think Philip would know, Lottie. He's already gone over to Liverpool. He's being taken out to lunch today.'

'By his father?' She knew Lazlo was sometimes included in invitations like that.

'No, a new friend he's made.'

That felt like a dagger in her back. 'It wouldn't be Sylvia, would it?'

There was a slight pause, then, 'Actually, her parents have invited him.'

'Oh!' It took Lottie a moment to pull herself together. 'Thank you,' she said hurriedly. 'Sorry to have bothered you.'

'I ought to go with you,' Charles said, 'but the *Denbigh* will be docking within the hour. Come on, I'll run you to the station to get the train over. Be careful, and don't go to Gwen's house on your own.'

Lottie had her fingers crossed as she hurried to Lazlo's lodgings. When his landlady answered the door, she said, 'I haven't heard him go out. I think he's still upstairs.' Lottie took the four flights of stairs at speed and arrived at his door gasping for breath.

'I was just getting ready to go out,' he said, 'but do come in and sit down.'

'I hope you weren't going anywhere important,' she said, and told him why she'd come.

'If Gwen needs help, there's nothing more important than that. Let's go. I'm glad I got a car; we can be up there in fifteen minutes.'

While he put his coat on, Lottie remembered the last time she'd been here. 'Did you ever find that note I left you?'

'Yes, once I started looking for it. When you pushed it under the door, it also went under the lino, so I didn't see it.'

Lottie sat in the passenger seat, relieved she'd managed to make contact with Lazlo. It was a lovely summer's day, the sort that made her think of holidays. She tried to relax. 'Do you think Jeremy really intends to poison Martin?'

'How could he possibly do that? Buying poison is one thing. Getting Martin to swallow it is another. He'd be better off thinking about what he'll say in his defence when he gets to court. Gwen says she can't get him to talk to his solicitor, even though he's worried stiff.'

'Thank goodness you've come,' Gwen said when they were shown into her sitting room. They could see she was very frightened. Lazlo put a comforting arm round her shoulders, while Lottie asked, 'Where is Jeremy?'

'He's out in the garden shed. He's in quite a state.'

'How d'you mean, ready to put his fists up?'

'No, there's no fight in him now. You saw how much he's changed. His problems have reduced him to a jelly.'

'So you aren't scared of him?'

'No, Lazlo, but I'm scared of what he'll do to Martin. He really means it.'

Lottie had had time to think. 'Why don't we go to the shed together and try to persuade him to give us the poison? If we can get it from him, he can't hurt anybody. We can return it to the shop where he bought it, and get the entry in the register cancelled.'

'He wouldn't give it to me,' Gwen said. 'I've tried and tried. He's been sitting out there nursing the package for hours.'

'When did he buy it?'

'Yesterday, I think. He was talking about it last night, but I didn't see it until after breakfast this morning.'

Lazlo shrugged. 'I can't think of anything better. Come on, let's try that.'

Lottie trailed after them. Jeremy's garden looked positively manicured compared to that at home, the lawns neat and trim and the borders full of colourful scented flowers. Gwen opened the door of the large shed and led them inside. Jeremy was slumped on a stool with his head on his workbench.

Slowly he looked up at them. 'Leave me alone, I don't want to talk to you.'

Lottie stepped forward. 'We can't do that,' she said. 'Gwen says you've bought poison in order to kill Martin.' He said nothing, but his eyes were dark pools of despair. She could see he had the package under his hand on the workbench. 'It won't help you to do that. It'll turn you into a murderer. You'll have the weight of the law after you.'

'I don't care.'

'How do you think Gwen will feel?' Lazlo put in. 'She'll care, won't she? And so will you, when it's too late.'

Silently Jeremy fingered the package.

'Uncle Jeremy, why don't you give me the poison?' Lottie asked. 'I'll take it back to the shop where you bought it and say you've changed your mind, that it's too dangerous to use in the garden. That Gwen fears for her dog.'

'She doesn't have a dog.'

'And you don't have moles in the garden. Look, I'll make sure the chemist cancels the entry you made in his register. Then you can be sure there'll be no added trouble for you from this.'

His troubled eyes met hers for the first time, and sent a shiver down her spine. He grunted. 'How do I know you won't poison me with it? It would look like suicide then because it was me who bought it.'

'I'd never do that,' she burst out. 'I'm not a murderer. I couldn't kill you. I couldn't kill anybody.'

'Neither could I,' Gwen said. 'We want to help you, Jeremy. You know me well enough to be sure of that, don't you?'

He seemed a man in chaos against the orderliness of the ranks of garden tools fastened to the shed wall. But slowly his fingers relaxed on the package and he handed it to Lottie. In block capitals was the word POISON, and printed below in heavy lettering: SALT OF POTASSIUM CYANIDE, followed by warnings about the dire effect it could have on animals. She wanted to drop it.

'How about coming indoors and having a cup of coffee?' Gwen asked gently, taking his arm.

Lazlo took his other arm and helped him to his feet. 'This is much the best way,' he said. 'You don't want any more trouble, do you?'

'I want to get my own back on Martin,' Jeremy said. 'He has caused all my troubles. He's a greedy man, always wants his pound of flesh. I want to give him his just deserts.'

'Better if you let it go,' Gwen said. 'Forget what Martin has done.'

'I can't,' he grunted.

Lottie wanted to get rid of the deadly package. 'Wouldn't it be better if we went straight to the shop now?' she said.

'It would,' Lazlo agreed, and led the way round to the front of the house to his car. 'We'll have that coffee when we come back.' He ushered Jeremy and Gwen into the back seat. 'You'd better sit in front with me, Lottie. Let me have a look at that package. Is the address of the chemist on it?'

Lottie held it up so he could read it. Gwen had to tell him which way to go. They set off, but it had all seemed too easy. She was fearful Jeremy might try to snatch the package back.

She put it on the floor and held her foot over it.

Lazlo parked right in front of the shop. Lottie went inside with the package, and the white-coated chemist wished her good morning. She was glad to find she was the only customer as she pushed the poison across the counter to him. Haltingly she told him the story she'd decided on. 'I don't want a refund,' she said. 'I just want to get rid of the stuff.'

'Very wise,' the chemist said, and reached for the register in which he noted all purchases of poison. 'When was it bought?'

She watched him find the entry and write in red: *Package returned unopened.*

As she went back outside into the sunshine, she felt as though a great weight had been lifted off her shoulders. 'All done,' she reported. 'No need to worry about that any more.'

'Thank you,' Gwen said. 'We all feel better now, don't we, Jeremy?'

He was struggling to get out of the car. 'There's an off-licence just along the parade,' he said. 'I'd like to buy some whisky.'

'There's no need,' Gwen said. 'You have plenty at home.' But he was already out and heading towards the shop, a shambling, bent and broken man.

Lazlo said, 'I still find it hard to believe that he actually bought poison to kill Martin.'

'He meant to do it,' Gwen said. 'Thank God you stopped him. I'm very grateful to you both.'

Jeremy came back with two bottles of Glenfiddich. Lazlo read the label. 'Posh stuff, single malt, twelve years old. Is it better than the average whisky?'

'I prefer it,' Jeremy said.

When Lazlo ran the car into their drive, it was almost lunchtime, but Jeremy refused to come into the house with them. He took the two bottles of Glenfiddich to his shed.

'He does keep a glass out there,' Gwen said. 'I know he enjoys a quiet drink by himself sometimes.'

'I hope he isn't going to get drunk and difficult to handle,' Lazlo said. 'I'd better stay with you in case he does.'

'Being out in the garden and having a tot usually calms him down,' Gwen assured them as they followed her inside. 'I'd be delighted if you'd both stay and have lunch with us.'

'Thank you, but I've got to go back to the office,' Lottie said. 'There'll be a lot of work for me and Dad to do this afternoon.'

'Then I'll run you to the nearest train station,' Lazlo said.

Both he and Gwen hugged her and thanked her for the help she'd given them. 'Such a relief to get that poison back to the shop,' Gwen said, 'and to know he can't use it.'

CHAPTER THIRTY-TWO

LOTTIE DID HAVE A BUSY afternoon. Dad had plenty of jobs waiting for her, but the success she'd felt at being able to help Gwen buoyed her up, and she did them with gusto.

At about four o'clock, Dad was down at the dock when Philip rang. 'Mother tells me you were looking for Lazlo this morning. Is there another problem?'

'There was,' she said and told him about it.

'Sorry I wasn't there to help.'

Lottie's conscience smote her again. 'I'm sorry, Philip, I owe you an apology. I was a pig to you last month, rude and ungrateful when you took me to see *Chu Chin Chow*. I can quite understand why you're keeping away. It's as though any problem I have shuts out everything else. I can't think of my friends, can't even be polite to them.'

'Lottie, that's not unusual. It happens to most of us. You've had a great deal to cope with.'

Dad burst back into the office saying, 'Lottie, could you—' She held up her hand.

'Sorry, Philip, we've got a ship in. It's one of those busy days. I'll have to go, but it seems ages since I saw you. I have missed you.'

'How would it be if I came down for an hour tonight? Just for a chat.'

'We'll be late home.'

'What about after supper, say eight o'clock? Would that be all right?'

'Yes,' she said. 'I'll be glad to see you then.'

For the rest of the day, Lottie looked forward to seeing Philip. She was sorry she'd been so horrible to him and afraid now that things between them could never be the same again. While she'd made things better for others, she'd fouled up her own life. Perhaps ruined things for ever.

They were late getting home, and she and Harriet were still washing up when he arrived. She was drying her hands on the tea towel as she went to the door. 'Hello, Philip, do come in.'

He was smiling and looked more attractive than ever. Dad and Grandma made a fuss of him and told him they'd missed him coming round. Lottie needed to speak to him on his own, so she said to Harriet, 'Philip will help me finish the washing-up.'

'I'll be more than happy to leave you two alone,' Harriet said with a rather coy smile at Philip.

Once the door clicked shut behind her, Lottie said, 'I'm sorry.'

He smiled. 'You've already apologised profusely on the phone. Let's forget all that. I'm sorry too.'

He was no longer at ease with her; that had gone. She turned her back on the unwashed plates and the cooling greasy water in the brown stone sink. She had to get this out of the way first. 'Glyn tells me you've got a stunning new girlfriend, a real beauty, but I hope you'll still want to be friends with me.'

'Friends?' He stepped forward and took her in his arms. 'I was hoping you were over this obsession about us being friends. You must know I want more than that; I always have.'

'But what about this new girlfriend – Sylvia, isn't it?'

'Lottie, I want you to know that I took up with Sylvia because I was getting nowhere with you. I was afraid you were giving me the brush-off. She's a raving beauty all right, but she thinks of nothing else but keeping her nose well powdered and buying new clothes. She doesn't like sailing and won't even go for a walk if it's raining in case it spoils her hairdo. She'd never be any sort of a replacement for you.'

Lottie clung to him, hardly able to believe her ears.

'I love you,' he went on. 'I try to tell you that every time I see you, but your mind is crammed with a hundred and one other things that you seem to find more important.'

'What a fool I've been.' Her smile was widening, and now it turned into a little laugh. 'When Glyn told me about Sylvia, I felt quite jealous. I was afraid I'd turned you off for good. I love you too, I really do.'

Philip looked at her seriously. 'I don't want to rush you, Lottie, but this is something I've worried over for weeks. It's not the right place either, but I do need to get this settled. Charlotte Mortimer, will you marry me? I'd be very honoured if you'd be my wife.'

'Yes, oh yes. I want that more than anything else in the world.'

His arms tightened round her and his lips came down on hers. Lottie was up on cloud nine.

It was some time before she whispered, 'D'you remember

one Christmas when you were about twelve? You asked me to marry you then, and I said yes.'

He laughed. 'Yes, I found a ring in a party cracker and put it on your finger.'

'You said I could consider myself engaged.'

He laughed. 'That was too long ago; I was afraid I couldn't hold you to it.'

Lottie laughed with him, brimming with happiness. 'You've always been the one for me. Now we really are engaged.'

'I need to update that ring. You must come out with me and choose it.'

'Lovely. Shall we tell the family now?' she asked.

'Why not.'

Philip took her by the hand and led her into the sitting room. Three faces turned to look at them with questioning eyes. 'Lottie has just agreed to marry me,' he announced.

Dad leapt up to kiss her and shake Philip's hand. 'I'm delighted,' he said. 'I wish you both every happiness.'

Harriet was close on his heels. 'So do I.'

Grandma was slower getting to her feet, but she came to kiss her. 'Thank goodness you've forgotten that Roddy,' she said. 'Philip is a much wiser choice for you. You'll be safe with him.'

Lottie giggled. 'Safety isn't what I'm after, Grandma.'

Jemima was stern. 'That's the trouble with you youngsters, you can't learn from other people's experience. You may not seek safety, but you need it.'

Lottie wanted to change the subject, but it was Philip who said, 'Tomorrow I'm going to take Lottie out and buy her a ring. I want everybody to know we're officially engaged.'

'A ring?' Grandma was showing her disapproval. 'This is no time to waste your money on jewellery. You need to think of setting up a home.'

'It's usual, Mrs Mortimer,' he said hesitantly.

'I have plenty of rings.' Jemima took a key from the chain on which her fob watch was suspended. 'Harriet, get the box from the safe in my bedroom and bring it here. I want Charlotte to choose one that she likes.'

'It's the prerogative of the groom to provide an engagement ring,' Philip said slowly.

'These are Mortimer family rings, good quality, better than a young man in your position can afford.'

Lottie could see he was embarrassed; even Dad was. Harriet brought the rings and spread them out along a side table. Lottie stared at them. She didn't want Grandma to upset Philip, but neither did she want to upset Grandma. She picked up a pretty ruby surrounded with pearls.

'That's more of a dress ring.' Grandma took it from her. 'And not this one either; opals are considered bad luck. Now this was my engagement ring. My husband was in Philip's position, unable to afford a good-quality ring. So my father gave him this.' She was pushing a heavy gold band with a large solitaire diamond on to Lottie's ring finger. It felt cold and heavy.

'It's not a good fit, Grandma,' Lottie managed.

'It is a good stone,' Dad said, 'but the setting is old-fashioned, and it needs cleaning.'

'Philip,' Grandma said, 'I suggest you take it to a jeweller and have it polished and reset. Recut if that's what you want. Have it modernised for Charlotte.'

'It'll be lovely when it's done,' Harriet said.

'Yes, it's a fine diamond,' Lottie said carefully, 'but if it was your engagement ring, why don't you wear it?'

Grandma spread her hands in front of her. 'This is what age does to your fingers; the knuckles swell up with rheumatism and I can no longer get my rings on.'

'You could have them made larger,' Charles said.

'I have done already, more than once. I can't be bothered any more.'

'Then thank you, Mrs Mortimer,' Philip said politely. 'I shall do what you suggest. It's very kind of you to give us this, and you're quite right, it is of a far better quality than I can afford.'

'I shall be proud to wear a Mortimer family diamond,' Lottie said, but she was concerned. 'You didn't offer one of these to Dilys or to Eunice, did you?'

'It didn't occur to me to offer one to Eunice, as Martin seemed to be wealthy. I did offer a ring to Dilys, but made the mistake of delaying until after Alec had bought one for her. She refused, of course.'

'I won't refuse,' Lottie told her and kissed her cheek. 'Thank you very much. I'll love that ring when it's done.'

'Your grandfather was an Irish doctor with little money. He worked hard to help the poor Irish immigrants who came to Liverpool looking for a better life. He was a very good husband. I'm sure you will be equally trustworthy, Philip.'

When Philip left, Lottie walked up the garden to see him off. 'Alone at last,' he said. 'I want to buy you a ring, so you'll have two. It won't be as good as that diamond, but tomorrow we'll choose something.'

'I'm so glad you didn't insist on that to Grandma. It was kinder to accept.'

'I had to, she meant to be generous.'

'D'you know, I've never heard Grandma admit she's made a mistake before. Nor has she ever referred to her old age or any infirmity.'

'She's mellowing,' Philip said.

Lottie smiled, feeling that at last things had come right for her. She wouldn't stop worrying about Eunice and Gwen, but for now, she and Philip were thinking about their future. She kissed him goodnight in a haze of joyous happiness.

CHAPTER THIRTY-THREE

T HE FOLLOWING MONDAY, LOTTIE drove Dad home from work and found she was following Dilys's car, which seemed to be packed tight with suitcases and parcels. Once they reached the back garden, Dad leapt out of the car. 'Has something happened?' he asked Dilys.

'A lot is happening,' she replied. They knew that after Dilys had phoned the girls' grandparents in the Lake District, they'd come down to stay in a nearby guest house. Dilys had helped them pack the girls' belongings, most of which they'd had to send by rail. All the time that was going on, Martin had stayed in his study and kept the door firmly closed.

'Eunice hardly seemed to know what she was doing,' Dilys said. 'She'd put things in the trunk, then take them out again. She couldn't make any decisions. I had to wake Martin from his lethargy and make him look for their birth certificates and various documents relating to their mother.'

After two very difficult days, their grandparents had taken the three girls away. 'When the time came to say goodbye, Frances clung to Eunice and wept, and Christabel was rebellious. Martin wouldn't even have bothered to see them off if I hadn't dragged him out of his study to do so.

'Eunice says he's spending almost all his time in there, that he's drinking and won't come out to eat meals with them. He's bad-tempered and miserable with her and the boys, and complains about the noise they make and about her cooking. She seems to be making little effort to clean the house, and order is rapidly descending into chaos.

'The good news is that she's agreed to leave him at last. She's going to tell him tonight that now the school holidays have started, they all need a break, and she'll bring the boys to my place for a few days. I've been helping her pack today; she's no longer capable of doing that on her own.'

They were walking down the garden to the back door when Dilys added, 'Oh, and Jeremy came round this afternoon, and he and Martin spent a long time talking together in his study.'

'I thought those two were sworn enemies,' Dad said.

Lottie couldn't believe what she was hearing. It was only a few days ago that Jeremy had been threatening to poison Martin.

'Well now it seems they've made it up,' said Dilys. 'The sounds I heard were quite affable. But Eunice certainly can't stay there any longer. I've said I'll collect her tomorrow.'

'Dilys, you'll need help. You won't get Eunice and the two boys into your little car, and they'll have a lot of baggage.'

'I've brought a lot of their stuff with me now, as you can see. Alec's school has broken up, and he said he'd come with me tomorrow. We've decided to go over on the train and get a taxi back.'

'I could come too,' Dad said. 'I haven't done much to help Eunice.'

'Alec and I will manage fine.'

Dilys had to repeat all this for Grandma and Harriet when

they reached the sitting room. 'I went over this morning and I've spent much of today with her. She told me Martin came to the dining room for breakfast this morning, and she'd made an effort to cook what he said he fancied. But he complained his bacon was half raw and his egg fried to a frazzle, and threw the plate across the room at her. Then he lost his temper with Tom because he laughed.'

'What a mess,' Grandma said. 'Martin is going to walk away from his responsibilities. He fathers five children and leaves it to others to bring them up.'

Dilys went home to unpack her car, and Harriet got their dinner on the table. Grandma couldn't stop talking about the problem. 'This probably means a divorce for Eunice, the first ever in our family. What a disgrace.'

They had barely finished eating when the phone rang. Lottie happened to be nearest to it, so she picked it up. It took her a moment to recognise Eunice's voice; she was screaming and shouting. Twice Lottie had to ask her to repeat what she was saying. It brought Grandma and Harriet to her side. When she eventually understood, she felt sweat breaking out across her forehead, and gasped out, 'She thinks Martin is dead!'

Grandma snatched the receiver from her hand. 'Eunice, calm down,' she boomed. 'Take a deep breath, and now another . . . Is that better? Now tell me what's happened.'

Lottie listened in a state of shock, and Harriet was open-mouthed. The noise had brought Dad to join them.

Jemima was saying, 'Have you called the doctor?'

Lottie could feel her knees sagging. Would a doctor be any good? Eunice had said he was dead, and seemed quite sure about that. She remembered with a sinking feeling that Jeremy had been with Martin in his study this afternoon. Could he have found some other way to kill him?

'Yes, Eunice,' Grandma said calmly. 'Lottie and Dad can come over ... Yes, dear, but perhaps you should ring Gwendolen. She's nearer and can be with you more quickly ... What? ... All right.' She put the phone down. Her face had gone paper white; she looked petrified.

'What is it?' Dad was impatient.

'She thinks Martin's dead. She took a tray of supper to his study and found him like that. She rang Dilys first, and Dilys told her to phone the doctor and then to call everybody else. Her doorbell rang, so she went to answer it.'

'We'll have to go over,' Charles said. 'She needs somebody with her.'

'Dilys and Alec are on their way,' Jemima said.

'I feel I ought to go,' Charles said. 'She is my daughter. I can't leave everything to other people.'

'I'll come with you, Dad,' Lottie said as she rushed to put her coat on.

Dad was in the driving seat for once, and she had to persuade him to leave the car in Hamilton Square and take the train from there. 'The luggage boat stops running quite early in the evening; we might find we can't get the car back.'

As they approached Eunice's house, she was relieved to recognise Lazlo's car parked close to the front door. Dilys let them in. 'Hello, I thought you might come over.'

'Is Martin really dead?' Lottie asked.

'Yes,' Lazlo said. 'The doctor thinks he might have had a heart attack, but he can't sign the death certificate because it was so sudden. The coroner will have to be informed.'

'But Martin was fit and well, wasn't he?' asked Lottie.

'The doctor told us that heart attacks can strike people out of the blue,' said Gwen. 'Martin might have had a heart problem but didn't know about it.'

'I was afraid . . .' Charles began.

'After listening to Auntie Gwen, and knowing there'll be an inquest, we're all afraid,' Dilys agreed. 'The doctor said he'll arrange everything; we're just waiting for the ambulance to come to take Martin to the morgue. Come and have some tea. Alec has just made a fresh pot.'

'How is Eunice?'

'In a terrible state; she's lying down upstairs. She'd put the boys to bed, but we're going to take them all back to our house. I've rung for a taxi.'

Headlights were coming into the drive. 'Is that the taxi or the ambulance?' Dilys opened the front door. 'Good, it's the taxi. I'll bring Eunice down. Can you bring the boys out?'

Eunice looked terrible, downright ill. Lottie wrapped her coat round her and got her on to the back seat, then put Eddie on her lap. Dilys joined her holding Tom, and with Alec beside the driver and two suitcases stowed, the vehicle pulled away.

Charles breathed a sigh of relief. 'We've done all we can. Dilys will take care of Eunice now. Let's have that cup of tea before we do anything else. I'm sure we're all in need.'

Lottie flung herself on to the sofa. She was tired, and she knew Dad must be too. Lazlo poured out and handed cups round. 'It might not be over yet,' he said.

'I wish it were,' Lottie breathed. 'It's one problem after another, and they're getting worse.' Nobody disagreed with that.

'There is another,' Gwen said slowly. 'Jeremy has disappeared, and his case is coming up tomorrow.'

Lottie groaned. Charles said, 'When did you last see him?'

'He had lunch with me at one o'clock,' Gwen said, 'and I haven't seen him since. Dilys said he came round here about half past two and spent an hour or so with Martin in his study; she didn't hear him go, so she doesn't know exactly when he left. We always eat at seven o'clock, but he didn't show up. This isn't like him.'

'Let's drink this tea,' Lazlo said, 'and then I want to have another look at Martin before the ambulance takes him away.'

Charles took two gulps from his cup and was on his feet again. 'Let's get that over with now.'

Lottie trailed behind them as they all went to the study. She'd never seen a dead body before, and was reluctant to do so now, but it was recognisably Martin. He was stretched out in his large and comfortable desk chair.

'Gwen and I both noticed this,' Lazlo said, picking up the bottle of Glenfiddich on his desk. 'Jeremy bought two bottles of this the other day when he was with us. He must have brought it here.'

There were two cut-glass whisky glasses on the desk; one was empty, but the other still had an inch of amber liquid in it. Charles picked it up and swirled it round.

'Don't taste that,' Gwen said.

'I just want to smell it,' he said. He took a sniff. 'It is whisky.'

Gwen held the glass against the bottle. 'It looks the same, but did he add something to it? Jeremy wanted to get his own back on Martin. He told us he intended to poison him.'

Charles looked confused. 'But Lottie told me she'd taken the poison back to the chemist.'

'She did. Lazlo drove us there. We wanted Jeremy to see her do it.'

'He didn't put up a fight to keep that package,' Lottie said. 'Could he have had more? Anyway, cyanide isn't the only poison. He could have arranged a backup. Had he something else in mind?'

'It looks horribly likely,' Gwen said. 'And I read somewhere that victims of poisoning die in agony. Just look at Martin's face.'

'Yes, though I understand a heart attack is very painful too,' said Charles.

Lazlo said, 'I suggest we pour all this whisky down the sink. Wash the glasses and put the bottle in the bin.'

'Should we do that?' Charles was frowning more heavily. 'We could be destroying evidence.'

'Evidence of what?' Lazlo demanded. 'The doctor thinks he had a heart attack; that means he died of natural causes. It would be entirely normal to tidy up, wouldn't it?' He picked up the bottle and glasses. 'Where is the kitchen?'

Lottie led the way and watched him pour the whisky down the sink. When he'd finished, she washed and dried the glasses. 'Where do these go?'

'I've seen a drinks cupboard in his study,' Gwen said.

As they finished putting everything away, the headlights of the ambulance lit up the window. Lazlo went to open the front door.

By the time the ambulancemen had loaded Martin's body into their vehicle and driven slowly away, the tea had gone cold in the cups. 'Come to my place,' Gwen said, 'and I'll make us a fresh pot.' She shivered. 'This house is giving me the creeps.'

While Lottie and Gwen washed up the tea things, Lazlo and Charles went round the house making sure that it was locked up securely.

'We ought to go home,' Charles worried. 'It's getting late.'

'Let's first find out if Jeremy is at home,' Lottie said. 'If he is, it's one less thing to worry about.'

'There's a railway station just round the corner from our place,' Gwen said. 'Less of a walk than from here.'

They all got into Lazlo's car and Gwen said, 'Since we went into Martin's study and I saw that whisky bottle on his desk, I've felt all of a flutter. It must mean Jeremy was involved in his death. He must have had more poison than we knew about.'

'Don't worry yet,' Lazlo said. 'If he's not at home, we'll ring the police and report him missing. That's what we'd do if everything was normal.'

'I'm keeping my fingers crossed that he's there,' Gwen said grimly, but when Lazlo pulled into the drive, the house was in darkness and there was no sign of Jeremy's car. She unlocked the door and threw it open, but there was utter silence. 'He's not here,' she said. 'There's nobody here.'

'Don't you have staff living in?' Charles asked.

'No, can't get anybody to do that these days.'

'Right,' Lazlo said, 'let's have a good look round first, and then Gwen, you must ring the police. I'd like to find that other bottle of Glenfiddich. Will it still be in the shed, do you think?'

'Probably, but that'll have to wait for daylight; there's no light in there.'

'Do you have a torch?'

'Somewhere, yes.'

'Never mind, let's start with his study.' Lazlo went in and switched on the lights. They all stood looking carefully round.

'No bottles on show here,' Lottie said, and began opening cabinets and drawers.

'This is a study to be proud of, so why was Jeremy spending hours in his shed?' Lazlo said.

'He has a drinks cabinet,' Lottie said, 'but there's no Glenfiddich here. Plenty of ordinary whisky, though – a full bottle and another three-quarters full.'

'So why did he buy the Glenfiddich the other day?' Lazlo pondered.

'Was it a favourite tipple of Martin's?' Lottie shivered. 'Was it meant to tempt him to drink poison?' The thought made her feel sick. She'd watched Jeremy buy it. They all had, but they'd thought their worries were over once the cyanide was back in the shop.

Gwen joined them looking worried stiff. 'The police have taken details and will start looking for him. They want me to take a photo of him down to the station in the morning. I'm going to make some tea, unless you'd prefer some of this whisky?'

'Tea please,' they chorused, and she went to the kitchen.

Lottie sat down at the desk and looked at the large book that was lying in front of her. After a few moments she jerked up. 'Oh my goodness,' she said, her heart turning over. 'Look at this – "Common Poisons found in the Average Garden".'

'Strewth.' Lazlo's mouth hung open.

Dad was visibly shaken. 'Then he did kill Martin! Must have done. And that Glenfiddich was to put the poison in. Oh my God!'

They all started talking at once; this was an important find. Gwendolen returned with a tea tray, but nobody was interested in that now. 'Has Jeremy gone on the run?' she suggested. 'The police would want to talk to him if they knew about this.'

When they'd calmed down, Lazlo asked, 'Lottie, what are these common garden poisons?'

She turned to the index and read out, 'Belladonna or deadly nightshade, digitalis, laurel . . .'

'There's a whole hedge of laurel along the front,' Gwendolen gasped, 'and I've seen deadly nightshade growing there too. Jeremy pointed it out to me once and told me it was dangerous.'

'There's loads more,' Lottie said. 'Hemlock, which has been poisoning people since Biblical times. Aconitum – that is said to be the most dangerous plant in Europe. The flowers are called monkshood, but I don't know what they look like.'

'I believe we have a patch of those too,' Gwen said.

'Oh gosh!' The pages of the book had fallen open. 'He's left a bookmark in the section on digitalis.' Lottie was struggling to get her breath.

They stared silently at each other for a long minute. Then Gwen said, 'Does that mean it was what he used?'

'It looks like it,' Charles said. 'That's probably the best indication we're likely to get.'

Gwen drew a deep, shuddering breath. 'What is digitalis?'

Lottie began to read it out. '"The common foxglove grows wild in Britain but is frequently cultivated in gardens because of its bell-like flowers of several colours. All parts of the plant contain digitalis and digoxin."'

'Oh my goodness. Jeremy's proud of his foxgloves.' Gwen was ignoring the tea tray. 'He grows lots in the borders, white ones as well as purple, and with a bit of plant food they get really tall.'

Lottie read on. '"To touch the stem can irritate the skin. If ingested, the foxglove causes delirium, convulsions, tremors and headaches. In humans it has a dramatic effect on the heart. For centuries it has been used in medicine to treat heart problems, and in humans an overdose mimics the medical condition it is used to treat."'

'That's it,' Charles said. 'The doctor thought he'd had a heart attack.'

Lottie could feel the sweat standing out on her forehead as she continued. '"It is safe today to use medically, but in the past it was dangerous, because the extreme potency of the foxglove meant it was very easy to give an overdose. Even the use of raw leaves of the purple foxglove, *Digitalis purpurea*, will kill in small quantities. A high dose can kill within minutes by effectively paralysing the heart. It leaves no obvious signs, but its presence is detectable by a pathologist if he knows to look for it."'

'Well I'd say that was what Jeremy used.' Charles looked stunned. 'It would be so easy for him. It's enough to make your hair stand on end.'

Lottie agreed. She'd had no idea the garden contained poisons like that. It made her feel sick.

'Come on, we have to go.' Charles stood up. 'We don't want to miss the last train.'

'They run until half eleven,' Lazlo said. 'Plenty of time yet.'

'I'm tired,' Charles sighed heavily, 'and this has been an alarming evening. Heaven knows what else will come to light. Lottie, you can come back tomorrow; there won't be much to do in the office.'

As they walked to the station, Lottie couldn't bear to think of what Jeremy had apparently done. Instead, she pondered on whether Lazlo intended to spend the night with Gwen. It certainly looked like it. She thought it would be the best thing for both of them. They'd be in need of comfort after the events of the evening. Grandma would be outraged, and possibly Dad too. She wouldn't mention it to either of them.

CHAPTER THIRTY-FOUR

LOTTIE GOT UP THE next morning feeling full of apprehension. The rest of the family looked strained. Today was the day Jeremy's case would be heard; he'd been told to attend court at ten o'clock.

Harriet was a bag of nerves and dropped a plate of porridge on the kitchen floor. Grandma barked at her irritably and made a fuss about the mess and the broken plate. It meant helpings were smaller than usual, but that didn't matter, since none of them had any appetite.

Jemima phoned Gwendolen before breakfast to find out if Jeremy had returned home during the night. He had not, and Gwen didn't know whether the hearing would be cancelled or whether it would proceed without him.

Lottie felt tense and worried. She went to the office with Dad to open the post, because Grandma said there was no point in getting to Gwen's house too early. She couldn't settle to do anything else.

Philip rang her at half past nine. 'I'm in Liverpool,' he said. 'I came over on the luggage boat this morning with Mum and Dad. They're motoring up to Manchester to have lunch with some friends. The thing is, I saw Jeremy's car parked near the river. It was raining and the hood was down, and it looked as though it had been there for some time, so I got out to have a closer look. He'd left the keys in the ignition; anybody could have taken it. I put the hood up and locked it to make it safe, but goodness knows where he is. I waited around for a bit, but he hasn't shown up.'

Lottie's anxiety burst into full-blown dread. This discovery opened up a whole lot of new, positively dreadful possibilities.

'I have a lot to tell you,' she said. 'There have been frightening developments. Can you drive that car?'

'Well I'd love to have a go.'

'Gwen and Lazlo are expecting me to come over. Dad'll run me to the station here. Could you meet me at James Street in half an hour? Unless you're planning to do something else this morning?'

'I've been told to buy some respectable clothes to wear to the office when I start work next month, but I'd rather drive you up to Arbuthnot's place.'

'Good, I'll see you shortly then.'

Although she was five minutes early, he was waiting for her when she came out of the station. He leaned over to kiss her when she got in. 'This is a lovely car,' he said. 'A shame to let it get wet inside. I've tried to dry it off a bit. Are you all right? You sounded frightened on the phone.'

'I'm scared stiff.' She recounted everything that had happened yesterday. 'We're all waiting with bated breath for the next disaster.'

'Will Jeremy be in court for his hearing? That's today, isn't it?'

'Phil, we have no way of knowing.'

'If he isn't, it'll only make things worse for him.'

Lottie shivered. 'They couldn't be any worse. Since you told me you'd found his car apparently abandoned near the river, I've been afraid he might have thrown himself into it.'

'Oh God! That's an appalling thought. Heaven forbid.'

When they rang Gwen's doorbell, Lazlo came to the door. His mouth dropped open when he saw Jeremy's car. 'Philip noticed it,' Lottie said, 'parked near the river.'

The significance of that was not lost on him. 'Strewth!'

'He'd left the hood down,' Philip said. 'I'm afraid it got wet inside.'

'Badly?'

'We're damp from sitting on the seats,' Lottie said.

Lazlo leapt across the wet gravel to open the back door. 'We'll need some towels. Perhaps take the carpets out, but better get it in the garage first.' He leaned inside and held up a bottle of Glenfiddich. It was now only half full. 'Oh my God!'

Gwendolen came running downstairs. 'You've found Jeremy's car. Where was it?' Together they brought her up to date. 'But where is Jeremy?'

Lazlo put his arms round her. 'Gwen love, my guess is that he's in the river. Come and sit down.'

Once in the sitting room, Lottie could see she was distressed, and went to sit beside her on the sofa.

'I'll ask Bridget to make us some coffee,' Lazlo said, 'and I'll put the car in the garage.'

'I was half afraid he might do something like this,' Gwen whispered, 'but then again, he's lost all his confidence and his courage; I thought perhaps he wouldn't be able to bring himself to do it. Perhaps he hasn't yet.'

Lottie took hold of her hand and said slowly, 'If he did kill Martin, to kill himself might seem the only thing he could do.'

'He must have felt full of dread at having to go to court and be publicly charged with homosexual offences,' Philip said. 'He might have thought this way easier.'

Lazlo was bringing in the tray of coffee. He put it on the table next to the bottle of Glenfiddich. 'It looks as though he needed Dutch courage,' he said.

'That depends,' Gwen said, 'whether this bottle contains neat whisky or whether he added poison to both of them. He might have poisoned himself and then jumped in the river to make doubly sure.'

Philip sniffed the contents. 'It just smells of whisky.'

'So did the other bottle,' Lazlo said. 'But he must have put the poison in one of them.'

'Unless it's just us being suspicious, jumping to conclusions,' Lottie said. 'It's all supposition, isn't it?'

'It could be more than that.' Lazlo looked Lottie in the eye. 'Early this morning we went out to the shed and found more things. A pint jug, spoons and a funnel. Scissors too, to cut up leaves or whatever it was. Things that could be construed as evidence that he had been concocting some sort of poison.'

'What have you done with them?' Lottie felt shocked.

'We brought them back to the kitchen and washed them up very thoroughly.'

'Everything seems to point to Jeremy being guilty of murder,' said Lottie. She was still finding it hard to believe.

'Lazlo and I have spent the last twelve hours trying not to think about it,' Gwen said. 'We've been telling each other that we must be patient, until things are more definite.'

'But now we've found his car,' Lottie said. 'That's a definite fact. Shouldn't you tell the police about that?'

'Jeremy wouldn't want any publicity,' Gwen said.

Lottie wanted to point out that if what they were surmising was true, Jeremy wouldn't know, but she didn't want to upset Gwen.

'I know it's none of my business,' Philip said, 'but wouldn't that be hiding evidence?' They looked silently at each other.

'Phil's right,' Lottie said. 'You should show them his book on garden poisons too, tell them he'd marked the page about digitalis.'

'But who is going to suffer if we do that?' said Lazlo. 'Gwen, for one, and Eunice, and haven't they suffered enough? I think it would be better if we said nothing.'

Lottie could feel her heart racing. Gwen squeezed her hand. They stared at each other wordlessly.

Lazlo broke the silence. 'The doctor said he thought it was a heart attack. As far as we're concerned, that's it, unless the post-mortem reveals otherwise. I think we should leave it to the police.'

'But what if the post-mortem proves Martin was murdered?' Lottie said.

'Even if that's the case, it will be almost impossible for them to find out how. His death could be seen as suicide too, and there'd be no story to unfold and therefore less publicity.'

'A good job Dad and Grandma aren't here,' she said.

'Yes,' he agreed. 'They believe fulfilling their duty is the be all and end all of everything. But I think Jeremy has brought his difficulties to a satisfactory close. Justice has been done. He can't be punished for murder if he's already killed himself. We should leave it there.'

Lottie pondered. 'I don't know, concealing evidence is—'

'Look at it like this. Jeremy may have murdered Martin, but Martin was involved in criminal acts and made others suffer, Eunice in particular. He attacked Gwen physically.'

'He really hurt me,' she said, 'but he was hurting Eunice psychologically by playing on her mind. That is much worse; he's taken away her confidence and she can't think straight any more.'

'If we take this evidence to the police,' Lazlo went on, 'the story will get into the newspapers. Investigations will take place and the story will unfold. It will make the headlines because Jeremy is an MP, and it will drag on for weeks. This way is better for Gwen and for Eunice, and for Martin's children. Better for us all. We can put it behind us more easily and get on with our lives.'

'Poor Eunice,' Lottie said, 'to be caught up in this.'

'But at least she'll be better off without Martin,' Lazlo said. 'And Gwen and I will be better off without Jeremy. He's kept us apart for twenty years. We have nothing to thank either of them for.'

After lunch, Lottie and Philip went home on the train. 'What a morning this has been for you,' he said several times. 'You must feel awful, but at least it's over now.'

'Not quite, there's still the post-mortem.'

'That's still a couple of weeks off. Two peaceful weeks, I hope.'

She smiled. 'There's been very little peace for me and the family in the last few months.'

When they reached Mersey View, Dad was already home, and he and Grandma were talking about the latest problem.

'The worst is definitely over,' Grandma said. 'We must concentrate on getting Eunice through this and settling her down.'

Later, Lottie and Philip went up to the old playroom, where they could be on their own. They sat on the sagging sofa with their arms round each other. Lottie heard the phone ring in the hall but ignored it, reaching up to kiss Philip instead. 'This is what being engaged should be like,' she whispered as he pulled her closer.

Shortly afterwards, they heard Harriet calling Lottie's name, then the sound of her hurrying footsteps. Lottie had moved away from Philip by the time she threw open the door.

She was really agitated. 'Lottie,' she said, 'Gwendolen is talking to your dad on the phone. I think they've found Jeremy. You'll want to hear all about this.'

Dad was still talking as they passed him. In the sitting room, Grandma was waiting white-faced in her favourite chair. Moments later, Charles came in. 'What is it?' Grandma demanded.

'The police have found a body they think could be Jeremy. They want somebody to identify it, and Lazlo has gone to do that. It seems that early this morning one of the passengers on the New Brighton to Liverpool ferry thought he saw a man fall overboard. The boat stopped and a lifeboat was lowered, but they saw nothing more of him. Then this evening, a body was found washed up beyond Runcorn.'

'Oh my goodness!' Grandma was mopping her forehead.

'Is Gwen all right?' Lottie asked.

'She says she is; that she half expected him to do something like this.'

'That's true,' Lottie said. 'We talked about it this morning.'

Philip nodded. 'At least it settles the matter for her. She knows for sure what has happened.'

'Frightening all the same,' Harriet said. 'Strange that he was carried all that way up the river.'

'Not really,' Dad said. 'It must have been an incoming tide when he went into the water. It's a spring tide at the moment, and the current is very strong, as you know.'

'I suppose it's understandable,' Grandma said thoughtfully. 'He couldn't face going to court, could he? That and all the fuss there'd be in the papers. What a mess he made for himself.'

Later, when Philip was leaving, Lottie walked up the back garden with him. 'You were a bit premature in hoping for two peaceful weeks,' she said.

'The peace will start from now,' he promised as he kissed her goodnight.

CHAPTER THIRTY-FIVE

O N THE WAY TO WORK the following day, Dad said, 'I've had a bad night worrying about Eunice and the boys. Let's go round by Dilys's and see how they are.'

They found the adults all sitting round the breakfast table still wearing their dressing gowns, while the children were kicking a ball about in the back garden.

'I'm feeling better now I'm here,' Eunice said. 'Don't worry about me, Dad. I'm not grieving for Martin. In fact I'm relieved in a way.'

'When school reopens in September, I'll take the boys with me,' Alec said. 'They'll do well there, I'm sure.'

'You're thinking of coming to live on this side of the water permanently then?' Dad asked.

'Yes, I grew up on this side and I want to be near to Dilys.'

'I'll be pleased to be closer to you and the boys,' Dad said, 'though you have a very nice house over there.'

'It's far too big for them,' Dilys said. 'You need servants to run a place like that.'

'Dilys thinks I'd be better in a house like this,' Eunice said, 'and it would be a price I could afford.'

'Somewhere nearby, where we can help,' Alec added.

Dilys said, 'Dr Humphries gave Eunice a sedative last night to help her sleep, and she had a good night. Tell them what he said to you, Eunice.'

'Yes, he's notified the coroner, and he'll ask for a post-mortem to be carried out by a pathologist to determine the cause of death.'

Lottie stiffened; suddenly she felt an added wave of fear in the atmosphere. They all knew that could bring bad news.

As soon as they were back in the car, Dad said, 'I could have done with a sedative last night. The big question is, what will the pathologist find?'

'We'll just have to wait to find out. At least Eunice seems better. And Dilys is persuading her to think of the future in a practical way.'

'It was a bit chaotic in there. The sooner Eunice finds a place of her own, the better.'

Lottie was spending more time with Philip, but she didn't want to visit the cinema or have meals out. She felt the need to talk, so they either sat in his car or, if the sun was shining, went for walks along the Esplanade.

At the weekend, she persuaded him to drive her over to see Gwen. Lazlo was in the study and saw them come to the door. He got up to let them in. 'I'm glad you've come. Gwen and I can't stop talking about Martin's death and Jeremy's suicide.'

He led them inside, and Gwen got up from a low chair to kiss her. 'It's all this waiting. It's hard not knowing what's going to happen next.'

'It's the tension,' Philip said. 'We're all feeling it.'

379

Lottie could sense it in the room. It was not nearly as tidy as it had been the last time she'd been here. There were books scattered about, and the desk was covered with documents. She sat down in the desk chair, since there was no other vacant. Jeremy's book of garden poisons was still open on the blotter in front of her.

'Do stay to lunch,' Gwen said.

'Thank you, is there any more news?'

'Yes,' Lazlo said. 'I've given up my lodgings. I went down yesterday and settled up with the landlady. She said she was sorry to see me go.'

'He's moved in here with me,' Gwen said.

'But don't tell them at home,' Lazlo went on. 'Not yet. Mother will have a fit. I'll make an honest woman of Gwen as soon as I can. It's just that with all this trouble hanging over us, we don't seem able to think of anything else.'

'I'm very pleased.' Lottie leapt to her feet to kiss them over again. 'You're my parents and I'd like to think of you being together and happily married at last.'

'This way we can comfort each other,' Gwen said with a smile in Lazlo's direction.

Lottie was looking at the book of poisons, a large, heavy tome with glossy pictures of the plants. 'I didn't realise that the common foxglove was so poisonous,' she said. 'I wonder if Uncle Jeremy really did use that.'

Gwen was on her feet. 'Don't let's talk about that again. I should have tidied up and put all this away.' She slapped the covers of the book together and pushed it back into the bookcase. 'I should have paid these bills, too. I see there's one here for the rates.' She shuffled the papers into a neat pile.

'What's this?' Lottie picked up an envelope that had been tucked into the corner of the blotter. Gwendolen's name was scrawled across it in heavy black writing. 'It's addressed to you.'

Silently they watched her open it. Her fingers were shaking, her face screwing with pain as she scanned it. Then with a sob she handed it to Lazlo, who read it out:

Dear Gwendolen,
   I'm doing the cowardly thing now by taking my own life. I can't face going to court on a charge such as this. I'm sorry I've not been a better husband to you, when I know you've always done your best for me.
   I do love you in my own way.
   Jeremy

'Gwen love,' Lazlo said as he put an arm round her shoulders, 'I know it's horrible to find out like this, but it's better for him and it's better for us.'

Gwen mopped at her eyes. 'He's not admitting anything, Lazlo, except suicide.'

'Exactly. We can show this to the police. There'll be no further questions about his death, and it doesn't give them anything to connect him with Martin's.'

'He would have known that.' Gwen sighed heavily. 'That's why he wrote it. Sometimes he did try to do the right thing for me.'

'I'll go and ring them now and tell them we've found a note.'

'A sad end to his life,' Lottie said.

Gwen sighed again. 'It was never a happy one.'

Anne Baker

When Lazlo came back, he said, 'They want me to bring the note in so they can see it. It means there'll be no further investigation. Jeremy's death will be accepted as suicide.'

They spent another three days worrying what the result of Martin's post-mortem might show. Lazlo busied himself arranging Jeremy's funeral. A paragraph about his suicide appeared in the newspapers, but there was no obituary, and they kept the date and place of his funeral as private as they could.

'I want no fuss,' Gwen said. 'Everything must be as quiet as it possibly can be. That's what he would want.'

'All right, and I'll arrange to have him cremated.'

When they told Grandma, she said, 'I don't think I shall go, and neither should you, Harriet. We didn't know him well and he was a disgrace to the family.'

'Gwen would like to be there; she says it'll be a final goodbye,' Lazlo said. 'We've kept it very private, and there may be no one else.'

Lottie said, 'I didn't know Uncle Jeremy, but you are my mother, Gwen, and I'd like to come if only to show support to you.'

'Good,' Lazlo said. 'We'll go as a family.'

Jeremy's funeral took place at twelve o'clock on a close, humid day. Summer rain lashed the churchyard and rumbles of thunder could be heard in the distance. Nobody else was there. Gwen was quiet and subdued. The three of them went straight home afterwards for lunch.

They sat over the table for a long time. 'He gave you a hard life, Gwen,' Lazlo said. 'I should have stood up to him and taken you away from him. Then we three would have had a more normal family life.'

'Water under the bridge now,' Lottie said.

'I can't believe he has gone so quietly,' Lazlo said, 'that it has all blown over so easily. He was never quiet about anything.'

'He kept saying he was going to kill Martin,' said Gwen. 'I wish I knew if he really meant it.'

Lazlo patted her hand. 'We'll just have to wait and see what the post-mortem says.'

Lottie was down on the dock, checking on the *Caernarvon*, when Dilys rang the office. When she returned, Dad was beaming. 'Good news. Dilys says Dr Humphries telephoned Eunice this morning to tell her that the pathologist has found that Martin's death was caused by a coronary occlusion leading to a heart attack. His body will be released for burial now, and Dilys says Eunice has decided to have him cremated.'

Lottie could feel relief flooding through her. 'Excellent, couldn't be better.'

She phoned Gwen to let her know. 'Dilys has already rung us,' Gwen said. 'We are so pleased; delighted, in fact. Lazlo says can you and Phil come over tonight? He says we should celebrate.'

Dad was in high spirits. 'Such a weight off my mind. Let's go home early and tell the family.'

'It's the most common cause of sudden death,' Grandma said when they gave her the news. 'Didn't I tell you, Charles, that those ideas you had about poison were ridiculous? I knew there was no need to worry.'

'Mother, you made our hair stand on end saying that you

thought Jeremy was about to kill Gwendolen. You got it all wrong, just as we did. This is a satisfactory end to a messy business. Now we can all concentrate on our own interests.'

Philip and Lottie went over to Gwen's house. Lazlo came to the door. 'Come along in. I'm so pleased that's all over, I could dance. It's a long time since we've had so much to be glad about.'

'After all our fears and speculation about what Jeremy might have done, it's hard to believe Martin's death was deemed to have been by natural causes,' said Lottie. 'Though Jeremy's book did say an overdose of digitalis in humans could mimic the illness it was used to treat. So was Martin poisoned or wasn't he?'

'We'll never know for sure, so there's no point wondering,' said Lazlo matter-of-factly.

'It's Eunice we must think about now,' Gwen said. 'She's been hurt badly by Martin, and she's been left her to bring up those boys on her own.'

'We're afraid he might also have left her big debts.' Lazlo was pouring drinks. 'She'll need all the help she can get to sort out the mess he's left.'

'Dilys has taken her back to collect more of her things,' Gwen said. 'They're looking for a small house on your side of the water. She needs to be near to Dilys, but the trouble is, all the houses on that estate have been sold, so they're having to look further afield. The sooner she gives up the lease on that big house, the better it will be for her finances. She just needs to decide what furniture she wants to keep, then Lazlo will arrange for the rest of it to go to the auction rooms.'

Martin's funeral took place two days later. Harriet stayed

home to look after the two boys, and Dilys and Alec drove Eunice to the church in Charles's car. Grandma insisted on going with them.

'It must have been divine intervention that he should die of a heart attack,' she told Charles later. 'Eunice should give thanks for that. I'm certainly not sorry to see the back of him.'

Chapter Thirty-Six

THREE DAYS LATER, HENRY Royden invited Charles to have lunch with him at the Adelphi Hotel. 'Not just one of our friendly get-togethers,' he told him. 'Wear your best bib and tucker. A director of my firm has suggested it.'

'Why? What for?'

'You'll have to wait to find out,' he said.

Lottie was intrigued. 'A director of Elder Dempster has invited you to lunch? That'll be a change from beer and sandwiches with Ted.'

She was expecting him to return to the office straight after lunch, but he hadn't come by five o'clock, so she locked up and went home. He was another hour behind her, but when he arrived, he was beaming. Jemima was full of questions.

'Harriet, make Charles a cup of tea,' she commanded.

'I've been drinking tea all afternoon,' he said. 'I'll get myself a bottle of beer before I tell you all about it.'

'What did you have to eat? I'd love to have lunch at—'

'For heaven's sake, Harriet, that isn't important now.' Grandma glowered at her. 'What did Elder's want from you?'

'They took me back to their office after lunch. They're interested in our business, the fleet.'

'You mean they're interested in taking it over, buying it?'

'Yes.' He took a long drink from his glass.

'They've made you an offer?'

'No.' He laughed. 'Let's say they've opened negotiations. Lottie, tomorrow will you look out the files on the last surveys we had done?'

'You mean on all the ships?' This was phenomenal news.

'Yes, and the insurance policies too. Elder's know the book value from our annual accounts, but of course they want to survey the vessels themselves.'

Grandma straightened up and said firmly, 'I don't think we should allow our business to be amalgamated into a larger business like that.'

'Why not?' Charles asked. 'It would give us capital. We'd be able to buy a modern house in a better area. It wouldn't be this size of course; four bedrooms maximum.'

Harriet was overcome at the thought. 'That would be marvellous, absolutely wonderful, and much more manageable. We could move to Heswall or West Kirby. It would be a new start in life.'

Lottie was thinking about the business. 'Isn't that what happened to the Roydens many years ago?'

'Yes.' Grandma was at her most severe. 'In 1921. It was the end of the Royden Line.'

'But Philip's family have prospered over the years since. More so than we have.'

'They wanted to buy our fleet then too,' Harriet said. 'Henry Royden tried to persuade us to accept.'

'Oh gosh! Why didn't we?'

'We Mortimers have been shipowners for nearly three

hundred years, and we aren't going to lose our fleet in my time. I feel strongly that we need to keep it running for the next generation.'

'Oliver and Glyn are quite happy working for other shipping lines,' Lottie pointed out.

'Yes, in order to gain the experience necessary to run the Mortimer Line when the firm needs them.'

'But everything changes,' Lottie tried to explain. 'Business has to move with the times. Ships get bigger, companies get bigger and Dad is struggling to make it pay.'

'Family is important, Charlotte. We have to think first and foremost of other family members. Harriet, isn't it time we had our dinner?'

Lottie's mind was teeming with questions, but when Grandma had had enough of a subject, it had to be buried. Over dinner they discussed Eunice's situation. A house had come up unexpectedly on Dilys's estate, and she had registered Eunice's interest straight away. It sounded perfect for the little family.

Once Grandma and Harriet had gone to bed, Lottie made up the fire. 'Dad, I want to hear about what happened in 1921, when Elder's first offered to take over our fleet. Why didn't we go the same route as the Roydens?'

'Henry Royden tried to persuade me. Lazlo was keen; he was backing me, urging me to do it. But I didn't stand up to Grandma, and she got her way.'

'Will you do it now?'

'I think we should. It seems like a lifeline the way things are now, though our company is worth less than it was then, and so are our vessels. They are older.'

'So why do Elder's want them?'

'While shipping generally hasn't been profitable since the war, it seems the West Africa trade is holding up. Lever Brothers are prospering; they have plantations out on the Coast and they need vast quantities of palm oil shipped to their factories up the Mersey at Bromborough. Their soap and margarine factories continue to make a profit, because everybody has to buy soap regularly, and margarine is a cheap substitute for butter. The slump hasn't affected them.

'Elder Dempster are now running a regular mailboat service to the main ports of Lagos, Takoradi and Freetown. As well as the postal service, they carry passengers and freight. They ship cotton fabrics from Manchester in designs to appeal to the people there, and things like enamelware dishes and guns. Trade has grown over the years all along the Coast, so they need smaller vessels to act as feeders to the main ports. That is what they want to use our fleet for. It's cheaper to buy our ships than to build new. Strictly speaking, though, it isn't Elder's who want them. You know how companies are bought up, taken over, merged and amalgamated, so nobody knows who owns what. Our ships would trade under the flag of the United Africa Company.'

'And Grandma doesn't like that? I thought she was always right.'

'She'd like to hear you say that.' Charles poked the dying embers in the grate back into a blaze. 'Mother believes she's always right, but sometimes she makes mistakes. That was a big one and it did the family fortunes no good at all. I think we should be grateful they've thought of Mortimer's again.' He smiled at her. 'I believe we can thank Henry Royden for that, though he hasn't said so. He's an important man in that company.'

Lottie went to the kitchen to fetch the biscuit tin, but all the time her mind was on Grandma. She'd ruled the family, made all the important decisions, expounded her strongly held opinions and could see no other point of view.

Lottie felt she'd grown up believing everything Grandma had told her.

'Dad, what Grandma said about homosexuality, was she right about that?'

'Her pet hobby horse, yes, it was a real trial to Jeremy Arbuthnot, got him down in the end. And your mother suffered because of it too.'

'I meant was Grandma right about what causes it?' Lottie was thinking of the time when Glyn had invited a friend from the *Conway* to stay with them.

'I don't remember what she said.'

'Yes you do. That we humans all develop in the same way, loving only ourselves, then our own sex, but then some don't take the last step and don't fall in love with someone of the opposite sex.'

'I think that over simplifies it, but on the whole yes, that's what happens in adolescence. Some believe it has to do with the chemical make-up in the brain.'

'Surely there aren't any chemicals in the brain?' Lottie laughed. 'That's harder to believe than Grandma's theory.'

'Oh dear, the human body is just one big bag of chemicals, Lottie. Didn't they teach you any chemistry at school?'

'No, I learned botany and biology.'

'I should have insisted on you girls going to a better school.

That little Dame School was Grandma's idea.'

'I liked it there.' But this time, Lottie thought Grandma was wrong to want to keep the business.

CHAPTER THIRTY-SEVEN

THE FOLLOWING DAY, GWEN rang Lottie in the office. 'Will you be free to come out for a celebration lunch the day after tomorrow?'

'Yes,' Lottie said eagerly. 'That sounds exciting.'

'Lazlo has rung Philip and he's agreed to come too. It'll just be us four; come in all your finery, you know, dress up.'

'Where are we going to meet?'

'Philip will bring you to our house at about half ten.'

'Sounds like an early lunch.'

Gwen laughed. 'There's something we want you to do for us first.'

That evening, Lottie and Philip went to the yacht club for a drink. They sat outside looking at the river and discussed their future.

'I'd like us to be married as soon as possible,' Philip said.

'So would I.'

'It costs a lot of money, though, and I've been a bit extravagant since I came home, buying the car and a whole load of new clothes. At least I have a job.'

'Well, I'm not sure that I'll have one for much longer,' Lottie said, and told him what was being negotiated with Elder Dempster. 'It means our office will close. Did you know?'

'No, it isn't the sort of thing Dad would talk to me about.' He smiled. 'I'm pleased for your family, but I don't want that to hold us up.'

'I might be able to get another job,' she said. 'I'll try.'

'I think I could manage a mortgage on a small house, or would it be quicker to find somewhere to rent?'

'Let's start looking round.' Lottie had the warm feeling that it was all going to happen for her soon. Later, she and Philip spent a lot of time with their arms round each other in his parked car, outside her back garden gate. That was the time that thrilled her most.

On Friday morning, he picked her up and they drove out to Gwen's house. Bridget let them in, but Lazlo was coming down the hall to meet them looking very smartly dressed, with a red carnation in his buttonhole. 'We have a tray of coffee ready; come in and we'll have that first.'

Gwen came to kiss Lottie. The first thing she noticed was her exotic perfume, and then she saw Gwen was wearing a summer-weight turquoise suit and a matching hat with an eye veil. 'Mum, you look lovely. Smart enough to grace a fashion magazine. You must be taking us somewhere very elegant for lunch.'

'No, we'll come back here to have that. I think it's more personal to eat here rather than in a restaurant.' She picked up the two carnation buttonholes she had ready, and handed one to Lottie and one to Philip.

'Fact is,' Lazlo said, 'we're getting married and we need you two as witnesses.'

'Oh my goodness.' Lottie began to laugh. 'This is a bit of a shock, but marvellous. A lovely idea, no hanging about, absolutely no waiting. What time?'

'Half eleven at the register office. Come and drink your coffee and then we must be on our way.'

'You've sprung this on us,' Philip said, shaking his hand. 'Congratulations.'

'I can't believe it.' Lottie couldn't stop smiling. 'You're getting married on the spur of the moment? But I'm so pleased.'

'Not exactly the spur of the moment,' Lazlo said. 'We should have done all this twenty years ago, and we see no point in waiting any longer just to give us time to arrange a big do.'

'We don't want a lot of fuss.' Gwen smiled at him. 'We're just longing to settle down to normal married life.'

'That's what we want too,' Philip said, holding on to Lottie.

Lottie had hardly got her breath back when they were going up the steps into the register office. They were shown into a small bright room panelled in dark wood, and welcomed by the two people there, a clerk who asked questions and wrote down their particulars, and the registrar, a very polite elderly gentleman who put them at their ease. The air was scented by a bowlful of roses on the polished desk, and more filled the empty grate.

The ceremony was quite informal. They all signed the register and shook hands, and it seemed no time at all before it was over and they were walking back to the car.

'I can't believe it.' Lottie felt light-headed. 'You're married. Just like that.'

'It is legal,' Lazlo said, 'and that's all we need.'

'Everybody else takes months if not years arranging their weddings,' Lottie said. 'Marriage seems such a big step, it has to be approached slowly.'

'It is a big step at your age.'

Back at home, Lazlo led the way to the sitting room. The French windows were open to the garden, to let in a cooling breeze. The coffee tray had gone and a bottle of champagne was cooling in an ice bucket. Lazlo expelled the cork with a loud whoosh.

'Congratulations. A very good way to get married; no fuss.' Lottie raised her glass to her mother. 'I'd quite like us to do it this way.'

'No, not for you,' Gwen said. 'Fine for us old ones, but I want to see you walk down the aisle in a white gown.'

Philip was smiling. 'So do I. I like the idea of going at it like an express train and getting it over and done with,' he said, 'but my mother would be horrified. And so would your grandmother.'

'She wouldn't believe you were truly married.' Lazlo laughed. 'And anyway, didn't you say you wanted your wedding to be like Dilys's?'

'I did.' Lottie thought about it. 'That would be the next best thing, but it would take much longer to arrange.'

'Only a month or so,' her mother said, 'and you've got all the time in the world. You'll enjoy the anticipation and the preparations. We wasted the years of our youth, but you're in no danger of doing that.'

'Your mother's right, Lottie. The traditional way is the best way for us.' Philip stretched out a hand to covers hers.

'Lazlo and I will enjoy helping you.' Gwen smiled at her. 'We've missed so much of your growing up; we don't want to miss seeing you walk down the aisle as a bride.'

'This is one time when we have to consider our families,'

Philip said. 'We will, after all, be leaving them and the family home for good. Well, we hope so.'

'Well, I for one have worked up an appetite,' Lazlo said, 'and Bridget will have set out our lunch before she went home, so let's tuck in. It's handy having other people to take care of our needs, but it's bliss when they go and we can enjoy the privacy of our own home.'

Lottie gasped when she saw the feast set out on starched white damask, accompanied by bone china, silver and cut glass. She took in the glittering spread of prawns and lobster, smoked salmon, salads and cold chicken, together with many other delicacies Grandma would think too extravagant to put on her table.

'A cold repast,' Gwen said, 'but just the thing for a warm summer's day.'

'Do help yourselves.' Lazlo passed the plate of lobster to Gwen and poured more champagne. 'We haven't yet managed to get everything organised for our new life. We have to wait for probate on Jeremy's will before Gwen can put this house on the market, but that isn't going to stop us.'

'You're moving house?'

'Yes, this house was Jeremy's choice,' Gwen said. 'When I came out of that sanatorium, I found he owed a lot on the mortgage. I had literally spent nothing for two years, so I just paid the whole thing off, though I didn't take his name off the deeds, but I don't want to live here, neither does Lazlo. I want our life to be different, a different house in a different place with no connection to Jeremy.'

'It's all very exciting,' Philip said. 'Where are you thinking of buying this new place?'

'Your side of the river,' Lazlo said. 'Somewhere near your family home, Philip.'

'We want a smaller and more manageable house than this,' Gwen said. 'More modern, with a smaller garden. This was meant to add to Jeremy's status, and we don't need to bother with that.'

'I'm oozing with envy.' Lottie was helping herself to lobster. 'It must be wonderful to go whizzing ahead with your plans like this.'

Gwen smiled. 'Tell us about *your* plans. Do you have a date in mind for your wedding?'

'Not yet,' said Philip. 'The main hold-up for us is that we have to find a home first, and we haven't decided what we should look for. To rent for a while, or bite the bullet and buy?'

'Is it a question of what you can afford?' Gwen asked.

'Yes,' Lottie replied. 'You see, I might find myself out of a job and be unable to help. It depends on what Dad does now.'

'Yes, I've heard something of that,' Lazlo said.

'No need to let that bother you,' Gwen said. 'I've done nothing for you up to now. I would like to make up for that. I want to you to look for a house you really like, something suitable in a pleasant area, and Lazlo and I will give it to you as a wedding present.'

Gwendolen and Lazlo's sudden marriage was seen as something of a bombshell by the family. But another was in the offing as Dad attended meetings in the Elder Dempster offices to negotiate the takeover of his fleet. When finally they made him a firm offer, he and Grandma were closeted in the study on their own for two hours, and Lottie and Harriet heard raised voices.

Two days later, Charles announced over the dinner table that he had accepted the offer. The *Caernarvon* and the *Denbigh* would still bring slate from Porthmadog to Liverpool, but Mortimer's would no longer run that service. The three freighters would be used in West Africa. Grandma was in a bit of a mood because she'd been overruled. She insisted on calling it a merger rather than a takeover.

When Dad told Ted Pascoe the news, he strode up to Lottie's desk and clapped her on the shoulder. 'If this means you are looking for a job,' he said, 'I want you to think of me first. A water clerk who will also help about the office and who gets on so well with our existing staff would be like gold dust.'

The next decision to be made concerned the house. Both Charles and Harriet were keen to move to a more comfortable, modern place. Jemima didn't share their enthusiasm.

Lottie said, 'Grandma, we all think it's time to go, but it must be very hard for you when you've lived here for so long. You must have seen changes, changes that you don't like.'

'Of course I have, Charlotte,' she said, and headed towards her bedroom. 'It is hard, but I've always faced reality and done what's best for us all.'

Suddenly several members of the family were looking for new homes at the same time. Houses were the main topic of conversation at mealtimes, and the kitchen table was covered with sales brochures. Lottie and Philip spent hours driving round the more affluent suburbs on the Dee estuary and collecting ever more details of houses for sale. Dad was taking his mother and Harriet round on the same mission.

Lazlo and Gwen were the first to find what they wanted. It was in Caldy, the most expensive residential district on the Wirral, and was about fifty years old. It was an attractive house from the outside and had lots of character inside, and it had been well maintained and kept up to date. There were four spacious bedrooms and a study, and views from the upstairs windows of the River Dee. The garden was lovely, and the place was surrounded by trees and well shielded from nearby houses.

'It's everything we could possibly want,' Lazlo said. 'We'll take you to see it.'

'We need something more modest,' Lottie said.

'No you don't,' her mother said. 'I want you to have a house you'll love, with space for a family if and when it comes, and then you won't ever have to move.'

They came across it the very next day, in West Kirby. It was a pretty whitewashed cottage with a roof of blue Welsh slate and roses round the door. Inside it was larger than it seemed from the front, and a more recent extension provided two more spacious living rooms. The windows looked out on to the pleasant garden, and it had a friendly, welcoming air. Lottie felt she'd found her dream house.

It took Dad and Harriet longer to persuade Jemima that she could live in a newly built house. Harriet said she didn't want to settle for anything more than two years old. 'It'll be much more comfortable than an old house,' she kept telling her mother. 'We'll have central heating and all mod cons.'

It was Lazlo and Gwen who found a solution that pleased all three of them. New houses were being built on the front overlooking the Irish Sea in Hoylake. There was a beach and a sort of rudimentary promenade, and then steep gardens going up to the houses. It was a quiet, undeveloped area, not a popular beach resort, and it was the position that convinced Jemima it might suit her.

Harriet was afraid it was rather a long way from everywhere, but Charles said, 'You must learn to drive and I'll give you my car.'

'That would be marvellous,' she said. 'Are you sure?'

He laughed. 'Of course. I fancy a better one, more like Lazlo's.'

'Won't Charlotte want it?'

'Everybody is running round after Charlotte making sure she has all she needs. It's time someone thought about you.'

CHAPTER THIRTY-EIGHT

ALL THE TIME THEY were house-hunting, the family were helping Lottie to make arrangements for her wedding. She and Philip went together to see the vicar of St Mark's church and asked if he'd marry them on Friday 18 September. He booked it for eleven o'clock.

The following Sunday, Grandma had invited Philip and also Lazlo and Gwendolen to lunch. Lottie had just returned to the table after clearing their soup plates and Charles was carving when Grandma said, 'Have you decided who will give you away, Charlotte? You seem to have two fathers.'

'Oh, I haven't got round to thinking of that.' She looked from Lazlo to Charles. Dad wouldn't meet her gaze. 'Yes I feel very lucky to have been blessed with two dads.' She smiled at Lazlo.

'I know I'm your biological father,' he said, 'but you've never really belonged to me. I can't give away what I've never had.'

'Quite right,' Lottie said. 'I think you're the proper person to do that, Dad, and I'd be very grateful if you would.'

Charles beamed at her as he handed up a plate with several slices of beef and Yorkshire pudding on it. 'I shall be more than happy to do that for you, love,' he said.

'But I still want to be very much the mother of the bride,'

Gwen said. 'I'm getting a very smart outfit to outdo all the others.'

'Of course,' Jemima said, 'and I think, Charlotte, you should ask your two married sisters to attend you as matrons of honour. Eunice may not want to walk down the aisle with you, but you must make sure she is involved.' Lottie and Dilys had already discussed that, but she smiled and said, 'An excellent idea, Grandma. That's what I'll do.'

'Good.' Jemima picked up her knife and fork. 'So that's everything settled.'

'Not entirely.' Lottie glanced at Philip. 'I know I said I wanted my wedding to be exactly like Dilys's, but it won't be so easy to have the wedding breakfast at home.'

'We won't have moved by then,' Grandma said.

'No, but with us all setting up new homes, you've given away a lot of furniture, and you've also promised us a share of your best cutlery and crockery.'

'So I have. Perhaps the house does look a little bare.'

The photographs of the two colliers, the *Olwen Thomas* and the *Gwendolen Thomas*, had been wrapped up in newspaper that morning for Gwen to take with her, and a mahogany sewing table that had belonged to her sister was already waiting at the back door.

Philip smiled at Jemima. 'My mother is suggesting a reception at the yacht club,' he said. 'That would be a lot less trouble for you.'

Grandma did not look pleased. Lottie said quickly, 'We quite like the idea. You'd be able to relax for once and enjoy it, instead of worrying about what the caterers are up to. What d'you think, Grandma?'

'All brides should be married from home. Mortimer brides always have been. This is a new-fangled idea. We'll have to see.'

Dilys had taken it on herself to oversee Lottie's wardrobe. 'Come to the shop and have a look at this year's wedding dresses,' she said. 'What style do you have in mind, a traditional romantic sweeping skirt or a slim-fitting one?'

'Slim-fitting,' Lottie said, 'like you had.'

When she went to the shop and the dresses were brought out for her to try on, Dilys had collected an audience of friends and fashion buyers to give their opinion. The first one she tried, a fitted number, was given the thumbs-down.

'You're too tall and slim for that,' she was told. 'White satin from shoulder to floor makes you look like a flagpole. You need curves to wear that kind of dress.'

One with a bouffant skirt was picked out for her, and Dilys helped her get into it in the changing cubicle. 'Better,' was the verdict.

Lottie studied her reflection in the mirror. 'No, I'd like something a bit more sophisticated.' She went back to the rows of hanging gowns swathed in cellophane. One of the fashion buyers pulled out a gown that had a slim skirt at the front but was gathered round the hips and taken back into a bustle of three large descending folds of silk behind.

'Try this,' she said.

Lottie liked it at first glance. The silk was oyster-coloured with a faint shine, and beautifully tailored. Her audience liked the style as much as she did. 'An interesting back view,' they told her, 'and that's what the congregation will see.'

Dilys frowned. 'It could do with being an inch longer.'

'I love the style,' Lottie said, 'but it isn't very comfortable.'

'Not your size,' one of the sales assistants suggested.

The head buyer looked out the manufacturer's charts and studied them. 'I can order one in a different size, and you can come back and try it on,' she said.

Lottie was looking at the price tag; the dress was wildly expensive.

'We'll do that,' Dilys said firmly. 'And while we're here, we'll look at veils and shoes.'

There were lots of other things that Dilys thought she should have, and Lottie went home with a lavender-coloured suit for going away, and bagfuls of frilly nightdresses and underwear.

The weeks were flying by. It felt like a roller coaster of a time, as Lottie and Philip set up and furnished their first home, and booked their honeymoon in North Wales. Dilys took her back to the shop to try on the replacement wedding dress they'd ordered for her, and they thought it was absolutely gorgeous.

Philip's mother had a friend who made and decorated wedding cakes, and she had ordered a three-tiered one to be delivered. She had also made all the arrangements for the reception to be held at the yacht club, while Grandma had insisted on an organist and choir to provide music at the ceremony.

With all the preparations and anticipation, the day arrived almost before Lottie felt ready for it. The matrons of honour arrived early in the morning to help her dress and get themselves ready. For the first time, Eunice seemed to be enjoying herself, and if not exactly her old self, she was certainly closer to it than she had been for a long time.

It was a sunny late summer day, but a day like no other. The family departed for church, leaving Lottie alone with Dad.

'Lottie, love,' he said, 'you've been a very rewarding daughter. I wish you all the very best for the future.'

She nodded, feeling a little fluttery. In the taxi she was trembling, and he patted her hand and said, 'No need to worry, Philip is exactly right for you.' But it wasn't worry. It was the little thrills that were running up and down her spine.

Dilys, Eunice and Harriet were waiting for them in the church porch in their finery, all excited smiles. Harriet kissed her and whispered, 'I'll let them know the bride has arrived.'

They paused there for a moment. Dilys smiled at her and straightened her veil. When the soft background music ceased and after a pause the organ burst into a rousing piece, Lottie knew the moment had come. Dad led her into the familiar church, which today was decorated with flowers. It was full of people, and they were all turning their faces to look at her. Faces filled with affection and admiration. Faces that she knew and loved: Glyn and Dorothy, Oliver and Harriet, Lazlo and her mother. Gwen was mopping at her eyes with a fragment of lace, and even Grandma shed a tear.

As she neared the altar, Philip turned round and she met his gaze. His eyes were full of love. Today love was all round her; she felt wrapped in it. All she could feel was overwhelming joy.

Liverpool Gems

Anne Baker

It is 1935 and as Carrie Courtney watches her twin sister, Connie, marry the man of her dreams, Carrie longs to find a love of her own. Having lost their mother at an early age, the girls were brought up by their maiden aunts and, with Connie leaving home, Carrie is desperate to spread her wings.

Using her skills as a bookkeeper, Carrie gets an exciting new job but her stunning beauty soon attracts the wrong kind of attention. And romance is the last thing on her mind when her beloved father finds himself caught up in an illegal jewellery business that threatens to destroy them all . . .

Praise for Anne Baker's gripping Merseyside sagas:

'A stirring tale of romance and passion, poverty and ambition' *Liverpool Echo*

'Baker's understanding and compassion for very human dilemmas makes her one of romantic fiction's most popular authors' *Lancashire Evening Post*

'With characters who are strong, warm and sincere, this is a joy to read' *Coventry Evening Telegraph*

978 1 4722 2534 4

HEADLINE

Wartime Girls

Anne Baker

Set in Liverpool during the Depression and the Blitz of the Second World War, Anne Baker's dramatic saga brings a close-knit community vividly to life.

It is the day of the Grand National, 1933, when Susie Ingram's fiance, Danny, is killed in a tragic accident. In a cruel twist of Fate, Susie discovers she is carrying Danny's child and, shunned by his parents, she turns to her mother for support.

Louise Ingram, widowed during the First World War, knows how hard it is to bring up a family alone, but with the help of her eldest daughter, Martha, who lives next door, they manage to survive.

When little Rosie is born there is no doubt that she is Danny's daughter, but it is destined to take many more years of heartache before the two families are united again . . .

Praise for Anne Baker's gripping Merseyside sagas:

'A stirring tale of romance and passion, poverty and ambition' *Liverpool Echo*

'Baker's understanding and compassion for very human dilemmas makes her one of romantic fiction's most popular authors' *Lancashire Evening Post*

'With characters who are strong, warm and sincere, this is a joy to read' *Coventry Evening Telegraph*

978 1 4722 1226 9

HEADLINE

A Liverpool Legacy

Anne Baker

On a spring day in 1947, Millie and Pete Maynard take their daughter Sylvie on a boat trip that is to end in tragedy. Poor Sylvie blames herself for the accident and Millie needs all her strength to comfort her children and overcome her grief. Then Pete's will is read and further heartache lies in store . . .

Meanwhile, Pete's younger brother and his good-for-nothing sons try to take control of the family business, but they've underestimated Millie's indomitable spirit. She's worked in Maynard's perfume laboratory for eighteen years and is determined to protect her husband's legacy no matter what obstacles are thrown in her way . . .

Praise for Anne Baker's gripping Merseyside sagas:

'A stirring tale of romance and passion, poverty and ambition' *Liverpool Echo*

'Baker's understanding and compassion for very human dilemmas makes her one of romantic fiction's most popular authors' *Lancashire Evening Post*

'With characters who are strong, warm and sincere, this is a joy to read' *Coventry Evening Telegraph*

978 0 7553 9960 4

HEADLINE

Now you can buy any of these other bestselling
books by **Anne Baker** from your bookshop
or *direct from her publisher*.

A View Across the Mersey	£6.99
Liverpool Gems	£7.99
Wartime Girls	£6.99
A Liverpool Legacy	£5.99
Daughters of the Mersey	£7.99
Love is Blind	£8.99
Liverpool Love Song	£7.99
Nancy's War	£7.99
Through Rose-Coloured Glasses	£8.99
All That Glistens	£8.99
The Best of Fathers	£8.99
A Labour of Love	£8.99
The Wild Child	£8.99
Carousel of Secrets	£8.99
Let The Bells Ring	£8.99

TO ORDER SIMPLY CALL THIS NUMBER

01235 827 702

or visit our website: www.headline.co.uk

Prices and availability subject to change without notice.